JIANG LI, RIVER BEAUTIFUL

A Novel By
Patrick L. Deu Pree

ACTION BOOKS

COPYRIGHT © 2012
BY
PATRICK L. DEU PREE

TO MY WIFE, DONNA, FOR HER PATIENCE AND UNDERSTANDING

OTHER NOVELS BY PATRICK L. DEU PREE

KSHATRIYA, THE LEGEND OF NATHANIEL J. SMITH

KSHATRIYA II, CAPTAIN STEEL

THE ANGEL AND THE HITMAN

REIGN OF THE GOLDEN GODDESS

BLACK JADE

BLACK JADE II "REDEMPTION"

BLACK JADE III "FULL PARDON"

STEEL GRAY

APOCALYPSE DAWN

DEPUTY RONDA MILLER/ THE PROTECTOR

TO MY TEAM

BRENT MCCAIN

LAMBERT CHEUNG

CHRISTINA CORTEZ FOR COVER EDITING

BERTHA ALBRIGHT FOR EDITING

JOHN CHASE FOR TECH SUPPORT

MIRIAM SYKES FOR TECH ADVICE

Cover by

Createspace Covercreator

PROLOGUE

He was moving along the street, weapon ready, it was house to house, he was leading his squad. All was quiet now. It was a house to house search for the enemy. It was anything goes here, they could enter at will if a suspected enemy was inside. No tangos so far. The walls of the buildings were pock marked with bullet holes, larger gaping openings left from RPG rounds. Some structures they passed were completely devastated, barely the framework remaining. In the distance he could hear gunfire, full auto, an M-60 was active out there somewhere.

They moved on.

"What now, Sarge?" Private Stevens asked, right behind him.

"Stay alert!" he answered as they moved along.

The silence was eerie, smoke lifted from one of the buildings nearby, or rather what was left of the building. He adjusted his heavy body armor, it was uncomfortable but a necessity here.

They moved on.

He heard a sound, he looked around. It was Neela, a young girl he had seen almost every day looking out her window at him from his assigned position in the building he and his outfit were occupying, she would stand across the street in her window looking out at him, her big brown eyes studying him. She had black hair, strands falling from her head covering, always dressed in her robes, so young and always with her mother and one other older man, a family member whenever she would go out onto the streets. It was forbidden for women to travel alone, always they were to be accompanied by a male family member. But as they would walk by she would look at him. He would smile at her and finally she smiled back. From that time on she would look at him from her window and smile. That was their relationship, looking and smiling.

Now here she was.

She was walking along the street with her older sister and one of her uncles, a man with a gray beard, wearing his turban and robes. They must have been to the market. What dangerous times to be traveling.

Then he heard it. The whoosh of an oncoming RPG round. The explosion. He and his men hit the deck as AK-47 rounds impacted all around them, shards of concrete flying in their faces, goggles protecting them. He felt the shards sting his face. He looked up.

"Return fire!" he yelled and they began firing away at the windows of the apartment where the rounds were coming from. He looked across the street. Neela's uncle was dead, lying, bleeding on the sidewalk, his head half off. Neela was screaming, her older sister was screaming. She looked at him.

"Keep down, Neela!" he yelled.

He could not risk his fellow squad members trying to rescue a civilian.

More rounds impacted around him.

"Cover me!" he finally said to his men. They kept up the barrage as he dashed from cover, crossing the street and hitting the wall and flattening against it. He was right near Neela. She was looking at him. With his hand he motioned for her to stay down. She pulled her sister down with her and they hugged the ground.

More gunfire erupted farther down the street. He heard a scream and turned. Neela's sister pitched backwards as a round tore into her chest, blasting out her back. She had tried to rise up, Neela did not pull her back down in time. Now she was dead before she hit the pavement.

More ear shattering automatic gunfire.

He could see tangos coming up the street, heavily armed and coming fast, a group of ten, two had RPGS. They fired and the rockets were streaking right towards him. He grabbed Neela to her feet and lunged through an open door. The rounds impacted outside, the blast sending fragments through the door into the entryway. He held Neela to him, her arms were around him, he could feel her face against his, feel tears in her eyes running down her brown cheeks. Her body shook with sobs.

More gunfire.

His squad was opening up on the tangos. He heard gunfire from above. The original tangos were in the apartment just above him. He heard the whoosh of an RPG and an explosion just across the street.

"Stay down!" he told Neela and he didn't know if she understood him or not.

"I will," she said in in her heavy accent.

"Good! Don't move!"

"Stevens! Are you okay?" he yelled.

"Okay, Sarge!" came Private Steven's reply.
"How about the rest of the squad?"
"Okay! Tangos coming up the street, Sarge!"
"Got it!"

More gunfire. More explosions. He headed for the stairs, climbing swiftly. A tango appeared at the top, drawing a bead on him, but didn't have time to fire as he opened up on him, watched him dance to the rounds impacting into his body and saw him fall, dropping his weapon. Now the sergeant bounded up the steps, it was now or never. He made the hall at the top and headed right for the apartment entrance, the door was slightly ajar. He kicked it in. Two tangos were in the room, one ready to fire another rocket. He took both out then slammed a fresh clip into his weapon. He went to the window.

"Stevens! I got the room secured!"

He saw Stevens lift his hand in a thumbs up salute. Now there were the advancing tangos on the street to worry about. He heard a sound and he whirled around. Neela was standing in the doorway.

"No, Neela!" he said and then a sound brought him back to the window. He could see more tangos advancing up the street. This was bad, they were now outnumbered. He looked across the street at his squad. Corporal Powell was readying an OSI reloadable tube launcher. He fired and the round streaked on target. The mass of tangos diminished now by five men.

"Good going, Powell!" the sergeant shouted.

He heard a sound. Neela was handing him the RPG launcher, it was loaded and ready. Two more launchers lay on the floor with extra rockets. He took aim down the street and fired. The rocket launched, it took the usual unsteady path right towards the tangos then veered off course and hit a wall, way short of the target. But the tangos had stopped their advance. He could see Private Connelly on the radio calling for backup. Good man!

He looked across the way.

Tangos were on a rooftop just across the street and more were about twenty yards down from his squad's position. They had several RPGs ready. He grabbed up another launcher and took aim.

"Hope this works better this time!"

He fired. The rocket streaked across the gap between buildings and impacted right in the middle of the tangos, a direct hit.

"Yes!" he said. "Right on, baby, right on!"

"Jeem!" he heard Neela calling his name in her heavy accent. He whirled. Too late, a tango was in the doorway, AK-47 in hand. The tango opened fire before he could get a round off. He felt the burning in his side. Neela had an AK-47 in her grip and she opened fire. The tango pitched backwards as deadly rounds impacted his torso.

He stood, looked down, saw the wound, saw blood seeping from his torso. It had pierced the light body armor. He could feel the burn where it had exited his back, a clean shot through mid torso. He looked back at Neela, eyes wide. She dropped the weapon and came to him, holding him, all was going black, he felt faint, his legs wobbled, like rubber. Neela's arms went around him.

"Jeem, Jeem!" she said.

"You know my name, Neela," He said and that was the last he knew as the blackness enveloped him.

CHAPTER ONE

He was standing on Market Street, San Francisco. There was a steakhouse there, cheap, he could see the flame broiler from the picture window. The steaks sure looked good, juicy, ready to devour and he was hungry, famished, starving for a good steak and an ice bold beer.

He went inside and got in line. Not many people here this time of the afternoon, around four o'clock. He could smell the flavor of the juicy, red meat. There were several steaks on the grill being prepared. As he approached the cook looked at him, a short, stocky man in a white jacket and tall white chef's hat.

"How do ya want it?" he asked then he noticed the ribbons on the young man's Army uniform, noticed the red beret on his head.

"Rare," the young man declared.

"Rare it'll be," the cook said and he started flipping steaks, seeking just the right one.

"You just get back from 'over there?'" the cook asked.

"Yeah," the young man, a staff sergeant, said. He had on his dress greens, shoes polished black and shining.

"How long you over there?" the cook asked.

"A year."

The cook looked at him.

"I bet a beer would go good with that steak, eh?" the cook said.

"A beer would hit the spot," the young sergeant answered. "A nice, cold Lowenbrau would do just fine."

"Lowenbrau it'll be," the cook answered. "Jill!" he called and a young Asian girl also dressed in a white jacket but minus the cook's hat appeared as if out of nowhere. "Pour this young man a Lowenbrau."

"Thank you," the sergeant said as Jill handed him the cold, frothy drink.

"Here you go, sir," she said.

The man took the beer, put it on his tray and moved down the line. He picked up his plate with steak, baked potato and salad and moved to a table next to a window where he seated himself. He looked down at the steak, taking it all in and he briefly closed his eyes. He had the first sip of his beer, felt the sting in the back of his throat as the liquid hit, felt it in the back of his eyeballs as it went down smooth. He was back, back from the dead, back but not yet home. That would come later. He looked at the counter. Jill was there, she had been looking at him and she smiled self consciously and went back to work.

Staff Sergeant Jim Saunders sat there at his table next to the window enjoying the meal, not really conscious of the people passing by outside. His mind was far off for a moment, Iraq, the hellhole reliving itself in his mind. No, it was over. Staff Sergeant Jim Saunders was out of the war for good now. A hot round through the upper torso which had just missed his heart had guaranteed that. And Jim Saunders had not wanted to come home, had not wanted to leave his outfit. He remembered lying there in the burned out building with rounds impacting all around him. Somehow the round had penetrated his vest, worthless piece of shit, he had thought to himself at the time.

"Is everything all right, sir?"

Jill's voice. Sergeant Saunders looked up, she was standing there smiling at him, she had been clearing the table next to him.

"Yeah," he said, "just fine."

He took another sip of his beer and finished his steak. He guessed it had been delicious but while he had been eating his mind had been on that burned out building, that fucked up, pitted, stinking burned up building on that fucked up street in Iraq, that fucked up street where his life had changed. He had been there over a year, his third year in the Army, had lived in that hellhole, had seen his buddies die. He thought he was dead in that moment.

"Sir, are you all right?" Jill's voice again through the fog.

"Oh yes, quite all right," Sergeant Saunders lied. He finished his beer and set the empty glass down.

"Would you like another beer?" Jill asked.

"Why not," Jim Saunders said. "Sure, why not."

It was brought with a smile. He watched Jill return to the counter to wait on more customers who were coming in, it was later in the afternoon now and some people were starting to get off work. Men and women in their business suits, they began piling in. Jim concentrated on enjoying the smooth taste of his beer. The feelings were just below the surface, the rage and the anger. Dropped out of the service because of a flesh wound. At least it seemed like a minor flesh would to him but the military physicians had stated otherwise and that had been that. His military career over in a flash. He felt like he had just been dropped off a cliff and was still plunging downward, the bottom nowhere in sight yet.

He took another sip. Jill was behind the counter serving a customer but she threw him a look. He noticed two Asian men enter the steakhouse, dressed in suits, they did not wait in line with the others. One was a burly man, tall, thick in the shoulders but not quite as built as Jim Saunders. The other one, short, thin, he wore the more expensive suit and carried a shiny, black briefcase. Jim looked over to see the cook looking nervously at the two men. Jill was also apprehensive as she tried to pay attention to her customers. The atmosphere had changed in the little restaurant. There was the feeling of menace. The cook leaned over and said something to Jill and she left the counter, going through a door to a back room or office.

Jim downed the last of his steak. Whatever was going on here was none of his business and he prepared to leave. Something held him here. Perhaps he would have another beer. Jill returned from the back with another man, an older man, probably the owner of the establishment. The older man motioned to the two Asian men and all three of them went on through the door. Jill looked towards Jim and smiled sheepishly. Jim held up his mug for another. Jill brought him a fresh beer and set it down on the table. She started to leave.

"Everything okay?" Jim asked her.

"Oh yes," she said but her tone told him differently.

"It doesn't seem like it," Jim said. "Who are those two guys?"

"They are just business associates of the owner."

"Business associates. They seem a little on the shady side."

With that Jill threw him a smile.

"You've been watching way too many movies, sir," she said.

"My name's Jim."

"Hello Jim." She had an educated tone.

"You go to school, Jill?"

"Yes, San Francisco State, forth year. I am majoring in psychology."

"A shrink, huh?"

"Not yet, exactly." Her tone had changed slightly.

"I didn't mean to be offensive, just joking..."

"No, that's okay, I get that all the time."

"No, I'm really sorry," Jim was angry with himself now for trying to be a wise ass.

Jill threw him a genuine smile now then she moved away across the room, clearing one of the tables. At that moment the two Asian men came back through the door and went to a table where they seated themselves, rather than get in the line at the counter like everyone else. Jill immediately went over to them and asked what they wanted.

"You!" the burly man said with a creepy grin.

Jill just smiled, a very forced smile, in Jim's opinion.

"I need a beer right now!" the burly man said.

Jill headed for the counter and poured the beer and brought it to the burly man. She set it down on the table.

"You didn't serve my boss first!" the burly man said as he took a gulp. The thin man said nothing.

"I...I'm sorry sir, but you said..."

"Who do you think you are to disrespect customers this way? Who are you?"

"Sir..."

Jim was now watching intently. Jill was struggling to maintain a calm demeanor. She looked at the thin man.

"I am sorry, sir, may I get you something?"

"A steak, I'll have a steak and be quick about it!" the thin man said, "and so will my friend."

"Right away, sir," Jill said and she started to leave. The burly man reached out and took her wrist.

"I don't like the disrespect you are showing us!" he demanded.

"Sir, there is..."

Suddenly a large hand gripped the wrist of the burly man. Jim was standing there, a firm grip on the man.

"I'd say that would be about enough of that, asshole!" Jim said.

The burly man tried to break away but Jim's grip was like iron.

"Please, sir..." Jill was trying to say.

In a split second Jim had the burly man by the collar, hoisting him up from his seat, his chair clattered over and the beer spilled. The glass shattered on the floor. Jim got in the burly man's face.

"Go wait in the serving line like everyone else, dickhead!" Jim said in a low, steady voice. And while still holding the burly man he looked at the thin man. "And that goes for you too!"

The thin man looked up at them, a calm covering the rage within.

Slowly he rose up, looking at Jim. He stood there.

"You have anything to say, asshole?" Jim asked.

Jill was standing back, a look of panic on her face. The other customers were also staring, some were leaving quickly.

The thin man looked at Jill. The owner and the cook had now come over.

"I believe we have concluded our business here for today," the thin man said to the owner. "We shall return later and continue." And with that he smiled at the owner and placed his hand on the burly man's shoulder. Jim released him with a shove. The burly man started straightening his clothes. The thin man looked at him.

"I thought I brought a man with me to back me up," the thin man said to the burly man who hung his head in disgrace. "We will be leaving now."

"Don't let the door hit you in the ass on the way out!" Jim said.

The two men headed out the door, the customers looked on, not knowing what to do. More of them had beat a hasty retreat. Jill was standing there, a look of shock on her face. She came over to Jim.

"I'm sorry," Jim said, "but I couldn't just sit there and let that creep mistreat you."

"You've really done it now," the older man, who was the owner said. "Now they'll be back and really cause trouble."

Jill sat down, she was shaking.

"You don't know who you were messing with," she said.

"And you liked the way he was treating you?" Jim asked.

"Sometimes you just have to put up with certain things!" Jill said, her voice ready to break.

"Bullshit!" now Jim was really pissed off. "You don't have to take that shit, maybe you do," he looked at the owner and over at the cook who was trying to get things rolling again serving the customers, who slowly were filtering back into the serving line.

"It's all over, folks," the cook said with a ready smile, "Just a little mis-understanding, that's all."

"Mis-understanding my ass!" Jim said and he headed for the door, barely controlling his rage. He did not look back as he stormed out onto the street. He looked around and did not see any sign of the two men who had been there. He started off down the street, going east towards the Embarcadero, it was time to catch the ferry. He had gone about a half block when he heard a voice calling to him. He turned to see Jill running up the street after him. She caught up to him, she had let her hair down and now it hung about her shoulders and down her back, black and silken, shining in the sunlight. It was getting into late afternoon now, people were starting to leave their offices, they all wanted to get home to their families as soon as they could.

"I thought I would miss you, you walk pretty fast," Jill said.

"I got places to be," Jim said.

"I want to apologize..."

"For what?"

"Back there, those men...it's complicated," Jill blushed and waved a strand of her beautiful hair back out of her face. "I just finished my shift. I hurried to catch up with you."

"There was no need to do that."

"I wanted to. You tried to help, even though it will do no good."

"What about calling the police?"

"I think you and I both know that would be a waste of time, Sergeant, don't you?"

"Extortion, Chinese gang?"

"One of the largest here in the city. Everyone pays them for protection. And now..."

"I screwed things up, didn't I?"

"I'm afraid so. They'll be back. I can only hope they will understand, but you insulted one of the kingpins and his bodyguard. He won't forget that."

"It sure isn't your fault or the restaurant owner's fault. It was me. And there is no way you are going back there to work."

"Excuse me?"

"Sorry, you've got to quit."

"Who do you think you are?" now Jill was frowning, anger flared in her eyes.

"You can't work there after this...oh hell," Jim threw up his hands, "here I don't even know you. But really, you can't go back. I'll walk you home, it's the least I can do, do you live far?"

"I live up in Chinatown, we're almost there now."

"I'll walk you home then."

"You don't need to do this..."

"I insist."

"Have it your way, we turn here," Jill said. They were at Market and Kearny Street. They made a left turn and started walking north.

"Jill, that doesn't sound very much like a Chinese name," Jim said.

"Of course not, I have my traditional name," Jill answered with a genuine smile.

"And it is..." Jim said.

"Okay, my name is Jiang Li."

"What's it mean?"

"It means, 'River Beautiful,'" Jill smiled and they kept walking.

They were now crossing Sutter Street and nearing the entrance to Chinatown, the huge, ornate archway towered over them as they passed through.

"You've been here before?" Jill answered.

"Oh yeah, I was raised across the bay."

They turned off the main street, away from the shops and headed up a steep side street. They stopped mid block and Jill turned to Jim.

"This is as far as you can go with me, I'm afraid. I live just up the street, my father and mother, they are very traditional, they would not approve of me being escorted by and American."

"But we are all Americans, this is the 21st century for God's sake."

"Not in this world here, I'm afraid," Jill smiled and looked up the street at a large apartment building ornately decorated with an Asian style facade.

"You live up there? In that apartment building?"

"Goodbye, Jim, and thank you," Jill said with a smile. She leaned up towards him and gave him a kiss on his cheek.

Then she darted off up the street and turned the corner. Jim started to follow her, that kiss on his cheek, he wanted see where she lived. He thought better of it. No use getting her in trouble with her parents. He looked down the street towards Kearny. He started walking, turned right and headed back to Market Street and turned left, heading east towards the Ferry Building.

The Ferry Building rose up before him, impressive, domineering, it had been redone in its original style from the early days since it had been built in 1892. The massive clocktower rose above the structure, the clock had been reactivated after repairs. It was a reminder of a bygone era before the original ferry boats had been discontinued, they had carried cars then. Now only passengers rode the smaller double decker boats. People were in line, waiting for their tickets and he joined them. He looked back up the street and he felt a longing deep inside.

He finally boarded, it was crowded inside on the first level. Jim made his way to the bar and ordered a beer then shoved his way past the other passengers and went out to the deck, he stood at the bow. It was warm, late spring, and a gentle breeze was blowing, daylight saving's time had kicked in so it would be light out until much later.

Jim felt the boat pull away from the dock and he took a pull from his beer, enjoying the relaxation of the moment and taking in the view. He had ridden the ferries back and forth as a high school kid, heading into the city for movies with his buddies and to just hang out like all kids do.

High school.

It seemed to be another world now and yet it had only been four years since he had graduated. Jim enjoyed the gentle roll of the boat as it made its way across the bay. When he finished his beer he stepped inside and ordered another then sat at the bar.

"A lot of ribbons there, sergeant," he heard a man say and he turned. A burly man of about forty was standing there at the bar enjoying a mixed drink. Jim shrugged his shoulders.

"Just getting back from Iraq," it was a statement.

"Yes sir," Jim said. He could tell by the man's rugged features that he had been in some branch of the service.

"I was there in the early nineties," the man said, "Marines. I'll bet those are hard won and deserved." He indicated the ribbons on Jim's chest again.

Jim shrugged his shoulders again.

"I don't know why I was singled out," he said. "Other guys deserve 'em just as much as I do, maybe more so."

"I understand, son, On your way home?"

"Yeah."

"Good for you. Take a word of advice from and old timer, just take it easy for awhile and let it all come to you."

"Sir?"

The man smiled and said nothing. The boat was pulling into the dock now.

"Been nice talking to you, son, take care, I'll be seeing you," the man said and he walked away.

"Be seeing me?" Jim asked himself then shrugged it off. It was time to leave.

CHAPTER TWO

Jim took the bus from the ferry station and relaxed in the back row seat all the way home, a half hour drive. He got off the bus before it got to the center of town. His neighborhood was in the lower income area. That's where his parents lived, where he had grown up. The bus had passed the old high school, the tall clock tower rising above the rest of the school and the trees.

Jim turned down a side street, off the main drag and walked a half block to the neighborhood bar. He had not been old enough to drink when he had joined the Army. Now he was so he stepped inside. He wanted a beer before going the rest of the way home. The bar was packed with working class types from his neighborhood, the old timers and the younger ones just stopping off for a fast one before going their separate ways. Some of the men had hard hats on, there were also a couple of women in hard hats, things had changed in the four years he was away.

"Hey Jimbo!" one of the guys said as he saw Jim enter the bar. It was Will, Jim's age, in work clothes seated at the bar. There was an empty stool. "Come on over and let me buy you a beer, huh buddy?"

"Hi Will," Jim said as he made his way across the floor to the bar, shaking hands as he went with many of the guys, his age and older. He knew them all, older men, parents to his friends, hard working men. Of the two woman who wore work clothes and had hard hats on, one was Jim's age or maybe a little older, the other one appeared to be in her late thirties. Jim was used to women in the work environment, he had known several over in Iraq although none had been on any patrols he had gone on in house to house fighting. The younger woman looked up at him, a pretty blond, she smiled. The older one was not as attractive, a bit on the heavy side, doughty looking, dull eyes. She did not smile.
Jim took his seat at the bar, an open tall one already in front of him. Will slapped Jim on the back.

"I'll bet it's good to be back," Will said.

Jim shrugged. He didn't even know if it was good or not.

"Was your hitch up?" Joe, another young man at the bar on the other side of Jim asked.

"I guess you could say that," Jim answered as he took a pull from his beer.

"Your dad said you were wounded," Will said.

"Yeah."

"You look to be in pretty good shape."

"That's what I kept trying to tell the Army but they didn't see it that way."

Sam, the bartender, made his way over, he had been busy with other customers down at the far end of the bar. A big smile filled his aging, rugged features, his rugged face, battered from years in the boxing ring in his youth and too many years afterward because he never knew when to quit.

"Jimboy!" he boomed, his voice overriding all the chatter in the bar and a bear paw of a hand reached across and took Jim's hand in a firm grip. "Great to see you home, Jimboy! Great to see you!" he pumped Jim's hand for all it was worth. "Have you been home yet, seen your dad?"

Jim shook his head. "No, I just got off the bus and I thought I'd come by here first and say 'hello.'"

Jim had worked in the back room for Sam as a young boy, cleaning glasses and running errands for spending money. He had never been allowed in the bar as a boy of course but the kitchen was his territory and Sam found he could count on Jim, who was a willing worker. Jim had worked for Sam right up until he had graduated from high school and gone immediately into the Army, answering the call after the events of 9/11.

"I'll have another beer, Sam," Jim said as he placed his empty on the bar and reached into his pocket for some money.

"You just keep your money, son," Sam said, "You'll never spend a dime in here, you have my word on that one, those ribbons earned you that right!" And Sam immediately placed a full beer in front of Jim. Sam had seen action in Vietnam as a Marine and had earned his share of ribbons, had come home to an ungrateful public who condemned him as a murderer, there had been no fanfare, no parades, just emptiness and isolation. Sam had swallowed the bitter pill and had taken his rage out in the ring, being a leading contender for a few years in the heavyweight division. Sam had known Jim and his family all his life in this town. When Jim had been a young skinny kid he had had some trouble with some bullies so Jim's dad knew the answer to that one, he had taken his shy young son to Sam who taught him

the basics of boxing and self defense. No bully dared mess with Jim after that.

Jim took a sip of beer, he felt the cold tingle in the back of his throat, to him, right now, nothing seemed better in the entire world than to be sitting here right now in Sam's Bar with a few buddies enjoying some ice cold beers. He shut his eyes for a moment. There were the images again, the broken buildings, streets strewn with debris and bodies, flames, streamers from RPG rockets as they came at him. He was about to open his eyes when another image came to him. Jill, waiting on the tables at the restaurant over in San Francisco, Jill hurrying quickly up the street in Chinatown to disappear around the corner never to be seen again.

"Hey, Jim, come on back," Will's voice brought Jim back to the present. He looked to see the empty bottle, another being put in its place. "Drink up, buddy, you're home now."

Jim took a swig. Someone was cranking up the juke box, tunes Jim couldn't even recognize, he had long lost his love of popular music. Just some group or other playing a fast tune. It screeched in his ears, he had heard the same tune and others like it blaring over the ghetto blasters over in Iraq.

"Hi Jim," a young woman's voice said and Jim turned on the stool. Rebecca was standing there, her black hair trailing down her shoulders, Rebecca Fabiola, her dark Italian eyes looking at him. She was dressed in a tube top and tight jeans. She was standing about three feet in front of him.

Jim nodded to her.

"Oh is that all I get? Just a nod? And I haven't seen you in over, what is it now, three years?"

"Yeah, three years," Jim said and he turned around to face the bar. She was just a bad memory now. He felt her slide up next to him, shoving between Jim and Joe. She placed her arms on his shoulders and hung there.

"Oh come on now, Jimboy, don't be like that, how about buying me a beer?"

Jim laid some money down on the bar. Sam served the beer but refused the money.

"It's for her, Sam, not me."

"Like I said, you don't ever buy another beer in here."

Jim could feel Rebecca's arm rubbing against his shoulder, feel her close to him as she picked up her beer. Then her arm went around him and her face was close to his.

"I've missed you, you know," she said.

Jim had nothing to say. She was looking at him, he was looking straight ahead.

"Am I a bad memory?" she asked.

"You're not a memory at all," Jim answered.

"I guess I deserved that," she answered. "Hey, I'm gonna put on some different music, I'll be right back." She smiled at him, then taking her beer in hand she moved across the bar towards the juke box. Jim noticed her sleek brown skin and the dragon tattoo snaking up her mid back disappearing up her tube top, could see the design descend past the top of her black high rise panties and into her jeans, intricate designs branching out along the ridges of her spine. The style of the day, he thought to himself. Every young woman and even those old enough to know better were getting themselves marked these days.

Rebecca put a few quarters in the slot and began selecting tunes. Then she downed the rest of her beer and returned to her place next to him. He felt something primal stir within his being as she nudged in beside him. Her arm went around his shoulder as another beer was brought to her.

"Oh Jimbo," she said, "you don't hate me do you?"

"I don't hate you Rebecca," he tried to keep his voice cold but the feelings were surfacing, slamming into his brain and his soul.

Jim took a long pull on the beer.

Jim heard a commotion at the entrance and he turned on the barstool to see Mike Walker entering the bar. He felt Rebecca stiffen next to him.

Mike Walker stood there, tall as Jim and just as big, stark red hair, short and bristly, he was dressed in jeans and a black "T" shirt which accentuated his bulging biceps. On his right arm, a rattle snake coiled, ready to strike.

"Well look who's here!" Mike Walker declared.

Jim's muscles tensed, ready, but he remained calm on the outside as he casually took another drag from the bottle.

"Hello, Mike," Jim said.

Mike Walker's watery blue eyes just stared at Jim, regarding him. He nodded and started across the bar. He stopped a few feet in front of Jim.

"Back in town one day and already makin' it with my girl, huh?" Mike said.

Rebecca's eyes flashed hot with anger.

"You don't own me, Mike!" she said.

"Oh yeah, well we'll see about that now won't we."

"Chill, Mike!" Jim said and there was menace in his voice, deadly, cold, calculating menace that rumbled deep from his gut.

Mike looked Jim up and down, nodding his head. Two other young men came up beside him, Tiny, who towered above them all and weighed over three hundred pounds and Greg, also a sizable young man. Greg handed Mike an open beer. Mike took a swig, some of it spilled down his face onto his "T" shirt and he wiped his mouth off with his forearm.

"If you're lookin' for trouble you'll find it here!" Will was off his barstool as was Joe. The other patrons in the bar were beginning to make way, clearing the floor and lining up along the walls.

"You want trouble we'll take it out of here," Jim said. "I'm not busting up Sam's place teachin' you a lesson you've had coming for years."

"Maybe there ain't no choice! I'm sayin' here and now!"

Jim turned back to the bar.

"I'll take another beer, Sam," he said.

Sam delivered the beer.

"Son, you want to mop up the floor with his face be my guest," Sam said in a low voice.

Rebecca placed her hand on Jim's shoulder.

"I'll get him out of here, Jim," she said.

"Don't bother," Jim answered.

Rebecca stepped towards Mike.

"Let's go, Mike, don't start trouble, please," she said as she reached for his arm. He jerked away.

"I don't think so, not now!" Mike said. Then he looked at Jim again.

"Whadda ya say, war hero! You and me right now!"

Jim just looked at him then took another drag from his beer.

"Mike," Jim said, "the problem with you is that you never got out of the seventh grade. Grow up."

Jim turned away from Mike and sipped from his drink. Mike

stepped forward and was about to grab Jim's shoulder when Jim suddenly spun around facing him. In that instant Mike was startled and it showed, just for that brief moment. Jim just smiled at him, satisfied at the result.

"I'll meet you down by the railroad tracks Friday night!" Mike said. "You'll either be there or you'll be a chicken shit, yellow bellied coward."

"You'll wait alone," Jim answered.

"He's yella," Tiny chimed in.

Jim came forward towards the towering giant. Tiny stepped back, obviously nervous. Jim stood there in front of him for a moment, looking him in the eye while Joe and Will came up on each side, ready for anything.

"Let's get outta here!" Mike said to his two companions and then he turned to Jim. "I'll be out by those railroad tracks at nine Friday night, that's three days from now and I'll be waitin' for you! We'll see who the real man is around here. You!" Mike indicated Rebecca to come with him. She moved over by Jim, taking his arm.

"I ain't goin' nowhere with you, Mike," she said.

Mike glared at her for a long moment. Then he turned and signaled to his buddies and the three of them left the bar.

"Would you mind walkin' a girl home?" she said to Jim with a smile.

"Guess not," Jim said as he finished his beer, went back and set the empty on the bar. "See you later, Sam, guys," he nodded to Will and Joe. He headed out of the bar with Rebecca.

"My car's over there," she said pointing to a ten year old Toyota four door parked nearby. "You can drive," she handed Jim the keys. Jim opened the passenger door, holding it while Rebecca got in, then he went around to the driver's side and got in. He inserted the key and was about to start the engine when he felt Rebecca's hand on his shoulder. In an instant her arms were around his neck as she came across the seat towards him, locking her lips on his in a smothering kiss, her tongue seeking his, her hands began to fondle his chest.

"Oh Jim, baby," she breathed in his ear then nibbled on his lobe teasingly. "I know you want me, Jim, it's been so, so long since I've been with you."

She moved back for a moment, pulling off her tube top, her large, rounded, brown breasts swinging free she came at him again, reaching for him, kissing his neck. He found himself responding to her, kissing her passionately, his hand going to her breast.

"They're yours, Jim, all yours, just like before in high school, remember Jim, oh Jim, you remember don't you!" her breath was hot and heavy as she fondled him, exploring him, caressing his thighs. She kissed him again. Jim opened his eyes, he pushed her away.

"No, Rebecca," he said.

"It's all right, Jim, I'm yours! I've always been yours..."

"What about Mike, it seems he has a claim on you and it would seem you were plenty willing while I was away."

"Jim, Jim, I was alone, Jim. But now you're back...oh Jim, it can be the way it was..."

"I don't think so, Rebecca," Jim said as she came at him again. Jim fought a great fight to keep from giving in, this was a beautiful young woman in the car half naked with him.

"You made your choice, Rebecca, put your top back on. You can drive yourself home."

Jim got out of the car, Rebecca gripping his hand, trying to pull him back in with her.

"Jim, Jim, don't go, Jim," she pleaded.

Jim took his other hand and peeled her hand from his wrist then made it to the street. Rebecca moved over into the driver's seat, not bothering to put on her top, now she glared up at him.

"You bastard!" she yelled. "You Goddamn bastard!"

Jim started walking away. She fired up the engine, the tires screeched as the car spun around, now it was coming right at him, he was caught in the headlights. Quickly, he leaped aside, rolling on the ground and regaining his feet with practiced ease while the car sped past. Rebecca drove to the end of the street and pulled a quick "U" turn, roaring up the street. Jim was on the sidewalk now, the car drove up and stopped. Rebecca stared out at him, her eyes burning into his.

"You'll pay for this you bastard, you'll see! You'll pay dearly, I promise you that!" with a screech of the tires she was speeding off down the block, turning at the intersection and disappearing up the next street. In the distance he could hear her tires screech again as she took another turn then the sound died down and Jim was standing there under the streetlight in total silence.

CHAPTER THREE

Jim was standing in front of his parent's house. He had been avoiding this moment. He had dusted himself off and had walked the quarter mile home. Now he stood on the sidewalk looking up the walkway to the front door. The lights were on in the front room, his parents were still up. They would not be expecting him back this evening.

He walked up the walkway and stopped at the front door, he felt he should knock before entering even though he had run in and out of this house since he had been a little kid playing with his friends. He went to knock but he found he could not move his hand. He shut his eyes. Then he knocked and waited.

The door opened and his father was standing there, graying, but tall and strong, an older version of his son, John Saunders stood there looking at him. Instant recognition crossed his face and he gave his son a strong bear hug.

"Welcome home, son," he said and he turned. "Jim's home, dear."

Jim's mother, Sandra, came to the door, also a tall woman, wearing her age well, graying blond hair and blue eyes, she threw her arms around her son as tears came.

"Thank God you're safe and home again," she said as she held him.

As his mother was hugging him his younger brother, Robbie, entered the room from down the hall. He was a slender, but muscular boy still in high school with longish hair and a handsome face not unlike his older brother. He stood there, his hands in his pockets, nervously waiting.

"Hi there, Little Bro," Jim said as he parted from his mother.

"Hi," Robbie said then he came forward and gave his big brother a hug, his eyes lighting up now. Jim held him at arm's length and looked at him.

"You're growin' up fast, Little Bro," he said. "A bit skinny though, the weights will fix that."

"Oh he's always on the go these days, Jim," his mother said, "he barely has time to eat anymore, just pops in and stuffs his face every now and then."

Jim just smiled at his brother.

"Speaking of stuffing faces, Mom, I'm starved right now, I realize

It's way past dinner time..."

"Come on in the kitchen and I'll fix you something, Jim," she said. Then a frown crossed her face, "You've been drinking, haven't you, son?"

"I stopped off at Sam's for a few."

"How is ol' Sam doin', Son, haven't been by there in a long time," Jim's dad asked.

"Seems to be doin' okay, Dad."

"Well, son, would you like another beer?"

"John, I think he's had enough for one night," his mother said.

"Oh nonsense, come on, son, let's have a beer," and his dad led the way to the kitchen. John passed his son a bottle from the fridge and one for himself and they were seated while Sandra heated some spaghetti in the microwave oven.

They sat there in silence for a while, John looking at his son.

"You okay, son?" he asked. He knew already, a Vietnam vet himself he and his son both shared wartime experience. Both knew the meaning of a fired RPG round impacting nearby, both had stared death in the face. At this moment no words were needed, they just sat sipping their beers. Robbie entered the kitchen and went to the fridge.

"Now there, you just wait until this meal is heated," Sandra said and Robbie seated himself.

"You okay, son?" John asked. "I heard you took a round."

"I'm fine, Dad," Jim said, "if only the Army realized that."

"Maybe they're not tellin' you everything, son, so maybe it's for the best."

"If it got you home to us in one piece then it's a hidden blessing," Sandra said. "I worried every day about you over there, hearing on the news of all the deaths, all the boys who came home in boxes, I was worried stiff..." her voice almost broke. "Your dad was too."

Jim looked at his father who sat there, his face unreadable but his eyes betrayed him.

"Son," Sandra said.

"Yeah, Mom."

"I'm sorry about what happened with Rebecca. I was always suspicious about that little slut!"

"Now Sandy..." John said.

"It's true, her taking up with that Mike Walker right after you went into the service and sending you that letter. That Mike Walker is nothing but a thug, always was as far as I am concerned."

"I know, Mom. I saw both of them on my way home, down at Sam's."

"I suppose she tried to get friendly again."

Jim said nothing.

"Of course she did, I know her kind, worthless trash, son, worthless, you were well rid of her."

"I don't really think about it anymore."

"Well I was glad, I feared for awhile that you were going to marry her, I was worried sick about it."

"Dear, it didn't happen," John said.

"But I was afraid it would. I'm so glad and son, I'm so glad you are home again."

"I just don't like the circumstances, Mom."

"I don't care what the circumstances are, Son, whatever happened, it got you out of harm's way."

"It isn't fair to the other guys who are still there, we were a good team, they needed me..."

"Oh enough now!"

"Okay, that's it, it's over and done with, Sandy and that's it," John said firmly as he took another sip from his beer.

Sandra served up the food and Robbie had a generous helping.

"I swear, Robbie, I don't know where you put it all, you had a big dinner and now you're eating again," Sandra said.

John and his two sons ate for awhile in silence then John spoke to his son.

"Any plans, son?"

"None, Dad, none for now."

"That's okay son, you just take it easy for now, take it slow, it'll all come to you."

"Funny thing, Dad."

"What's that, son?"

"A guy on the ferry boat said the same thing today to me. A war vet from the Gulf War."

"He was right, son, just take it easy for awhile. You'll figure it out."

"Is that what you did, Dad?"

"No, son, I didn't have the time to figure anything out. Your mother came along at that time and I knew exactly how my life would go." John looked at his wife who was blushing now, "Best thing I ever did in my life."

A thoughtful look came over Jim's father's face for am moment. Then he finished his beer and his meal.

"Well, I'll be turnin' in, son, gotta full day ahead tomorrow."

"G'night, Dad," Jim said. "I'm feeling kind of tired myself. Great meal, Mom," Jim got up and kissed his mother on the cheek then looked at Robbie, who was still eating. "Take care, kid, see you tomorrow."

Robbie smiled and Jim headed down the hallway to his old room.

Jim entered his boyhood room and closed the door, turned on the light. He looked around. Sports banners decorated the walls, pictures of him in his football uniform, even a picture of him at his prom with Rebecca at his side. He looked at the group picture of the football team. He was in the back row, along with the other taller players. He was at one end. And at the other, Mike Walker. The room suddenly became stifling, claustrophobic. For an instant Jim wanted to bolt out of there. Then he sat on the bed. He started unbuttoning his shirt and took it off, he took off the green undershirt and stared in the mirror, his muscular torso bare. He could see the small scar on the left side of his chest. He turned around and looked at his back, he could see the larger scar of the exit wound. He felt the slight sting there, deep inside as he twisted back and he winced slightly. Not bad, he thought, this was not a bad enough wound to cause him to be released from duty. He undressed, turned off the light and slipped beneath the covers, closed his eyes and drifted off.

***

He could see her dark eyes looking right at him. Neela. She was holding him, trying to stem the flow of blood. He had blacked out. No, he was not out completely, there she was holding him. She had eased him to the floor.

"Neela," Jim whispered.

"Jeem, Jeem," she kept saying and there were tears in her eyes.

"How did..."

And he struggled to get the words out, he could feel the blackness closing in all around him, he concentrated on her, forced his mind to focus.

"How did..."

Again the blackhness was closing in on him.

"How did you know my name?"

Her face was near his now, yes he could remember now, remember things he had thought he had had no awareness of.

"I asked your soldier friends," she answered and he thought he saw the hint of a smile. Then all became blackness.

***

Jim was lying awake in a cold sweat. He could feel the burn in his chest, feel the scarred pathway through his torso the round had left, feel the deep burn. He had twisted in his sleep and the pain had caught him. He jerked upright. It was still the middle of the night. He shook it off and lay back down.

Neela.

He wondered what had happened to her. He had never seen her again. When he had regained consciousness he had been in a field hospital O.R. then he had blacked out again. After that he was aboard a transport plane heading stateside to a waiting hospital. He had asked why he had been taken there, he felt good, he was back on his feet pacing the hallways and wanting to know when he could rejoin his outfit. There had been no answer for days. Just endless therapy, changing bandages until the wound had healed. Then he had been given the news.

He was to be medically discharged, honorably and with decorations for valor in the face of extreme danger. That was it, his military career was over.

He faded into sleep again.

***

He could see her face, an Asian face, long, black hair framing a beautiful face. Jill. Standing there in Chinatown on the main street looking at him. She was reaching out her arms to him and he was coming towards her. Then she turned away and faded, she wasn't there when he reached her. He looked around, she was nowhere in sight, she had simply disappeared. Up a side street? He went up a street and came to a dead end. Then he saw movement out of the corner of his eye, a flash of garment disappearing around the side of a building. He headed in that direction.

"Jill!" he called.

There was no reply. He headed around the corner of the building and there she was, standing there in the middle of the narrow street, no one else was around. She smiled at him and again opened her

arms. He came to her and she embraced him, held him.
***

Jim opened his eyes. A dream, it had only been a dream. Sunlight was streaming through the gap in the window shade, it was morning now. Jim rose up and shook his head, shook off the sleep, the dream, and got to his feet. He felt unsteady for a moment. He went to the closet and took out a pair of his faded jeans hanging there and put them on along with a white "T" shirt and his sneakers. He looked at his uniform hanging there, never to be worn again, then he shut the closet door. He figured his dad had gone to open the shop he owned, a garage and body shop out on the other end of town.

Jim headed into the hallway and walked into the living room. He could see the weight set out on the patio, the barbell, loaded with iron plates on the bench and a movable squat rack off to the side against the wall to the garage and laying beside it a pair of heavy dumbbells. What memories he had, his dad teaching him how to lift weights and he teaching his little brother. He had noticed his brother had put on a little solid weight over his slender frame, he had obviously been hitting the workouts. He was at school now.

Jim heard a sound from the kitchen and he went there. His mother was washing the dishes and placing them in the cupboard.

"Hi Mom," Jim said.

She turned and smiled at him.

"Good morning Jim, how are you feeling? Did you sleep well?" she asked.

"Yeah, I guess," he answered.

"Dad's out in the garage, he hasn't left for work yet."

"Okay."

Jim went through the door into the garage. There was his dad busy polishing a shining, white, freshly waxed 1964 Chevy Impala Supersport, raised in back with wide tires on gleaming chromed rims. It was a thing of beauty.

"Wow!" Jim said.

Then he looked at his dad.

"Dad, you aren't at work today?"

His dad smiled as he put the polishing rag on the workbench.

"I'll go in later, son, Tony can run things."

Tony was his dad's chief mechanic down at the garage, Jim knew his dad could always count on Tony to run things but it was still rare to see his dad ever taking any time off.

"I just wanted to get her polished up for you," his dad said.

Jim had worked for his dad and also for contractors during summer vacations doing construction work in addition to working for Sam at the bar to buy this car, he had set his goal ever since seventh grade and he had bought the Chevy finally, his dad had helped with the rebuild but when he had left for the war the car had needed a paint job and body work. Now here it sat, looking better than new, a gleaming, shining masterpiece.

"All registered and insured in your name, Son," his dad said.

"Dad...I am amazed... I don't know what to say..."

"How about just taking it for a spin? Lets' look at the engine."

They went to the front of the car and his dad popped the hood. The engine was a clean 427 with a new fuel injection system, all upgraded, high performance to the max. Jim's dad had gotten rid of the carburetor and had replaced everything.

"Jeeze, Dad, you shouldn't have..."

"Glad to do it, son, me and your brother worked on it night and day, it was a way to keep close to you. And your mom even helped. She knew this car was a part of you, son, and now it's ready for you to take for a ride."

Jim was still dumbfounded as he stared at his like/new car.

"Well, son, I gotta be off now so you take her out and have a great time."

His dad patted Jim on the shoulder. Jim looked at him, his eyes almost tearing.

"I don't know what to say," Jim said.

"Say nothing, son, just enjoy the ride. I'll be home this evening so don't be late for dinner, okay?"

"Sure dad."

His dad smiled and headed out of the garage to his pickup truck with John's Garage and Tow painted on the door. He got in and fired it up, looked at his son, smiled and drove off down the street. Jim just stood there a while looking at the car, running his hand along the body, how smooth and perfect the paint job.

"It's a fine job your dad and brother did," his mother was standing there in the doorway. "When we heard you were coming home your dad and Rob worked exhaustingly to get it ready for you."

"You did too, Mom," Jim said.

"Oh I really didn't do anything, son, I don't know much about cars."

Jim knew better but didn't say anything.

"Would you like some breakfast, son?" she asked.

"That's okay, Mom," Jim said. "I'm going down to Stan's for breakfast."

Jim gave her a kiss on the cheek. "Thanks."

He was out the door and back in the garage. He got into the car and adjusted the seat, fastened the seatbelt around his shoulder, the garage door was already open.

"Well, here goes," he said, "it's been a long time."

He turned on the key and hit the electronic ignition. There was a buzz, a whine and then she caught, firing up with a deep throated rumble that vibrated the garage and probably the whole house as the mighty engine thundered to life. Jim let it idle for a few moments as he turned on the radio, selecting the proper station, heavy metal, the speakers came to life, further vibrating the garage and house, the huge base speakers in back thundering along with the engine as the whole car vibrated with renewed life. Jim depressed the clutch and shoved the four on the floor into first, letting it out slow as the car lurched forward down the driveway. A neighbor across the street, an older man who was out watering his lawn looked up and waved. Jim waved back. He turned down the street and took off, shifting into second as the car rumbled down the block to the first stop sign. He stopped and waited a moment for all cross traffic to clear.

"Well, let's see what this baby can do," he said to himself as he gunned the engine, hitting first and letting out the clutch then starting forward, slow at first then flooring it, the tires caught with a screech as rubber burned. He moved quickly into second gear and then into third then backed off, cruising along in third as several people watched from their houses. Yes, Jim Saunders was home. Finally.

He headed up the main drag through the center of town, not much had changed during his three year absence, then headed out to the main highway and pulled into the parking lot of Stan's.

CHAPTER FOUR

Stan's was a little greasy spoon breakfast and lunch restaurant out on the edge of town along the main highway. Jim was hoping he was open today, Stan usually ran things his way, opening whenever he felt like it and Jim hoped it was his lucky day today. There was nothing better than steak and eggs and home style hashed browns served by Stan himself.

There were other vehicles parked there, he was in luck, Stan's was open for business. He parked and got out. Stan's was a small place with a large picture window in front with the name, "Stan's," painted across it. There was a sign on the door that said "closed." It always said that, open or not but Jim could see that the place was packed. Everyone loved Stan's home cooked food and they went there every chance they could, whenever Stan had a mind to open for business. Jim could see Stan behind the counter, a lean man in his sixties with longish steel gray hair, his face narrow, deep set eyes that smiled, every line in his face deeply etched. He wore a white "T" shirt, his arms, though thin, showed well defined muscle under his aging skin as well as tattoos decorating his forearms, one of a ship on his right forearm and on his left, a red heart with an arrow through it and about an inch away, a winged, little fat Cupid holding a bow, extra arrows in a quiver across his back. Above the heart, the words, NAVY SEAL enshrined in flames.

"Ah the returning hero!" Sam broke into a big smile, his mouth seeming to fill the entire narrow face, he was missing a front tooth, his eyes, black as night, sparkled with joy. He hurried around the counter and gave Jim a bear hug which almost took his breath away, there was a lot of power in his lean arms.

"Hello, Stan," Jim said.

"Welcome home, kid!" Stan said, "Have yourself a seat, breakfast is on the house."

Other customers had turned to look, mostly familiar faces, working men Jim had known ever since he had been a kid, also a few middle aged wives who had joined their husbands for breakfast. Some of the men rose up and greeted Jim as he made his way to the counter and took a seat. He shook hands all around nodding and saying "hi." He had known these men and women all his life, knew them growing up, played with their kids, got into scrapes with those kids.

"Like I said, breakfast is on the house," Stan said as he returned to his place behind the counter. There was a woman working the counter also, she was busy taking orders, a young woman Jim recognized, Sarah, he had known her in high school. Sarah looked at him and gave a smile.

"Hi Jim," she said.

He nodded. She had been the girlfriend of one of his buddies in high school. He noticed she was wearing a gold wedding band.

"How's Dave," Jim asked, he figured Dave Stevenson had married her.

"Don't know, Jim," she said, "haven't seen him in two years. I married Guy Reynolds."

"Oh."

Guy Reynolds was another guy Jim had known but not real well. He'd been a smart kid, headed for college at the time. Sarah gave Jim a smile and went about taking orders.

"Never knew you to hire help," Jim said to Stan, "and I'll have steak and eggs, rare and over easy."

"Over easy it is, kid," Stan said, "I needed some help here, I'm open all the time now, not like the old days and Sarah, well, they're, her and Guy are just starting out and all so I figured..."

"Okay," Jim said. Come to think of it he had noticed that the old place had had a repaint and looked a little neater.

"Still closed on weekends though, gotta get my fishing in," Stan smiled. He owned and lived on a boat docked at a local harbor nearby and he loved cruising around San Francisco Bay although he never caught much fish and those he did he usually threw back in the water. It was just a relaxing pastime for him. He had a Navy pension, had taken a few bad hits over in 'Nam. He had been decorated for bravery pulling his wounded buddies out of the line of fire with no regard for his personal safety.

Stan returned to the grill, flipping flapjacks, sausages, and hash browns. He tossed a huge flank steak down, it hit with a sizzle.

"Steak and eggs comin' up," he said.

Sarah brought Jim a cup of coffee, Jim sipped it black. There was no finer cup of coffee than the coffee from Stan's place as far as Jim was concerned. Sure, there were those new latte places he had noticed as he drove through town with all the fancy flavored stuff and the yuppie types sitting out in their chairs concentrating on their laptops, plugs in their ears as they listened to their IPODs.

Breakfast was served, steak blood rare, eggs over easy and plenty of home cooked, thick cut hashed browns, not the prefab, flaky stuff most chain restaurants served. Also a side of pancakes. Jim poured a generous amount of maple syrup on these and plenty of butter.

It was great to be home again.

"Heard from Sam that you had a little trouble last night," Stan said in a low voice.

"Oh not really," Jim answered. Though they would never admit it, Stan and Sam, the bartender, were the best of buddies and Sam often accompanied Stan on his excursions around the bay on his fishing boat.

"Watch out for that Mike Walker," Stan warned, his voice still low.

"He doesn't really bother me," Jim answered as he slurped up some eggs mixed with hashed browns.

"Well, anyway, kid, watch your back."

Jim looked at Stan, his eyes betrayed a moment of dead seriousness.

"No problem there, Stan, I've been watchin' my back plenty for the past three years."

"I know what ya mean, son, I know what ya mean," and Stan reached over and patted Jim on the shoulder. "Just watch yourself with him."

He went back to the grill and Jim finished up, washing the last of the pancakes down with a swallow of coffee.

"Man, that was great, Stan," Jim said. "Over there I used to dream of coming in here, the food was so bad there you would not believe..."

"Oh yeah I would," Stan said.

"Yeah, I guess you would, see ya later, Stan."

Jim headed out the door and across the parking lot to his car. When he reached it he heard tires screech and looked around. A candy apple purple 1965 Pontiac GTO was just pulling into the lot, wide tires, chromed rims, raised high, chromed exhaust pipes, engine thundering it came to a halt near Jim. The door opened and Mike Walker stepped out. The passenger door opened and out stepped Rebecca, dressed in skin tight jeans and a black tube top, her straight, black hair whipping about her shoulders as she came up next to Mike.

He put his arm around her. She smiled at Jim then up at Mike. Mike put his lips to hers and her arms went around him. Mike looked at Jim, challenge in his eyes. Jim said nothing.

"Just a reminder," Mike said, "the railroad tracks, Friday night."

"You'll be waiting a long time, Mike," Jim answered.

"I certainly never figured you for a coward!" Rebecca said as her eyes blazed at Jim.

Jim just shook his head and got in his car. He fired it up. Mike came towards him, the window was rolled down. Mike leaned towards him, Rebecca at his side.

"The tracks, Friday night."

Jim said nothing, he hit first and screeched away, Mike and Rebecca jumped back, startled. Jim peeled out of the lot and hit the main road. He knew his destination.

CHAPTER FIVE

Jim was driving across the Oakland Bay Bridge hitting 90 miles an hour. He slowed down to 70, remembering that there could be cameras recording his speed and he didn't really need a speeding ticket right now. He passed Yerba Buena Island and crossed the final span into San Francisco, taking an exit and driving up Market Street to Stockton, hanging a right and driving north several blocks to Union Square, he headed down the ramp into the underground parking lot, took a ticket, punched the button, the guard arm lifted and he found a parking space. He locked his car and headed out of the lot heading directly for Market Street.

Jim knew right where he was heading, the steak house, it wasn't hunger driving him, having just had breakfast at Stan's an hour ago. It was her. He wanted to see her. He could picture her in his mind as he turned up Market heading west.

He saw the sign for the steakhouse and turned to go in. The door was locked. Jim stepped back and discovered why. There was a sign on the door which read: "Out of Business." He put his face to the glass and peered inside at the darkened interior. All the tables were still there, the grill was there, everything in place but completely deserted. Jim knew why. It was his fault. If he hadn't interfered this would not have happened. He felt sick to his stomach suddenly as he reeled back and landed against a lamp post. He shook his head. This could not be happening, yet it had. And in less than twenty four hours. Real fear, that's what would cause the owner to cut and run like this, nothing else, those men in there the day before had been real bad news.

Jim turned around and started back down Market Street passing dozens of people and not even being aware of them. He was trying to get a bearing on what to do now. He needed to clear his head, to think about what had happened, figure out how to make things right.

There was no making things right, it was much bigger than anything he could possibly do.

Jim was standing in front of a bar. He went inside and sat at the bar. He ordered a beer and sat sipping it slowly, trying to sort things out. He found himself thinking of Neela. He remembered her dark eyes as she had looked at him, he remembered when she had smiled at him. He had felt he had known her more than any other girl he had ever known in high school. There hadn't been many, mainly Rebecca. But he had not cared for her in the entire year he had known her like he had found himself caring for Neela in the brief time he had seen her.

"Another?" the bartender was asking.

Jim looked down at his empty glass. He knew what he must do now.

"No thanks," he said and he rose from the barstool and left the establishment.

Jim headed right for Kearney Street walking right up into Chinatown. He went to the street he remembered Jill turning on and went up one block trying to figure out which building she had gone into. They all looked pretty much the same. People came and went along the sidewalk ignoring him as he searched the block. He figured he could knock on every door but that wouldn't work for very long, a lot of people would be getting upset. He should just forget it, she was as gone as the restaurant was. He hardly knew her anyway and yet he couldn't get her out of his mind. He decided to head back to Union Square to his car. From there he had no idea where he was going to go.

He decided to take a short-cut. He turned into a narrow ally and started walking. He saw two figures up ahead blocking the way out. They were short, Asian, stocky build, standing with hands on hips. Jim turned to go back the other way. There were three others now blocking the way he had just come. One was the burly one he had had the confrontation with in the restaurant. The three were now advancing towards him. Jim turned and started down the alley towards the two men at the other end. They stood, waiting. He felt the hairs go up in back of his neck, felt himself shift into "combat mode." Survival! The key most thing in his mind right now.

As he approached the two men they shifted into a fighting stance. Jim stopped and looked at them, then turned sideways to them and hit a low horse stance, hands ready, he looked in the other direction.

"Might as well give it up, honky!" the one he had confronted yesterday said, "You're a dead man!"

The burly one began advancing with his partners, the two in front also did the same, but cautiously, they had read the look in Jim's eyes correctly. Jim sensed movement and shifted as the three in back came at him, the burly one in the lead. Jim slammed his heel into the man's chest and heard the audible crack, the burly man screamed, cut short as Jim nailed him in the temple with a single knuckle strike. As the man hit the ground Jim was over him and burying his heel into one of the other men's ribs, he felt them give way, that man also caving in, going to ground with his buddy. Jim was airborne now, his body twisting as he did a flying wheel kick, his heel connecting solidly with the third man's Jaw, knocking him backwards against the wall. Jim landed on his feet, coming in low, spinning and coming around with a knifehand strike to the man's neck. The man was down. Now there were two more to worry about as Jim spun. Jim heard the rushing of air as one of the men pulled out a pair of maru gata nunchacku sticks, two sticks joined with a short chain capable of delivering 2000 lbs of striking pressure per square inch. The other man pulled out switchblade knife, flicking it open. They came at him, the nunchucks flying. Jim ducked as they missed, striking the bricks on the building sending a chunk flying. They came on, one of the men behind Jim on the ground was trying to regain his feet and as Jim passed he delivered a kick to his head to keep him out of action. The other two armed men stepped over their downed partners.

"We don't go down so easy, honky!" the man with the nunchucks said as he lunged forward.

Rather than stepping back Jim dove to the ground in his direction, spinning on his hip, his legs knifing across the attackers shins sending him to the ground. Jim was up in an instant delivering a chop to the mans throat, the man dropped his nunchucks and rolled around clutching his throat and fighting for air. The man with the knife looked down at his partner then at Jim and there was fear in his eyes. But he raised his arm. There was a "crack" and the man hit the ground clutching his forearm, his knife lying on the ground about ten feet away. The man rolled around screaming in pain. Jim looked up. A figure was standing there in the alley dressed in a black trench coat holding a 9mm in both hands. Jim recognized him immediately. The man from the boat, the man who had talked to him briefly and now here he was, standing there with a smoking gun.

Jim looked at him, then down at the man who had the knife. He was now whimpering in pain, he looked up at Jim then back at his ruined forearm. Jim looked at the man in the trench coat.

"Nice work there," the man said. "You handle yourself very well, I figured you would."

"Who are you?" Jim asked.

"A friend. That's all you need to know right now. You better get out of here fast."

Jim looked at the men lying on the ground.

"Don't be worrying about them, just get going," the man in the trench coat said as he stepped aside. A siren could now be heard in the distance.

"Take off!" the man in the coat said.

Jim nodded to him.

"Thanks," Jim said.

"Don't worry about it, I'll be in touch."

Jim ran past him and turned up the street. When he looked around the man in the trench coat was gone. Jim ran on and cut through another alley then made his way casually down Stockton Street to Union Square. As he walked into the underground parking garage an idea came to him. He smiled to himself. There was hope after all. He reached his car and got in.

***

Jim was heading west, a shortcut over Twin Peaks towards the coast. He reached 19th Avenue and headed south arriving at the campus of San Francisco State University. He parked in the guest parking lot and stepped out, the large buildings intimidating, towering, dominating, he didn't know where to begin. He started walking along pathways that wound through expanses of manicured lawns, students were rushing everywhere pre-occupied with their studies, hurrying to classes and here he was, the returned warrior, alone among the masses, feelings of isolation impacting on him suddenly. The second day home and so much had already happened.

He saw a girl, her back to him, long, black, silken hair falling about her shoulders dressed in a very short skirt and tube top, a backpack full of books over one shoulder, she was walking along, cell phone to her ear. Jill? Jim ran up along side her, pretending to be hurrying to a class. No, it wasn't her by a long shot. The girl turned and looked at him momentarily, her face caked with a ton of makeup and he noticed a dragon tattoo snaking up her spine disappearing into the tube top.

Not Jill, not Jiang Li.

A familiar sound assaulted his ears. The familiar sound of iron

Olympic plates being loaded onto an Olympic bar. He turned and faced a large building. The gymnasium. He headed towards it, towards the sound of iron and steel. He looked inside, he was in a hallway with an open door off to the left. He peered in. The weight room, squat racks, heavy duty benches, plenty of raw iron, rows of dumbbells ranging from three pound weights all the way up to a pair of one fifties. There were a few students in the weight room, football players from the look of them, large young men over by the squat rack and the bench loading plates. They looked in Jim's direction. Jim cut quite a picture himself at six foot two and two thirty, his massive arms bulging out of his white "T" shirt, his massive thighs straining at his faded jeans.

He crossed the floor, looking around for any sign of a coach or other authority figure who could possibly kick him out. He needed this, needed to feel the pump, needed to feel the surge that comes from driving raw iron. He approached the bench. There were four young men there, one was seated, they wore sweatsuits and tank tops, impressively muscled but not in Jim's league. They eyed him suspiciously.

"Hey, mind if I work in?" Jim asked.

"Go ahead," one of the young men said, he had just finished a set, there were two big plates on each side of the bar, two hundred and twenty five pounds. A good warm-up. Jim didn't need a lot of warming up after what had transpired in the alley just forty five minutes earlier.

Jim eased himself down onto the bench, it had been a couple of months since his last workout, a light, machine type for his re-hab in the hospital. He had not attempted anything this heavy in over a year. He gripped the bar, the cold steel in his hand felt good, he hoisted it from the racks and held it at arm's length over his head. No pain yet in his side, a good sign. He took a deep breath and slowly lowered the bar until it touched his chest then pushed upward with ease. A deep breath and another one, it felt nice and light. He did twenty while the others watched. Then he sat upright, racked the weight, and shook it off, oh it felt good. He could see the others looking at him. He stood and they all took their turns under the bar, getting five to ten reps among them, struggling with the last ones.

Again, they looked at him. He had hardly strained on that set he had done.

More plates were loaded, three on each side now, three hundred and fifteen pounds. Jim slid under the bar, gripped it and did ten easy ones, still no pain. The others did their sets, averaging five reps and one guy doing eight. It was Jim's turn again.

"Two more forty fives," he said and an extra forty five pound plate was slammed on each side, the sound of raw iron slamming onto the bar music to Jim's ears. He sat down on the bench. He had four hundred and five pounds on the bar. More than he had done in a quite awhile although he had done it regularly in his last year of high school and on base. They had had a makeshift gym with old rusty weights set up in one of the buildings over in Iraq and he had hit it pretty regularly between missions. There had been a lot of downtime.

Jim took a deep breath and lay back, gripping the bar and rolling it from the racks. Another deep breath, yes, it felt nice and heavy now. He lowered it to his chest and with a mighty heave rammed it upward. He did five then sat up. Man! It felt good. He looked at the others.

"Thanks, guys," he said as he got up off the bench.

"No problem," came the answer from one of them. Jim noticed that everyone in the entire weight room was looking at him as he left. He heard the last two plates being taken off the bar as he walked through the entrance to continue his search.

He walked along among the students, many Asian young women were going to and from their classes but none familiar. Jim felt pumped from his workout and from the alley fight earlier and he walked swiftly, covering as much ground as he could, ever searching but still, no luck. He found a cement bench near a lawn and sat down. He was thirsty. He looked across the way, there was a snack bar. He now had a hunger growing as a result of the brief workout. He walked over and ordered a Coke and a meat and bean burrito then returned to the bench and sat down to eat. The burrito was good, nice and spicy the way he liked them. The Coke soothed his mouth and throat and he could feel the tingle in back of his eyeballs. He closed his eyes for a moment to enjoy the taste. Nothing like a nice lunch.

When he opened his eyes he saw her. She was directly across from him getting in line at the snack bar. He almost didn't recognize her, she had on baggy jeans and a very loose fitting, oversized dark blue sweatshirt with SF embroidered on the front, a backpack on her back. Her black hair was loosely done up on the back of her head and strands escaped to fall about her face and shoulders. Same beautiful face, dark, dark eyes, full lips, no makeup like she had been wearing before, but Jim knew it was her, no mistake. She had not seen him, she was going through her purse when Jim walked up holding his Coke.

"May I buy you lunch?" he asked casually and she looked up. Her eyes met his and she almost dropped her purse as she moved back out of the line, startled. She turned and started walking away.

"Jill, wait," Jim said as he walked after her. She hurried along the pathway between two buildings.

"Please leave," she said without looking back.

"Jill," Jim said but she kept going.

"Jiang Li," he said her real name and she stopped suddenly, still not looking back. He came up to her and stood behind her.

"Please," he said.

She turned to face him.

"Haven't you done enough already? What do you want now?" she demanded.

"Hey, I went by the restaurant this morning..."

"And you saw that it went out of business, you caused this by interfering..."

"Hey wait a minute, I'm not going to take the blame for that one, those guys in there were bad news..."

"It was none of your affair! And now I have no job to go to. I found out this morning, I would have been working this afternoon otherwise. Now what am I to do? You think it's so easy..."

"Your boss shouldn't have backed down, that was his fault!"

"You don't know the hold these men have on us! You have no idea what you got involved in!"

"Oh I think I do! I saw those men just about an hour ago, plus a couple of friends of theirs..."

"Where were you?"

"In Chinatown, looking for you!"

She turned away from him and started moving away.

"Just leave me alone, I have to get to class now."

"No you don't, you were getting ready to have lunch and I'd like to buy you lunch, please, Jiang Li...Jill."

She hesitated. A young man came walking up to them.

"Jill, is this man bothering you?" he asked.

Jim looked at him, medium height, average build but not afraid as he looked at Jim, towering over him, his massive build dominating the situation.

"No, Steven," Jill said, "no really, everything's all right, this is a friend of mine, it's all right, thank you."

Steven looked at both of them, Jim said nothing. Jill took Jim's hand.

"Really, Steven, this is a good friend and we were just going to lunch, I'm ready, Jim," she looked up into Jim's eyes then smiled at Steven. Steven nodded and walked away.

"Just lunch! That's all," Jill said.

"I ask nothing more," Jim said and he smiled at her. She struggled not to but suddenly managed to smile back, a real smile, genuine, her dark eyes sparkling.

"But let's have a real lunch," Jim said, "is there some kind of restaurant around here?"

"A good cafeteria over there," Jill said indicating another building.

"It isn't cheap."

"I'm not cheap either, let's go," Jim said as he offered his arm. Jill hesitated then took it.

They walked to the building and got in line, it was busy, people turned to look as they entered, Jill was dwarfed by Jim, holding his muscular arm. She smiled at him then nodded to several students she knew as they got into the line. They both chose roast beef, mashed potatoes and gravy, peas and carrots and large Cokes and then took a seat near a window. Jim set his tray on the table and then pulled back the chair for Jill, she smiled and was seated.

"A gentleman," she said and she smiled at him again.

They took a few bites and Jim looked out the window at the school grounds, the passing students, then he looked at Jill.

"The cook in the restaurant, he didn't look like the type of guy who would fold."

"He isn't, it's his family, and the owner, he has a family also, they have to think of them, you know."

"And how do they feed their families if they have no business? No income?"

"They'll find a way, they have probably left town. I'm telling you, these men are very dangerous. And there's my family as well..."

She looked down, Jim could see fear momentarily cross her face.

"They've threatened your family?"

"Not yet, but I'm sure it could happen."

"Over one incident that I caused, it was really my fault, I can see that, but then, what those men were doing was wrong."

"Right or wrong doesn't matter to them, it's all just about what they want and they have the power to get it. And my family..."

"What?"

"My father has businesses in this city, and real estate, and he has to be careful."

"He pays 'protection?'"

Jill said nothing, she just kept eating.

"Like I said, I had a run in today with several of them, not the one who was running the show but the other one and his buddies. They won't be bothering anyone for a while."

"And they recognized you."

"That's why they stalked me."

"You look like you can take care of yourself but it won't be enough. Don't return to Chinatown, Jim. You survived this time."

"I have no intention of staying away. Let's have dinner tonight, after all, you won't be working."

"You saw to that!"

"Well?"

"No, this lunch was enough. You would have to meet my parents and they would not approve, I already told you that."

"You have your own choice in the matter, let me hear it from you, Jiang Li, let me hear you say you don't want to see me again and I'll leave, I won't come back, but you say it to me right now, to my face, no bullshit!"

Jim started to rise from the table, having finished his lunch. Jill grabbed her backpack and slung it over her shoulder. She was looking at him. Jim moved closer to her, his face near hers. Here was this young girl, he hardly knew her yet here she was, it was like he had known her for a long time.

"So go ahead and say it," he said, "and I'll walk away, promise."

She looked dead at him, her eyes intense, piercing, he couldn't read what she was thinking. She was studying his face, his eyes, his soul, he felt.

"Why? Why do you care, why?" she asked.

"I like you, that's it. I like you and I want to see you again and I think you like me."

"You're certainly sure of yourself, aren't you?"
"I'm sure of how I feel."
"You haven't known me for even a day."
"I like what I see."
She looked down, thinking, pondering.
"You should leave," she looked up at him, her eyes almost pleading. There was hesitation in her voice.
"That's not the question. Do you want me to leave, really want me to leave? Just say the word."
"It's dangerous for you and for me and for my family."
Jim felt like a jerk now. It was true. He had placed her in danger, had caused a man to quit his business and run for his life. Jim knew he had no right.
"You're right, I'm sorry."
Jim started to turn away then he turned back to her.
"You have a class?"
"I am on my way there now, I am almost late."
"I'll walk you there, if you don't mind."
"Do I have a choice."
"Say the word, like I said."
She smiled and then she reached over and took his hand, holding it firmly, her touch was warm, her hand soft. His large hand folded around hers.
They left the cafeteria hand in hand and strolled across the campus to one of the buildings, stopping outside. They turned to face each other, he took both of her hands in his.
"How many more classes do you have today?"
"This is the last one," she said. "I'll be finished in an hour."
"How did you get here?"
"I took the bus."
"I can give you a ride home."
"No..."
"Please, I'll let you off before we get there, you can walk the rest of the way. But I'll keep an eye on you until you go in."
"And then you will know where I live."
"And that's bad?"
"No."
She took her hands from his and fooled with the straps of her backpack. She was looking down, then she looked up at him.

"What time are you due home?"

"They don't know I have no job to go to yet, I didn't tell them. I guess a ride would be all right..."

"I'll be waiting right here."

She smiled up at him, then she entered the building, looking back and smiling at him just before going through the entrance.

"See you in an hour," she said.

***

Jim had been seated on a nearby bench for an hour. Still, she had not come out the door. Was she ditching him? He had that thought. Still, he waited.

He looked at his watch. Now fifteen minutes had gone by and he was starting to get worried. He was getting the idea, she didn't want to see him and was taking the easy way out. He rose from the bench. She came running through the door, her hair half unraveled and falling about her shoulders, struggling to keep her backpack on as she almost tripped at the entrance. She looked up at Jim, breathless, and smiled, running up to him.

"I'm really sorry," she said as she stood in front of him, still breathless, "I had to talk to the teacher about the upcoming assignment, he wasn't quite clear in class, and there were other students in front of me and..."

"It's okay," Jim said to her with a smile. He was quite relieved to see her and he secretly admonished himself for doubting her. He looked at her eyes and he realized that if she had really not wanted to see him she would have told him so. But then, she had actually done just that and he had been so insistent. No matter now, here she was right in front of him.

"Here, let me take that," Jim said as he eased the backpack from her shoulders and hoisted it over his. He took her arm gently and she did not pull away. They walked along the pathway between the buildings, between lawns and a plaza with a fountain, he could feel the mist as they passed.

"Tell you what," he said.

"I'm afraid to ask," she answered.

"No, it's a good thing," he said.

"What?"

"I'd like to take you to my town to meet my parents, we'd have plenty of time and I could get you home with no problem. I'm just across the bay. How about it?" He was prepared to back up his request with a persuasive argument. Jill looked at him and smiled.

"I'd love to," she said.

* * *

Jim took the exit from the freeway, heading along the old highway into the outskirts of town, then down the main drag into the town center, going slowly, pointing out all the main features of the place which he had grown up in, it was an upbeat town now, there were four trendy coffee houses competing with one another, an influx of business executives, writers and even some movie personalities and producers had taken up residence in the once simple small town, there was plenty of new construction going on and older buildings were also being upgraded. It was not the same small town Jim had grown up in anymore. Jill looked about, taking it all in. He noticed that she leaned slightly across the bucket seat towards him and every now and then she would look at him. Their eyes met from time to time.

"That's where I went to grade school," Jim said as they passed the elementary school, one of several in the town. It was afternoon now and school was out, the grounds empty. They passed on down the street, he hit a few turns and they passed the high school. There were students as well as adults out on the track running and walking. Some were stretching and others were standing in groups. Jim pulled into the parking lot and parked. He got out and went to the passenger door opening it for Jill. She got out, stood there in front of him for a moment looking up at him, looking into his eyes. He looked back and grinned.

"Come on," he said, "I want you to meet someone."

They walked along beside the chain linked fence and went through a gate to the track area. Several students were in jogging suits, just coming around the turn. One of them was Rob.

"Hey kid!" Jim yelled and Rob separated from the group, running up in front of them.

"This is my kid brother, Rob," Jim said as he patted Rob on the shoulder. Rob was quiet and nodded.

"This is Jill," Jim said, "she will be joining us for dinner tonight so be on time."

"Hello Rob," Jill said with a smile as she extended her hand. Rob took it, self consciously, not looking up, he seemed, to Jim, to be preoccupied with something.

"Okay," was all Rob said then he nodded to both of them and took off down the track, double-timing to catch up with his buddies. Jim watched him go, wondering at his quietness. He shook his head and looked at Jill. He reached out and took her hand, he felt her fingers fold around his, and they went back to the car.

"Now where?" Jill asked.

"Now, home, Dad should be getting home in about an hour."

"Won't I be intruding?" Jill asked. "I don't want to..."

"Nonsense, no problem at all, you'll have a great time."

Jill thought a moment.

"What is it?"

"Can we..."

"What?"

"Those coffee places in the center of town, can we go to one, I feel a little strange right now about meeting your parents, if we could just have a cup of coffee."

"No problem, we have all afternoon yet, but tell you what, my dad is still at work so why don't we swing by my home for a few minutes so you can meet my mom..."

Jill was almost in a panic. She pulled a cell phone out of her purse and handed it to Jim.

"Why don't you call her to tell her we're going to be there, please. I...am not dressed for..."

"Oh nonsense, you look..." Jim was at a loss for words, this young woman with him, dressed in jeans and a loose fitting sweatshirt, her hair tied loosely on her head with stray strands streaming down brushing her face was the most beautiful sight he had ever imagined, he suddenly realized.

"You look perfect, Jill, just perfect."

"But..."

"It's okay, we'll stop for a coffee and you can prepare yourself, okay?" he smiled. Jill returned his smile.

"Oh thank you," she said as she placed a hand gently on his shoulder.

Jim headed into the center of town and parked in front of the old bus depot, it had been rebuilt but it's old adobe style remained, originally built in the 1920s as a train station before the old rail line was taken out and buses replaced the passenger train as a means of transportation. In those days a train had taken commuters to Oakland where they would then take the old ferry boat across the bay to San Francisco.

Jim escorted Jill across the street to one of the coffee houses and they went to the counter and ordered two fancy, flavored lattes complete with whipped cream and a cherry on top. They seated themselves at a sidewalk table. Jim frowned at his coffee, Jill was already sipping hers. She looked at him and frowned.

"What's wrong?" she asked.

"I'm not used to this kind of coffee, if you can really call it a coffee at all," Jim answered.

Jill laughed and took another sip.

"Not your type?" she asked.

Jim picked off the cherry and devoured it then tasted the blend and shrugged his shoulders.

"Hmmm, not bad," he answered. "So this is what a four dollar cup of coffee tastes like."

"Oh I'm sorry,..." Jill stammered. "I didn't mean to make you spend..."

"Oh no...no problem at all, I was just saying..."

"Hi Jim, what's up," a voice said and Jim looked up. Will was standing there, a grin on his face.

Jim made a brief introduction. Will took Jill's hand in greeting.

"Pleased to meet you," he stammered. He was staring at her, and realizing it, looked down.

"So what's up?" Jim asked.

"I was just down here in town and saw you, thought I'd say 'hi.' Oh yeah, Mike Walker's been hanging around town, saw him a little while ago."

"Interesting," Jim answered, giving Will a look saying to go no further with the conversation. Will got the message.

"Well, I gotta be goin'," Will said, "Say 'hi' to your folks."

"Sure thing," Jim said turning back to Jill. Will walked off down the street, Jill watched him go. She looked at Jim.

"So this, Mike, he is also a friend of yours?" Jill asked.

"Oh," Jim was hesitant, "well, kind of, I guess you could say that..."

Jill looked deeply into his eyes, Jim suddenly felt uncomfortable and shifted in his seat.

"Somehow I doubt he is really your friend," Jill simply said as she sipped her coffee.

"Well, nothing to worry about," Jim said. "Some people are just nicer than others."

"And this 'Mike' is not so nice."

Jim just smiled at her and found himself reaching across the table and taking her hand, her hand going willingly into his. It felt soft but there was firmness to her grip.

"We should be going," Jim said as he finished his coffee.

"I guess it's finally time, I am very nervous you know."

"You have nothing to worry about, really, you'll see."

"Your brother..."

"Yes," they were rising from the table.

"He, well, there was something..."

"Oh he's just shy, that's all."

But there was more to it than that, Jim knew his brother and he realized something was bothering him. Oh well, it could wait until later, he would talk to him about it maybe tomorrow before his brother left for school.

They started across the street. As they did Jim heard the screeching of tires. He pulled Jill back just in time as the 1965 candy apple purple Pontiac GTO hurtled by. It spun around the turn and was gone down the street. Jim had caught just a glimpse of Mike Walker's grinning face just before the car was gone.

Jill was clinging to Jim's arm, he put his hands on her small waist to steady her, he could feel her firm midsection as she stood, leaning against his shoulder.

"Are you okay?" he asked her.

She nodded, she was still shaking. Jim got her across the street to his car. Rage shot through him for a brief instant. He would liked nothing better at that moment but to race down the street after Mike Walker, push his car to the side of the road and bodily drag his sorry ass out and kick his worthless butt.

Jim took a deep breath.

Jill leaned towards him from her bucket seat and he placed his arm around her. She looked up into his eyes at that moment, a deep look, an entire world in those beautiful, dark orbs.

"I'm really sorry about..."

He didn't finish. Jill's lips were on his, her arms around his shoulders, her eyes closed, he could taste her as she kissed him deeply, feel the warmth of her lips on his. She parted, looking at him. Then she let go and straightened in her seat, looking straight ahead.

"I'm sorry..." she stammered.

Jim said nothing. His blood was surging, partly from his lingering rage and mainly from the hot kiss Jiang Li had just given him. He fought to control himself, to keep himself from reaching over and pulling her to him.

"I'm so sorry..."

He placed his arm carefully around her shoulders. She still looked straight ahead.

"Hey," Jim said softly.

Slowly Jill turned to face him. She was across the seat again in an instant, her arms around him, her lips on his again, her breath hot and gasping as he held her, kissing her, holding her to him, feeling her against him and it felt so good.

"I can't do this," she whispered, "I never do this, I'm not like this..." she kissed him again. "I must be crazy..." another kiss. They held it for a long time then parted, looking into each other's eyes. Jill brought her hand up and gently stroked Jim's cheek. He stroked hers. Now Jill looked away, blushing.

"I have never kissed an American man before, and I never kissed any man before in my life like that..." she said.

"But you're an American," Jim replied.

"That's true," and she broke into a smile. "I shouldn't have..."

"Why? There was nothing wrong with..."

"No, you don't understand..."

Again she was in his arms, her lips near his.

"You just don't understand...why we can't..." and again her lips were on his.

Jim could hear the rumbling of an engine. They parted and he looked towards the street. It was the GTO again, right next to his car. Mike Walker was looking at him, and Rebecca was seated next to him glaring at Jim and Jiang Li intensely.

"Just want to remind you about Friday night," Mike said.

"Do another stunt like that again and you won't have to wait until Friday night. I can promise you that!" Jim warned. He was about to open the door, Jill's hand was on his shoulder.

"Who's the bitch?" Rebecca yelled and Mike pushed her back.

Rage now shot through Jim's being as he opened the door and

leapt out, feeling Jill trying to restrain him. Mike gunned the engine and the tires screeched, the car fishtailed then caught, speeding away as pedestrians leapt aside. Jill bounded out her side of the car and was beside Jim, her hand on his arm.

"Jim, what is this about?" she asked him, looking up at him intently, Jim could feel her hand on his tense arm and he relaxed.

"Nothing, really," Jim said. "Some people should learn some manners."

He turned and looked at Jill, put his hands on her shoulders, looked in her eyes.

"I'm really sorry you had to hear that."

"Who was she? She sounded like a jealous girlfriend."

"Believe me, she is no girlfriend of mine."

"Oh, you have more than one?" Jill broke into a playful pout. "Just teasing, really, it was nothing, I've heard worse."

"It was uncalled for," Jim answered as he escorted her to the passenger side of the car, the door was still open. He got in the other side and fired up the engine. He drew a breath as Jill placed her hand on his shoulder.

"I'm ready to meet your parents now," she said, smiling.

Jim broke into a smile.

"Sounds good to me," he answered.

They pulled away and left the center of town, heading down the main drag. A brand new, shiny, black Cadillac was heading up the street in the opposite direction, a convertible, top down, a man of around sixty driving, he had slightly unruly pure white hair and a white mustache, a heavy white brow with eyes so intense Jim could see them even from the closing distance as the car approached. In the seat next to the white haired man was a gorgeous, platinum blond, big breasted in a skimpy tube top. As the car passed the white haired man nodded to Jim who nodded back. They continued on down the street. Jill turned and watched as the car receded in the distance, almost at the center of town where they had just been. Jill turned back to Jim.

"Who was that?" she asked.

"Steven Denning, richest man in town," Jim said.

"Really, and was that blond his wife?"

"As far as I know, he's never been married. He owns many businesses in this area, a one of them is strip club, she is probably one of the dancers. His son goes to school with my younger brother.

Denning went to grade school and high school with my dad."

"And college?"

"He never went to college. According to my dad he has always been a hustler, in fact he was working on his fortune even back in high school. I guess you'd call him a 'self made man.'"

CHAPTER SIX

Jim pulled into the driveway of his parent's house. His dad's car was parked in front of the garage. Jim shut off the engine and hopped out, he went around to the passenger side and opened the door for Jill. She sat frozen in her seat.

"Come on," Jim said.

"Oh I can't," Jill replied. "I am very nervous, what if they don't like me?"

"Jiang Li, how could anyone not like you? Come on, you'll see."

"Well, it is because, you know..."

"Know what?"

"I'm...different, you know..."

"Oh come on now, you aren't 'different.' My mom will be delighted to meet you, really."

"Meet who, dear," it was Sandra Saunders' voice, Jim's mother, standing right behind him. "Who is this lovely young lady? Come, dear, I am Jim's mother and you must be..."

Jill looked into the smiling woman's eyes and she got out of the car, extending her hand to the older woman.

"I...my name is Jill," she said as Sandra took her hand then her arm.

"Jill, what a beautiful name, dear, Jim never told me about you, you will, of course be staying for dinner?"

Jill blushed. Jim stood awkwardly to the side, not knowing what to say.

"Uh, Mom," he stammered and both Jill and his mother looked at him.

"Yes, Son," Sandra said.

"She also has another name, her actual name is Jiang Li which means River Beautiful."

Jill was blushing deeply now.

Sandra looked at Jill and smiled into her eyes. "River Beautiful, what a wonderful name, and what a beautiful young girl."

"What's up here?" came Jim's father's voice as he came out of the garage, Rob was in the garage not speaking, just looking on.

John Saunders came forward extending his hand.

"Hello, young lady, I'm John, Jim's dad."

Jill took his hand.

"Oh my," she said, "I can see why your son is so handsome."

Now John Saunders was blushing. He looked at his wife.

"Well, don't just stand there, you two," Sandra said to both her son and her husband, "Get down to the store, I need some things, Jill and I will start dinner while you two are gone. Dear, what would you like to have for dinner," she asked Jill.

"Oh whatever you are having is good," Jill said.

"What about steaks?" John put in his two cents worth and Sandra's eyes flashed.

"John..."

"I love steak," Jill put in.

"And baked potatoes?" Jim put in his and again Sandra's eyes flashed.

"That too, I love baked potatoes."

"Steaks and baked potatoes is what it will be then!" Sandra said, "And take your brother with you."

"Come on, Robbie," Jim said as he opened the door to his car.

Robbie hesitated, hanging back.

"Have you met Robbie?" Sandra asked.

"Yes, we met earlier," Jill said.

"Oh, he didn't mention it," Sandra said as she threw a look Robbie's way.

"Have you nothing to say?" Sandra asked him.

He came forward, heading for the car.

"Hi," he said not looking at Jill. Sandra's eyes burned into him but he avoided her.

Robbie went straight to the car and got into the back. Jim got behind the wheel and his dad got into the passenger seat. Jim fired it up and they started backing out of the driveway. They waved to Sandra and Jill, they waved back then Jim headed down the street.

As they headed down the street they passed the neighborhood bar, it was quitting time for the workers so the place was packed, many cars and trucks were parked along the street and in the parking lot.

"Busy afternoon for Sam," John said. "Why don't we go in and have a beer, son?"

Jim looked at Robbie.

"I don't think..." Jim started to say.

"We can buy Robbie a Coke, what do you say, Robbie, a Coke

sound good?"

At the suggestion Robbie's face suddenly lit up.

"Sure," he said. A kid anxious to grow up and drink in a bar with the other men.

"I don't know, Dad," Jim said, "He shouldn't be in the bar, Sam'll be in big trouble if he's busted."

"Sam won't mind, I've brought Robbie in there before, isn't that right, kid?"

"Sure," Robbie answered, still all smiles.

Jim found a place to park and they entered the establishment. It was packed as they had figured. Jim noticed that the attractive blond in the hard hat was there with her friend. She smiled at him as they entered. Jim scanned the place, he saw his friends, Will and Joe seated at a far table. Will was waving them over, there were several empty chairs. Jim, his brother and his dad were seated.

"Hi, Mr. Saunders," Will said.

"It's John, Will," John said as they shook hands across the table. Joe shook hands with John as well.

"May I take your orders, gentlemen," a familiar voice said and Jim looked up. Rebecca was standing there in tight, cutoff jeans revealing her nicely tanned, silken thighs. She was holding a tray.

"Since when did you start working here?" Jim asked.

"This afternoon," Rebecca answered. "Sam always needed help so I kept at him until he gave in and hired me. The crowd last night was what decided him. And how are you, Mr. Saunders."

"Just fine, Rebecca," John answered as he glanced over at Jim.

They placed their orders and Rebecca went to the bar. John looked over at his eldest son.

"She's bad news, you know, son," he said.

"You don't have to tell me," Jim said.

"I'm glad you broke up with her, I remember she called the house all the time when you were in high school. In fact, she called this morning, your mother said. So she knows you're back already."

"She knows."

Rebecca returned with the drinks, beers for Jim and his dad and a Coke for Robbie. John paid for the round, leaving a five dollar tip which put a smile on Rebecca's face.

"Why thank you, Mr. Saunders," she said then moved to the next table.

Jim noticed that Robbie was all eyes, watching Rebecca.

"Wow, she sure is hot!" Robbie said.

John shot his younger son a look and laughed to himself.

"Kids," he said then he looked at his older son. "Now that young lady you brought home this afternoon, son, now that is a young woman of quality. She's a winner, son, don't let that one go."

Jim took a sip of his beer then he scanned the room. There he was, seated in a far corner of the bar. The same man who had talked to him on the boat, the same man who had helped him earlier today in Chinatown. He was dressed casually in a polo shirt and slacks and was having a beer. He seemed to be minding his own business.

"Just a moment, Dad, I see a 'friend' over there."

Jim rose from his seat and crossed the barroom. Rebecca passed in front of him, giving him a look then went to the table she was serving. Jim walked up to the small table the man was seated at, alone. Something about the man's presence told everyone he wanted solitude and as if by instinct, no one had bothered to try to sit across from him in the only other chair.

Jim stood over the table, looking down at the man. The man looked up at him and raised his drink.

"Hello young man," the older man said, "please take a seat."

"I am with..."

"I know, your dad and your younger brother."

"How do you know that?"

The stranger smiled.

"I know a lot of things about you, son."

"I think you aren't the one here to be calling me 'son.' The only man who can say that is that man right over there. I don't know what your game is, or what you were doing in Chinatown or on the boat but I am going back over to my table now."

Jim started to turn.

"You were captain of your football team in high school. That girl over there waiting tables has a thing for you, her boyfriend has arraigned a fight Friday night, he has always been a rival. Your father runs a successful business, a garage and body shop out near the main highway, Sam, the bartender here taught you the rudiments of self defense, boxing, when you were a kid. You have had further training in hand to hand combat, you showed your ability well in Chinatown this morning. That girl at your parents house, she is a nice young girl, you have good taste...shall I go on?"

"How do you know so much about me? And as far as that fight at the railroad tracks, well I'm not playing that game. I got out of high school four years ago."

"You're not afraid of Mike Walker, that's for sure, I saw how you handled yourself in Chinatown and at the restaurant yesterday. No, Mike Walker is just a small town punk. You show maturity in not bothering with him."

"So what's your game, why are you following me and why did you dig into my family history? What's going on?"

The older man smiled again.

"We'll talk later. Just watch yourself, okay?"

Jim turned away and went back to his table and sat down.

"Friend of yours?" John asked.

"No friend of mine," Jim said.

"I've seen him around town," Robbie said.

"When?" Jim asked.

"Last couple of weeks, when we got word you would be coming home."

"How come you didn't mention it to me or your mom?" John asked.

"I donno, didn't think it was important I guess," Robbie shrugged his shoulders. Then he looked at his brother.

"What?" Jim asked him.

"I heard word around town that Mike Walker called you out."

"Yeah, what of it?"

"You gonna fight him?"

Jim momentarily thought of the rage that had shot through him earlier when Mike Walker had come at him and Jill with his car in the center of town. He took a sip of beer.

"No," Jim answered.

"No? No? How can you back down?"

"Robbie!" John said.

"No, I heard you weren't gonna fight him! You could take him, what are you afraid of? So it's really true, you're chicken!"

"Robbie!" John said, "That'll be enough of that shit right now!"

"No, Dad, let him have his opinion. So that's what's been buggin' you for the whole afternoon."

"Your brother is no chicken!" Will said.

"He didn't get those medals because he's chicken," Joe said.

"At your age I wouldn't expect you to understand," Jim said.

Jim looked up. He saw the blond in the hard hat looking his way. She smiled then rose from her table. She crossed the room and stood near Jim.

"Hi," she said.

"Hi," Jim answered.

His brother sat seething over his Coke.

"My name's Suzie," the blond said. "I noticed you in here yesterday, I asked around about you. Heard you just got back from the war."

She held out her hand. Jim rose and they shook.

"Pleased to meet you Suzie," Jim said.

"I just wanted to come over and introduce myself. I'll get back to my friends now, see ya, okay?"

"Sure," Jim said.

Suzie went back to her table to join her friends including the woman she had been with last night.

"Jimbo Jimbo!" Will said with a laugh, "Still got the touch. Why I asked that cute blond out twice last week and no dice."

"Yeah, I asked her out too," Joe said.

"Oh what a buddy you are!" Will shot back.

"Hey man, love and war and all that stuff, right? She turned me down flat also so don't be feelin' bad.

"And yeah, now that you mention it, I've seen that guy over there in here before and also down at the town center."

"Did he talk to you, any of you?" Jim asked.

"Not a word," Will answered.

They looked across the bar. The stranger had gone.

"Hey Dad," Jim said, "Don't you think we outta be getting' back?"

"Take it easy, son," John said.

"But Mom is expecting us to get things from the store."

"Bullshit she is, she already has everything she needs right in her kitchen."

"But..."

"But hell, son, you don't get it, do you, I guess you couldn't be expected to, not being married for many years."

"What's that got to do with anything? Jill is probably getting nervous right now..."

"Not at all, son, not at all. Right now they're having 'girl talk.'"

"Girl talk?"

"Mom's getting to know your girlfriend, why else do you think she sent us on this little 'errand?'"

"To get stuff for dinner," Robbie answered.

John shook his head.

"And speaking of your girlfriend..."

"Dad, she really isn't my girl..."

"She's nice, son, really nice. Like I said earlier, don't let that one go."

John looked at his watch.

"Well, Jim, Robbie, it's time to go to the store."

"I thought you said mom already has everything she needs..."

"Kids," John said as they rose from the table. "We don't show up with something from the store then it'll be obvious."

"What's obvious?" Robbie's jaw hung open.

"Kids," John said as he led the way out of the bar. As they were leaving Jim turned around to bid his friends good night. Suzie waved to him and smiled. Jim nodded and left.

***

They stopped by the store, bought some potatoes and a twelve pack of beer then drove back home, all the while Robbie sulked in the back seat. When they arrived they were greeted by Sandra and Jill.

"Well, finally you're back, just in time for dinner," Sandra said and they headed into the dining room where they were seated at the long dining room table, John at the head of the table, his sons on either side facing each other while Sandra insisted Jill be seated beside Jim while she served.

Steak. Rare for the John and his sons, medium for Jill and Sandra. Steak and baked potatoes, and home made rolls fresh from the oven. They ate a pleasant meal, everyone talking except for Robbie who pieced away at his meal, sulking. Sandra noticed him.

"What's wrong, Robbie, you always love steak," Sandra said to her son.

Without a word Robbie rose from the table and moped down the hall to his room, slamming the door.

"You'll have to excuse our younger son, Jill," Sandra said. "I just don't know what gets into him lately."

"He's just growing," Jill said as she finished her meal. She had moved closer to Jim as they ate and made small talk and several times her thigh brushed his, she did not look over at him. He could feel her nearness.

Dinner over, Jim and his dad helped the women clear the table. Jill was about to help with the dishes.

"No, you are our guest, John and I will take care of this," Sandra said.

Jill looked at Jim and smiled.

"How about a little walk?" Jim said.

Jill nodded and they went out the front door and strolled down the sidewalk. Jill placed her hand in his.

"I really like your family," Jill said.

"Even my moody brother?"

"It's just a part of growing up," Jill said as they walked along.

They strolled down to a small, local park with sandbox, swings, monkey bars and a slide. Jill sat in one of the leather seats to the swing. The sun was dipping below the horizon. Jim stood behind her and gave the her a gentle shove. She swung back and forth as he pushed her then she stopped as she swung back towards him. He put his arms around her and they kissed, a long and passionate kiss, her hands went to his face, eyes closed. She opened them and looked into his eyes. He looked deep into her dark eyes.

"I should be getting back," Jill said. "Soon my parents will be expecting me."

Jim kissed her again.

"Jiang Li," he whispered.

She stepped from the swing and held him tightly, her arms went around his neck. Then she gently pushed away.

"Really..." she said.

Jim took her hand and they walked back to the house. Robbie was still in his room. Jill said her good-byes to Jim's parents then they got into the car and drove off.

***

During the drive across the bridge into San Francisco Jill was silent, looking straight ahead. When they approached Chinatown Jim turned up her street.

"Park here," she said.

"I understand," Jim said.

Jill opened the door and got out before Jim could go to the passenger side. He stepped up to her.

"I can walk the rest of the way," she said. "I can't let my parents see us."

"I understand," Jim said as he reached for her hands. She drew away, looking into his eyes.

"I really enjoyed myself this evening, Jim, you have wonderful parents."

Jim reached for her again, pulling her towards him, she placed her hands against his chest, keeping herself away.

"We can't," Jill said.

"I don't see why not," Jim answered as he tried to pull her to him. Finally she relented and threw her arms around his neck, kissing him long and deeply.

"I can't see you again," she whispered to him.

"You can," he said.

"No, you don't understand, we are from different cultures..."

"That's bullshit!" Jim said, anger in his eyes. "You're as American as I am."

"That's not the point, I still live by our old world standards and expectations, Jim, tonight should never have happened..."

Her eyes were misting over and she held him again and kissed him.

"It's wrong for us to be together," she whispered.

"No it's not," their lips met again.

Her eyes were misty. She forced herself to push away again, backing up, making distance between them.

"No, Jim, I can never see you again...'

"I don't think..."

"Jim..." she started to choke on her words.

"What?" he came towards her again and held her, she held him briefly then kissed him. She turned her face away, tears were running down her cheeks.

"Jim, no. You don't understand."

"Understand what?"

"Jim, I'm going to be married soon."

CHAPTER SEVEN

Jim was driving back across the bridge, confused, feeling lost, feeling sick inside, life seemed to have lost its meaning. How could he have been such a fool? What had he been thinking anyway? That he could have a relationship with someone so different, from such a foreign tradition? But this was America, people had choices. Family ties were the strongest force and Jill was a victim of those ties. She had been in tears when she had run from him up the street. He had tried to follow her, to hear more about this "marriage" but she had demanded that he not follow her. She had told him it would be only trouble for her if her family saw her with him. He had respected that, though he had wanted to run after her, to hold her again.

Now he was alone.

He was really alone, that is how he felt as he drove home, barely conscious of the other cars, in a daze. It had started out to be so wonderful. He had been overjoyed that he had found her. Then she had kissed him. He had kissed her. How could a woman about to be married to another man kiss him so, hold him so. He'd heard older men talking about how a man could never be able to ever understand a woman. He agreed. He felt lost now.

He drove into town and parked in front of the local bar. Not many cars there this time of night. He noticed Mike Walker's car was not there. He almost hoped it would be, he was indeed in a mood to kick some ass. Just one wrong word is all it would take.

Then he remembered.

Tomorrow was Friday. Mike Walker had made an "appointment" with him. Jim thought about it. No, he must not stoop to that level. High school was over. It had been different in Chinatown. Jim had had to fight for his life, for survival, no ego involved, no having to prove himself, just survive. Had he not been trained he was sure he would be dead or wishing he was.

He had survived, thanks to all the training he had received, the intense martial arts training. He had figured he would never have to use it, not now that he had been ceremoniously relieved of his military duties. But he had had to fight anyway and he had done well. He had done what he had been trained to do.

Jim wandered into the bar. Rebecca was no longer there serving tables, the afternoon rush now long over. Jim was relieved. He just wanted to sit and get drunk, just dead drunk, to forget Jill ever happened. He walked up to the bar and sat on a stool. There were only a few people in the establishment, an older couple at a table and several other men at the bar. Two men were playing pool.

"Back again?" Sam asked.

"Yeah, I'll take a draft."

Sam poured and handed him his beer. Jim reached into his pocket.

"Like I said before, Jim," Sam said, "you'll never spend another dime in here again."

"But I intend to get very drunk right now, Sam."

Sam looked at Jim for a moment, their eyes locked, then he busied himself washing some glasses at the sink. Jim sipped his beer as he looked in the mirror. He saw his rage looking back, hot rage burning in his eyes. He took another sip then downed the rest of the beer in one gulp, slamming the mug down on the bar.

"Another," he said.

Sam brought up another frosted mug of draft. He looked Jim in the eye again.

"Son, you feel like talking about this?" Sam asked.

Jim looked at Sam for a moment as he took a sip.

"Not right now, Sam, not right now."

Sam shrugged his shoulders and went back to his tasks.

"Hi," it was the voice of a young woman. Jim saw her in the mirror, standing at the bar, right next to him. It was Suzie, she had returned and was no longer dressed in her work clothes and hard hat. She wore a red halter top, her waist bare and wore cut-off jeans that were pasted to her nicely formed and athletic legs. Her bare shoulders were bronzed and toned with rippling muscle just beneath the surface of her silky skin. Her hair was a slightly unkempt mop about her shoulders.

Jim took another sip of his beer.

"Mind if I sit here?" Suzie asked.

Jim shrugged and downed the rest of his beer. He held up two fingers and Sam brought two beers, setting them on the bar. Jim started to reach into his pocket and Sam waved him off.

"What I said, it goes for who you drink with," Sam said.

"Thank you," Suzie said.

"No problem," Jim answered as he took a large gulp, feeling the sting at the back of his eyeballs, feeling himself begin to mellow, a deep relaxation seeping into his entire being.

"You're new in town," Jim said.

"Yeah," Suzie answered. "I work across the bay. Two year job, just started a month ago. I decided to move here for the duration, nice small town, and not too far from work."

"Why not in the city?"

"I was talking to some of the other people on the job and some of them live here, they suggested it to me and I fell in love with the town. Old style, yet also upbeat, among the redwoods and the mountain. And the public transportation can't be beat, a bus ride then the boat ride across the bay. I love it."

"What kind..."

"High rise construction."

Jim's eyebrows raised, then he noticed her build.

"Was it tough to get in, I mean, I don't mean..."

"For a woman? Don't worry, I'm not offended. It was tough at first, my dad was in high rise and I grew up helping him fix up the house at home and doing other hard chores, I played baseball, soccer and I wanted to play football but of course that was out of the question."

Jim nodded.

"What about you," Suzie asked. "I asked around, Sam said you grew up here. What a great place to grow up in."

"I liked it. Where..."

"Los Angeles. And in Huston and in Chicago, we moved a lot, the nature of the work."

"And your parents..."

"Mom and dad live in Denver. Mom wanted me to go to college and I did two years at the Community College then decided to go to work. Dad couldn't help, he told me I would have to get in by myself, but I already knew that. I accepted it."

"What's your dad think now?"

"He doesn't say much. But I think he's proud. That's why he didn't help me, he wanted to see what I was made of."

They finished their beers and Jim ordered two more.

"I'll buy this..." Suzie started to say but Sam waved her off.

"I heard you served over in Iraq."

"Yeah?"

"Oh, I was talking to your two friends, Will and Joe. They really are your good friends you know."

"I know that."

"So what's eatin' you? I can tell you are upset. Is it about that incident in here last night, that guy..."

"Mike Walker? No, he doesn't bother me..."

"I didn't figure he did. You don't have to go you know..."

"Go..."

"The railroad tracks, you don't..."

"I don't intend to, although right now if I saw him I might go at him."

"But it's not him, is it, he'd be just a focal point for what's really eatin' you."

Jim didn't answer her. He just sipped his beer.

"It's a girl."

He said nothing.

"I can tell. I saw you driving out of town earlier with her. Pretty."

"You notice things."

"I just happened to be driving home from here to shower."

"Why'd you come back?"

"I guess I just got a little bored so I figured I'd pop in for a quick drink." She finished her drink and set the empty down. "In fact, I think I'll be running along, I gotta get up real early tomorrow."

She started to rise from the table. Jim rose up with her, "Yeah, I guess I better get goin' myself," he said. He downed the rest of his drink and both of them headed for the door.

"G'nite Sam," Jim called and Sam waved them off. They walked to Suzie's car, a late model Nissan. She paused as she unlocked the door. She looked at him, thinking.

"Well," she started to say then she shook her head.

"What?" Jim asked.

"I was going to ask...no, it really isn't appropriate right now..." she reached over and touched his arm. "I could take advantage of the moment but I think it would be a mistake on both of our parts."

Jim said nothing as she opened the door to get in, she was looking into his eyes, her lips seemed so inviting.

"Yeah," Jim said, "You have a good day tomorrow."

She smiled then got in and started the engine. Jim watched her drive away then went to his car.

***

No one was awake when Jim walked into the house and silently made his way to his room. He sank down on the bed and slipped into a deep sleep instantly.

***

Jim awoke the next morning, got dressed and made his way to the kitchen. His dad had already left for work and Robbie had gone to school. His mother had a cup of coffee on the table waiting for him. He sat down and slowly sipped.

"Anything you want to tell me?" Sandra asked.

"About what?"

He already knew.

"She's a nice girl, I really liked her. When are you going to bring her here again?"

Jim said nothing, his mother's eyes were burning into him, boring a hole right through him.

"I'm not."

"I see..."

"She's getting married, Mom, there's nothing there."

"You don't think so? I would beg to differ with you. That girl is gone on you."

"Sure she is, that's why she told me never to see her again. Real gone for sure. And..."

"Things can change..."

"And why should she care for me? Why? I have no job, no prospects..."

"Jim, you just got discharged, you have to give it time."

Jim just sat there. He was pondering his future. He could go to the community college, the government would pay for that. And work, he would find something. He just had to get his head straightened out.

He finished his coffee and rose from the table.

"I'm heading down to Stan's for breakfast," he said as he kissed his mother on the cheek and left.

***

Jim had breakfast at Stan's. He was seated at the counter finishing up when he heard the familiar sound of Mike Walker's GTO outside. He didn't look around to see him enter.

Mike Walker had his two side kicks, Tiny and Greg, with him. They walked past Jim and were seated at the counter a few seats down. They looked over at Jim. Tiny smiled a sneering smile.

"Well lookie who's here," Tiny said.

"Yeah, never can tell what kind of trash comes in here," Greg said.

"All right, boys," Stan said as his eyes narrowed, "that'll be enough of that shit in here."

Mike Walker looked over at Jim.

"You're treading on thin ice, Pal," Jim said.

"It's Friday," Mike said, "you know what that means."

Jim finished his breakfast, took a last sip of his coffee.

"I think he's 'chicken.'" Tiny said.

"Yeah, look at him, shakin' like a leaf," Greg added.

Across the restaurant an older man, lean and fit looking, looked over. It was Steven Denning, seated at a table all by himself. He watched Jim with inquisitive eyes. Then he looked at Mike and his friends. He laid a ten dollar tip down on the table and stood up. He walked up to Jim.

"Hello, Jim," Steven Denning said.

Mike Walker and his friends looked away, now silent.

"You boys got a problem?" Denning asked Mike and his friends.

"No sir, Mr. Denning," Mike Walker said and he was decidedly nervous. Jim caught the changed attitude.

"Hello, sir," Jim said to Denning.

Denning held out his hand and they shook.

"Good to have you back in town, son," Denning said, "I heard you made a real good account of yourself over there."

"It was nothin'," Jim said.

"Not from what I heard, good to see you back. And you boys," Denning was addressing Mike and his friends, "Don't you have something else you have to be doing?"

"Yes sir, we were just leaving," Mike said as he and his friends rose and put their money down on the counter. They nodded to Denning and left real fast.

Jim looked at Denning.

"Those boys work for me, down at my club some nights."

Denning operated a strip club down the road, one of many of his business interests. "They would be working for me tonight but I have the place closed this entire weekend for some repairs. There was a kind of mis-understanding among several of my customers..."

"Oh, I think I understand, sir," Jim answered.

"Mike and his two cohorts did their job well enough but it was still quite a brawl. Mike's the head bouncer, knows his stuff well enough. Tiny and Greg, they just do what they're told.

"Which brings me to you, son."

"Me?"

"You're built plenty strong, trained in hand to hand combat and you've always seemed to have a good head on your shoulders. I'll bet you're good in a tight spot so how about it?"

"About what, sir."

"Working for me, down at the club. I noticed a little friction between you and Mike. He's good but you'd replace him as head bouncer. He's a hothead."

"And I'm not?"

"I have an instinct about people, Jim. And though you may seem a little brash at times, no, I would not call you a hothead. My boy, Dave, is friends with your brother. Goes to school with him.

"And," Denning went on, "I've heard some talk."

"Talk?"

"A 'main event' to be staged down at the railroad tracks tonight."

"Won't be any 'main event.' I don't do street brawls. That's high school stuff."

"I heard Mike challenged you."

"That's his problem."

"See, that's what I mean."

"Mean?"

"You're no hothead. Mike Walker is an asshole, he has his uses but you, on the other hand, you have great potential."

"How so?"

"Mike will always just be a bouncer. He's head bouncer now because he's the strongest guy who ever worked for me. So far. And besides, he's just muscle. You know that. In high school who was the team captain? Not Mike Walker. You were.

"Point proved. Do you want the job?"

Jim thought about it. Then an idea began forming in his mind. He thought of Jiang Li, Jill.

"I don't think I really want to be a bouncer, no dis-respect intended, sir, but no. I'm looking for something else solid."

Denning smiled.

"I can see why," he said. "Very beautiful girl you had with you yesterday."

"My, word gets around."

"I can see why you want something solid, son. I'm not offering you a lifetime job but you need something to get started with until you find something else. It's a night job, it would be only four nights a week. Give you plenty of time to go to school during the day."

"I'll think about it, sir," Jim said as he finished his coffee. "I've really gotta be going right now."

Jim rose from the table.

"Let me know, son, job's always open," Denning said as he also stood. They shook hands.

"Don't worry about tonight. Mike's just a stupid bully, you are right not to get involved. I can take care of it..."

"No need. Let him stand out there and wait all night."

Denning laughed.

"See you around, son. And don't forget, the job is open."

Jim nodded and left the restaurant, bidding good-by to Stan who watched him go with narrow, contemplating eyes, wary eyes.

Stan looked over at Denning and then went back to serving his customers.

***

Jim was headed across the Bay Bridge, he had a goal in mind, he was determined, focused, he knew what he had to do, to attempt to do.

He drove directly through the city to Nineteenth Avenue and parked in the guest parking lot of San Francisco State College. He went to the information desk to inquire as to what classes Ms. Li was taking and then realized he did not know her actual last name. Feeling like a fool he wandered out of the offices and across the campus. He didn't even have a photograph to show anyone. He couldn't just say he was looking for an Asian girl, the place was filled with Asians, it was like searching for a needle in a haystack.

Frustrated he headed back to the weight room where he had worked out the day before. The usual crowd was there and that is when he noticed and dark haired young woman far off in the stretching area, dressed in leotards, doing a shoulder stand on the mat in front of the mirror which ran along and dominated the entire wall. He could see the pile of her black hair around her head on the floor, see her perfect form, well toned legs in the black tights, see the small, prominent muscles in her shoulders and arms visible under a light, healthy layer of bodyfat, not sharply defined as in a competitive bodybuilder.

He realized he was staring at her.

"Hi," said one of the young men by the weight bench. It was one of students who had been working out the day before when Jim had benched so much weight it had blown everyone away.

Jim nodded to him in acknowledgement then started across the floor towards the young woman in the shoulder stand. She moved one of her legs down now into a figure four, then the other leg, flipping over and silently gliding to her feet. Her hair was in her face as Jim stared. She shook her head, the hair flying back and she reached back and tied it into a loose ponytail. Jim was staring right into the eyes of Jill, Jiang Li.

Momentary anger flashed across her eyes and she quickly walked past him and made for the doorway. Jim ran after her, she was now making her way away from the building.

"Jill, wait," Jim said.

She kept walking.

He caught up with her.

"Jiang Li," he said as he reached for her arm. She tried to jerk away but his hold was firm. She spun around, looking directly in his eyes.

"I already told you," she said, "I told you we can't..."

Her arms went around his neck, her face near his, their lips met. She reached back and undid her hair, it flew about her face and shoulders as she kissed him. He held her there, feeling her against him, her lithe body on his. He held her to him as she kept kissing him. She opened her eyes, looking right into his. He took her face in his hands.

"Jiang Li," he said.

"No," she said, "don't say anything right now."

Her lips were on his again.

"You know this is impossible," she said to him.

"I don't care."

"You don't understand," she said.

"Then you explain it to me."

She looked down. "My choices are not in my control."

"Bullshit they're not! You make your own choices in life!"

"Maybe you have that freedom but I do not. The marriage was

arranged. He is from Taiwan. I have never met him but it will help unify our families. It is an obligation I have to my family."

"That bullshit went out a hundred years ago!"

"Maybe here..."

"You're living here! Not over there, you're living right here in this country!" he had her by the shoulders, his eyes burning into hers.

"Let me go!" she said as she shook herself away from him.

"Who ever told you you had to marry someone you had no desire to marry? Who told you this?"

"It has never been my choice. There are many factors involved!"

Jim reached for her. She tried to turn away, he caught her by her shoulders. She turned and was in his arms again, tears were in her eyes.

"I don't have the choice!" she said.

Then she kissed him again. They held each other. Jim closed his eyes. What was he doing? He had no prospects to offer her, she would obviously be secure in life in this arranged marriage. Who was he to interfere and yet he kissed her again. He thought of his options. Yet he could not see this beautiful, wonderful young girl just go and live a life she had no choice in. He knew he wanted her. It was not right. But what she was being forced to do was not right. She was looking into his eyes. She kissed him again.

"Come with me," Jim suddenly said. "Come away with me right now! We'll work it out somehow. I have some money still and..."

"Then let's go!" she said just as suddenly. "Let's go before I change my mind, before the fear of what I am doing really dawns on me!"

"You're books..."

"No! Let's go, I'll grab my clothes but let's hurry before I change my mind, before the fear of what I am doing really sinks in."

She looked deeply into his eyes, a burning look, looking for truth.

"Do you mean it?" she asked, her eyes penetrating his soul.

He flashed back on Neela, the young girl in Baghdad. He remembered his deep longing, those dark eyes, trusting him. Now another set of dark eyes were looking at him, trusting him.

"I mean it! Let's go."

"I'll go to my locker and be right back!" she kissed him again and dashed off.

She was gone no more than five minutes, dressed now in her jeans and loose fitting sweatshirt, her backpack on one shoulder she came up to him, leaning up to him and kissing him. He took her hand.

"We'll go by my parents place and I'll get my money and we'll be gone," Jim said.

Then he turned to her and right there, he kneeled down, taking her hand.

"Jiang Li," he said, looking up at her, "Jiang Li, marry me, Jiang Li, I am asking you to be my wife. We'll go right to Vegas..."

She dropped her backpack and went down on her knees in front of him, holding him, looking into his eyes.

"You really mean it?" she asked.

"Really," he answered and he leaned towards her, kissing her. They rose together, arms around each other. She smiled at him then looked beyond him, past his shoulder. Her expression changed.

"Jiang Li, what's wrong?" Jim asked and he sensed someone behind him. He turned, still holding Jiang Li's hand. Two Asian men were standing there, dressed in dark gray suits, one young and the other in his mid-thirties, the younger one was slender, had longish, black hair. The other one had a tight flattop, a bull neck and intense, beady eyes, his shoulders strained at his suit. Both were blocking the pathway. Jim felt Jiang Li's hand tighten on his, felt her trembling.

"Where do you think you are going, my future sister in law?" the younger man asked. The stocky man remained silently threatening.

"Just who the hell are you?" Jim asked as he stepped forward. The burly man placed himself between Jim and the young man.

The young man did not take his eyes off of Jiang Li.

"Jim, please, no..." Jiang Li said as Jim stepped forward another foot, ready for battle.

"I suggest you get out of here ever so quickly!" Jim demanded.

The bull necked man's eyes glazed over with rage, his fists tightening.

"David!" Jiang Li said, "What are you doing here?"

"I heard you were seen with a young American man yesterday and the day before. So this is the one. He better have not touched you, if you know what I mean. We would not want to offer ruined goods to my brother, he would be greatly dis-pleased, my sister."

"You bastard!" Jim was ready now, the burly man tensed, also ready.

"You might tell your young American friend that if he values you, respects you, then he had better mind his manners, or dire consequences could result."

"Jim, please..." Jiang Li said, taking Jim's arm.

"I asked you to marry me!" Jim said as he turned to her. "I am asking again..."

Jiang Li looked into his eyes, taking his hands, tears ran down her face.

"Let me remind you again, of how much you love your father and mother, and your younger brother and sister. A lovely family, it is hoped they will stay that way," the one called David said as he placed a cigarette in his mouth.

"That sounds like a threat to me, asshole!" Jim stormed.

David smiled and lit his smoke.

"I do not threaten. I merely remind one of certain consequences. Of course, Jiang Li, feel free to marry this young man. And will you both be attending the funeral of certain family members?"

"I heard the threat! Jiang Li, we'll go to the authorities, this is extortion!"

"Go ahead, my young American friend, go on and call the authorities," David smiled as he blew smoke out.

The burly one started forward.

"No, Han," David said. "I will remind the American only once that if I am harmed in any way, then Jiang Li's family will pay a dear price. This is so, is it not, my future sister?"

Jiang Li lowered her head, eyes down cast.

"You don't have to do this, Jiang Li," Jim said. "Come with me, Jiang Li. We can take care of these threats!"

"Go ahead, my sister, run away with him, I am not stopping you," David smiled, taking another puff from his smoke.

Jiang Li's head remained lowered. Then she looked up at Jim.

"I'm sorry, Jim, I'm sorry..."

Jim looked at her, faced her, took her hands in his.

"I understand, Jiang Li. I understand."

She looked up at him. He leaned forward and kissed her lips, her eyes closed as she kissed him.

They parted.

"Good-by, Jim," Jiang Li said.

Jim parted.

"I believe you have a class to attend, my sister," David said. Then he turned to Jim, "Han and I will escort the young gentleman to his car."

Jim said nothing. He set his jaw, looked one last time at Jiang Li, then he walked away. David tossed his cigarette to the ground and he and Han followed him.

Jim walked quickly to his car, David and Han right behind him. When he got to his car he turned and faced his "escort."

He stepped forward, right up to David. He saw a moment of fear in David's eyes.

"Don't worry, asshole," Jim said. "I won't touch a hair on your head, I won't bust up your scrawny little body, no, I wouldn't want to do that, I remember what you said. But..."

Jim wheeled, his fist crashing into Han's jaw, taking him unawares, Han reeled back and Jim spun around, delivering a wheel kick, again, to Han's jaw, sending him to the pavement where he lay very still.

"You said nothing about him!"

David paled now, shaking as Jim came towards him.

"Now, you listen to me!" Jim said. "If I ever hear of any harm coming to Jiang Li, her brother, her sister, her parents or anyone else in her family, I will find you! Believe it, asshole! I will find you!"

Jim let what he said sink in for a moment. Then he got in his car, the engine roared to life, the tires screeched as he backed out, engine idling as he looked at David.

"Remember it well! I'll find you!"

With another screech of burning rubber Jim peeled out of the parking lot and down Nineteenth Avenue.

As he drove away a deep sense of hopelessness overcame him. Once again, he had lost someone dear to him. Lost her forever.

CHAPTER EIGHT

Jim sat in his car by the water. South bay, along the peninsula south of the city. Confused thoughts ran through his mind, he felt truly lost. To come so close, but then, again, he remembered that he really had nothing to offer. No job, the only prospect of a job was Steven Denning's offer of a job at his topless nightclub, out on the edge of his town, right over the city limit where the law couldn't touch him. The sheriff's department patrolled the area but they didn't really care as long as no big fights broke out, as long as wealthy citizens were not inconvenienced. Jim had never been there, only seen the place as he was driving by.

So Mike Walker was the head bouncer there.

And Steven Denning had offered the head bouncer job to Jim, just like that. If he took the job he would definitely be stepping on Mike Walker's toes bigtime. There was the matter of tonight down at the railroad tracks. Jim did not do street brawls. That incident in the city the day before had been an issue of immediate survival. And this morning in the college parking lot, he had been making a point to David, not to mess with Jiang Li or her family. He could do nothing about her decision to marry whoever it was she was supposed to be marrying. It was obvious that someone had a strong hold over her entire family, an unbreakable bond. The tongs, he figured. Tradition, hundreds of years old, never broken, not even here in America. And Jiang Li was a prisoner in that ancient system.

Jim shook his head.

It was all too complex for him right now. He took a final bite of his roast beef sandwich and a sip of his beer. He had bought both at a local deli before driving out to the levy, just south of the San Mateo Toll Bridge where he had parked to just watch the seagulls and the water, to clear his head. He could see the bridge in the distance, the mid point rising high to allow shipping, the rest of the span low to the water, barely visible over a shimmering sheen above the water, the heat waves creating a mirage.

Jim chucked the last of his beer and tossed the empty into the back seat. Illegal as hell probably but right now he didn't really give a damn.

Jim felt it again, he was being watched. And he was right. Of the several cars parked nearby one stood out. A gray Toyota was occupied. A man inside was watching him. Jim knew who he was. The man who had been following him from place to place, the man who seemed to know so much about his life. The door to the Toyota opened and the man stepped out. He was dressed casually in tan Dockers and a polo shirt. The man walked towards Jim. Jim got out to meet him halfway. Both stopped and faced each other.

"Howdy, Jim," the stranger said.

"Cut that 'howdy' bullshit!" Jim demanded. "Just what the fuck are you doing following me around?"

"Nice job you did in that parking lot today, son," was all the man would say.

"And what the fuck do you know about that?" Jim answered, his fists balled up at his side.

"Looks like you're ready for a fight, son," the man said.

"Yeah, with you as the target if you don't watch out! Now you tell me just what the hell is goin' on here!"

"Nice little gal you got there," the man said, ignoring Jim's threat. "I wouldn't let that one go."

"It's none of your fucking business, asshole!"

"Maybe not, but I'd say she's a winner. You don't have to give up, you know."

Jim looked out at the bay.

"Easy for you to say."

"Not at all. And son, I'd say you have a lot of anger you need to work out. Maybe you should keep that little appointment you have with Mike Walker tonight. Might do you some good."

Jim was silent. He turned away and walked out towards the edge of the water, along the levy where the small waves lapped against the piled up stones and cement slabs.

"That Mike Walker is just a small town punk. He needs an 'ass whippin',"' the stranger went on.

"It's none of your business. Who the fuck are you anyway?"

"You'll be finding out real soon. And maybe we can find a way to solve the problem of you and that little lady from Chinatown. I wouldn't give up on her just yet."

"And what would you know about it, you seem to know everything else, so tell me, what do you know?"

"We'll talk soon, son. Just take care. And remember, sometimes a good fight is good for the soul, know what I mean? Be seein' you, son."

With that the stranger walked quickly back to his Toyota, got in and drove away. Jim just stared out at the bay then picked up a flat stone and held it in his hand. He gave it a toss and watched it skip three times across the waves. Then he got in his car and drove away.

***

"Jim, wake up," he could hear his mother's voice in the far distance as if funneled through a tunnel, echoing off the boundaries of his fogged mind. He was awake now, he had been in a deep sleep on the couch for over two hours after returning home. He opened his eyes, the TV was on but there was no sound, the afternoon news was on KPIX Channel 5.

Jim was awake now.

"What is it, Mom?" he asked.

"Your brother, he hasn't come home from school yet."

"Maybe he's just hanging out with his buddies."

"No, he's usually here by this time. And he hasn't come back. He's usually out in the back lifting weights, sometimes his friends join him but no one has come home."

"Well, Mom, I'm sure he'll be home soon. I don't think you have anything to worry about."

"It's just not like him."

"I'm sure there is some kind of explanation, if he doesn't show up by evening I'll go look for him, it's okay, I'm sure."

"Maybe you're right. But I'm still worried. Oh, you're dad's pulling in."

Jim heard the car. In a moment his dad came in the door, kissed his wife.

"Hello, son, how are you today?"

Jim shrugged his shoulders.

"Going to visit your girlfriend?"

"There is no 'girlfriend' Dad."

"What do you mean?" his father asked.

"Just that, there is no girlfriend," Jim was now on his feet heading for the door. "Maybe I'll cruise around and see if I can locate Robby."

"Robbie? What's wrong with Robbie?"

Sandra explained briefly.

"I'm sure he's okay," John said. "Just out with his buddies is all.

Don't worry, he'll be home for dinner, that he never misses."

"I hope you're right," Sandra said as Jim gave her a kiss on the cheek on his way out the door.

***

Jim fired up his car and left. He drove through town, around the park and down by the high school. He asked several kids if they had seen his brother. One said he had been with Denning's son, they were friends, Denning had told Jim this morning. That was all they knew. Jim figured that Robbie had gone over to his friend's house, maybe for dinner. He decided to get something to eat so he parked in the center of town and went into Subway for a roast beef sandwich and a large Coke, everything on it. He sat at one of the outside tables under an awning to eat.

As he was eating Joe came walking up and sat down opposite him.

"How's it goin'?" Joe asked.

Jim shrugged his shoulders and went on eating. He looked up at Joe.

"You haven't seen Robbie around have you?"

Joe thought about it for a minute.

"Yeah, come to think of it, I have, he was with Denning's kid."

"Thanks, at least I know he's okay, Mom was concerned because he didn't come home right away."

"Ah, don't worry, hell, it's late spring, he's probably got lot of things goin' on. He'll be home soon enough."

Jim had finished his sandwich and Coke. He rose from the table.

"You headed for the bar this evening? I'll buy you a beer. Hey, Jim, that little blond in there seems to be sweet on you, she sure as hell doesn't turn her head when I walk in, but then, there's that Asian gal you were with. Wow, she sure is fine. She your girlfriend?"

"Nope."

Joe was waiting for more but Jim rose from the table.

"See you later?" Joe asked.

"Yeah, later."

***

Jim arrived home. His mother was now in a cheery mood.

"What's up, Mom," Jim asked her.

"Robbie called, he's over at a friend's house for dinner, the Denning boy, you know..."

"Yeah, I know his dad, met him this morning."

John came into the kitchen.

"I knew he'd be okay, the Denning boy's a good kid."

"There, Mom, everything's okay."

"I'll have dinner ready soon," Sandra said.

"That's okay, Mom, I already ate, I'll be down at Sam's."

"Again? Don't you think you're starting to hang out there a little too much?"

"Oh, Sandra," John said, "give him a break, he's been in a war, he deserves to kick back and live a little."

Sandra gave her husband a look.

"That was a nice girl you brought home yesterday, you should be seeing her instead."

"Mom, like I said, she's getting married soon."

Sandra said nothing.

"Be back later, Mom."

***

Jim walked into the bar, the place was packed this time of the afternoon with the usual working crowd. Rebecca was waiting on tables and looked in his direction for a moment. Another pair of eyes were also on him. Suzie was seated with the other working woman she usually came in with. Jim walked over to her table.

"Hi, Jim," Suzie said, "would you like to join us? Let a working girl buy you a beer?"

"Sure," Jim said as he took a seat.

"This is Trudy, we work together," Suzie said. Both had their hard hats on still. Jim could tell Trudy was used to hard physical labor, she had strong looking hands and forearms.

"Hi," Trudy said. "Suzie's been telling me about you. I was in the Army, actually I served briefly in Afghanistan before my hitch was up. I heard you are just back from Iraq."

"Yeah," Jim said. "Back earlier than I expected."

"So I heard, sorry to hear that, I know what it's like to miss your comrades, although I wasn't really in the front action, I was backup support, all female personnel are."

Suzie had held up three fingers and Rebecca brought the long necked bottles and set them on the table. As Suzie paid Rebecca threw her a look then left.

"Wow, that lady sure doesn't like you," Trudy said to Suzie. "I would guess she has a case on you," she said to Jim.

"I guess," Jim answered.

They had a few rounds and then Suzie and Trudy got up to leave.

"It's getting a little late," Suzie said, "I gotta drive Trudy home, I'm her ride this week, we switch. Saves gas. We always drive to a park and ride where we catch the bus to the city. If you're here later I'll come in and join you."

"Okay," Jim said, "I got nowhere to go, I guess I'll see you soon."

***

Jim had had several beers but wasn't feeling them. He ordered another and Rebecca brought it over. She sat down opposite him.

"She your girlfriend, or is the gook..."

"That'll be enough of that! I don't want to ever hear that from you again!" Jim's eyes burned with momentary rage.

"Okay okay," Rebecca said, "Sorry. So, you gonna be out at the tracks tonight?"

"No, you know better than that!"

"Mike's gonna be waitin' you know."

"He'll wait all night then."

"Don't you even care about how you'll be looked at if you don't show up? Don't you care?"

"Rebecca, I got out of high school quite some time ago. I've been in a real war where people get killed. I don't have time for any bullshit like this. Mike can wait till sunrise for all I care. And I don't really give a shit, understand?"

"Mike'll be lookin' for you if you don't show up."

"Great."

"Hey, Rebecca, we got customers!" Sam's voice thundered across the room. Rebecca threw him a look then got up to go back to work.

"I'll be down at the tracks, waitin'. You'd do well to show up."

"Later, Rebecca."

Jim took another sip of his beer. He looked up in time to see Joe come in the door. Joe made right for his table and sat down.

Rebecca came over and Joe ordered a beer. She left and Joe leaned towards Jim.

"What a piece of work she is, you did well to be rid of her. She still has the hots for you but watch out, she's treacherous."

"I know, Joe, I wouldn't trust her as far as I could throw her. What's up."

"That's what I'm here to tell you about. I saw Mike Walker

driving out of town towards the tracks and his two buddies Tiny and the Greg were with him, plus, I saw other cars following him. Guys he was always friends with, guys up to no good. There were three other cars and maybe twelve or more guys packed into them."

"A bunch of punks with nothin' else to do," Jim took another sip.

He looked across the room and saw Rebecca with her purse across her shoulders. She gave a look towards Sam then left. Sam came out from behind the bar and came over to Jim and Joe's table, carrying two long necks. He set them down in front of Jim.

"Like is said, Jim, free drinks for you and your friends. And besides, I'm feelin' pretty good right now."

"What's up, Sam?" Jim asked.

"Oh not much, I just fired that gal, she was gettin' a little too mouthy with the customers. I don't know what I had in mind when I hired her anyway."

"Hell," Joe said, "she's gotta job down at Denning's club anyway. Dancer and waitress."

"Oh yeah, well I guess it suits her, she's got the body for it, too bad brains didn't come along with it, or at least an inkling of common sense. Anyway, boys, enjoy."

"Sam," Jim said, "If you keep servin' up free beer to us all the time you'll go broke."

"I'm not worried. I got more business than I know what to do with. I guess that's why I figured I'd hire a waitress. But it didn't work out."

"There's other girls in need of a job that'll work out for you, Sam, and you need to hire someone to help out," Jim said.

"Oh time will tell, I guess, and that blond, she doesn't know it yet but I'll be refunding all the money she paid for the rounds she bought you."

"Sam, Sam, Sam," Jim smiled as he took a drink.

Sam returned to the bar. The place was beginning to empty out now, the rush hour long over.

***

Jim and Joe drank their beers in silence for now. Jim remembered the boxing lessons Sam had given him as a kid. Sam had been hard as nails on him and Jim had cried at first. But Sam remained firm and Jim learned his lessons well, he had cried no more. When Sam had figured Jim was ready he had brought in other kids, bigger, tough kids and had Jim fight them. Jim had taken some hard knocks but after a while the bigger, tougher kids had been afraid to show up, Jim was fast gaining a rep. He had never abused his ability, instead he had focused on sports and did fairly well on his studies. He and his two pals, Joe and Will did get into a bit of mischief but nothing that was serious. Not like some of the punks that Mike Walker had hung out with. It had almost cost Mike his place on the football team. Jim had even intervened for him but still, the competition between them had been fierce, coming mostly from Mike. Mike had always been a good team player in the games however.

Then had come Rebecca. She had been Jim's girlfriend for awhile but after graduation Jim had joined the service and had opened the playing field for Mike who had obviously jumped right in. Mike had been jealous, had always tried to pick up on her. Jim's joining the service had opened the door wide for Mike. Now that Jim was back, Mike felt threatened.

Jim's mother had never really approved of Rebecca and had been greatly relieved, the only positive in her mind for Jim's joining the service. Jim had not been serious about any girl after that. Jim had been determined, he had had to answer the call to duty after 9/11.

Now he was home. Now he was also alone.

"Hi," it was Will, entering the bar and coming over to the table and seating himself. Sam brought over another round of beers before Will could even get up to go get one for himself.

"Here you go, boys, another round," Sam said and went on back behind the bar.

"Sam's gonna go broke this way," Will said.

"Yeah, I know," Jim answered.

"Saw a bunch of guys drivin' out towards the end of town, by the railroad tracks," Will said.

"So I heard," Jim answered.

"You aren't worried about what everyone will say if you don't show up?"

"Doesn't bother me at all," Jim answered.

"And it shouldn't," Suzie's voice broke in and they all looked up. "Mind if I have a seat," Suzie asked, she was dressed casually in jeans that fit just right and a black "T" shirt.

Before anyone could move she slid right in next to Jim.

"feeling better?" she asked him.

He made no comment.

"I meant it," she said. "You don't even need to go there, I've been hearing the talk around town. It's like it's become some kind of big show. I saw cars heading out of town."

"More cars?" Joe asked.

"Seems like it."

Jim just shook his head.

"Don't worry about Jimbo," Joe said to Suzie, "he can handle any of those guys if they want to start up."

"I believe it," Suzie answered as she snuggled closer to Jim. "Like I said, you don't need to be there."

"I know."

They sat in silence for a few minutes, sipping their drinks, Suzie would occasionally look at Jim. The silence was broken by a thundering sound at the front entrance, the familiar roar of a Harley Davidson filled the bar then stopped. Everyone looked towards the entrance.

Jim's face lit up with recognition.

Standing there was an awesome sight, as big and built as Jim, but with long black hair trailing down his back in a ponytail, his wide brown shoulders jutting from a cut-off jean jacket vest, dressed in jeans and black motorcycle boots.

Jim was momentarily overcome with joy.

"Charlie White Eagle!" Jim said as he rose from his seat and crossed the room to give the big Indian a warm embrace.

"Well, you gonna buy a thirsty Indian some firewater, white eyes?" the one called Charlie White Eagle said.

"Come on in!" Jim said and he led his friend across the bar to the table. "Charlie White Eagle," Jim said to everyone, "watched my back over there. His tour was up just as mine was beginning but in the two months he was there he showed me the ropes."

Jim made the introductions as Sam made his way over with yet another round of drinks. Charlie drained the first beer in a single gulp.

"Man, I been riding up the Five Freeway all day, I'm parched," he said and another beer was thrust into his hands.

"How'd you find me?" Jim asked.

"Us Indians are good trackers. Actually I had the address you gave me and your father told me where to find you. Not hard to figure out, the local watering hole. Oh yeah, some kid is outside, said he wanted to talk to you."

"A kid, what's he want?" Jim asked.

"Dunno, he just asked me to tell you he was outside. Guess he figured I knew you for some reason."

Jim looked up.

A kid his brother's age was standing in the entrance.

"You want to see me?" Jim asked as he beckoned the kid to enter.

Nervously, the kid walked over to the table and stood.

"What can I do for you?" Jim asked. "Go ahead, you're among friends here."

"It's Robbie."

"What about him."

"I thought you outta know...he..."

"What?" a sternness came into Jim's eyes. "What about Robbie?"

"Well, he...he..."

"He what? What?"

"He went down to the railroad tracks with Dave Denning, he's gonna take on Mike Walker!"

Jim was on his feet in an instant.

"I guess that changes things!" he said as he headed for the door. Joe, Will and Suzie were right behind him, Charlie quickly downed the rest of his beer and followed.

"What's up?" Charlie asked.

"Just a little problem!" Jim answered as he reached the door.

"Sounds like a rumble, I'm in!" Charlie was now beside Jim, Suzie on his other side. Just as Jim came through the entrance a body collided with him, arms around him.

Jiang Li.

Her lips were on his in an instant, her arms around his neck. Jim backed up, almost tumbling over.

"I went to your parents house but you weren't there, they said you were here," she gasped then she looked over at Suzie who was staring, amazed. A look crossed Jiang Li's face in that moment and Suzie backed up.

"Hey don't worry about me, he's all yours, I had no chance," Suzie said.

"You shouldn't be here!" Jim said, looking down at her as she gazed up at him.

"But I am! What is going on?"

"I don't have time to explain! Wait here!"

Jim headed for his car. He could see Charlie's gleaming Harley parked right in back of it. Jim was opening the door.

"You lead, I'll follow, Bro!" Charlie said as he hopped on the bike, instantly thundering it to life. Joe and Will packed into Joe's car.

Suzie was about to get in Jim's car when Jiang Li squeezed in right beside Jim, her arms around him.

"I'll ride with Joe," Suzie said.

"You shouldn't..."

"Hey, I work high rise remember?"

Suzie ran to Joe's car and got in.

"You can't," Jim was saying to Jiang Li.

"I have no time to argue with you!" Jim said as he fired up the car and peeled out down the street. He had to admit to himself that it felt good having Jiang Li next to him.

He peeled onto the main drag, followed by the roaring Harley and Joe's car. They sped along, Jim hoped the cops weren't around. The last thing he needed right now was to be pulled over.

"What's going on?" Jiang Li asked.

"Robbie's in trouble!" Jim said no more as he sped along, watching for cruising cops. Jiang Li didn't ask any more questions. Jim wanted to ask her a million questions, why she was here, but now he was focused on one thing.

***

The small caravan headed out to the edge of town, crossed the main highway underpass and then the tracks. They hit the dirt road that ran along the tracks and bounced along it for about a quarter of a mile, dust rising in the air as they went.

The road widened into a large dirt parking lot. There were about a dozen cars there now, hot rods, old Chevys, Buicks and Oldsmobiles. Mike Walker's Pontiac. No one was in sight, they would be down by the tunnel. Jim slammed on the breaks and Charlie's Harley pulled up along side, Joe's car on the other. Jim was out the door. He looked at Jiang Li.

"You better stay here!" he said.

"I did not come to find you only to hide! I'm with you!" she said, looking deep into his eyes. Joe, Will and Suzie were now up beside them, along with Charlie.

"Lead the way, Holmes!" Charlie White Eagle said.

It felt good knowing a fellow battle hardened warrior was there with him, a comrade in arms, ready for anything.

Jim ran on.

The tunnel loomed ahead, several cars were parked, engines idling, headlights on to light up the area. The place was packed. All the wrong guys, troublemakers from the word "go."

Along with Tiny and Greg there were Jack Fraser, Bob Gianechi, Dean Carlson, Brad Chapman, Tony Giovani and Jack DePoli, with his semi long, greasy, black hair slicked back against his head, wearing his gaudy, spangled shirt and gold chains.

"Hey lookie here, the 'chicken' has finally showed up!" Dean Carlson stepped towards Jim, the others behind him, menacing. Dean was a big young man, but not quite as big as Jim or Charlie White Eagle. In a slit second Dean was on the ground, unconscious, Jim had hit him hard across the jaw with a right cross. Lights out for him!

"Anyone else have anything else to say?" Jim asked and the others took a second look, at him, at his friends, and at the big Indian who now looked towards them with eyes of death, just on the edge!

They stepped aside.

Up ahead Jim could see Mike Walker, right at the tunnel entrance. Standing near him was Rebecca and in front, Robbie. Robbie's nose was bleeding. Blood also was coming from Mike Walker's mouth. He was wiping it away, Robbie was standing, shakily, his fists balled at his sides. The Denning boy was also there with him, his fists also balled and ready. Both of them looked at Jim.

"Good job, Robbie, looks like you got him good!" Jim said to his younger brother.

Mike looked at Jim, defensive, he stepped back.

"Thought you could whip my brother?" Jim asked.

"You were too yellow to show! At least he's here!" Mike answered.

"I generally don't go to high school street brawls, but now that I'm here, well, for old time's sake I guess I'll just have to whip your ass!" Jim said.

"In your fuckin' dreams!" Mike said.

"Get him, Mike!" Dean had regained his feet and had stumbled up to them. "What are you all waitin' for? We outnumber these guys."

"Hey, come on, Holms, lets get it on!" Charlie said as he came up beside Jim.

The other young men now started to circle around Jim and his group.

"Well," Joe said, "I guess it's time to get it on!"

"Right!" Will answered.

Robbie and Dave Denning also moved into position with Joe and Will. Jim looked toward Jiang Li and Suzie.

"There are ladies here…"

"I'm okay!" Suzie said.

"Me too!" Jiang Li answered confidently as she stood, hands at her sides.

"I'll have some of you, bitch!" Rebecca said as she came forward, right towards Jiang Li.

Mike was now stepping forward, fists ready.

"I've been waitin' for this for a long time," he said with a smile.

Rebecca broke through the circle heading right at Jiang Li. Jiang Li simply flew into the air delivering a spinning wheel kick, striking Rebecca square on the jaw. Rebecca dropped to the ground, out cold.

"Nice work, sister!" Suzie said.

The other guys moved in now, except for Jack Depoli, who watched with an air of detachment. Charlie was in among them throwing his fists expertly, he downed Jack Fraser instantly, Joe ducked as Bob Gianechi took a swing at him then he hit Bob in the gut, doubling him over. A right to Bob's jaw finished him. Dean Carlson made a move at Will and went down, second time this evening. This time he stayed down. More of the young men moved in, Jim's group was highly outnumbered. Two guys were heading for Jim as Jim was advancing on Mike. Suzie stepped in, Jiang Li beside her. Suzie spun expertly and came around with a hammerfist strike to one of the men who fell backwards into the dirt. Jiang Li ducked under one man's attempted blow and spun on him, getting him in an arm bar, she forced him down and hit his temple with a single knuckle strike. The man was out. She was now back to back with Suzie. Charlie took down both Tiny and Greg with ease.

Jim was circling Mike, ready, Mike looking intensely in his eyes.

"You gonna use that fancy karate fightin' on me?" he asked.

"No. This will be a simple boxing match! But call off your goons!"

"Your friends came for the party, let 'em party!"

"Hey!" a voice yelled over the melee. It was Jack Depoli's.

Everyone stopped and looked at him. Robbie and Dave were side by side, they had been in the thick of the fight as well. Dave's face was bloodied now but he stood strong. Brad Chapman was lying on the ground near him, his mouth bleeding.

"We came here to watch a fight!" Jack Depoli said. "Not to get into a brawl."

"Hey, he brought backup!" yelled Bob Gianechi as he stumbled to his feet.

"As if Mike didn't?" Jack said. "youse guys outnumber these guys and yer getting' yer fuckin' asses kicked! Now let's watch the fight!"

Both groups backed off, cautiously watching each other. The sound of a train whistle could be heard echoing from the train tunnel and there was a reflection of the headlight, several miles away as the train was entering the tunnel from the other end.

"Okay," Jim said, looking around and then at Mike. "Let's get on with it!"

At that moment Mike lunged at Jim, hitting him across the jaw with a strong right. Jim reeled with the blow, lessening the impact as he absorbed the shock. He wheeled around and stood strong. Mike lunged again but Jim stepped aside. Mike whirled around and took a punishing right to his jaw, he went down and rolled but quickly regained his feet.

"Kick his ass, Kick his ass!" came Rebecca's voice, she had regained consciousness now and she came running up to them, glaring at Jim. "You're gonna get your butt kicked now, you bastard!"

She lunged at Jim and he shoved her aside. Suzie and Jiang Li ran up and seized her arms, holding her back. Jim and Mike circled each other, feinting and lunging, Jim blocked a punch and jabbed with his left, hitting Mike, who shook it off. Mike was quick and he was strong. This was a good match. Jim fought against the instinct to use all his knowledge. Boxing only! As long as Mike followed the rules so would he.

"Come on, Mike!" Tiny yelled, mouth still bleeding.

The train whistle sounded again, the roar of the engines now echoing off the tunnel walls.

Mike came at Jim again, jabbing expertly, he had also had boxing training. Jim blocked and jabbed back, then stepped in with another right, Mike ducked back, on the tracks now. Jim stepped after him, both were on the tracks now, they had moved just inside the tunnel entrance.

"Jim! The train!" Suzie yelled.

Neither Jim nor Mike heard her. Mike jabbed again and Jim caught him hard in the face, right on his nose, blood spurted anew and his eyes teared. He went insane at that moment and dove at Jim, his arms going around his waist, driving him back into the tunnel. Both of them went down onto the tracks and rolled farther inside the tunnel. They could feel the vibration of the tracks and could hear the ever growing sound of the approaching iron and steel juggernaut as they rolled, Mike tying to gouge Jim's eyes. Jim put the heel of his palm under Mike's chin and tried to force his head up, Mike's thick neck muscles tensed like steel cords as he grabbed Jim's hand. He dislodged his hand and they rolled. The light was flooding the tunnel now, the roar growing greater and greater, the train thundering down on them. It was almost upon them. Jim heard a scream in the distance, a girl's scream. He shoved Mike off of him and rolled aside. The train was bearing down on them at full speed, the headlight blinding them, the whistle blared a deafening sound as Mike stood looking at it, transfixed, a confused look on his face. He was right in front of the approaching engine, the roar filling the tunnel, the vibration intense. Jim dove on Mike, spilling both of them off the tracks just in time, falling to the side as the train sped by, gleaming, steel wheels just inches from them. Jim held Mike down and they buried their faces in the dirt and gravel, hands over their ears as the train kept rumbling by. Jim could smell the diesel smoke trailing behind the two utility engines.

Finally the last car passed them and the train was gone. Jim was still holding Mike down. He released him, he could hear footsteps approaching as young men came running into the tunnel expecting the worst. Jim and Mike stumbled to their feet, clutching each others arms, they staggered out into the night. Suzie and Jiang Li were there, both running their hands across Jim's face, tears were in Jiang Li's eyes. Charlie, Joe and Will were also there.

Jim released Mike who stood dumbfounded.

"Get his ass, kick his ass!" Rebecca was beside Mike. "Go on! Don't wimp out, kick his fuckin' ass!"

"Shut the fuck up, you slut!" Mike's voice thundered at her and she backed off, shocked, looking at him then at Jim.

Jiang Li had her arms around Jim now, wiping his face with her hand. Tears were still in her eyes, she was trembling.

"I thought you were dead!" she said as she buried her face in his shoulder. Then she kissed him, her lips hot on his. They parted.

The crowd started to come nearer.

"Well, Mike, want us to get him?" Tiny asked.

"Back off!" Mike said. "All of you back off!"

He looked at Jim, at Jiang Li and Suzie and at the rest of them.

"Go for it! Come on, we're ready!" Charlie yelled as he got into his fighting stance.

"Hang on!" Mike yelled as he staggered forward. He looked at Jim again.

"This guy just saved my life!" he said as he wiped blood off his face. "I thought I was dead in there. I've never been so close to death before!"

He looked in Jim's eyes.

"Bein' in a war, I guess you've come close many times," Mike looked at the group, "I could have died in there. This guy beat me fair and square, I broke the rules by trying to wrestle him because I was losing. I had already lost the fight. He beat me."

He held out his hand to Jim.

"Apologize to her!" Jim demanded as he looked at Jiang Li, "Apologize for what you said about her background. Apologize for almost running her over with your car! Apologize to her face!"

Mike looked at Jim, then at Jiang Li. He looked at Rebecca. She glared at him and then at Jiang Li. He came forward and looked at Jiang Li, right into her eyes.

"I apologize," he said, "For what I said about your race and for coming at you with my car. I am sorry, I mean it."

Jiang Li looked in his eyes. She nodded.

"You saved my life," Mike said to Jim. "And you won. There's no way I could ever have beaten you fair and square or any other way. I guess I always knew that, you were the leader in football because you're a natural leader, you were better than me there also. I hated you for it. But not now. I could be dead right now but you pulled me out. I don't think I would have done the same for you and I am ashamed of that. I am ashamed.'

"Don't put your playing ability down, Mike. You were good on the field. And you fought well, and yes, you would have done the same for me." Jim said.

Mike held out his hand. He was looking right in Jim's eyes.

Jim took his hand and they shook firmly.

"Far as I'm concerned I'll be there if you ever need backup. Anytime," Mike said.

Jim looked around.

"Way to go," Jack Depoli said as he surveyed the crowd. "We saw a good fight tonight, let's all go home!"

One by one everyone began to head for their cars, engines started up as cars started turning around. There was the sound of sirens in the distance and Jim could see the red and blue lights on the approaching police cars, arriving too late. He took Jiang Li's hand.

"Let's get going," he said to her. She looked up at him, reached up and kissed his cheek, he put his arm around her.

Three patrol cars pulled up, blocking the way out, search lights flooding the area in a brilliant glare. Jim heard car doors closing, saw silhouettes approaching, clubs and flashlights in hand.

"Just hold on there!" a stern voice spoke from the glare of the lights. It was Captain Crane of the local police department.

"Everybody freeze!" another voice barked a command. It was Sergeant Stone. Jim had grown up knowing these cops.

More figures were emerging from the glare of the lights. Jim shielded his eyes against the glare with one hand while he placed Jiang Li's head against his shoulder. They were quickly surrounded by uniformed officers.

"What's the problem, Officer?" Jack Depoli asked.

"Well, well, so it's Depoli," Captain Crane said. "I figured there was trouble and seeing you here I'm convinced."

"Hey Captain Crane," Depoli said, "we're just out here havin' a friendly get-together, that's all."

"Is that so?" Captain Crane answered.

"Sure, no problem, Captain," Mike Walker spoke up now.

Rebecca was right behind him, quiet for once.

"Why I thought you worked down at the club on Friday nights," Captain Crane said. "Oh, that's right, it's closed down."

"It'll be up and runnin' again in no time," Mike answered.

"I can imagine. Too bad it's across city limits or it'd be closed down for good. I'd personally see to that! Nothing but trash hangs out or works there."

"Hey, I work there!" Rebecca spoke up, angry.

"Watch it!" Mike said, anger now flaring.

"It's okay," Jim patted Mike on the shoulder and stepped up, still holding Jiang Li. "It's like Jack said, just a get-together, a friendly get-together."

Captain Crane approached Jim, looking him over, up and down, Sergeant Stone did the same.

"Saunders, it's the Saunders kid, and look over there, it's the younger one as well, Robbie Saunders, and Denning's boy!" Sergeant said. "I never figured you for a trouble maker, Jim."

"No trouble at all, Sergeant, Captain, no trouble at all, just like I said..."

"Yeah," Captain Crane said, "Just a friendly get-together, that's all."

"Yeah, but I seem to have heard a rumor going around town about a certain fight that was supposed to take place out here. And look! I see bloodied mouths on some of you. Doesn't look so friendly to me."

Sergeant Stone was looking over everyone as two more patrol cars pulled up, more officers getting out and coming forward.

"We're doin' nothin' wrong, officers," Depoli spoke up again.

"Depoli, every move you ever make is wrong," Crane said. "Let's see, we can charge you all with trespassing, for one, illegal assembly for another."

"Hold on here!" Jim said now.

"I'm surprised at you, Saunders," Crane said, "You were never a trouble maker before! Why now? The war fuck your mind over, kid?"

"Watch your mouth!" Jim said, indicating Jiang Li.

"Don't give me any shit, kid!" Crane's eyes burned with anger now and he pulled out his club.

"Hold on!" Suzie stepped up now, anger flaring in her eyes.

"What do you want, young lady? Do I know you?"

"No, but I can vouch for everyone here, there's no problem."

"And by what authority do you speak? You're just one of them as far as I am concerned.

Jim noticed the momentary fire in Suzie's eyes. Then she calmed down.

"Look, officer, we were just leaving, no problem here at all," Jim said. "And as far as trespassing, I saw no signs."

"Don't need any. Fifty feet on each side of railroad tracks is private property, it belongs to Southern Pacific. I'd say you were all trespassing. But I'm letting it go for now. I will be keeping an eye on all of you, that's for sure. I don't want to see anyone of you out by these tracks again! It's dangerous here, you outta know that. You've been warned. I outta take down all your names but I already know who most of you are. I'm surprised at you, Saunders, but maybe it was your kid brother, maybe he was in danger of getting into a scrape, I see blood on his face, so I guess you were here to bail him out, like any good older brother would do.

"So all of you get the hell outta here and I don't ever want to catch you out here again!"

"Hey, we got rights..." Tiny started to say.

"Shut the fuck up, fatboy!" Depoli shouted then he looked at Suzie and Jiang Li, "Beggin' your pardon, ladies."

"Outta here! Now!" Crane's voice now boomed over a megaphone.

"Don't worry," Joe said to Jim, "I'll get Robbie and the other kid home."

Everyone headed for their cars and they quickly cleared out. Suzie rode with Joe and Will, Jiang Li got into Jim's car and he fired it up. Charlie White Eagle came thundering up beside him on his bike and stopped, engine idling.

"Sorry about tonight," Jim said, "I didn't mean to involve you in..."

"Hell, man, a good fight was just what I needed. I had a great time!" Charlie grinned. "I gotta be goin' but hey, I'm in a booth at a pow wow at the Cow Palace next weekend. Why don't you come by."

"A pow wow?" Jim asked.

"Yeah, a gathering of the tribes for celebration. Good food, lots of good stuff, come on by, I'll get you in free." He dug into his pocket and came out with two tickets which he handed to Jim. "For you and the little lady. Nice to meet you, ma'am."

Jiang Li started to acknowledge him but he had thundered off down the road, following the tail lights of the other cars. There were several patrol cars behind them, making sure everyone was leaving. Jim looked at Jiang Li, then straight ahead as he put the car in gear and drove off.

***

Jim pulled up down the street from his parent's house and parked on

the street. They had not spoken as he had driven away from the tracks, Jiang Li had just sat beside him, her hand on his at times.
Jim was silent for a minute, collecting his thoughts.

"What happened?" he asked her.

"The Toyota parked over in front of the bar, you probably didn't notice it. It's my car. I usually take the bus to school. I snuck out tonight to see you."

"But what about your parents, those punks in the parking lot who warned you."

"I don't know right now," she said. Then she leaned over and put her arms around him. "I only know this," she said as her lips met his. They kissed a long, lingering kiss, Jim's arms went around her, holding her to him across the shifter and consol between the bucket seats.

"I saw how you took care of David in the parking lot this afternoon, I hid behind a building and watched. And I have heard stories also."

"Stories?"

"About an American guy in Chinatown yesterday who took out several hoodlums belonging to a certain triad. Dangerous men but they were nothing to this young American. The incident you told me about."

"Really? I wonder who would have seen anything like this."

"Probably someone watching from a window. But these guys had no chance against this one American. He was that good, they said."

"How would I know, I was out at the college that day."

Jiang Li smiled, "You already told me about it in a few words."

She kissed him again.

"Now what about you? What about the threats against your family?"

"I have never met the man I am supposed to marry. My father became indebted to one of the triads when he was in financial trouble, years ago. He was unable to pay the price they required..."

"So you became the price..."

Jiang Li lowered her head.

"But..." she turned away for a moment. "But then you came along. I was about to graduate with my degree. But I would still have to marry that man."

"And now? You're here tonight."

"I don't know. But I knew I had to see you again. I knew how I felt about you I think from the time you walked me home. I thought I would never see you again but then, there you were, standing there at school. I was so glad you were there. And again, today, when I saw you. I was glad. I had such a heavy heart having to tell you I was to be married."

"And so now..."

"I don't know. I just know I can't be without you."

"Maybe you should leave, maybe...no...I don't know what to say right now."

"For now I'll stay in school, I graduate in three weeks. I will drive home and sneak in. My parents don't know I left tonight."

"These people, this triad, how much power do they have over your family?"

"They have the power of life and death."

"You could go to the authorities."

"Do you really think that would help? Do you think the authorities really care about what goes on down in Chinatown?"

"What you are talking about is like life lived in the dark ages."

"It is the 'dark ages' in many ways. I don't know..."

"I know this, you aren't marrying this man! Not if it isn't your choice. Jiang Li...I choose you, I want to be with you, I know that!"

They kissed again and he looked into her deep, dark eyes, black pools of wonder, looking into his soul.

"Do you mean it?" she whispered.

"I mean it! I won't have you marrying some man you don't even know, against your choice, and even if it were your choice I will put my bid in right now!"

Now he took her in his arms hungrily, kissing her deeply. Then they parted.

"Your mother said a strange thing tonight when I came by looking for you," Jiang Li said. "She knows doesn't she, I mean, about me getting married? But she seemed very glad to see me and then she said something strange."

"What did she say?"

"She said that if I needed to get away I could stay there in your house."

Jim was astonished.

"She said that?"

"Yes..."

He shook his head. Jiang Li came across the seat again and raised her sweatshirt up exposing her black bra, she had small, rounded breasts. Jim bent down as she held his head and he kissed the uncovered parts as Jiang Li's head leaned back, she was moaning with pleasure then her lips found his again as he felt her, holding them in his palms, they were firm but yielding in his hands. He felt the fever rise in him as they kissed, losing themselves in each other. Jim saw the headlights of an approaching car and he clumsily ducked down across the consol out of sight as they continued to kiss, his hands still on her. She took his wrists and had him push harder against her body.

"I'm yours," she whispered to him, her lips brushing against his ear. He could hear the roar of her breath. "I'm yours, no matter what happens please believe that I am yours, Jim."

"I believe you, Jiang Li, Jill, I believe you."

"Jill, Jiang Li, whatever you call me, it's okay, both Jill and Jiang Li are yours."

Then they parted and Jiang Li lowered her sweatshirt, her hair was a mess around her shoulders, Jim liked the way it looked that way, all messed up. He ran his fingers through her hair then held her face in his hands.

"I must be going," Jiang Li said.

"Tomorrow's Saturday, you don't have school tomorrow do you?"

"No. But I do have to be in soon. It's a long drive back. Maybe I can get away tomorrow afternoon. I have to study in the morning and I really should look for another part time job. I don't want my parents getting any ideas right now."

"Meet me tomorrow then, in the afternoon. There's a lake near here, a nice small inland lake with a sandy beach on one side. The weather's getting nice and warm now, summer's just around the corner..."

"I'll do everything I can to be there tomorrow. Tell me how to get there."

Jim reached across her to the glove compartment. She kissed him as he opened it and their lips lingered for a moment. He took out a small writing tablet and a pen and wrote on it. He handed the paper to her.

"I'll be there," he said. "Now I better drive you to your car."

He fired up his car and they headed down the street to the bar. It was eleven thirty now and the bar was still open as it would be until 2 a.m. Jim pulled up behind Jiang Li's Toyota and parked. They both got out and he walked her to her car. She was about to open the door when she turned to face him. He reached for her and she threw her arms around his neck. He pushed her back against her car, taking her breath away as his lips smothered hers, their tongues wrestling, their breathing coming hot and heavy, his lips found her neck and she gasped as he kissed her neck. She kissed his. Jim felt her teeth on his neck pinching the skin. Then they parted. He felt his neck.

"I gave you a hicky!" She smiled, "And I have never given a hicky before to anyone. My mark of 'ownership!'"

"I'd give you one but I don't think it's a good idea right now, you wouldn't want your parents seeing it," he laughed and they held each other again, kissing deeply.

They managed to part again and she got into her car and fired up the engine, she rolled down the window and he reached down. They kissed again.

"I'll be at the lake," she said.

Then she drove off, Jim watched until she turned off onto the main street heading for the highway home.

CHAPTER NINE

Standing there on the street under the streetlight Jim suddenly felt parched, intensely thirsty. He looked across the street to the bar. He decided to go inside. Mike walker was the only one there besides Sam, he was seated at a table in the corner and he looked up as Jim came in. He motioned for Jim to come over.

"Let me buy you a beer," Mike said, a smile on his face. He seemed, to Jim, a changed young man.

"Sure, but the thing is, Sam over there, he keeps insisting that every beer I drink is on the house."

Sam was looking in their direction. He was already on his way over with two beers which he set on the table. He looked at Jim and then at Mike. He had a puzzled look on his face.

"You guys okay?" he asked.

"Just fine, Sam," Jim answered.

Sam shook his head then returned to the bar, it was getting late and he was beginning to clean things up for the night. Sam would keep the bar open until two but he would make sure all his side work was done.

"Well," Mike said, "I guess Rebecca's career here was short lived."

"Yeah, I'd say so."

"She was always bad news," Mike said, taking a pull from his beer. "I should have seen it then. You did."

"Yeah," Jim answered, feeling the cold feel of the brew cooling his throat, "it didn't take too long."

"Yeah, I saw that tonight. And anyway, she was always going to be hung up on you. There will be no changing that."

"I hear you're working down at Denning's club."

"Yeah. Not a bad job, I can get you in if you like. But it's not what I want for the rest of my life, that's for sure."

"Are you in school?"

"Started at the local JC but didn't stay with it. Maybe I should go back. What about you? Don't you get some kind of benefit from the service? Some kind of educational benefit?"

"Yeah, I plan to do something."

"See you gotta girlfriend. I'm sorry about what I said about her..."

"It's done with, Mike, what was past is done with now."

"It is," Mike raised his bottle in salute then finished it off. Jim finished his, Sam was already placing two more on the table. Mike reached for his money but Sam put up his hand and shook his head.

"God I wish he wouldn't do that," Jim said. "I'm thinking of not coming in here anymore. I feel like some kind of bum."

"Sam's a veteran. You were in a war. You know how he is about vets. You earned it, you were over there puttin' your life on the line. I wasn't, that's for sure. Maybe I should join up."

"It's like this, Jim, when that train was comin' at me tonight it's like my whole life was in front of my eyes and suddenly all the bullshit I believed about myself and believed in just didn't matter anymore. And I saw that Rebecca didn't give a rat's ass. She doesn't give a rat's ass about anyone but herself, but you already knew that.

"You were always smarter, Jim..."

"Hey, don't go puttin' yourself down..."

"No, it's true, you always knew the right thing to do, me I was just trying to get my own way and feeling threatened by you all the time. I guess I felt that if I could beat you that it would make my life good. I was obsessed with beating you. I felt that when I had Rebecca with me I had won something, taken something that had been yours. But it was no gain, I guess I always knew what she was but I couldn't let go.

"And then when you came back, I saw her going right for you. I saw her eyes light up just at the mention of you so I figured I had to beat you again. When those train lights were looking me in the eye and the train whistle was sounding a death toll it all changed. Maybe I should look into school or something. Or maybe work for a power company, I could handle a lineman's job I think, good pay and good benefits.

"And you, you should look at something soon too. Like I said, that's a nice girl you were with. I could tell she has real class, just lookin' at her I can tell that. And I just had to run my mouth."

"It's okay, Mike. What happened down at the tunnel, it's finished. It turned out well."

"I'm sorry I hit your brother. He's a scrapper though, he got a good one in on me."

"Robbie had to learn a lesson the hard way, Mike. He chose to get involved in a brawl so he had to take his medicine. He's okay."

"I'm glad I didn't hurt him. The whole idea was really stupid, brawling, railroad tracks, high school stuff. You never did that stuff. I used to say it was because you were afraid but deep down inside I knew better. No man was better on the football field than you."

"Mike, I only fight when I have to fight. When there are lives on the line. And I've had plenty of that the past year and a half."

"Yeah, gettin' shot at is no picnic."

Mike set his empty down on the bar and stood up. Jim stood.

"Well, I gotta be goin', I gotta get up early, help in the repairs at the club, Mr. Denning wants to open tomorrow night. I'm tellin' you, you outta check out a job there. You'd be good. Lot's of rowdies in there, we'd be a good team. It's not job with a future but it's good for now. think about it, okay?"

They shook hands.

Mike left and Jim made his way over to the bar. He hadn't mentioned Denning's offer this morning, about the job, about taking over as head bouncer. He wasn't going to be going for that job, he didn't want to displace Mike or anyone else. For now, he just wanted to relax, to put his mind at rest, to figure some things out.

Jim heard a sound. Someone had come in and he heard a chair being pulled back. He looked over his shoulder. He was there, the stranger, seated in a corner, looking at him.

"Two more, Sam," Jim said and Sam placed two beers on the bar. Jim took them and made his way over to the stranger's table.

"Well, don't mind if I do," the stranger said as Jim sat down, placing one beer in front of him.

Jim pulled up a chair and sat directly opposite the man, looked him right in the eye. The man was smiling, his clear blue eyes were smiling as well.

"Let's just cut the bullshit right fucking now!" Jim said to him.

"You handled yourself very well tonight down at the railroad tracks," the stranger answered.

"And how would you be knowing that, I never saw you there."

"I know all about it and you did very well. Like I had expected you to handle it."

"So what's it too you? What the hell is going on? Level with me now or I'm puttin' you against that fuckin' wall over there!"

"No need to get threatening," the stranger said and now his blue eyes changed, the laughter was gone and there was an intenseness there. Jim noticed the man's thick neck muscles tense almost imperceptibly but they had tensed.

"Level with me!" Jim demanded. "You strike me as someone who defends himself but I wouldn't count on beating me!"

"I wouldn't either, and we don't need to go there," the man said. He reached into his coat pocket and pulled out a wallet, holding it up to Jim and opening it. There was a badge and his picture. Jim scrutinized it. It read:

MARTIN THOMAS
DRUG ENFORCEMENT AGENCY

The stranger named Martin quickly replaced the wallet in his pocket.

"So what does that have to do with me?" Jim asked. "If you are investigating me on suspicion of using drugs then you will find that booze and coffee are my drugs of choice and perfectly legal."

"We've been keeping an eye on you ever since we knew you were being discharged from the military, son," Martin said.

"Like I said before, only one man has the right to call me 'son.'"

"Well, former Sergeant Saunders, would 'Jim' do?"

"'Jim' will do fine."

"Like I said, Jim, we've been keeping an eye on you, especially me and also, a few other people. I'd like you to come down to the Federal Building in San Francisco on Monday afternoon at, say, about one o'clock."

"Am I being investigated?"

"Not at all, Jim. I will tell you this, and I would like this conversation to remain confidential, we have been watching you, how you handle yourself and the report is good. Now let me ask you this, would you like a career opportunity landed right smack in your lap? A job with a future, with benefits, medical benefits, a dynamite retirement after twenty years of service, the chance for advancement?"

"What are you talking about, you're offering me a job? Don't I have to go through some kind of civil service testing, have a college degree, stuff like that? And be physically fit? I was kicked out of the Army, they said I was no longer fit for combat."

"Army bureaucracy. All bullshit, you and I both know that, S... I mean, Jim. All bullshit. You have more than qualified as far as we are concerned for what we would like to have you do for us. But I need you to come down to the Federal Building to talk it over and meet a few people who have been watching you. The way you handled yourself in Chinatown, and the way you took that punk out at the college was mighty impressive."

"You had my back, didn't you?"

"But I wasn't really needed. And the way you handled yourself in the situation at the railroad tracks shows good judgment. Your ego doesn't get involved. You have that detachment."

"Really, I was about to kick your ass a few minutes ago, that's not detachment."

"You had every right to be angry, Jim. I would expect nothing less at that moment. That's why I leveled with you. So tell you what, if you want this job, a job with an excellent future, then come to San Francisco Monday afternoon. If not, the offer's off the table. Let me add this. That's a nice girl you found. A girl like that would give a young man like you an incentive to want to better himself, find a career, and we have just the career that would fit your talents. Be there Monday and we'll talk about it further. Sound good?"

"That girl is..."

"I know about the family. I know about the tongs in Chinatown. It is not a hopeless situation. We can help you get her and her family out of this mess, I can promise you that. You'd like that, wouldn't you?"

"If you're bullshitting me..."

"Find out. Be down at the Federal Building Monday afternoon."

CHAPTER TEN

Jim curled the bar towards his chest, there was one hundred and twenty pounds on it, he was finishing his twelfth repetition with the weight on the curling bar, he was standing astride a workout bench, he could feel the blood gorging his bulging biceps as he strained to grind out that final rep. He finished and set the bar on the bench then sat down to get his breath, wiping his forehead with the towel he had around his shoulders. It was eight in the morning and he had awakened with the desire to workout. He was working arms today, having done the bench press at the college gym the other day while he had been searching for Jiang Li.

"Hi," Jim heard Robbie's voice and he looked around while taking a gulp from his plastic water bottle. Robbie was standing at the doorway to the patio.

"Hi kid," Jim smiled. "How you feeling today?"

"Okay," Robbie smiled. "I just got back from Dave's."

"I figured you'd stay there all weekend with your buddy."

"I was going to, mind if I do a set?"

Robbie looked at the loaded bar.

"Go ahead, how much?" Jim asked him.

"Seventy five I guess," Robbie answered. He helped Jim unload some of the plates from the bar then he did a very hard ten repetition set.

"Two more!" Jim commanded when he had finished the tenth rep and Robbie strained hard on the bar, his arms were growing, Jim could tell. Jim helped by placing his fore finger from each hand just under the bar to give just a little bit of help. Robbie got the two extra reps then sat down on the bench, exhausted with the effort.

"Good job," Jim said as Robbie fought for breath. "I can tell you've been hitting it regularly."

"Every day," Robbie answered.

"Good job last night, too," Jim said.

Robbie looked down.

"I'm sorry," he stammered, "about the things I said, I'm sorry about that, I was being pretty stupid I guess."

"Somewhat, and somewhat not."

Jim placed his hand on Robbie's shoulder.

"I know at your age it's seems so important to prove yourself. And you did that, you got a good piece of Mike last night, got a good hit in. But street fighting is never acceptable. In high school I never got involved in those fights."

"You fought..."

"When I had to. When I had no choice. Look, Robbie, you're a strong kid, I can tell, you've put on a lot of size since I've been away, you don't have to prove anything to yourself anymore. Everyone knows you can take care of yourself now so avoid trouble like that. If someone challenges you, walk away. You already know you can fight."

"I thought...I thought you weren't going..."

"...because I was scared so you felt obligated to fight the battle because someone had to...right?"

Robbie looked away and nodded. "But it wasn't that way at all. You could have taken everyone there if you had to."

"I don't know about that..."

"I can tell you could have. Mike's lucky to be alive, if you ask me. And then you saved his life."

"And as you can see, me and Mike shook hands afterwards. Mike isn't a bad guy, he's just unsure, but he's not a bad sort of guy. And he definitely knows my little brother can do some damage. I'm proud of you, Robbie, you showed guts when it counted. You don't ever have to do that again."

"Thanks," Robbie nodded.

"Now, kid, let's work triceps, okay?"

"Sure thing!" Robbie said as they loaded some weight on the bar.

***

It was eleven thirty as Jim drove up the winding road through the trees at the base of Mt. Diablo. He turned off on the road leading to the lake and stopped at the guard gate. He paid the park ranger the five dollar entry fee and drove on through. He reached the parking area and pulled into a space. The place was not as packed as he thought it would be, in fact very few people were there at all. He was glad. He had stopped at Stan's for breakfast after a great workout with his brother. His mother had offered to fix both of them breakfast but Jim had begged off. His dad had gone into the shop today, unusual for he almost always took Saturday and Sunday off. He had said there had been extra work. He had smiled at Jim and Robbie and then had left. His mother had tried to pry information out of both him and Robbie but Jim had said nothing about the scene down at the railroad tracks. He had kissed her on the cheek and left.

He picked a spot on the man made sandy beach that occupied the west side of the lake. There was a snack bar nearby and the lifeguard tower. The lifeguard was seated on the platform overlooking the water. There were a few people about, mainly families and the kids were frolicking in the water having a ball. They stayed in the shallows. Farther out were the floats supporting the roped area allowed for swimming. A pier jutted out into the water just down from the guard tower and several older kids had just jumped from the end of the pier and were swimming towards the raft that floated in the center of the roped off swimming area. The lifeguard watched with heightened interest as they made the swim, hoops and hollers announced their arrival at the raft as they pulled themselves up and relaxed in the sun. The weather was picking up, not the usual June glooms for this time of year, it was getting warm. The water was probably still pretty cold and Jim saw the smaller kids now running to their parents who were putting towels around them and giving them sandwiches.

Jim had placed a towel on the sand, he was wearing cut off jeans and a tank top, revealing his well defined and massive shoulders. It felt good to be getting some sun on them.

Jim checked his watch. A little after twelve now. He wondered if she would be there, maybe she had been prevented from leaving by her parents. Then he saw the Toyota just pulling into the parking space and he felt his heart leap for joy. He was on his feet in an instant. She had now gotten out of the car and was crossing the lot. She was dressed in cutoff jeans, showing her smooth, tanned legs to advantage, she had on sandals and she wore a large, white sweatshirt with the words SF State in large red letters. She also wore a large, straw sunhat and, large, round dark glasses with blue lenses. Her long, silken black hair trailed around her shoulders, carelessly from under the hat. Across her shoulders she carried a canvas bag. When she saw Jim she waved excitedly and started to run towards him, she almost tripped as her sandal started to come off, she turned to replace it.

Jim was in front of her now, holding out his arms to steady her, she turned and looked up then she was in his arms, kissing him.

"You were able to get away," Jim said, "I'm glad."

He kissed her again, he could feel her against him as both her arms were around his neck. He held her tight and her feet came off the ground, out of her sandals. He set her back down and she stepped back into them.

"I am having a terrible time trying to keep these things on..." she stammered then took his arm.

"I'm right over there," Jim said as they walked across the parking lot and onto the sand. "Did you have trouble getting away?"

"No problem at all. Although my father was looking at me strangely this morning. My mother also. I think they know something's up."

"That guy, David? Maybe he told them something."

"I don't know..." she kissed the side of his face, "...and I don't care."

They walked over to Jim's towel and Jiang Li set her things down, removing her sun hat and undoing her hair, it fell the rest of the way around her shoulders and she shook her head. Jim felt he had never in his life seen a more beautiful woman as this one before him. She slid off her sweatshirt, she was wearing a one piece, black bathing suit underneath, her browned skin had a velvet sheen, the sun shown off the gentle curves of her well toned shoulders and arms. She reached down into her bag and pulled out some sun tan lotion and applied it to her arms, smiling up at Jim. She offered him the bottle and he put some on his arms and shoulders. She turned her back and Jim squeezed some of the lotion onto his hands. He began rubbing it on her back, the back of her neck as she raised her hair out of the way, down the tops of her shoulders, feeling the small muscles beneath her silken skin. His palms circled her shoulders, she leaned her head back, turning her face towards him. He kissed her then kissed her face and worked down to her neck. She reached back and held the back of his head, stroking his hair. Their lips met again and she moved against him, sending tingles through his being. She reached down and undid the snaps on her cutoffs then let them fall. She moved away from him and stood there in front of him in her one piece, more revealing actually than any string bikini could ever be. The suit rode high along her hips, her small breasts were round and full under the material. She came to him and pressed against him, her arms going around his waist and locking against his lower back so she could press herself more firmly against him. His arms were around her waist as they kept kissing, his tongue wrestling with hers, her eyes were barely open and glazed over with passion. He ran his hand through her hair and then placed her face in his hands, looking into her eyes. Such deep brown pools they were, almost black. She reached for his tank top and moved it up, he helped her and pulled it over his head then felt himself against her, felt her breasts pressed against his chest, he could feel her breathing. She let out a gasp, then they parted again. He took her hand.

"Let's go in the water," he said.

She smiled and they ran down the beach and right into the chilled water, both of them gasping as they broke the surface and plunged in, now swimming side by side. They headed out to the raft, now deserted. They reached it and Jim pulled himself up onto the raft and reached down for Jiang Li's hand, pulling her up with him. They lay on the raft now as it bobbed in the water. She lay on top of him as they kissed each other. Jim noticed the lifeguard was no longer on his platform.

Jiang Li's hands roamed his back then moved downward to his waist, to the tops of his cutoffs as she moved against him. He kept kissing her breasts and feeling them, working the nipples in his thumbs. She brought her hands along the front of his waistline and undid the snaps of his cutoffs. He arched upward against her now, surging against her, feeling the litheness of her body against his. She undid another snap then he felt her hands roam lower. He pulled the straps of her suit down along her arms, baring her beautiful breasts, her nipples were erect. He kissed them and her hand slid down undoing yet another snap, reached down further and finding him now, holding him firmly, feeling his manhood, all of his manhood. She gasped as she gripped him firmly in her hand.

Their lips parted and they looked around. No one on the beach was really paying attention to them, most had left and the lifeguard was still not on his platform, Jim could see him over by the snack bar having a hotdog. All the kids had gone and a gentle, cool breeze now wafted across the gently rippling water. Jiang Li released him and moved on top of him, his freed manhood now against her wet bathing suit. She moved against him, smiling down at him, her breasts bare. Jim rolled her over under him, facing away from the beach. One of her legs wrapped around his, her hips jamming against him, feeling his heat against her, she moved against him. Their tongues met again in a long kiss and then he put his lips on her nipple as she leaned her head back and gasped as the passion was unleashed within her being.

"Jiang Li, I love you," Jim whispered into her ear.

"I love you," she gasped back at him, now looking into his eyes.

They surged against each other again, Jim hot against her wet suit.

"Go ahead..." she gasped. "Go ahead..."

He released in a blinding surge, every nerve in his body on fire as she moaned against him in her own release. It felt like a thousand suns exploding in his being, in his mind, in his body, in his soul.

They lay together, calm now, he could feel her breasts against his chest. She moved up on him, kissing him, feeling his face with her gentle hands, tracing the line of his face, feeling his hair, tracing along his forehead. She kissed him again. She closed her eyes and lay on him, both of them dozing together in a sea of unbounded bliss, the world had ceased to exist for now.

***

Jim opened his eyes. There was still a breeze drifting across the water but it had gotten colder now. He looked towards the shore. Everyone had gone and the sun was now lower in the sky. Jiang Li was nestled on his chest. She opened her eyes. She was shivering. He kissed her.

"We have to get back," Jim whispered.

Thank God they had put the sunscreen lotion on, water proof, it had protected them from the burning rays. They dove off the raft and swam across the water to the shore. Jim took Jiang Li's hand and led them to his spot on the beach. Jiang Li reached into her large bag and pulled out a large towel. Jim sat down next to her, they lay back and pulled the towel over them, both of them were shivering with the cold now, Jim's teeth were chattering. He pulled Jiang Li to him under the towel and they held each other, feeling each other's warmth. The sky was beginning to cloud up, the June glooms, the weather never really predictable at this time of year, hot one day and cool the next.

Jim drew Jiang Li closer to him and their lips met in a soft kiss.

"We made love," Jiang Li whispered. "we...we didn't really make love, but I have never been this far with any man before." She kissed him again. "Yes, it was lovemaking, truly lovemaking. I hope we can have it completely soon."

"So do I..." Jim whispered. "I never felt more complete than I felt out on that raft."

Warmth was beginning to spread through them now and the

shivering had stopped. Jim felt a deep relaxation come over him and he closed his eyes. He opened them and saw that Jiang Li was closing her eyes as well.

"Sleep," she whispered, "let sleep take us now..."

Jim surrendered to the pull of deep sleep as it washed over him. He heard her whisper to him as he drifted off... "true lovemaking..."

***

Jim was in a dream. Neela was there, sitting across from him, her deep brown eyes looking into his soul. He was lying on a gurney and he seemed to be drifting along, weightless. She spoke to him. "Jeem," she said, "Jeem, I am at peace now. For me there is no more war. Jeem, stay with her, Jeem. I weesh eet could have been me, I weesh, oh Jeem, I weesh...but it doesn't matter now, for the war ees over for me now. I smile on you, Jeem...I smile on you..."

***

Jim's eyes opened. A dream. Neela. She had come to give him a message, he believed that. He felt a sadness as he remembered the dark eyed beauty saving his life. He had had such a terrible longing for her. He knew she had died.

Jim felt Jiang Li lying against him, sound asleep. The sun was setting now. Jim rose up slightly and saw that her Toyota and his Chevy were the only cars left in the lot. No one had tried to wake them, everyone had just left. The cool breeze still blew across the lake and he could feel the coolness on his arm.

Jiang Li moaned slightly and moved against him, snuggling in closer to him, deep in sleep. Jim knew it was time to leave. He nudged her and she slowly opened her eyes, looking up at him with a dreamy, misty look, her hair messed up around her shoulders, she never looked so beautiful as right now, there under the large towel in his arms. He didn't want this to end, this blissful afternoon, almost evening now.

Jim kissed her, a long, lingering, blissful kiss as Jiang Li brushed his face with her hand.

"We have to be going," Jim said to her.

"I know," she whispered to him. "I want to stay here forever. I never want to leave."

They kissed again then Jim stood up, holding out his hand to Jiang Li. She rose next to him and threw her arms around his neck, kissing him again. He was beginning to get aroused again and he took a deep breath.

"What's wrong," she smiled up at him, an innocent look in her playful eyes.

"You know what you're doing..."

"Of course!"

And she kissed him again.

The sun was even lower now, the sky darkening. Jim glanced at his watch. Eight o'clock, it would be completely dark soon.

Jiang Li moved against him again and again he felt a surge of desire that almost overpowered him.

"You are my first," she whispered to him, "...and my only..." moving against him again. Then she backed away from him and stood before him on the sand, the breeze blowing her hair around her shoulders. She undid the straps to her bathing suit, sliding them down over her shoulders, her breasts freed now, glistening in the remaining light, she slid the suit further down and stepped out of it, letting it remain on the sand. She stood there, naked before him, her hair blowing around her shoulders, her skin sleek and smooth. She held out her arms.

Jim undid the snaps to his cutoffs and slid them off. He stood there before her then went to her, feeling himself against her smooth skin, his desire driving him mad at this point. Her arms went around him as she pressed herself against him, moving on him, driving him crazy with his desire for her. She parted from him, holding his hand and leading him back to the towel, she knelt down, pulling him down with her, she was beneath him now as he settled on her. He kissed her breasts, licking her firm nipples, rolling one gently in his teeth as she moaned with growing pleasure.

"Jim, I want you, Jim, I want you now..."

He moved down upon her.

"Easy, Jim, easy," she gasped as he slowly entered her, he could feel her gripping him, feeling her tensing, she drew a deep breath, he paused. Her arms went around his neck and her mouth covered his, her tongue darting against his. He sank in farther, she let out a cry and then, slowly, very slowly, she accepted him as she caught her breath.

"I am truly yours," she gasped.

***

It was dark now. Jim opened his eyes, she was laying on his chest, her arms around him under the towel. Jim checked his watch. It was ten thirty. They had made love for over an hour and had then drifted off into a blissful, deep sleep together. He had held himself from completion, bringing her to climax after climax before pulling out to protect her. She had caressed his face, neck and shoulders as he did hers as they had drifted off together.

He nudged her gently and she awoke with a blissful smile, looking at him with dreamy eyes barely visible in the darkness. The weather had changed now and the night was dead still and warmer. Jiang Li reached down and fondled him gently and lovingly.

"What a nice job he did," she whispered in his ear, breathing deeply. He felt himself start to leap to life but fought the urge. She pressed him against her and they kissed long and deeply.

"We really have to get back," Jim whispered but she kissed him again.

"Oh of course we do," she answered.

She gripped him now as he felt her naked nipples against his chest.

"Just one more time..." she gasped as he rolled over on top of her.

***

Eleven thirty now.

Jiang Li shot upright, the towel falling from her shoulders.

"Oh my!" she exclaimed.

Jim rose up beside her. She was fumbling in her bag. She pulled out her cell phone.

"What?" Jim asked her.

She leaned over and kissed him.

"It's okay, but I have to have an excuse," she answered.

"An excuse?"

"Hello, June? June?" she was speaking into the phone. "Yes...it's me...I was wondering...yes it is..." she let out a girlish laugh... "We're fine. We're at a lake right now, in fact we will be leaving soon...I was wondering if you would...what?...really?...then you won't be there...okay, it's under the plants...which one?...okay...I can't thank you enough..." Jiang Li shut off the phone and put her arms around Jim, kissing him.

"What was that all about?" Jim asked.

"It's June, a friend of mine from school, an American friend, sometimes I spend the weekends there studying with her, I was going to ask her to cover for me but I have great news."

"Great news? What kind of great news?"

"She has invited us to stay at her apartment in San Francisco, out in the Sunset district near the beach."

"Us?"

"She knew I was with you."

"Me, she knows me?"

"Well, yes. She saw us together at school and asked many questions so I told her all about you, well mostly all about you."

"Really."

"Yes, I told her how I met your parents. She and all my friends are happy for me."

"All your friends."

"At school. You're so cute that word spread quickly!"

"Cute?"

"You know you are," Jiang Li kissed him, her arms going around him. "She invited us to stay there, she was on her cell phone, she isn't home this weekend, she's with her boyfriend down in Palo Alto for the entire weekend but she has a spare key hidden under one of her planters outside the apartment door, it's a two bedroom flat, first floor. You could follow me there?"

Jim held her, they kissed again, a long, lingering kiss.

"We'd better get going," Jim said, "Or else we'll be here all night if we get started again."

Jiang Li smiled at him and fondled him.

"Better not," he answered.

"We still have the rest of the weekend," Jiang Li said.

***

Jim parked his car about mid block. He had had to drive several car lengths to find a parking space. Jiang Li had already found a spot and was running towards him as he locked his door. They put their arms around each other's waists as they strolled to a stairway leading up to a covered porch with two entrances. One door to the upstairs apartment and the other to the ground floor flat. Jiang Li tilted one of the planters and found the key. She turned to Jim, smiling and holding it up. She put her arms around him and they kissed, Jim pulling her against him, the fever rising again.

"June usually keeps 'protection' in her medicine cabinet," Jiang Li said. "I have seen them there before." She smiled and kissed Jim again. "I wish we didn't have to use it."

She turned and unlocked the door, they stepped inside and she closed and locked the door behind them. A table light was on, dimly lighting up the spacious living room.

"Nice place for a college girl," Jim said.

"She's on a scholarship and her parents pay for the flat. They also bought her a nice BMW."

Jim scanned the room, there was an entertainment center, big screen LCD TV, DVD player, a Bose radio/CD player and large speakers. Jiang Li turned on the radio to a popular station playing soft love songs which drifted out of the speakers in a low, mellow tone. Next, she closed all the shades and drew the drapes shut then turned to face Jim.

"Here we are," she said.

Then she was rushing to him, throwing her arms around his neck and kissing him as he held her tight.

"How about a nice, warm shower?" she said to him with a smile as they parted.

She took his hand and led him down the hallway to the master bedroom, Jim noticed the other bedroom had a desk with computer and a corner mounted Bowflex™ exercise machine. They entered the master bedroom, the bathroom was adjoining, the door slightly ajar.

Jiang Li paused by the bed and slipped out of her sweatshirt, letting it fall to the bed. Next came her cutoffs. She stood there in her still damp bathing suit. Jim undressed quickly and came to her, pressing against her, feeling himself against the wet material as they kissed and caressed each other. Jim peeled the shoulder straps away, pulling the suit down, feeling it fall to the floor between them, Jiang Li kicking it free then pressing herself against him, her wet skin felt so good against him. She parted and took his hand, leading him into the spacious bathroom with white tiled floor. She opened the shower door and turned on the water. Steam rose as she adjusted the temperature. They stepped inside the shower stall as the water rained down on them and steam flooded the room. Soaking wet, they held each other close and kissed as beads of water cascaded off them. Jiang Li reached for the soap and stepped away, soaping herself. Jim took the bar and soaped her breasts then she started on him, his chest and shoulders, his thighs and then she moved higher to his lower abdomen, then back down to him, soaping him well. Jim pressed himself to her, kissing open mouthed as their heat rose, as steamy as the shower itself. They rinsed off and stepped out of the shower. Jiang

Li opened the medicine cabinet, the entire room was fogged up with the steam. She withdrew the small package, turned to Jim and smiled.

"Now you don't have to be careful," she said with a smile as they walked to the bed still soaking wet. She lay down and Jim sank down on top of her, her arms going around him. He placed the protection on himself as her legs wrapped around him and drew him into her, she gasped with unending pleasure as they made love there in the darkened bedroom on into the night.

***

Jim opened his eyes. Outside the sky was beginning to show the first light of morning, the window was facing west towards the ocean two blocks away. A cool breeze was drifting through the curtains, blowing them slightly about the window frame. Jim and Jiang Li were lying with just the sheet barely over them, she was lying on his chest, her leg draped over his loins, he could feel the smoothness of her silken skin against him. Her face was covered by her tangled hair and she looked so incredibly sexy, lying there, naked with him. He closed his eyes a moment, this was truly a moment of eternal bliss, and he really did want it to last for an eternity.

He felt Jiang Li stir, and she gave out a low moan and moved on him. She half opened her eyes and raised her head up, looking around then she looked up at him, her hair all disarrayed around her face and she smiled the sexiest smile he had ever seen. She rose up, looking beautiful in the dim, pre-morning light and she reached for the nightstand, picking up another package. She set it down on the bed next to them and then she moved over on top of him, he could feel every move of her supple body on his. She rose up, seated on him, leaning on her hands, one to each side of his head.

"Well, good morning there, sleepy head," she whispered.

She bent down and kissed him a long kiss, her lips wet on his. He reached up and felt her bare breasts and rose up and kissed one as she leaned back her head with a moan of pleasure. She reached down and felt him, then she tore open the package and he could feel her place it on him, rolling it along his length. He felt her settle on him.

"I wish we didn't have to use this..." she gasped as her body shuddered.

"We must, for now, we..." Jim took a sudden breath then she leaned down, he could feel her hair tickling his face. Their lips met as he moved in her, her firm body rocking on his, he could sense all her delicate, toned muscles at work on him.

"Staff Sergeant Jim Saunders, I love you..." she gasped.

"Jiang Li, I love you..."

***

Jim sipped his coffee, a large mug Jiang Li had placed in his hand. She sat beside him on the bed, a coffee mug also in her hand. The sun was well up in the sky now, it was almost noon and growing warm out, no June glooms today.

"Nothing like home brewed coffee," Jim said to her as he took another sip. He set the mug down and leaned over and kissed her cheek. She set her mug on the nightstand and placed her hands on his face, gently caressing his skin, running her fingers over his days growth of stubble. She brought her face over and rubbed her cheek against his.

"Rough," she whispered.

"Rough?"

"Your face, rough."

"I should shave..."

"No," she whispered, "I kind of like it like that right now. Are you hungry?"

"I'm famished."

"There is a really nice little breakfast place right down the block."

In and instant Jiang Li was out of the bed, standing naked before him on the bedroom floor, the sunlight playing across her bare, silken smooth skin, playing through her tangled hair.

"I must look a mess," she said.

Jim was on his feet in front of her, feeling her against him as he drew her to him.

"You look positively lovely, you are the loveliest sight I have ever seen."

"You wouldn't be lying now, Sergeant Saunders."

"Former Sergeant Saunders. Lying, there is no way I would be lying."

"I think we should go have that breakfast, although it's really lunch."

***

They sat at a table outside the small mom & pop restaurant. One of the few mom & pop restaurants left in the world, Jim was thinking as he shoveled a generous helping of home cooked hashed brown potatoes into his mouth followed by his coffee. Before him was steak and eggs, steak rare, eggs over medium. Same for Jiang Li and she ate with a voracious appetite.

"I am so unbelievably hungry today," she commented. "I usually eat like a bird but this is so, so good."

She looked at Jim who was busy devouring his steak and eggs now.

"Something tells me you eat like this all the time," she said to him.

"Huh?" he asked, looking up at her.

She laughed.

"I believe all men are alike when they eat."

Jim frowned, looking at her quizzically. Then he looked into her eyes.

"I want to marry you, Jiang Li," he said.

She dropped her fork, it clinked into her almost empty plate, her eyes on his. Jim's heart was pounding now, he just lost his appetite, he was scared out of his wits now, had he gone too far? He had already asked this question once at the college. But now it seemed to him to be more real.

She came across the table, her arms going around him and they stood, holding each other, she was looking up into his eyes.

"I accept, Staff Sergeant Jim Saunders, I gladly accept!"

She reached up and placed her lips on his and the whole world stopped in that moment as he pressed her to him.

"What about..."

"It's finished," she whispered to him, her lips on his ear, "it's time the game ended. I will never belong to the one my father intended me for, never and I never wanted to. I never even met him before. No, it's time this ended."

Then they parted and she stepped back. Suddenly she was shaking, realizing what she had just said.

"My family...what have I just done?"

"You have your life, Jiang Li, your own choices, whether with me or not, make your own choices!"

She came into his arms again.

"I just have." She said as she kissed him.

"Why don't we go down to the beach for a walk."

"Sounds good, Sergeant Saunders."

"Former Sergeant Saunders."

***

They walked along the sandy beach, there were quite a few people out today, as bright and sunny as this afternoon was turning out to be but they were oblivious to the crowd as they strolled, they held their shoes in their hands and were wading along as the waves splashed up over their feet and lower legs, Jim's jeans were getting soaked but he didn't care. They held each other's hands as they walked along.

"How did this all happen?" Jim asked her.

"What?"

"This obligation your parents hold over you. How could this happen here?"

"It actually goes back to before I was even born."

They walked along.

"I know of a nice place we can go to and talk," Jiang Li said.

***

They crossed Great Highway, the highway that ran along San Francisco's Ocean Beach. They were at the far west end of Golden Gate Park. There was a towering old windmill, an ancient landmark. They walked around its base and found a bench nearby. They sat and Jiang Li leaned over and kissed Jim. Then she took his hand.

"Tell me about it," Jim said.

"It goes back to before I was born, like I was saying," Jiang Li began her story...

***

My father's father came here to San Francisco from Mainland China. He escaped and was smuggled in with connections he had made in Hong Kong. It was rough for my grandfather here at first. He worked as a busboy in several restaurants in the city, he was lucky, he was finally able to obtain legal status here and was also able to gain entry for his father and mother seeking personal asylum right after the takeover and the downfall of Chiang Kai Shek.

He continued to work hard living in Chinatown and he saved his money. He and other relatives pooled their money and were able, in time, to open a restaurant and several shops in Chinatown. He was helped by one of the tongs.

My grandfather met a nice young girl from a good Chinese American born family and they were married. Thus, my father was born, the first of seven children. My grandfather brought my father up to run the businesses and my father learned well. He met a nice young girl, my mother, and they were married. I am the oldest of three children, I have a brother and the youngest, my sister.

When I was born my father ran into hard times. My grandfather had grown ill and there were many medical expenses to be paid. My grandfather finally died leaving my father nearly bankrupt. The businesses were not doing well either. There was a lot of trouble in Chinatown with the gangs. There had been some shootings and for awhile the tourist trade in Chinatown was down. At that time the gangs began to gain a stronghold in Chinatown. My father had been approached before by representatives from gangs for "protection" money and he had resisted. There had been some trouble, employees had been threatened and some acts of sabotage had been committed. My grandfather had always resisted the gangs and had the help of the tongs who, of course, received a fee and the problem was "taken care of."

With these new, more violent gangs it was a different story.

Business was down and I was just a baby. My father had taken in my grandmother to care for her. My father was desperate for money.

That's when The Cobra appeared.

The Cobra was a ruthless and fast growing crime organization with ties to Hong Kong. They had heard of my father's financial problems and offered to bail him out with a loan. My grandmother and my mother both begged my father not to accept the loan but we were in danger of losing everything so my father agreed. He paid all his bills and kept his businesses alive, he sold a restaurant and kept some dry cleaning businesses and started doing well again.

At first the loan payments were not too steep and my father did okay. I was now about five years old and I had my younger brother and baby sister with me.

But things started to change.

The Cobra began to raise the interest on the loan and my father started to go deeper and deeper into debt. Finally he could not make the payment. He missed one payment and that angered The Cobra. They demanded the immediate loan in full plus one hundred percent interest. double the amount!

My father pleaded with them to lighten the burden but The Cobra demanded the full amount in one week!

Of course, my father could not pay.

There was an explosion at one of my father's dray cleaning

businesses late one night. No one was hurt but it was a total loss. An "accident." The police, of course, investigated but my father told them nothing of his suspicions. Of course it was The Cobra's work but my father was now terrified. There was no way he would have gone to the authorities. The police were not much interested in what went on in Chinatown as long as the trouble never spread to the white community.

My father was warned that the payment was due in a week's time.

My father turned to the tong but the tong offered no help. They were intimidated by The Cobra.

That is when Gordon Lau, a major representative of The Cobra approached my father with an offer. My father would be safe if he promised his oldest daughter in marriage to the son of Harry Xiang, the head of the Cobra. He lived in Taiwan and made "business trips" back and forth to America. He was raising his two sons to take over The Cobra one day. He was raising them to be as ruthless as he was and Harry Xiang is the epitome of ruthlessness.

My father had no choice, there were also threats made against me and my brother and baby sister if he did not agree. So he had no choice but to go along. It broke my grandmother's and my mother's heart. But they had no choice. I was raised with one thing in mind. That my future was sealed and that I had no choice in the matter. The agreement was that the marriage was to take place after my twenty second birthday.

***

Jiang Li sat looking at Jim, there on the bench under the giant windmill looming over them in Golden Gate Park.

"Jim," she said, "I just turned twenty two this month."

Jim looked into Jiang Li's eyes seeing the hopelessness there now.

"But Jiang Li," Jim said, "surely you must have rebelled. I mean, growing up here in America, this is unheard of..."

Jiang Li took Jim's hand.

"There are many arranged marriages here, old customs do not die out so easily. And I was always raised with the constant threat over my family. I was raised to accept it as my duty to my family.

"Even though my mother had objected she knew there was no other way and she would point to my brother and sister and remind me of the threat against them. At first I hated them, my parents, but as I grew older I came to accept it, there was really no other choice for me. The threat was always there to remind me."

"So now?"

Suddenly Jiang Li began to tremble.

"What have I done, Jim what..."

Jim held her.

"Jiang Li," Jim said to her, "this was never your responsibility! Never!"

"I have wronged my parents! Oh what have I done? What was I thinking?"

Jiang Li leapt up, pushing away from Jim. She started running.

"Jiang Li! Jill!" Jim yelled and he leapt up and ran after her. She was heading out of the park, right for Great Highway and the speeding cars. She kept running, like she didn't care.

"Jiang Li!" Jim yelled as he ran after her, but she was fast, light on her feet as she hit the highway.

Tires screeched!

Horns blasted!

"No!" Jim screamed at the top of his lungs.

Cars were swerving as he dashed onto the highway and grabbed Jiang Li's arm, yanking her back, pulling her out of the way, pulling her along the pathway in the park as she struggled with him.

"No!" she screamed as she tried to pull away. "Let me go! If I am run over and killed my parents obligation will be over!"

Jim struggled to hold her, her panic and desperation was giving her amazing strength. She used a forearm block to dis-lodge his hold then ran back and turned to face him, tears streaming down her face.

"It's no use, Jim, I love you but the dream is over. It's over and it never was! Never!"

"Jiang Li, listen to me!"

"No! I'm sorry, Jim."

She turned to run and he dashed after her. She was fast but now his old football mode kicked in, he was running for the most important tackle he would ever have to make. He lunged forward and was momentarily airborne, taking her legs in the flying tackle. They both hit the dirt pathway and rolled. Jiang Li struggled, crying, then they lay there on the path and she threw her arms around him, her lips meeting his as they held each other. Jim kissed the tears away from her eyes.

"There will be a way out for you, Jiang Li," Jim whispered.

"You'll see, I promise you there is a way out."

"You are brave and you are wonderful, my love, and your belief is strong but you are wrong."

"Just give me a chance," he said to her, kissing her lips and face.

"I promised I would marry you," Jiang Li said, "I will marry you. I will, I was so scared just then."

"I know, I know all about it, Jiang Li."

"Sometimes it becomes overpowering, my decision. It's suddenly hard to breathe..."

"I know. I'm here, Jiang Li. I'm here for you."

He looked into her eyes.

"Jiang Li," he said.

"Yes."

"Jiang Li, will you trust me?"

"Of course I trust you..."

"No, Jiang Li, I am going to ask you to trust me now, whatever may happen, just trust me. I know a way out but I can't talk about it just yet, but, please trust me on this. Will you do that?"

She nodded, looking deeply into his eyes.

"What is it?"

"I can't tell you right now but soon I will be able to. Promise me that no matter what happens, you will trust me, I know it's a lot to ask."

"I'll trust you, Jim. I remember how you stepped in at the restaurant on Market Street the first day I ever saw you. You were doing the right thing. And I saw how you took care of Dave Xiang back at school in the parking lot. There is also something else I know. Word is going around Chinatown about an American stranger who took out several of The Cobra henchmen one morning, I believe the same morning you looked me up at school. Talk is going around."

"Yes, you mentioned something about this before but I wouldn't know about..."

"Oh come on now, Jim, you know...you even told me about it." Jiang Li's lips met Jim's again. Then they parted and looked at each other.

"It was my brother who told me all about it. It seems someone was looking out a window and saw everything. They say this stranger was very good, fast, a big man, young, never seen here before. Then he was gone."

"Was he now?"

"I know it was you. It could have been no one else, I know that. I saw you there at the restaurant and I knew as you walked me home that you were a man of integrity. I also wanted to see you again but I knew I mustn't. But you found me and I knew then that I loved you. And meeting your parents and also seeing the way you handled that fight at the railroad tracks. You settled it in another way rather than violence. You saved that young man's life and the entire situation between you and he changed in that moment.

"I trust you, Jim. Whatever you have to do, I trust you. I will marry you no matter what."

They held each other, just standing there in the park, her head on his chest, holding him tight. She looked up into his eyes and they kissed again. They left.

***

They walked hand in hand back to the apartment and stopped at the doorstep while Jiang Li fumbled for the key. The door opened and a petite, young girl with brown hair and brown eyes was standing there.

"Well, hello there," she said to them as she invited both of them inside. "So finally I get to meet this fantastic guy that my good friend has been going on about for the past several days. I'm June."

She held out her hand and Jim took it. He flushed.

June giggled. Jiang Li's arm went around Jim's waist as they walked into the living room.

"I can see that you two are inseparable. It must have been quite a weekend," June said and Jim blushed. Jiang Li gave him a kiss and looked at her friend.

"It certainly was!" she said.

"I'll be right back," Jiang Li said as she reached up and kissed him again. She turned and went down the hall and into the bathroom.

Jim stood for a moment, he looked at June. June motioned him over by the living room window. She looked directly at him.

"She loves you, you know," June said. "I hope you know that."

"I love her," Jim answered.

"I hope you do."

June thought for a moment. "She's really an innocent you know, well, maybe after this weekend not quite so much so. But still, I know she gave herself to you and she's yours one hundred percent. I hope you respect that!"

"I respect that very much."

"I know she's supposed to be getting married, an arranged marriage. I and all her friends have tried to talk her out of it. I don't know the whole story..."

"I do."

"Whatever it is, I'm glad you came along. You're all she's talked about the past few days. You're going to have to be strong for her, Jim. You're going to have to go with her to her parents and tell them."

"I asked her to marry me."

June looked stunned.

"And..."

"She said 'yes.' I told her she was free to say no but I wanted her to be free of that obligation."

"I can't figure out why, in this day and age, and in this country, that she would agree to an arranged marriage in the first place."

"It's rather complicated."

"This won't be easy for her, you know. You seem strong, I hope you are."

"Jim," June's eyes burned into his. "She needs you."

At that moment Jiang Li re-entered the room and came up to Jim, taking his hand.

"I'll leave you two alone," June said.

June left the room.

"I guess it's time I was going," Jim said. "I need a way of getting in touch with you."

Jiang Li thought for a moment.

"Darn it, Jiang Li, I want to go with you right now and have a talk with your family! This has to be done sooner or later and it might as well be right now!"

"No! No, Jim, not yet, please," Jiang Li's hands tightened on his, her eyes imploring him.

"Jim, I'll call you and you can call here, June will give me your message. Oh wait, silly me, I have my cell phone. You can call either number, June's or my cell."

"I want to see you again soon," Jim put his arms around her, holding her close to him, smelling the fragrance of her hair, drinking her in.

"I want to see you, Jim, I am closing in on finals now and I graduate in two weeks. I'll have my degree then, it will help us, Jim, help us get started."

"You said the time had come now for you to keep your word."

"I know...it is expected of me right after graduation, we can tell my father then, Jim, and you said..."

"I said to trust me, that I have an answer, I can't tell you about it now, but I also have a career opportunity. Jill, Jiang Li...Jill..." he kissed her, looked into her eyes, "...two names, Jill, Jiang Li, you're amazing..."

"No..."

"Truly amazing, you really are, you know."

Their lips met in a long kiss.

"I'll miss you the next two weeks. It will be very hard to study but I'll pass and it will all be over. Then we can face them."

"I'll be right beside you."

They parted and Jiang Li walked over and reached into her bag. She took out a tablet of paper and wrote June's phone number on it, and her cell phone number as well, handing it to Jim. He took the pad and paper and wrote his home phone. She clasped the piece of paper between their palms, then she took it and placed it in her bag and she walked with him to the front door. June entered and came up to them.

"If you need anything, both of you, be sure to let me know," she said.

Jim and Jiang Li walked out onto the porch, it was late afternoon. Jiang Li's arms went around Jim's neck and they kissed a long kiss. Jim backed down the steps, slowly releasing Jiang Li's hand.

Jiang Li was watching as Jim walked off down the sidewalk to his car.

***

Jim was in an almost dream state as he drove back across the bridge as the sun was setting. He drove back to town and went to the bar. Hardly anyone was there this evening, just a few old timers. He ordered a beer from Sam, offered to pay as usual and, as usual, the offer was denied.

Jim took a table in the corner, sitting alone and savored the first sip, the dream was alive in him, he was filled with joy. There was a great challenge ahead, many obstacles, but for now, he could relax. He took another sip and leaned back, closing his eyes. He could see an image of her in his mind, just as real as if she were right in the room with him. In his mind he relived every moment of the weekend with her.

"Mind if I join you?"

Jim opened his eyes. Suzie was standing there in "T" shirt and cut offs, a foaming draft beer in her hand.

He nodded and she seated herself next to him, looking into his eyes.

"Haven't seen you all weekend," she said then she looked deeper. "And I know why. I am looking into the eyes of a man in love."

CHAPTER ELEVEN

Jim drove into the underground parking garage beneath Union Square in downtown San Francisco. It was Monday morning. He had stopped at Stan's for breakfast, the usual, steak and eggs and coffee. The night before he had had a few beers at the bar but had told Susie nothing about his weekend. He said "Good-night" and had gone home. Robbie had greeted him with a smile, he had eaten a warmed over spaghetti and meatball dinner his mother had left in the refrigerator for him. His dad was watching TV and his mother had served him the dinner, no words were spoken but she had given him a knowing smile.

Now he was walking out of the parking garage and heading on foot for the few blocks that would take him to 425 Lombard Street and the Federal Building. He would avoid crossing through Chinatown, not wanting to be seen there, not wanting to cause any trouble.

That would come soon enough.

***

He crossed the street and entered the lobby, went to the elevator, going up to the forth floor and exiting into a well furnished reception room. A young, smartly dressed Asian girl was seated at the reception desk. She looked up at him.

"You would be Mr. Saunders?" she asked. "Correct?"

"That's correct," he answered.

"You may go right on in, you are expected."

Jim passed through a door into the inner office. Martin Thomas rose from his desk as Jim entered, extending his hand.

"Welcome, Staff Sergeant Saunders," Thomas said, "Please be seated. Can I get you some coffee? Anything?"

"No thank you, and I'm afraid it's former Staff Sergeant Saunders."

"Fortunately for us, that is quite true, Jim, Mr. Saunders..."

"Jim will be fine, Mr. Thomas."

"Call me Martin, Jim."

Jim looked across the desk, eyes level with Martin's steel gray eyes, smiling eyes for now.

"Let's get down to business, shall we, cut through all the bullshit.

What can you do for me and what can I do for you in return?"

"Fair enough, Jim, spoken like a man, I admire that. You are indeed the right man, I feel I chose wisely."

"Right man for what?"

"You had quiet a weekend."

Jim leapt up, anger in his eyes.

"You fucking bastard! Don't tell me you..."

"No no, Jim, sit down, relax...you were not followed last weekend. You were out of town, obviously with a certain young lady, more about her later."

"You said you could help me with her situation, if you even know the story!"

"Probably more than you realize, Jim, but more about that later."

"Straight out, Jim, we've got your war record. Everything about you, as I told you before. You're well trained in all weapons and, as Chinatown proved and that little scuffle out at SF State proved, you're more than an expert at hand to hand combat. You are well qualified for the job I am offering you."

"Tell me about this 'job.'"

"A little background first. As you know I am with the DEA and I am involved in a major investigation of a highly entrenched crime organization which has roots right in your home town."

"My hometown?"

"Exactly!"

Martin Thomas reached behind his desk and pulled out a manila folder which he tossed on the desk in front of Jim.

"Go ahead and take a look," Martin said.

Jim opened the folder. Looking at him in a full color glossy 8 ½ X 10 was a picture of Steven Denning.

"Denning? He's the richest man in town, his kid goes to school with my kid brother. Just what's this all about? He owns many businesses, and so what's wrong with that? He's an upstanding citizen in the community."

"Not so 'upstanding.' He owns and operates a topless club just outside city limit."

"It's still a legitimate business, look at the nightclubs right here in North Beach."

"Those are pretty shady too, Jim, if you want my opinion."

"It's not my business, really. So what's the story with Denning then?"

"I suppose at this point I'll have Agent Bradly join us to help fill you in."

Martin pushed a button to the intercom. The receptionist's voice answered.

"Send in Agent Bradley ," Martin said.

"Right away, Mr. Thomas," the receptionist answered.

Jim heard the door behind him. He turned. Standing there in a gray business suit, skirt a little short, a Glock 9mm and a badge and ID at her waist, her blond hair done up in a professional manner, stood Suzie. Jim's jaw dropped.

"What th..."

"Hello, Jim," Suzie said as she came forward.

Martin offered her a seat next to Jim, who stood as she walked up to the desk. Suzie extended her hand and Jim took it, a million questions in his eyes.

"Jim, meet Agent Susan Bradley, Secret Service."

"Secret..."

Suzie smiled and was seated next to Jim who also sat back down.

"So you've been keeping tabs on me!" Jim said. "Friendship! Bullshit! What a ruse, pretending to be a construction worker and buddying up to me in the bar."

"Actually, I have quite an extensive knowledge of high rise construction," Suzie said. "My dad was a contractor and my uncle was a crane operator. Both of them still work in their professions. I worked various jobs during my summers between semesters in college, Jim. And Jim, I was already working this job, hanging out in your town before you got back from the service."

"I hope we can work together, Jim."

Jim shook his head, this was way too much information for one day, and a Monday at that.

"Okay, so what's the story here? What's this got to do with Denning?" Jim asked.

"First, before we go any farther," Martin said, "we have to have a guarantee that you want to work with us."

"What's it to me, why do I care what Denning does? I just want to live my own life and he's got his."

"Jim," Suzie said, "We're offering you a job with us."

"I don't get it, you are each from a different branch of the Federal

Law Enforcement Agencies. You," he indicated Martin, "are DEA and you, Suzie, are Secret Service. So who would I be working for?"

"I realize, Jim, that there are some complexities involved here. But we are offering to deputize you as a 'special agent' to work with both of us in our investigation. You will have full pay, benefits which include medical, and a dynamite retirement plan."

"Yeah, the service had a dynamite retirement plan as well, you take a bullet and it's all over. Great way to retire."

"I am not saying that this job doesn't carry its share of risks, in fact this particular job is very high risk. But Jim..."

"Jim," Suzie interrupted, "think of the benefits. You love that young lady you've been seeing, I can see it written all over you, Jim..."

"Yeah, and you said something about an offer to help me with her situation as well, if you even know the story..."

"We know the story, Jim," Martin said. "We know the whole story of The Cobra."

"And that's part of what we are getting at," Suzie said.

"But first, Denning," Martin said.

"Okay, what about him?"

"Denning runs an extensive crime network, drug dealing on a large scale, and is also involved in human trafficking, extortion, illegal gaming, stolen vehicles, etc. All run right from your town. It is a mainline to the rest of the country, a major conduit and for the last fifteen months we have been trying to uncover his operation, to bust it wide open. He owns many of the police in your town and also has ties with the Sheriff's department, I am afraid to say."

"Denning?"

"Denning," Suzie said.

Jim looked at Suzie, striking in her business suit with badge and gun at her waist.

"I was planted in your town to try to find out whatever I could," Suzie said. "A construction worker, living in the town and commuting to the city for all anyone knew. I have been getting close now but we need inside help, Jim."

"I don't understand what it is I can do. Sure, I live in the town but why does that make me any closer to Denning? I hardly know him except for the fact that his kid brother goes to school with my brother. I've seen Denning driving through town many times in one of his fancy cars."

"Jim," Martin said. "You are a local hero, returned from the Iraq war, the 'conquering hero' kind of. You are in a unique position to get close to Denning. I am going to suggest that you go to him and ask for a job as a bouncer at his nightclub."

"Strange you say that," Jim answered.

"How so?" Suzie asked.

"Friday morning at Stan's, you know the place..."

"I have breakfast there often," Suzie said.

"He talked to me and offered me a job working for him at his club. He wants me to start right away."

"Perfect!" Martin said as he clapped his hands together.

"A few weeks ago, before you came home, Jim," Suzie said, "Denning saw me at Stan's and he asked me if I would like to work there as a dancer in the evenings. I told him I would think about it. I had to make him think I was 'hard to get' as you say. Now would be the perfect time for me to 'decide to accept' the offer. We would be working together, and we could find out more that way."

Jim thought about it.

"Okay. So I work for you, and I accept the offer to work at the club. But you said you could help me with my 'problem' as you called it. What does that have to do with my girlfriend's situation?"

"Now we're getting to that," Denning said.

"So, I'm waiting..."

"As I said, Denning is a major conduit for drug running and human trafficking, that's human cargo, Asian illegals smuggled in and sent on to various cities to find work. Huge fees are paid by those wanting into our country and a huge network exists to bring them here.

"And then there is the drug network, The Golden Triangle from the U.S. to Asia, the importation of pure heroine to be cut and distributed to the streets of every major city in America.

"Denning is a direct connection to these activities with The Cobra. He is a partner with Harry Xiang and his sons. The Cobra is one of the most ruthless crime organizations ever to infiltrate Chinatown and they are branching out into mainstream America through Denning and others, but Denning is their main connection.

"You already had several run-ins with Harry's boys. At the steakhouse when you first arrived back in the U.S. Harry's boys were extorting money from the Market Street restaurant. Unusual the way they were targeting a non-Asian business, don't you think?"

"I don't know much about how they operate," Jim said.

"Jim," Suzie said, "these organizations rarely target non-Asian businesses knowing that Asians are reluctant to go to the authorities. But now, Harry Xiang is branching out. The Cobra is a bold organization, Jim, and getting more bold every day. Harry Xiang is a citizen of the United States, Jim. So are his sons, even though Harry lives most of the time in Taiwan and also travels to Hong Kong, Singapore and Bangkok. David, you met him, is his number one son who operates right here in America. Harry is bringing his second son over soon. We know about the arranged marriage to your girlfriend. Extortion. Loan sharking at it's highest level. Jill's father is afraid to come to us."

"And why should he?" Jim answered. "Hell, you didn't get involved until it became a 'non Asian' matter. Otherwise the victims would have no place to turn to."

"That's not true, Jim," said Denning.

"Bullshit it isn't. Mainstream America doesn't give a rat's ass about the problems in the Asian community as long as it doesn't spread to them and you know it."

"Jim," Suzie said, "until recently it was a local police matter. Now, in recent months that has changed. And as far as the local police, the San Francisco Police Department takes crime in the Asian community very seriously. But if no one will ever come forward then what can they do?"

"They come forward, they die. And no one can prove anything," Jim said. "And you know that's the truth."

"Perhaps that will soon change," Martin said.

"Jim," Suzie said, "right now you are in a unique position. You are somewhat of a hero in Chinatown right now. That brawl you had with those thugs in the alley was witnessed by several people from their apartment windows. These guys were top thugs for The Cobra, feared men in the community and the witnesses really enjoyed seeing them getting their asses kicked. You are known locally as 'The Stranger' now."

"Sounds like some cheap karate movie to me," Jim said.

"But it's true, Jim," Denning said.

"Jim," Suzie said, "if we can blow this organization wide open then your girlfriend and her family are free. It's a way out for all of them, Jim."

Jim thought about it for a few moments then looked at Martin and then at Suzie.

"Okay, I'm in," he said.

"Great..." Martin started to say.

"But," Jim said, "I want help and I want to choose my help."

"But this is highly irregular..."

"Then forget it, I'll just go my way and work things out in my own way..."

"You don't have much chance alone, Jim," Martin said.

"I'll have to be the judge of that," Jim said as he rose from his chair.

"Martin..." Suzie said.

"Okay, okay, what is it you want, Jim, maybe we can talk about it..."

"A friend of mine, I knew him in combat, in Iraq, former Sergeant Charles White Eagle. I want him in on this, deputized."

"I've heard of him, he was at the fight with you at the railroad tracks," Suzie said. "Seems able for the job but also seems like a loan wolf, a bit of a loose cannon..."

"So am I!" Jim said. "And also, maybe one more guy, Mike Walker..."

"No way, he's the town bully from what I heard," Martin said, "not the kind of person with the qualities we are looking for..."

"Not the kind of qualities? He's a good man, just a little mixed up, but after last Friday, not quite as mixed up as he was. Look! We played football together! That counts for a lot when looking into a man's character. He's good backup! He's a team player. Whatever differences we always had in high school he put them aside when it was gametime! I'm not saying I want him in right now, but later maybe, let me play it by ear.

"Charlie White Eagle and Mike both are without much direction right now and this is a good career opportunity for them. And they have what I need, both of them, but right now I want to bring White Eagle in, I can find him.

"And another good man as backup would be Stan Henke, ex..."

"Chief Petty officer Stan Henke," Martin said, a smile on his face.

"You know him..."

"Served with him in Vietnam, good man, Stan, been keeping an eye on him for quite awhile. Of course we would not be hiring him on as..."

"No, I realize he wouldn't be wanting a career with this organization, but to deputize him if needed. I feel he'd be good backup in a pinch..."

"That he would. I've been by his restaurant a few times, talked over the old days, had a few beers with him," Martin said, a distant look in his eyes, he was remembering.

"Okay," Martin said. "Then you're in."

"I'm in," Jim answered and Martin rose and shook Jim's hand, then looked over at Suzie.

"I am going to swear you in and then turn you over to Agent Bradley here and she can get you situated," Martin said.

***

Jim was walking down the hallway with Suzie. He had just taken the oath to uphold the Law of the Land and the Constitution of the United States of America. As they walked down the hallway Suzie took his arm, stopping him and looking into his eyes.

"Jim," she said.

He looked at her.

"Jim, I wasn't just using you..."

"Using..."

"By getting friendly at the bar, and backing you up at the fight...I mean, what I am trying to say is...Jim..." her face flushed, "...Jim, I mean...I really do like you...if things don't work out with...you know...I am not doing this very well..."

"I understand," Jim said as he took her hand.

"I hope you do, Jim...and I am really glad you came on board and are going to be at the nightclub...Martin wasn't going to allow me to go in there as a dancer alone...too much risk and to tell you the truth, Jim, I'm scared to death to do this...dancing naked in front of all those leering eyes...it's never something I would ever do on my own if I was out there looking for a job..."

"I understand completely, I don't like the idea of you being there either."

Suzie squeezed his hand.

"Thank you, Jim. I'll feel a lot more comfortable knowing you're there...hey, you get to see me naked after all."

She gave him a big smile and reached up and kissed his cheek. Now Jim's face flushed.

"Well, we better get you situated. Come on, you'll meet my boss."

They stepped into an office, the receptionist looked up, a young girl, she smiled.

"Go right on in, Agent Bradley ," she said as she hit the buzzer. She spoke into the intercom. "Our new recruit is here, Ms. Williams."

Suzie led Jim through the door to the inner office. There, seated at her desk was Suzie's boss, Trudy, the same woman who had accompanied her to the bar, now dressed in a dark gray business suit. She rose from her desk, a smile on her face.

"Welcome aboard, Agent Saunders," Trudy said as she extended her hand, "I am Director Trudy Williams."

"Director..." Jim started to say.

"I know I was at the bar with Suzie, I rarely get to get out to do any field work anymore but we wanted to be sure of you, Jim, sure you were the right man for this job and believe me, we weren't wrong about you."

"Gee," Jim said, "I hope I can live up to everyone's expectations..."

"I don't think we have a problem there, Jim, and again, welcome. Suzie will get you supplied with what you'll need."

Trudy smiled at Suzie.

"Come with me, Jim," Suzie said and they headed out of the office and down the hallway to an elevator, not the main one though. She pushed the button and in a few moments the elevator arrived. They entered and she hit the "basement, level four" button. The elevator began descending. She turned to him, a smile on her face, she stood near him.

"Oh the things I'd like to do to you in here right now," she said, looking into his eyes and moving even closer. Jim felt a rush. Despite himself he was aroused.

The bell sounded, they had arrived.

They emerged into a hallway, concrete walls, no wood paneling here, just bare bones basic construction, a utility hall. They made their way along the hallway to an open door at the end. Going through the door Jim saw a man seated at a desk wearing a uniform, he was armed with a .45 in a holster at his waist.

"Hello, Bill," Suzie said. "Jim, this is Bill, Bill this is Jim

Saunders and we need to get him supplied right away."

The uniformed man named Bill rose from his seat behind his desk and extended his hand. Jim took it and they shook. Bill looked at Suzie.

"And what would he be needing, Agent Bradley?"

"It's 'Susie', Bill, you know that, and I want the 'works.'"

"Please follow me," Bill said and he led the way through another doorway.

They stepped into another room. Most of the room was blocked by a barred wall with a cell doorway which Bill unlocked. Jim looked at the bars and saw why they were there. There were rows and rows of shelves heaped with all kinds of weaponry. Bill led them down an isle, Jim marveling at the arsenal before him. Everything from Glock 9mm handguns to OSI reloadable rocket launchers! Jim even saw a couple of RPG launchers on a shelf. His eyes widened.

"Jesus!" he said.

"Impressive, isn't it?" Suzie said.

"'Impressive' is not the word, really," Jim answered. He was awed.

On one wall hung full suits of Kevlar body armor, riot helmets, the works.

"I want him issued a .45 and also a Heckler and Koch MP5 submachine gun with case for immediate transportation," Suzie said.

"Then we'll get him ID'd."

"No problem, Agent..."

"Suzie!"

"Suzie..."

Bill was making his way along the shelves, carefully picking out the weapons Suzie had ordered for Jim. When he had finished he placed the items in a carrying case, the MP5 broken down, the .45 in a shoulder holster.

"Right this way," Bill said and he led them into another room where a computerized camera was set up on a stand in front of a white background.

"Please stand right there, Mr...or rather, Agent Saunders," Bill said as Jim stepped in front of the background. There was a brief flash and Jim blinked his eyes to clear them. Bill walked over to a desk with a computer. Suzie gave him a page of information and Bill went right to work typing and moving the mouse, clicking on various programs.

There was a hum and a machine spit out a plastic ID card. Bill reached into a drawer and pulled out a badge, recording the badge number then placed the badge and ID in a holder suited for wearing on a belt at the waist and presented it to Jim. Jim inspected it. The photo was a good quality likeness of him. The badge said "special agent," not designated to any one department.

They returned to the weapons room and Bill placed the carrying case on the table, open for inspection. Jim looked over the broken down MP5. Impressive, Jim thought to himself. Included were also several smoke grenades. Jim picked out the holster and drew the .45, holding the weapon in his hand, testing the balance.

"Now we'll go to the shooting range so you can get some practice in," Suzie said. "I need some practice as well, let's go. Thank you, Bill."

Bill nodded and shook her hand, he shook Jim's hand again and Jim followed Suzie out of the room and back down the hallway. They came to another adjoining hallway and made a right. As they made their way along Jim heard the muffled sounds of gunfire. A door opened at the end of the hallway and several men with white shirts and ties, .45s in holsters at their waists along with ID and badges came walking down the hallway. They greeted Suzie and looked questioningly at Jim.

"New guy, huh?" one of them said as he sized Jim up with a glance. Jim was doing the same. Instinct. Suzie greeted them briefly then led Jim on through the doorway. There was a long row of booths in a large, dimly lit room. At one end was the target area, well lit up. To the side a booth with a technician, an African American woman of about thirty five, attractive, her hair worn long and straight but tied back.

"Hello Bernice," Suzie called to the tech behind the glass picture window.

"Greetings, Agent Bradley ," the woman called Bernice spoke into a mike.

Suzie motioned with a nod of her head to the shooting booths. She stepped in one and Jim stepped into the other next to her. He found headphone type hearing protectors and he put them on, also a pair of safety goggles. He slammed a clip into the .45.

He was ready.

Suzie turned on the intercom.

"Okay, Bernice, we're ready," she said.

On the wall in front of the booths two targets popped up, human cutout forms designed to look like terrorists, complete with turbans and they were armed with AK-47s.

"I suppose you're more used to the real thing," Suzie said to Jim through the booth to booth intercom, her voice ringing metallic and muffled because of the ear protectors.

"Somewhat," Jim said.

BAM! BAM! BAM!

He heard Suzie fire off three rounds in quick succession.

"Pull!" Suzie ordered and the target slid along a wire right to her booth for her inspection. There was a fairly close pattern mid-chest.

"Hmmm, not bad," Suzie said. "Okay, Jim, go for it!"

BOOM! BOOM! BOOM! BOOM! BOOM!

The .45 roared in his hands, he used a two handed grip same as Suzie had.

"Pull," Suzie yelled and the target traveled along the wire to Jim.

"Wow!" Suzie said, noticing a close pattern, all headshots. "I can see you're not out of practice."

"I'm rather disappointed," Jim said. "That hospital stay and long layback really took its toll."

"Pretty good for being out of shape, I'd say. I can see I need more practice. Although I've been down here a lot lately, nothing to really do during the day while I'm supposed to be at that 'construction' job. Just tons of paperwork and so I come down here to break the boredom. I guess soon I won't be quite so bored.

"Let's have another go at it, shall we?"

They fired several full clips at targets, Jim exhibiting the same close pattern, all headshots, and now Suzie was coming up to speed as well. She came into Jim's booth.

"Want to give the MP5 a go?" she asked.

"I never fired one before," Jim said, "Mine was an M16."

"Check it out," Suzie said.

Jim took the parts from the carrying case and quickly assembled them, slamming in a full clip from the many that had been supplied for him.

"I thought you said you never handled an MP5," Suzie said.

"Haven't, instinct I guess, I was practically married to my weapons over there."

"I guess that would account for it. Okay, now, Jim, single shots! We're ready again, Bernice."

Up popped three targets at once and Jim, firing from the hip fired three times. When the targets arrived all of them had headshots.

"Wow," Suzie said, "you know you're really turning me on right now."

Jim tried to pretend he hadn't heard her remark.

"Now, full auto," Suzie said. "Ready again, Bernice, give him the works!"

Up popped six targets and Jim cut loose, the MP5 chattering away in his grip. The targets were disappearing in chunks as Jim kept firing and Suzie could see the sudden killer instinct in his eyes. Her face flushed hot.

Bernice didn't bother to run the targets to them, there was literally nothing left of them.

Suzie moved closer to Jim, taking off her goggles and headphones, Jim took off his.

"What can I say, Jim," she said. "I'd say you're prepared to do the job, no problem. I suppose your friend has equal ability, I judged him a man who can definitely take care of himself."

"Charley White Eagle?" Jim asked. "He definitely can outdo me anytime."

"Oh don't be so modest, Agent Jim Saunders." Suzie moved even closer to him and he could smell her perfume. It was almost intoxicating.

"I'm sorry, Jim, I guess I just can't help myself. I was attracted to you the day you walked into the bar. Don't worry; I know you have eyes only for your Asian sweetheart but a girl can dream."

Jim was breaking down his weapons, cleaning them with expert efficiency.

"Out of shape my ass," Suzie said with a smile as she did maintenance on her weapon.

"I'd say we're finished here," she said.

***

Finished, they returned to Suzie's office. Jim was seated opposite her at her desk while she went through some papers. She brought up two manila folders.

"Jim," she said, "This folder contains a complete profile of Steven Denning, his history, his known connections, especially his recent connections with The Cobra.

"This other file contains vital information you are required to know in your job as an agent for the Federal Government. Normally an extensive course of study and an intensive written test is required for you to work for us, that and an equally intensive physical exam. This has all been waved, of course. Your physical attributes for this job are beyond question, Jim. We know your entire history from the time you were born.

"But Jim, there are things you have to know, rules and regulations. When to break and enter, when it is permitted to draw your weapon, rules governing its use. You are going to be on a crash course of study, I'm afraid, Jim, and later on a written test will be required for you to stay here.

"We waved all that for now because of the immediacy of the situation at hand. I want you to pass this test when the time comes, Jim, I want you with us."

She took his hand in hers as she passed the files over to him and she looked into his eyes, hers were sincere and a bit dreamy, he thought.

"When that time comes..." Jim said.

"Yes, Jim?"

"When that time comes, you will know I was released from the Army as no longer fit for combat..."

Suzie took both his hands in hers, her hands felt warm, "This will not be a problem, Jim, you are considered fit by our standards already. There is a requirement that you keep yourself in top condition, and cigarette smoking is now forbidden on or off the job."

"Not a problem for me."

"Now, what about this friend of yours, this Charlie White Eagle..."

"Believe me he's fit for this job. I don't know as I ever saw him smoking cigarettes or any other substance for that matter. As far as passing the tests later, for him, he'll have to decide that, I have to approach him about this whole deal yet and see if he'll bite. I hope he does, I need him as back up, sorry, but I just don't have the same faith in your agents, not yet anyway. Charlie and I have been in combat, we've covered each other's asses time and time again so I know I can count on him."

"I understand, Jim. I'll do everything in my power to make it happen, I promise you that."

Jim glanced at his watch as did Suzie.

"It's probably time I was going," Jim said as he rose from his seat.

"I know," Suzie answered. "I have to go to a meeting in a few minutes myself."

She rose also, "I'll walk you out."

She came up next to him, standing close as she escorted him out of the office and to the elevator. Jim was carrying all his assigned gear in two, large leather bags suspended by straps from his shoulders. He had placed his Federal Agent ID and the two folders in one of them.

"You're carrying a lot of firepower there, Jim," Suzie reminded him. "Also, Jim, we are arranging some hand to hand combat training for you here later on in the week."

"I don't think..."

"Jim," she said as she stood close, "It's absolutely mandatory..." her eyes were looking into his, "...absolutely."

"Yes, ma'am," Jim answered.

"I'll be in touch, in one of those bags is a cell phone, paid for by the Federal Government. I'll leave messages for you and you can call me. You may also use it for you personal calls although I'm really not supposed to say that."

"You never said a thing."

"Of course not."

The elevator door opened.

"I'll ride down with you."

They stepped inside. There were two other men in the elevator. They exited on the next floor and it was just the two of them left as the car sped to the 1st floor. Suzie moved close to Jim, her body lightly touching his, looking up into his eyes, she kissed him on the cheek.

"Just remember, if you ever break up with that girl friend of yours, I'm here..."

The bell sounded and she moved back as the door opened. Jim stepped out into the lobby, Suzie stayed in the car.

"I'll call you, Jim," she said and then the door closed.

CHAPTER TWELVE

Jim was standing on Kearney Street at the entrance to Chinatown. He had walked from the Federal Building back to his car where he had locked his bags in the trunk. He had been about to get in and drive home when he had abruptly changed his mind.

Now here he stood.

He walked beneath the gate, crossed the threshold into the unknown, into another world. He walked casually along the street, taking in the shops and restaurants until he came to one and decided to go in and have lunch. It was a simple place, not one of the fancier eateries and he stood in the entrance. A young Asian girl walked up and escorted him to a table in the back of the room. As he was seated she handed him a menu. He ordered a beer for starters and it was brought to him. He sipped the Chinese brand beer slowly, enjoying the flavor and for a brief moment he pondered whether this could be considered "drinking on the job" now that he was officially a Federal Agent.

A Federal Agent.

Not in his wildest dreams did he ever imagine he would end up being a Federal Agent. He had figured on perhaps a military career, he had really liked the Army. When he had been discharged he had really felt abandoned, out in left field without options. Lying in the hospital he figured perhaps he would work in his dad's bodyshop and garage, learn the business, take some classes at the community college on the GI Bill and maybe help to improve the family business. Robbie would be getting out of high school and also, probably working in the shop.

Jim thought about his little brother. Not so little anymore and he had really come through in the fight at the railroad tracks. Robbie was a brave, although somewhat foolhardy, kid and Jim had to admit that he was proud of him.

He also knew he didn't want Robbie going into the Army.

Now life had thrown Jim a completely new curve. He suddenly saw far greater horizons for himself. He wanted to marry Jiang Li as soon as possible, he was sure of his feelings for her. He was in love with her completely. Suzie's strong "come on" had not veered him from his course.

He sipped his beer.

The waitress approached and waited to take his order but he just ordered another beer instead. He took a sip. It went down smooth. He pondered his situation. There wasn't much time. Jiang Li would graduate in less than two weeks and then the obligation to marry Tommy Xiang would come due. He wondered about that.

Why would her father have gone to the expense of putting her through college if she were to be literally "sold" in marriage to some Triad kingpin's son? Jim took a sip from the beer and set the bottle down on the table. The answer was quite clear.

Her father never wanted her to obey him in marrying Tommy Xiang! He had hoped his daughter would develop a sense of independence.

That was it!

Jim ordered Mongolian Beef for lunch with rice and noodles. He ordered an extra order of beef and had a full meal. As he was finishing his meal he noticed an Asian man sitting across the room from him near the large, picture window. The man was studying him with intense eyes. He was athletically built, perhaps in his forties. The man did not look away when Jim Noticed him. Another Asian man entered the restaurant and also looked at Jim. He nodded to the man a the table, they spoke a few words then the other man left.

The man who had been watching Jim rose from the table and crossed the room. He stood in front of Jim.

"Mind if I sit down?" he asked in perfect English.

Jim nodded to the empty chair opposite him and the man was seated.

"Beer?" Jim asked him.

"I'll buy," the man said and he held up two fingers. The waitress immediately brought the beverages and set them down on the table then hurried away. Both Jim and the man took a sip from the beers. Jim noticed how the man was dressed, a tan suit, European cut.

"What can I do for you?" Jim asked.

"Why are you here again?" the man asked.

"Again?" Jim asked.

"Don't act dumb with me!" the man said.

Anger momentarily rose in Jim but he let it pass.

"I'm having lunch," Jim said.

"And maybe looking for more trouble?" the man stated.

Jim took a sip, looking in the man's eyes.

"You're good," the man said.

"Good?"

"You're the stranger they're talking about."

"The 'stranger?'"

"Look! You took down several of the best members of The Cobra triad! It was witnessed and word spread. That waitress who works here? Her mother and she both saw what happened from their apartment window. She called me the moment you came in here. But I already knew you were here, others saw you."

"I didn't realize I was that well known."

"Oh I really wouldn't call it fame."

"Look, I happened to be walking along and this group decided to attack me, muggers I figured, out to rob me."

"You know that's bullshit! You had a run in with them the day before at a steakhouse on Market Street."

"Yeah, well a couple of them were fuckin' with the poor guy who owned the steakhouse. In fact, it looks like the guy left town in a hurry the next day."

"I wouldn't blame him, would you?"

"I guess not. I was glad I put a hurt on those assholes!"

"And they will not be forgetting soon. You realize you are at risk here?"

"Let 'em come! I handled them before and I'll handle them again!"

"Or maybe you'll end up lying in an alley with your penis cut off! They'd do that in a split second you know!"

Jim felt a momentary fear flash through him.

Having his penis cut off! He'd seen men lose their penises in battle, usually from land mines, young men, with wives and girlfriends back home, men who would never enjoy married life, never have children. He thought of his weekend with Jiang Li, to have that forever taken from him.

"You're not afraid?" the man asked.

"I didn't say I wasn't afraid," Jim said.

They had finished their beers and the man had ordered two more, hurriedly brought. Jim could see the man carried a lot of authority here.

"You own this place?" Jim asked.

"Perhaps, in a manor of speaking."

"I got it, another 'protection racket. You're with The Cobra."

Anger briefly crossed the man's face.

"What's your name?" Jim asked.

"Johnny, Johnny Lee," the man said. "And you?"

"Former Staff Sergeant Jim Saunders. I'm out of the service and unemployed. I'm just biding my time. I thought I'd come here and have lunch. I didn't realize It would be such a big deal."

"I'll lay it all on the table, former Staff Sergeant Saunders, who do you represent and what kind of deal are you after?"

"What are you getting at?"

"We know the Cobra is seeking expansion as are other organizations. You show up and make a show of force to bluff The Cobra. You want to cut a deal. But first you need a way in."

"You're wrong."

"We'll see about that. If you can help us we'll cut a better deal. The Cobra is already dealing with a big outside organization. We will make you an offer."

"Johnny Lee, what triad are you with?"

"We are the second largest here. We are The Tiger Clan and we want to cut a deal, what have you got to offer?"

The wheels were turning a mile a minute now. A way in! A plan began to form in Jim's mind.

"Okay, you're right," Jim said.

"I am always right,' Johnny Lee answered.

"I'll talk to my people and then I'll return here. I can't exactly say when."

"I'll know when you pass through the Kearney Street gates," Johnny Lee said.

***

Jim drove back across the Bay Bridge headed for home. A game plan was forming in his mind, just beginning but definitely there. He would have to remain in deep cover, his father and mother would not even know. Nor would Jiang Li for now.

He thought about it.

He might even have to work against her parents. She might end up hating him when she found out he was a Federal Agent, especially if he found out her father was involved with The Cobra in any but a victim role.

***

Jim drove up the main street into the center of town. He saw Will and Joe seated at Starbuck's® and he parked and walked over to them, he was eyeing the apartment above the coffee shop.

"Hey Jimbo, what's up," Will said.

"Been out interviewing for work," Jim answered. "Over in the city."

"Lookin' for work? Don't you have enough back pay to just kick it for now, I mean, why rush it?" Joe asked.

Jim sat down.

"I'll go crazy if I don't start doing something soon," Jim said.

"Yeah, Joe," Will said, "and he's also got a certain honey on his mind, ain't that right, Jimbo?"

"I wouldn't lie about it."

"Well," Joe said, "she seems okay to me. And that hot blond from the bar's pretty sweet on you."

Jim just shrugged his shoulders.

"Heard Rebecca's workin' down at Denning's club now, 'exotic dancer' is what she's callin' herself," Will said. "She sure is bad news. Mike Walker was right in droppin' her."

"You sure straightened him out," Joe said.

"Mike always was basically a good guy," Jim said.

"He seemed pretty much like a asshole to us," Will said, "Hell, I'd of let the train run his ass over."

"No you wouldn't, Will, you'd of done the same thing I did."

Will shrugged.

"Hey Jim, let me buy you a coffee, what'll it be, a mocha cream..."

"Just black coffee," Jim said.

"So how'd the job search go?" Will asked.

"Nothin' yet, pretty bleak out there."

"I bet your dad could use the help at the shop."

"Dad's doin' fine, he's got a good crew workin' for him down there and besides..."

"I know," Joe said, "You want to strike out on your own. Me, I got feelers out with the Phone Company."

Will returned with the coffees and Jim sipped his slowly as he eyed the windows above him.

"I wonder who I could talk to about renting one of those rooms," Jim said.

"Ol' Larry Gilmore, he owns the property, you remember him, owns the local movie theater too and he lives in the back," Joe said. "Your parents gettin' on your nerves?"

"It's a bit stifling there, I mean, I've been on my own for four years..."

"Yeah, and with the little gal..."

"Shut up, Will!" Joe said lightly cuffing Will's ear.

"Hey!" Will said, "I didn't mean..."

"I'm going around back and talk to Larry," Jim said as he rose from his seat carrying his coffee.

Joe and Will rose and followed him, coffees in hand.

Jim knocked at the door to the rear apartment and a medium sized, balding, graying man answered.

"Hello, Jim," the man recognized him.

"Hi Larry," Jim said.

"What can I do ya fer?" Larry asked.

"I'm interested in the room right above the coffee shop overlooking the street," Jim said.

Larry broke into and instant smile.

"I just so happens I been tryin' to rent that rat trap for over a month! You came to the right place, Jim my boy! It'll be three hundred fifty a month."

Jim reached into his wallet and pulled out a wad of bills, counting them into Larry's outstretched hand.

"Here's three months," Jim said and Larry was overjoyed.

"Here's the key!"

***

"Man, you look like you're luggin' some pretty heavy stuff there, at least you could have let us help!" Will said as the ascended the steps and Jim opened the door. It was a simple, one bedroom place with a bathroom and a small kitchenette.

"What ya got in there, Jim, a load of guns or somethin'?" Joe said.

"...or somthin'," Jim answered as he set everything on the large, queen sized, brass bed.

The walls were a dull beige with cobwebs decorating one corner and a faded picture of a farmhouse with farm animals in the barnyard.

"What a dump!" Will said.

"Man this place is depressing," Joe said.

"It'll do for now," Jim said, "I won't be around much anyway, I just need a place to plant my head at night."

***

"Jim, you really don't have to do this," Jim's mother was saying as Jim was carrying his clock radio and duffle bag out the door.

"He'll be fine, dear," Jim's dad said to his wife, "and if you need anything, son, you just let us know."

Robbie was also helping to bring some things, two dumbbell bars, the iron plates had already been loaded up. Will was carrying Jim's small color TV.

"Well you be sure you come for Sunday dinner!" Jim's mother ordered him, "You've got to eat at least one good, home cooked meal a week!"

"Sure, Mom," Jim said as he gave her a kiss and shook his father's hand.

"We just get him home and off he goes again," his mother went on.

"I'm right up town, Mom, and I just gave you and Dad my cell phone number."

His mother still couldn't get the worry out of her eyes.

"Remember, honey," John said, "he's got a girl now."

"And a right decent girl she is," his mother said, "you should marry that girl!"

"I intend to, Mom," Jim said and his mother's jaw dropped open.

"My they grow up so fast, John," Jim heard her say as he was going down the walkway to his car.

"I'll meet you guys over there," Jim said as he got in his car.

As Joe and Will drove away with Robbie Jim pulled out his cell phone. He punched in Jiang Li's cell phone number.

"Hello, my love," came Jiang Li's familiar voice, soft and deeply sexy and lovely at the same time, "I just got off the streetcar on Market Street right now, Jim, oh Jim, it's so good to hear your voice."

"It's good to hear yours too. I just moved out of my parent's house into an apartment in town. I've been moving all my stuff. It's kind of a dive but it will do for now."

"Jim, I've got to go now, I'm turning up the street to my parents place. Oh Jim, I've got so much studying to do, I am overwhelmed...I miss you so much..."

"I miss you too...It'll be over soon..."

"I've got to go, Jim, I love you..."

"I love you too," Jim said and they hung up.

***

"Oh man this place is cool!" Robbie was saying as he looked over the dismal apartment.

Jim was moved in now, TV set up on a small table, his clothes hanging in the closet, a bench, piles of iron plates stashed against a wall with the dumbbell bars, a compact stereo/radio/tape/CD player on the nightstand next to the bed along with the clock radio.

"Cool?" Joe was saying, "It's a dive, a roach haven as far as I'm concerned."

"No man, this is cool, your own place! Can I come by and visit, watch some TV?"

"Later, Robbie," Jim said, "but not right yet."

"Oh man..."

"Okay guys," Jim said, "Thanks a lot for helping out."

"Helping out?" Joe said, "There wasn't that much stuff. All those weight plates were a bit much."

Jim had not taken any of the weight equipment set up in the patio, that was for Robbie, he took just what he had had in his room. He knew it would pay to stay in shape.

Jim said "good night" to his brother and his two friends. When they had gone Jim sat on the bed facing the open windows, it was now growing dark, past eight o'clock on this June evening.

Jim suddenly felt the aloneness come over him. He had had such an amazing, fantastic weekend. Now he was alone. He glanced at the closet, went there and picked up the lighter bag and placed it on the bed. He took out the billfold and replaced the bag in the closet. In the dim light he studied the badge and the photo of himself.

James Steven Saunders
Federal Agent

He closed it and placed it in his front pocket. Federal Agent, he thought to himself. Never in a million years, he thought, never in a million years did he ever see himself as being a Federal Agent.

***

Jim sat across the street under the awning to the steakhouse next to the bus depot. He was enjoying a lean, rare, porterhouse steak with salad, baked potato and a cold beer. The night was warm and a slight breeze was blowing. He looked across the street, up at the windows to his new home. A dim light shown through the window, he had only the small table light on. After dinner he walked across the street to Starbucks and ordered a large, black coffee to go. He had many hours of study ahead of him tonight. Just like Jiang Li, he thought.

***

Jim sat on his bed, up against the headboard against several pillows, the shades drawn and the TV on but silent. His shirt was off and he was studying one of the folders Suzie had given him.

He began reading.

Steven Denning, 60 years old, was brought up in the town, born to a typical middle class family. From an early age Denning seemed to have a tendency to get into trouble. He stole things from back yards as a kid and got caught. His parents made reparations to the families. They took him to counseling. Denning learned real fast to work the system, he was always able to out think the therapists. He became more and more cunning, now he learned to hustle, to take stolen items and turn them over for other things, to sell or trade them. He began collecting bicycles, starting from several stolen bikes and then using trade to get others. He learned to be cagey, he found connections into the black market when he was in high school and began a small bank account. He did yard work as a cover and put money in his account then opened a safety deposit box where he stashed the extra cash he was making. He was investigated by the local police and they opened the safety deposit box with a search warrant. The money was confiscated and Denning was questioned but he held firm and as a result no charges could be filed. The money had to be returned.

By the time Denning was a senior in high school he had a nice, late model Cadillac convertible which he proudly drove to school. He managed to graduate with barely passing grades and was voted least likely to succeed by his peers. He did not attend any colleges. Instead he continued to perfect the art of the hustle, it was rumored that he had committed several large scale burglaries but it had never been proved. He continued to do yard work and built that business into a full time yard service business, he rented an office in town, obtained a business license and was seemingly legit. There were rumors, never proven, that he was involved in the drug trade, funneling marijuana harvested from northern California in Humboldt County, a prime area for the crop, grown in hidden fields in the massive redwood forests in both Humboldt and Trinity Counties.

Meanwhile Denning branched into other businesses, a garage and gas station, a liquor store. He had a store in town that dealt with imports from around the world, very pricy goods. He owned a bar in town. He eventually sold that and started his nightclub out just past the city limit where the local authorities couldn't touch him.

Denning never married but had had a string of girlfriends, many of whom were dancers at his club. Early on he had gotten a girlfriend pregnant and he had decided to raise the child. The woman left him, it had been rumored that he had beaten her up a few times but she had never come forward so nothing was ever proved. Denning managed to gain custody of the little boy, David, and he raised him. Denning bought some property in a remote, wooded, part of town and built a custom home, three stories high, ten bedrooms, swimming pool and spa, a massive six car garage to house his extensive car collection. He had several antique cars from the 1930s in perfect running order, he had a brand new Ford Expedition, a new Lincoln Town Car and a new Cadillac convertible, always his favorites. He liked to cruise town in the Caddy with the top down, parading one of his exotic, beautiful girlfriends at his side. His son, David, now drove the Lincoln. David, or rather, Dave, was a popular boy and had never been in trouble, he got good grades in school and was due to graduate soon from the local high school.

It had never been proved that Denning had any ties to organized crime and he always paid his taxes from the legitimate businesses he owned and operated. Denning had connections to city council in town, one of his friends, Shawn Grady, was a city councilman. Grady himself had earlier in life had a shady past, had, in his youth, run with an outlaw motorcycle gang, had been arrested for drug dealing but then he had seemingly cleaned up his act and had become active in community affairs and owned a garage in town and also the bar that Denning had once owned. The bar had been turned into an upscale establishment right in the center of town next to Starbucks and was frequented by many of the towns upscale residents, screenwriters, movie producers, even a movie star or two, who had moved into the town. Property taxes had risen due to the upscaling of the town and new buyers had to be in the money to afford to live there. Thanks to Prop. 13 the older families who had owned property from the very beginning and had bought in the fifties paid only the scale of the purchase price of that time. Jim's dad was one of those as were the families of his school mates from high school.

Jim's cell phone rang.

He picked up.

"Hi."

It was Suzie.

"Hi."

"What's up?"

"I've been going over the Denning file. Wow! The things I never knew about him."

"Hopefully we'll be finding out a lot more."

There was a moment of silence.

"Jim, want company? You could come over to my apartment..."

"I gotta place now," Jim said.

"When?"

"This afternoon. That's where I am now."

"I could come over. Jim, I'd like to see you. I want to talk..."

"I don't think it's a good idea."

"I just need to talk, Jim."

"Okay," Jim sighed and he gave her his address. Then he went back to work.

Now he opened the Cobra file.

As he had been briefed, the head of Cobra was Harry Xiang, he had two sons, Dave and Tommy, Tommy was the betrothed to Jiang Li. Anger flashed through Jim at the thought. All were citizens of the United States and had clean records, Harry visited Taiwan regularly as well as other Pacific Rim countries on business, supposedly legit and never proved otherwise. But there was always suspicion and now it was rumored he was getting ready to partner with a major American crime organization to expand his trade, drugs, mainly heroin, and human trade.

Was Denning a key player in this merger?

That was what Jim had to find out. And the key was the nightclub. Harry and his sons had been frequenting the club lately, had been wined and dined at Denning's expense. Denning had been seen driving into San Francisco several times in the past month. In the past he rarely went into the city. That had changed.

Jim thought about his meeting with Jonnie Lee. The Tiger Clan?

Rivals!

There was a knock at the door. Jim rose and opened it, not thinking to put on his shirt. Suzie was standing there, dressed in her "T" shirt and jeans, a lazy smile on her face.

She looked him over and he was self conscious for a moment. She pushed open the door.

"My my," she said with a smile as she looked at him. "I'd say that Asian sweetheart of yours is a very lucky girl indeed."

CHAPTER THIRTEEN

Suzie stood there in front of Jim in his room, looking at his bare torso and smiling a sexy smile. She looked into his eyes. Despite himself Jim found himself getting aroused.

"Your face is beat red you know," Suzie said.

"What do you want, Suzie?"

"I think you know that..."

Suzie came up to him and put her arms around his waist, pressing herself close to him, he became instantly aroused as she smiled up at him.

"Oh my," Suzie said, "maybe the heart is loyal but the body betrays..."

Jim backed away.

"I make you nervous?"

"Yes you do," Jim said as he reached for his "T" shirt, pulling it over his head.

"Darn, and I was just starting to enjoy the view..."

"Seriously, Suzie, Agent ..."

"I like 'Suzie' better."

"I don't think..."

"Don't think what, Jim," Suzie moved nearer to Jim again, he was now backed against a wall.

"Isn't this 'sexual harassment?'" Jim asked.

"Is it? I didn't notice..."

Suzie's arms went around Jim's neck now and her face was near his, her lips inches from his. She pressed herself against him and he hardened. She smiled.

"If Jill walked in here right now..."

"She'd see us and leave, and you'd be all mine..."

"Damn it!"

Jim pushed away from Suzie. She smiled.

"I'm sorry, Jim, I just..."

"You just came over here to make my life miserable! I've got work to do."

Suzie's face was serious now.

"I'm sorry, Jim, a girl's gotta try, you know...so what are you looking over, besides me?"

"These," Jim pointed to the files on the bed.

"Doing research I see."

"Pretty extensive. And no real proof. We've got our work cut out for us."

"I know..." Suzie suddenly had a far away look in her eyes.

"What's wrong?" Jim asked.

"Oh nothing, just..."

"...just..."

"Working for Denning, at the club...I feel..."

Jim saw the sudden panic in her eyes. Then she shut it off and her face was a mask, unreadable.

"Suzie, that job at the club...if you can't..."

"No, it's the only way to get close to Denning's organization, to find out what we need to know."

"Suzie, you really don't want to do this..."

"Of course I don't! I don't want to be dancing naked in front of a sea of ogling lecherous men...that's the last thing I want, but it's something that has to be done."

"Not if it's going to get to you it isn't!"

Suzie came to Jim now, her eyes almost tearing up.

"Jim, you're really the only man I ever want to see me naked!"

Jim put his arms around her.

"Suzie, you know..."

"I know, Jim. I'm sorry but I can't help how I feel. Every time I see you I feel the same way. And to go into that club..."

"I'm going to have a talk with Martin or Trudy about this..."

"No, Jim, don't you dare..."

"You're falling apart over this. This is not something you should be doing."

"I can do this, Jim, I have to get over this fear...this is an important case..."

"Not if it's destroys you and from what I am seeing right now, this isn't good, Suzie."

Suzie shook her head.

"I'm okay, Jim, I'm okay," she sat down on the edge of the bed and held her head in her hands, she shook her head then looked at the reports Jim was going over. She thumbed through the pages.

"I see you've been doing your homework," she said as she looked up at him.

"I've been doing more than that," Jim said. "Does the name Jonnie Lee ring a bell?"

"Why?"

"I went into Chinatown this afternoon after our meeting."

"Jim, I warned you to stay out of there!"

"But does the name Jonnie Lee ring a bell?"

"Jonnie Lee heads a smaller triad operating in Chinatown. They are rivals with Cobra but right now an uneasy truce exists between them. Cobra is going after bigger game right now, as we know."

"So's Jonnie Lee."

"How so?"

"I had lunch with him."

Suzie's eyes widened.

"It was a result of the confrontation I had had last week. Word did get around and they think I am representing someone right now and that I was making a power play to get their attention."

"Wow, what else did you talk about?"

"Well, I was warned..."

"Warned?"

"I was told that I could wind up with my penis cut off."

Suzie swallowed hard then rose and put her arms around Jim, pressing against him.

"Jim! Be careful, he's not kidding, it happened to another agent a year ago. He committed suicide afterwards."

They parted and Suzie sat back down on the edge of the bed. Jim sat in the chair.

"I can use this," Jim said.

"This is a very dangerous path, Jim."

"This whole thing is a 'dangerous path,'" Jim answered. "And now, Suzie, I think I should be getting some sleep."

"You're kicking me out?" Suzie smiled at him.

"Afraid so."

Both of them rose and Suzie went to the door. She hesitated there, her hand on the doorknob, she looked back at Jim.

"Say the word, Jim, and I'll stay..."

"Good night, Suzie."

"Jim, you need to be back at the Federal Building tomorrow morning at ten. Meet me there."

"See you then," Jim said as Suzie opened the door, still looking at him, her lips inviting. She sighed and closed the door behind her. Jim breathed a sigh of relief.

***

Jim was seated at Stan's having breakfast the next morning. It was eight o'clock. He was at a table by the window munching down steak and eggs and hashed brown potatoes with a side of pancakes. He had a big day planned ahead of him.

"Hello, Jim."

Jim looked up. Steven Denning was standing at his table, looking down at him, a friendly smile on his face. Jim nodded to the seat across from him and Denning slid into the booth, the waitress was there in an instant with his coffee. Steven smiled up at her, thanking her, then he sipped his coffee, looking at Jim.

"Big day ahead?" he asked.

"Yeah, I've got lots to do today," Jim answered.

He took a bite of his pancakes. Then he looked at Denning.

"I've been thinking about what you said," Jim said.

Denning was all ears.

"About the job. I think I'd like to give it a go."

A broad smile crossed Denning's face.

"Glad to hear it, son, glad to hear it, you won't regret it. Why don't you come on down to the club later today, or early this evening and we'll get you squared away. You're hired."

"Probably early this evening."

"Whenever you can make it, Jim. This afternoon, this evening, the job's yours."

Jim shook his head, forced an innocent smile.

"Wow, Mr. Denning, this is great, I hardly know what to say..."

"Say 'thank you' I guess and just be down at the club this evening."

"Well, then, thank you, Mr. Denning."

"Glad to have you aboard, son, you'll go far working for me, I can tell, someone with your potential."

"Well, I hope so, I really need to get going with my life now."

"I understand completely, son, and if there's anything I can do to help you out, well, you just say the word, okay?"

Jim finished the last of his pancakes and rose from the table, Denning rose also and offered his hand. They shook firmly and Jim reached into his pocket to pay for his breakfast.

"I got it," Denning said. "I'll write it off to Uncle Sam as a business expense, interviewing a potential employee."

Denning broke into a hardly laugh and slapped Jim on the back as Jim turned to leave.

"This evening then," Jim said as he walked towards the door.

***

Jim was seated in Suzie's personal office on the forth floor of the Federal Building. The window faced west, the sun was high in the sky but not yet pouring into the office as it would be in the afternoon. Suzie was dressed in a light gray business suit, the skirt a little on the short side, her hair styled and blow dried to perfection, her make up just right. Her eyes were dazzling. Jim wore his usual "T" shirt and jeans, his badge in his wallet. He was not carrying his firearm. Suzie smiled at him from across her desk.

"The reason I had you come here this morning was because I want you to meet someone," Suzie said.

"Who?"

"Mean Gene."

"Mean Gene? What are you talking about?"

Suzie smiled her sexiest smile at Jim.

"Follow me," she said as she rose from her desk.

Suzie led Jim out of her office to the elevator. They descended to the second floor and got out. They went across the hall and through a door. Jim found himself in a completely equipped gym that put commercial gyms to shame. Free weights, benches, three power cages which could be used for bench pressing, squats, and presses. There were also leg press machines, lat machines, machines for every bodypart, tons of plates, the latest in high tech exercise bikes and treadmills. Jim was amazed.

But that wasn't all.

Across the main training room was another room and Suzie led Jim across the gym floor towards the doorway. Inside was a large empty room, the entire expanse of flooring was covered with hard foam mat squares fitted perfectly together. To one side were several heavy bags and also several speed bags. In the center of the floor was a massively built black man, shirtless, wearing the bottoms to a black karate uniform, a black belt around his waist. His head was shaved and he wore a neatly trimmed goatee and mustache. He was in a full stretch position, his forehead against his thigh, leg straight, holding his foot and forcing himself down into the fully stretched position. Suzie bowed as she entered the room, eyes front. Jim stood at the entrance. He knew the martial arts protocol and he also bowed, keeping eyes front for one never looked down when bowing.

The massive man on the floor looked up and a wide grin crossed his face. He sprang to his feet with amazing agility for such a massive musculature. He was ripped to the bone, not an ounce of fat on him. His muscles glistened in the dim light of the dojo for that is what this training room was.

"Agent ," the man said as he strode over and shook Suzie's hand.

"It's Suzie, Gene, you know that."

"Suzie." The man smiled then he looked at Jim.

"I brought you your latest 'victim,'" Suzie said as she smiled at Jim. "This is Agent Saunders, he's new."

The man called Gene put out his hand and they shook, each man with a firm grip, eye to eye, Jim could tell that behind the wide grin the man was sizing him up.

"This is Gene," Suzie said.

"Gene, call me Jim."

Suzie place her hand on Jim's shoulder.

"Well, boys, I'll leave and let you two get acquainted."

She smiled at Jim and then walked back across the room and went out the door.

Gene looked at Jim.

"There's a training gi in the dressing room that ought to fit you. Go ahead and get dressed."

In a few moments Jim was back on the mat, he was wearing white gi bottoms. Gene looked him over.

"You're in good shape, I'll say that. Here!"

Gene tossed Jim a pair of lightweight boxing gloves, the Everlast® emblem on them. Gene put his own gloves on.

"Maybe you better warm up," Gene said.

"Don't need to," Jim said, "in a real fight you don't have time to warm up."

"True!" Gene came at him with a blinding attack of fists and feet. Jim ducked aside, spun around, and delivered a punch to Gene's torso. The blow glanced off and Gene faced Jim.

"You'll have to do better than that!" Gene said.

Jim attacked, a step in side kick aimed at Gene's ribs, it was blocked effectively and Gene delivered a punch to Jim's head, a direct punch, a hard punch and Jim spun and almost hit the mat. He stepped away, using footwork, buying time to clear his head. Gene came at him again in a flurry and this time when Jim went to move aside Gene stayed with him, using a circular attack rather than a linier one.

"Fooled you this time!" Gene said and in the next instant Jim buried his heel in Gene's ribs. It staggered him for an instant and he danced away using a foot shuffle.

"Pretty good, I'm impressed," Gene said, shaking off the blow. "But you'll have to do better than that."

He came at Jim, catching him in the ribs with a side kick, Jim shook it off. Both of them came at each other in a flurry of punches. Jim spun away, and caught a punch to the side of his head, it staggered him and he saw stars. Gene could hit hard. Jim shook it off and he and Gene faced each other across the mat.

"Heard you were pretty good," Gene said. "Heard about your little confrontation over in Chinatown. Impressive!"

Gene attacked again, landing punches, right and left, right and left, each one pounding Jim, his torso, his head, his torso, Gene was unrelenting in his attack. Finally Jim hit the floor, winded, exhausted, sweat pouring off of him. He had never fought such a fierce opponent. He shook his head. He was in a daze. He looked up. Gene was grinning at him.

"That's how it's done," Gene said, offering a glove. Jim took it and was pulled to his feet. Then Gene landed a hard one on him. The last thing Jim remembered before everything went black was Gene saying, "Never trust an opponent."

***

Jim was standing in the shower, letting the cool water hit his face. He was bruised and battered. He ached all over. He turned up the temp and let the hot water soak his sore body.

What a workout!

Jim dressed and was crossing the mat. The room was empty. He heard the familiar clanking of iron and as he came into the weight room he saw Gene bringing up the last rep on the bench press. He was using about four hundred pounds. He sat up, looked at Jim and grinned. He rose up and walked up to him, offering his hand.

"Great workout, man," he said, "you're good, real good, one of the best I've ever trained with. You actually lasted more than five minutes. Most don't get a minute."

Jim was wary as he looked at Gene's extended hand.

"Oh, don't worry, man, we're off the mat now and you know the rule, I expect you do."

"Yes," Jim said, "on the mat you enter the theater of life and death, there are no friends and no one can be trusted."

They shook hands and Gene slapped Jim on the shoulder. It hurt.

"Sore?" Gene asked.

Jim nodded, sheepishly.

"Good, don't worry, it'll pass, here, do a set, I figure that's a good weight for you."

Jim looked at the four hundred and five pounds on the bar, the four big plates on each side. He sat down on the bench and lay back. He gripped the bar and repped out five good reps, setting the bar back on the racks. It felt good and some of the soreness was beginning to ease up.

"I knew you could do it," Gene said. "Good weight. You're strong, you'll need to be for what you're gonna be doin' and that's why I'm here. Suzie, er, Agent Bradley..."

"Suzie..."

"Yeah, right, okay, Suzie. She gave me the rundown on you and your assignment. You're goin' up against some pretty tough customers. You did a good job the other day in that alley in Chinatown though. You probably left a pretty good impression. They know they can't mess with you without dire consequences. I'm here to make sure you're even better. Suzie put me on special assignment with you."

"You're a field agent?" Jim asked.

"Sure am, also the hand to hand combat expert here. I head up all the training programs."

Gene took his place on the bench and repped out five. Then Jim took another turn and did five. It felt good, the blood was coursing through his veins now, he was pumped.

"Well, I gotta be going," Jim said, "That's it?"

"For today," Gene said, "Just for today. Same time tomorrow."

"Tomorrow then," Jim said and they shook hands again.

Jim returned to Suzie's office. As he entered she rose with a smile from her desk.

"You boys have a good time?" she asked.

"Good time, hell!"

Suzie laughed.

"I knew you'd both get along well. I knew Gene would be the one to get you in shape. I didn't think anyone else would be able to teach you anything, much less be able to last with you on the mat."

"I can't wait to get Charlie White Eagle down here to meet Gene," Jim said with an evil grin on his face.

"You think he'll join?"

"I hope so. I'll see him this weekend at the Cow Palace."

"I'll go with you."

Jim was thinking of Jiang Li. No, he wouldn't be able to take her, he felt a pang of guilt knowing he had to keep his real job a secret from her for now. And also, the fact that he would have to investigate her father's involvement with The Cobra.

Jiang Li.

She was out at the college now.

"I gotta be going," Jim said.

Suzie placed a hand on his cheek.

"You have a bruise," she said.

"It's okay."

"Take care..."

She reached up and kissed Jim on the cheek.

***

Jim pulled into the parking lot to the college and got out. He had no idea where Jiang Li's class was today. Then it dawned on him. He pulled out his cell phone and rang her number.

"Hello?" her voice sounded sweet.

"Hello yourself..."

"Oh, Jim!" now she sounded excited. "Oh it's good to hear from you. I was just leaving one of my classes, oh Jim, it's so good to hear your voice."

"Where are you?"

"Just outside the Business wing. I am on my way to the student center to take a break. I have an hour before class."

"I'll meet you there, where is it?"

"You're here?" it took her breath away. She immediately gave Jim directions.

Jim walked quickly across the campus and he saw her, standing in front of the business building entrance. She was dressed in a short dress, her bag across one shoulder, her hair trailing down her shoulders, she was wearing her sunglasses. She was the most beautiful sight he had ever seen, he thought to himself. He walked quickly up to her and she threw her arms around him, her lips smothering his in a long kiss. They held each other tightly then they looked into each other's eyes. A smile crossed Jiang Li's face.

"Come with me, quickly," she said as she took Jim's hand and led him up the steps into the building. Once inside Jiang Li reached into her purse and took out two quarters.

"I'll be right back," she said as she ran quickly into the women's restroom. She emerged a few seconds later and came right up to Jim, throwing her arms around him again and kissing him.

"You didn't take long," Jim said.

"I didn't need to," she answered.

She took Jim's hand and quickly led him down the hall, peering into classroom after classroom. They were filled with students. Finally she found and empty room and opened the door, pulling Jim inside and closing the door after then. The shades were drawn in the classroom, it was dark. The desks stood in neat rows, those little desks students had to squeeze into with hardly enough room on the desktop to hold their books and papers. Cramped little desks.

At the front of the classroom was the large, mahogany desk used by the teachers, sitting in front of the blackboard. Written on the blackboard were mathematical equations, Jim had no clue as to what their meaning was. Jim had always been a bit math challenged.

They stood in front of the desk and Jiang Li threw her arms around Jim again, her lips met his as she backed against the desk, pressing herself into him.

"I've missed you so much," she breathed into his ear then her tongue darted into his ear and he could hear the roar of her gasping breath as she moved against him. He held her tightly to him, kissing her as he put his arms around her lower back, pressing her closer, feeling her movements against him, exciting him, his fever rising as he kissed her neck. She had set her purse down on the desk next to her and she fumbled inside it with her free hand, extracting a small package as she continued to move against him.

"So much, so much I've missed you," she breathed as she began undoing his belt, unfastening his snaps, one by one, then reaching in and finding him ready. Jim hiked her dress up and reached for her panties, feeling her moist and ready for him as he pulled them down, down around her ankles, he stepped away as she reached down and tossed them across the room then she lay back across the desk, her dress hiked up to her waist now. She broke open the package and took out the object, fitting it on Jim, he almost lost it as she touched him. He entered slowly as she gasped, then he made a thrust and she let out a cry of pleasure as she received him, her legs going around his waist as she kissed his neck. Then she bit his neck, working the skin with her teeth. Jim was careful not to do the same to her, not to put a mark on her for she lived in a dangerous situation. He was lost in her, taking her all in, their lips met again and his tongue plunged into her mouth, wrestled with hers now as she jammed against him, tightening on him, squeezing. Then the final moment of release and he collapsed on her as several objects fell from the desk. Their lips met again, her hair was soaked with sweat as she kissed him, kissed his face, felt his cheeks with her hands.

Slowly, he slid out of her, and he stood up, fastening his snaps and belt and pulling her up to him as she pulled down her dress. Her arms went around him and she looked into his eyes.

"I want this to be over soon, Jim, I want to marry you soon!"

"I want the same thing, Jiang Li, Jill, I want the same thing as soon as we can. I'd like to just go to your father right now and tell him..."

"Jim, that has to wait..."

"I know..."

Their lips met again. Jim held her face, stroked her wet hair, smoothing it back.

"I am interviewing for a job this afternoon," he said. "Then I am going to be taking some classes at the local college..."

"I will graduate next week, Jim, and then I can start working as well..."

"Your marriage..."

"No, that will never happen, I'll have to tell father then...and whatever happens, well it happens...oh Jim..."

"Don't worry, Jiang Li, don't worry, I will be there all they way for you, you have my word."

Just at that moment the room was flooded with light. Jim and Jiang Li looked around to find a young woman of about thirty standing in the doorway. She had a carryall she had been rolling along with all her books and papers and she was dressed in a gray business suit, her hair a sandy blond and cut in a professional manner, shoulder length.

"Oh, excuse me..." she said, looking embarrassed.

"Oh it's okay," Jiang Li said, "we were just leaving, we were...studying together..."

"Studying..." the woman, obviously a teacher, said.

Then she teacher looked around the room and her eyes lowered, she saw the panties lying there, between the rows of desks. Her face flushed red for an instant.

"Studying...okay, well, ah...I hope you learned a lot from your studying..."

"Oh yes...I think we certainly did," Jiang Li stammered then she picked up her purse and backpack from the floor where they had fallen, took Jim's hand and headed for the door. The teacher was looking directly at them as they passed her.

"Aren't you forgetting something?" the teacher asked but Jiang Li had Jim's hand firmly and was making a hasty retreat down the hallway and out the far door.

They broke out into the sunlight and Jiang Li broke into a laugh as she whirled to face Jim. He was laughing also, both of them now busting up uncontrollably.

"Oh that was so funny..." Jiang Li said as she threw her arms around Jim, "I love you, Staff Sergeant Jim Saunders." And she planted a kiss on his face.

They held each other for a moment then parted.

"I'll have to be careful in class," Jiang Li said.

"Huh?"

"You know, I'd better make sure my dress is down..."

Jim's face flashed red.

"Oh...yeah..."

"Oh my, and we also left something else there..."

"What...oh...yeah..." Jim thought about the little package.

Jiang Li laughed again and they walked hand in hand across the campus. They arrived at one of the other buildings and Jiang Li turned to face Jim.

"Well," she said, "I have to get in there, I'm a bit late as it is."

She kissed him, holding him tight. They parted, she held his hand for a moment then let it pull away. She gave him a smile and then she trotted up the steps and through the door, giving him a wave just before entering the building.

***

Jim was, again, standing at the entrance to Chinatown. He had parked at Union Square again, and, following his instinct, had left his Federal Agent ID in his car. He entered Chinatown and headed to the restaurant where he had met Jonnie Lee. He sat down at the table and the same waitress came up to him and took his order. He ordered Mongolian Beef and a beer. He sipped the beer while he waited for his meal to arrive. He looked around the room. There were only a few customers there, all Chinese, eating their food and minding their own business. There was still no sign of Jonnie Lee.

His food arrived and he began to eat, ordering another beer which he sipped in between bites.

"Hello my young friend," a familiar voice said and Jim looked up.

Jonnie Lee was standing there by his table. Jim nodded to the seat opposite him and Jonnie Lee sat down. Jim kept on eating.

"You eat like you are starving," Jonnie Lee said.

"I am," Jim answered, taking another sip of his beer.

Jonnie Lee said nothing, just watched.

Jim finished and Jonnie Lee held up two fingers. The waitress immediately brought two beers. Jonnie Lee took a sip of his.

"Well, my young friend, have you thought about what I said yesterday? Did you talk to your people?"

Jim took a sip before answering, "No, not yet. I'll let you know when but I have to have something to bring to the table. What can you offer that Cobra cannot?"

"A fair question, my friend. We will be able to offer our 'products' at a lower price than Cobra."

"Lower price doesn't always mean quality," Jim said as he took another sip. He was looking directly into Jonnie Lee's eyes. "My people are going to want to see proof that you can deliver on time."

Jonnie Lee looked Jim in the eye.

"Are you a cop?" he asked.

Jim's face did not change expression.

"You look like a cop. The short hair, just the way you present yourself speaks 'cop' to me. Need I say that a cop nosed around here before, several months ago. It is said that when he was found he would never be able to enjoy women again."

Jim took a another sip, still looking at Jonnie Lee.

"If I think you are a cop, my friend, you will not leave Chinatown alive today."

Jim set his beer bottle down on the table.

"Well then, you have to do what you have to do, my 'friend.'"

Jim rose from the table.

"I can see I wasted my time," he said. "And I wouldn't count on my not being able to get out of Chinatown."

Jonnie Lee also rose from the table. They stood eye to eye.

"If I, for one moment, think you are going to try to prevent me from leaving, I will take you out right here and now!" Jim said and his eyes carried the threat. Jonnie Lee didn't even flinch.

"My friend, come with me," he said.

Jonnie Lee headed for the back of the restaurant, through the doors to the kitchen, Jim following. There was a flight of stairs leading up and Jonnie Lee ascended these, Jim right behind him. At the top there was a narrow, darkened, hallway. They proceeded down the hallway and through a door at the end. Jim found himself in an ornately decorated office with a window overlooking the main street, right above the restaurant. The room was a brilliant, glaring, Chinese Red. On one side of the room was an altar with a golden god of some type, a massive figure in gilded bronze and gold, a bearded man and in his hand he was holding a broad, curved sword. There was incense sticks mounted in front of the figure.

Jonnie Lee paused before the altar and pulled out his lighter. He lit the incense then gazed at the statue for moment. He looked at Jim.

"Please be seated," he said.

Jim sat in the plush chair in front of the solid, oak desk in front of the window overlooking the street. The blinds were partially drawn. Jonnie Lee made his way over to the desk and also seated himself. He opened a drawer and pulled out a pack of cigarettes, offering one to Jim, who refused. He lit one for himself and inhaled deeply, relaxing for a moment. He nodded to the altar across the room.

"Guan Yu, also known as Yunchang, called the patron saint of martial arts. The 'General Who Eliminates Bandits' among his titles. He was a mighty warrior who attained enlightenment after his execution by a lord who had demanded that he change loyalties. He refused, the consequence of that action was his death. A great hero."

Jim nodded.

"Interesting," Jim said.

"Interesting?"

"You admire a great warrior god who fought bandits and other criminals but yet you are a criminal yourself."

"You are not? And, again, the sound of the policeman is heard."

"Not so. I am a criminal just like you but I don't buy into any 'gods' or anything like that. It would be hypocritical, don't you think? You deal drugs and women, import human slaves yet you worship at the altar of an honorable man."

Jonnie Lee's eyes narrowed for a moment, studying Jim. Jim saw the flicker of rage there.

"I could have you killed for such insolence," Jonnie Lee said.

"It's the truth. And go ahead, kill me then. But that would spoil your chances for a deal and that's why we're in this office isn't it?"

Jonnie Lee's eyes softened and a smile crossed his face.

"I see why they use you. You speak well, and stand strong. But then, you did make a good account of yourself in the alley the other day with members of The Cobra. You made your statement.

"And about Guan Yu, he was a warrior, just as we are. Maybe I break certain 'laws' of the land. But we are involved in warfare, the war for survival in this world. The government will not help us, no one will help us unless we help ourselves. We have families that demand our care and attention, we have to do well in life, provide for them. We are only surviving like everyone else and the law of survival is that the fittest live and the weak die. Is this not so?

"Of course it is so, you don't have to answer me, young man. We are in the game of survival, to attain the highest level in life so our survival is assured. And right now we are at war, the Tiger Clan, The Cobra and a few others. We are fighting over a great big pie and the strongest will get the major portion of that pie.

"You are in this business to thrive, not just to survive, is that not right?"

Jim kept looking at Jonnie Lee.

"It is so. And you are doing well, starting out well, you are strong, physical strength goes a long way and you also seem to me to have a keen sense of survival. You spotted an opportunity to get into the battle. Your boss saw that in you or he would not have sent you here to Chinatown to make your 'statement.'"

"So what have you to show me?" Jim asked. "What have you got that The Cobra cannot provide?"

"We deal with the same things, The Cobra and The Tiger Clan but we can land the deal for less. I have better connections with the Far East, an established conduit."

"So do they, or so they claim."

"They have to deal with other 'middle men' that I do not have to deal with. I have family connections they do not. Yes, they are ruthless, they have to be because they deal from a lesser position and make up for it in their ruthlessness. Extortion is a main profit conduit for them. I do not need to deal in extortion.

"What we both lack is an opening to the main stream of this country and your organization can provide this conduit. We can all profit together."

"Talk's pretty cheap, you know."

"So you want to see 'the goods.'"

"It would be a good start," Jim said.

Jonnie Lee stubbed out his smoke. The smell of the incense was filling the room, a sweet smell. Jonnie Lee pushed a button on his desk and spoke in Chinese into an intercom.

Jim heard the door open and he looked around. Standing just inside the door was a petite, extremely beautiful young woman dressed in a short, garish red, silk dress, she had long black hair, cut in straight bangs just above her eyebrows. Jonnie Lee spoke to her and she shut the door. She came into the center of the room and stood. She looked at Jim, into his eyes, her dark eyes said nothing. Jonnie Lee gave a command. The girl undid her dress and it fell to the floor, she was standing there in scanty black pushup bra and high rise black panties and black, see through stockings that clipped to the panties. Jonnie Lee nodded and she turned to profile, her petite breasts and shapely bottom cutting a perfect silhouette. Then she turned her back, her narrow waist blossomed into a perfect, tiny hourglass, her buttocks shapely and yielding, soft, inviting.

Jonnie Lee gave another command and she undid her bra and tossed it to the floor, her smallish breasts were perfect, her nipples erect, pointing slightly upward. She slid out of her panties and stockings and now stood there naked in front of Jim and Jonnie Lee.

Jonnie Lee gave another command. The girl came forward and stood behind Jim's chair. She began to massage his shoulders and neck and brought her face down near his. She kissed his cheek with her moist lips and Jim felt himself getting strongly aroused as her fingers worked at his neck and traps, her thumbs digging in, easing all his tension. He could now feel her breasts against the back of his head. Then she was in his lap, her legs suddenly around his waist, her breasts inches from his face.

He flushed with a growing passion he could not stop. He could feel her moving on him, feel himself harden and he saw the knowing smile cross her face. Her nipple jutted inches from his mouth. He thought of Jiang Li, how she was even more beautiful than this young girl. The girl shifted expertly on him again, driving him mad with desire that he fought against. She looked into his eyes and for a moment Jim thought he saw a glimmer of fear, an almost pleading look, then the eyes were blank.

Jonnie Lee gave another command and the girl rose from Jim's lap, he was greatly relieved. She moved over behind Jonnie Lee, first pulling down the shades all the way and she began to work on his shoulders, a smile on her face. She looked at Jim again, and again, Jim saw the glimmer in her eyes.

"This is Samantha Yi," Jonnie Lee said. "I recently had her brought over from Bangkok at a good price. Exquisite isn't she? And there are so many more. And I have them here already, ready to be sold. They are all my property. Do you want her? I can give you a good price. She will live with you and satisfy your every need, my young friend."

"You talked about family," Jim said.

"Family. Yes, of course. I am not married but I have two sons, fine sons, each from a different woman. I actually own a house down in South San Francisco and also some legit rental properties. A good place to launder cash. Also, I actually have a few legit businesses, Laundromats in the city and one over in Oakland. Yes, I have many legitimate businesses in which to hide money out. And many of the girls work there for me. That waitress, for example, the one who took your order? She is also from Bangkok, she is Samantha's cousin. Human traffic. You should have seen their lives over there. They lived in complete poverty. Here they have a chance. I have papers on them, they have a chance here. Their hope is to one day pay back their debt to me for making their entry into this country possible and to also get their other family members over here. There is nothing they would not do for their families to get them out of the hell holes they live in."

"The Cobra has the same thing to offer," Jim said as if he knew.

"You set up a meeting with your people and I will make my bid."

"I'll see what I can arrange."

Samantha smiled at Jim across the desk as she worked her hands down Jonnie Lee's arms now and kissed his neck. He smiled and paused, enjoying the sensations for a moment.

"It's good to relax, to meditate, go within one's being and such expert hands can send you there so fast and so completely..." Jonnie Lee was saying.

There was a crashing sound outside, it sounded like it came from the restaurant below. The shattering of glass, the sound of gunfire.

Jonnie Lee was on his feet, guiding Samantha behind him as he peered through the window to the street below. Rage crossed his face as he snapped the blinds shut. There was another crash and more gunfire.

"Quickly!" Jonnie Lee said as Jim was also on his feet.

Jonnie Lee led the way to the door, pausing at the altar and retrieving a 9mm from beneath it. He also retrieved another weapon, a .45, which he tossed to Jim, Jim caught it expertly. Jim grabbed Samantha's arm, she had not had time to put on her clothes. He felt her grip his hand and saw the fear in her eyes as she looked at him. He squeezed her hand to reassure her, though he felt no reassurance himself.

They were in the hallway and running.

"In here!" Jonnie Lee said.

He flung open a panel in the wall, there was another stairway leading down. There was the sound of heavy footsteps on the other main staircase as the three of them fled through the doorway and started down the stairs, Jim holding Samantha's hand tightly. She shut the panel just before they headed down the stairs. They could hear the footsteps in the hallway above, the sound of the office door being kicked open.

When they reached the bottom they were in an underground passageway dimly lit by lights placed several yards apart. Jonnie Lee led them along this passageway then up another stairway. They emerged into another hallway, Jonnie Lee opening the false wall panel. They stepped into the hall and he led them through a door.

They were in a gift shop across the street from the restaurant. Samantha Yi hugged her naked body against Jim's back, she was shaking with fear. He looked around at her, her eyes showed her fear.

Jim saw a rack of clothes and he grabbed a simple dress and handed it to Samantha. Jonnie Lee was concentrating on the scene across the street. Samantha slipped on the dress, looking at Jim.

"Don't worry, I'll pay for it," Jim said.

"No need," Jonnie Lee said as he turned around. "This is my shop, the dress is hers. She can't understand you."

"I didn't figure she could."

Jim looked at Samantha, she smiled at him then looked in a full length mirror on a wall nearby, admiring the simple dress. With her body she looked good in anything. Jim came up beside Jonnie Lee.

"Who is it? The Cobra?" Jim asked.

"No, The Dragons, a small no nothing bunch of pests, they are trying a powerplay."

Both of them still gripped their firearms, Jonnie Lee, his 9mm and Jim, the .45 Jonnie Lee had tossed him.

"With all this commotion the cops will be here any moment!" Jim said.

"Not so, they'll take their time, they don't give a rat's ass what happens down here as long as it stays down here in Chinatown. Look!"

Several stocky thugs emerged from the restaurant, they had broken the picture window. They had the waitress hostage, dragging her along by the arm as she struggled.

Jim found himself surging with a sudden rage. He bolted out the door.

"Wait..." Jonnie Lee warned but Jim was running across the street, gun in hand.

Jonnie Lee ran out behind him. There were four of them, all carrying. Jim came at them fast as tourists screamed and parted for them. Jonnie Lee and Jim were now side by side running down the street. People screamed and headed for cover. The four men who held the waitress hostage turned and opened fire. Three had 9mms and one had a MAC 10. The 10 sprayed bullets like water from a shower head and Jim and Jonnie Lee ducked and rolled as shop windows shattered and people screamed. Both Jim and Jonnie Lee came up firing and two of the Dragons went down, one of them releasing the waitress who ran on down the street, screaming. The two remaining men fired again, bullets whizzed by Jim's head, it was Baghdad all over again, the war zone. The MAC 10 chattered, bullets impacting on walls, hitting the street, most of the people had ducked down alleys, hid behind cars or had retreated into shops. More windows shattered, the man with the 10 was on a roll. He was empty and immediately had another clip ready. But his hesitation was his undoing as Jim and Jonnie Lee both opened up, rapid fire, riddling the man with lead, his body danced, spun and dropped. The remaining man ran down an alley in a panic.

Sirens could now be heard approaching. Flashing blue and red lights could be seen down the street, but they were being blocked by the traffic which had hopelessly jammed the street.

"Quickly!" Jonnie Lee said and he led Jim back up the street. They ducked into the restaurant, the place was destroyed, tables knocked over, the picture window completely obliterated, glass everywhere, tourists and local customers huddled against the wall, shaking in fear, the women crying in hysterics, clutching their husbands who showed total panic. One man had peed his pants and was shaking uncontrollably while his wife screamed and screamed.

Jonnie Lee led Jim through the doorway to the kitchen, popped open a drain on the floor.

"Here, quickly!" he said and Jim handed him his .45. Jonnie Lee dumped both firearms into the drain and put the lid back on. They were in the kitchen, the cook was hiding behind the dishwashing machine with the dishwasher, both of them huddling in fear. Tears were in the cook's eyes, he was a man of about fifty five. He spoke to Jonnie Lee and Jonnie Lee answered him in a comforting voice then looked at Jim.

"He was asking about my waitress, she is his niece, I told him she got away."

Jim nodded. He was glad she was safe. He looked at the cook. There was relief in his eyes but he still was shaken. The sirens were growing louder now, the police cars had gotten through. They all converged on the restaurant and armed officers were suddenly everywhere, handguns and shotguns drawn the cops moved in, securing the area. Unmarked cars were arriving, clamp on red lights spinning on their roofs. Plain clothes officers were emerging from these, all had on body armor and had their weapons drawn. Out of one car Jim saw Gene, his martial arts instructor from that morning, and Suzie emerge, armed and in body armor.

"Time to go into my act," Jonnie Lee said to Jim as he winked at him.

Jonnie Lee emerged into the restaurant in a panic, screaming loudly in Mandarin, yelling at the officers and waving his hands as he looked about at the destruction of his place of business. Jim emerged from the kitchen and several uniformed officers approached him.

"You!" an officer yelled. "What are you doing back there?"

"Trying to avoid getting shot!" Jim answered. "A guy just can't have a quiet lunch anymore around here."

"FBI!" Gene yelled as he was holding up his badge and ID for all to see.

"DEA!" Suzie yelled holding up her ID.

They entered the restaurant, both of them looked at Jim, Jonnie Lee continued to act the panic stricken owner, now he was letting the tears come, what an act, Jim thought to himself as Jonnie Lee kept rattling away in Mandarin while waving his arms at the total destruction.

"You!" it was Suzie, she was looking straight at Jim.

"Who? Me?" Jim asked innocently.

"I don't see anyone else in front of me right now! Outside! Now!"

Jim walked forward and Suzie spun him around, slamming him against the wall.

"Hands behind your head!" she commanded.

"Hey lady, I was just having lunch..."

"Not another word!" Suzie commanded as she brought one hand, then the other down and cuffed him, cinching the cuffs as tight on his wrists as she could.

"Hey! That hurts!" Jim blurted.

"You're gonna hurt a lot more if you don't shut up. Outside!"

Suzie hustled Jim outside while Gene and a detective were trying to calm Jonnie Lee down. Suzie hustled Jim over to the Fed car and slammed him against the side.

"Hey take it easy..."

"Take it easy my ass!"

Suzie began searching him, letting her hand hesitate near his upper thigh then continuing on down. She grabbed his wallet and opened it. She now talked in lowered tones.

"Well at least you left your Federal ID in your car, along with your .45."

"I never brought my .45 with me," Jim answered in a low tone.

"You were warned to stay out of Chinatown and now look at the mess you're involved in!"

"I was just having..."

"Lunch? Lunch my ass! Oh, I'd like to crush your balls right now, I am so pissed off at you!"

"Easy!"

"Easy my ass! We have three men dead out here, mass destruction of private property, dozens of tourists and locals in a panic and you say 'easy!' Oh I'd like to..."

"I know, I know, my balls..."

"You'll be lucky if you get out of all this with them at the rate you're going!"

Gene walked up to them now.

"How's it goin' in there?" Suzie asked.

Gene grinned.

"Old Jonnie Lee puttin' on his act for the local law enforcement agency, the poor shop keeper who has just been vandalized. And you..."

Gene stared hard at Jim.

"We are questioning the 'suspect,' that's all," Suzie said as she uncuffed Jim. "I guess we have nothing to hold the 'suspect' on. We might as well let him go. I guess we'll never really know who shot those men over there."

"They're Dragons," Gene said.

"I know that," Suzie answered as she looked at Jim again. Jim shrugged.

A detective was leading a middle aged white couple out of the restaurant. He brought them over to the two Federal officers, Jim was standing there.

"These people see anything?" Suzie asked the detective.

"We didn't see a thing!" the middle aged man answered.

"You have no idea who shot these three men?" Gene asked.

"Nope!" the man said and he snuck a look at Jim. "But whoever it was deserved a medal, he put a stop to this right fast. I ever meet him I'd like to shake his hand."

"But you didn't see who it was?" the detective asked.

"Nope, not at thing." The man smiled. His wife looked at Jim briefly and then she took her husband's hand and smiled also.

"May we leave now?" the man asked.

"Go on, get out of here," Suzie said. Then she turned to Gene. "I guess we'll never get the lowdown on this one. Looks like a gang shootout to me. The ones who did this are probably long gone now." she looked at Jim. "And you, get out of here!"

"Sure thing, lady," Jim said as he smiled at her. Her gaze was like ice, her eyes glaring into his. She walked up to him, still looking in his eyes.

"Maybe I'll come by your place tonight so I *can* crush them!" she said in a low voice.

Jim smiled again and walked off down the street, leaving the destruction behind.

***

There it stood, the large building with the billboard mounted on the roof showing a beautiful scantily clad blond woman with a big smile. The sign on the billboard read: "Gentleman's Club."

Jim pulled into the parking lot, not many cars here this late in the afternoon. He had driven home first and showered, and then had taken a nap. He had awakened refreshed and ready for the interview. Jim parked the car and got out. He headed for the main entrance, a burly bouncer stood there, it was Jack De Poli, his hair greased back, wearing a tight, black "T" shirt to accentuate his lean muscles, muscles impressive enough but not as massive as Jim's.

"Hey, Jimbo!" Jack said as Jim approached. "Come on in, the boss is expecting you. He's also getting ready to interview some new girls."

Jim said nothing, he nodded and walked on into the club. It seemed pitch dark at first as he entered, he could see neon beer signs and he could hear music playing from a stereo system with speakers that ran throughout the building. He saw the bar, a beer and wine bar only, behind the bar Rebecca was stocking beer bottles, she was dressed in a skimpy top and very, very brief panties. She glanced over at Jim but said nothing. She went back to work. Jim passed the bar and looked out on the main showroom floor, there were small tables and chairs set up, Mike Walker and Bob Gianechi were busy making repairs to a wall. They hung a picture of an oil painting, a beautiful, naked blond woman with lustrous, long hair reclining on a couch and smiling out at the audience. Mike Walker stepped back to inspect the work. He made a motion and Bob adjusted the picture. Jim looked around the main floor, there was a stage with a shiny pole, to each side were two cages and a ramp ran partly out into the audience from the main stage. The room was dimly lit in garish blue and red lights. Steven Denning was seated near the stage enjoying a beer. In former times there would be ash trays on each table but with the new laws no smoking was permitted in any building open for business to the public, or in any offices for that matter.

"Hello, Jim," Steven Denning's voice boomed across the room and Mike Walker and Bob Gianechi looked over. Mike nodded to Jim and Jim acknowledged him then crossed the room. Denning offered him a chair opposite him. They were in the front row.

"Well, so you've come for the interview," Denning said.

"Here I am," Jim answered.

"And we're glad to welcome you aboard, Jim, you can start right away, we open Thursday, if you want, to get the feel of the place. Everyone here already knows I am hiring you on as head bouncer, Mike won't be taking a pay cut though, he'll be your second in command, unless you say differently. I'm not going to go into a lot of details, I think you can get the idea, you seem to be pretty much on top of things. Just be polite to customers and be easy on the trouble makers if you can, just get them to calm down or get them out of here. Of course, sometimes trouble can't be avoided, we've just about repaired the damage here from that last brawl so we're ready to open for business tonight. I've taken a bit of a loss but it's a business write off so I am not too concerned, and I have insurance which helped finance the repairs. This place can get rowdy at times. Remember to be polite at all times, I realize you might get a mouthy customer who just can't seem to get the idea and it's up to you to 'convince' him, get what I mean?"

Jim nodded.

"I am also going to be training you to manage this place, I know you've got that girlfriend, little Asian gal."

Denning looked over at Rebecca, who was still stocking the bar. He smiled and shook his head. He looked back at Jim.

"Nice little Asian gal, as I was saying, and you say you're going to be in school so this job will really help you out. I can use a good head to help run things around here so we'll see how it goes.

"Say, tell you what," Denning raised two fingers and Rebecca brought two long necked bottled beers and set them on the table. "Thank you hon," Denning said as he took a sip and nodded to Jim who also took a sip from his beer.

"I gotta gal coming in here right now to interview for a job as a dancer. You can watch and learn. In fact, here she is now."

Both men looked towards the entrance. Suzie was just entering, dressed in tube top and tight jeans, her hair ratted and teased, she wore more makeup than Jim was used to seeing on her. Suzie halted at the edge of the main floor.

"Come on in, sweetheart," Denning said with a smile and Suzie hesitatingly came forward, looking around nervously. She looked at Jim and her eyes said nothing. Jim moved aside and pulled another chair up to the table.

"Have a seat, dear," Denning had a soothing sound to his voice and he smiled broadly. Suzie gave a smile back and then seated herself, holding her small purse in her lap.

"You know Jim here from Sam's bar down in town," Denning said to her and Suzie nodded to Jim.

"Hi," she said and she looked briefly at Jim.

"So, hon, you've finally decided to take me up on my offer," to Jim he said, "I've offered her a job here several times but she prefers that construction job in the big city."

"Um...Mr. Denning..." Suzie said.

"Oh hell, girl, call me Steven."

"Well...Steven...you see...I kind of got laid off my job..."

"Laid off, oh no, how sad," Denning said with all sincerity. "Well, you've come to the right place, now I can see you're a little nervous, would you like a beer, a glass of wine?"

"Well..." Suzie looked at Denning and at Jim.

"Go ahead, it'll help you to relax a little," Denning said as he signaled and Rebecca brought a beer, "Beer will be okay?"

"Oh, just fine..." Suzie said as Rebecca set the beer down, not looking at Suzie. Jim saw a brief glimmer of hate cross her dark eyes but then she skipped quickly back to the bar. Denning watched her for a brief moment.

"Poor girl," Denning said, "kind of mixed up but she works hard and is an excellent dancer. Now to you, young lady," and Denning turned his full attention to Suzie, "tell me a little about yourself, have you had any dancing experience? I know what most people think, all a girl has to do is get up on a stage naked and gyrate around a little bit but that's so far away from what I am looking for. I need good dancers, girls who will tantalize and, if you will excuse the expression, titillate the customer, keeping him coming back for more, keep him here until all hours buying drinks. The pay is good, maybe not what you were getting in construction but the tips are simply amazing. Drunk customers will throw handfuls of bills on the stage and its all yours to keep! You will have earned it. So tell me about yourself, I know, I tend to run on at times, forgive me, my dear."

"Oh, quite all right, Mr. Denning..."

"Steven, please..."

"Steven, well, Steven, I grew up in the mid west, my dad was in construction and I took to the work. But my parents had me in dance classes at an early age, ballet, modern dance, I danced all way through high school."

"And from what I heard from the little scene down at the rail road tracks, you can fight also."

"Oh, that, well, yeah I also had Taekwondo lessons, black belt."

"Oh my, maybe she outta be a bouncer, hey, Jim?" Denning smiled at Jim. "Well, my dear, why don't you go get ready and we'll see how you do. Rebecca will show you to the dressing room, Rebecca!" Rebecca looked over, "Please show this young lady to the dressing room. Go ahead and get ready and then we'll see you out here in a few, okay?"

Suzie nodded, looking briefly at Jim.

"Don't worry, dear, you're completely safe in here," Denning said with a reassuring smile. "Now run along."

Suzie left the room, following Rebecca down a hallway.

"Now we'll see how she does. How long have you known her, Jimbo?"

"I just met her when I got back, she hangs out at the local bar. Worked in the city as you know."

"Heard you made a little escapade to the city the other day, had a little rumble in an alley from the word on the street."

"You know about that?"

"Sure do, made a good account of yourself. I have eyes in Chinatown but more about that later. So, Jim, what do you think of my setup? Pretty good, eh? What do you think?"

Jim looked around the large room, at the bar, at the paintings of nude women on the walls, he noticed one was of an Asian woman.

"I am really impressed," Jim said, "I think I'll like working here for a while, you understand I'll be going to school..."

"I completely encourage it, my boy, completely, you're a young man who's going places and I am glad I can help for awhile. Oh, here she comes now."

Jim looked up, Suzie was standing on the stage by the pole. She was dressed in a see through with a black string bikini underneath, her hair was wild and she had on a little extra makeup, and longer eyelashes. Denning signaled the man in the disco booth and the music began, modern, fast, a heavy beat, the sound filled the room and the colored lights began to flash, a dazzling disco ball hanging from the ceiling began to spin, it's hundreds of tiny, square mirrors sending flakes of the colored lights spinning around the room. Denning signaled and Rebecca brought two more beers and set them down.

Suzie began to dance about the stage then she spun expertly around the pole, Jim saw that she had been practicing her moves, he could tell she had been an excellent dancer, he noticed the perfectly developed muscles on her thighs and calves, smooth but firmly muscular.

She shed the see through, it slid off down her arm and she tossed it to the side, now only in her string bikini she danced and as she did she looked seductively right at Jim. She danced out to the edge of the stage now, the floor lights at the edge illuminating her beautiful thighs, her skin a silken, velvet sheen, she wore spiked high heels. She danced back to the pole, spun around it, holding on with one hand while the other went to the back to unfasten her top, the top was now held only by her hand as she again danced to the edge of the stage, looking right at Jim, confidence in her eyes, she took the top off, her beautiful breasts swinging free as she tossed the garment to Jim, who caught it.

"Bravo!" Denning shouted as he raised his beer in her direction then grinned at Jim.

Suzie now danced back to the pole, spinning, moving down to roll on the floor, then she did a flip and was on her feet dancing across the stage. She pulled at the bottom garment while she turned her back on the audience, her body in constant motion she eased out of the bottoms, holding them between her fingers, spinning them as she moved about, her back still turned. She turned to face them now, she was an astounding sight, dancing there completely naked. She had shaved herself and she glistened with her perspiration.

"Oh Baby! That I like!" Denning shouted as he clapped his hands. Suzie was looking right at Jim now, her eyes penetrating his soul. He was intensely aroused, he couldn't fight it, he was aroused almost beyond control as she moved out to the runway then kneeled down, hitting the main floor and dancing right over to Jim, putting her arms around him, she placed herself in his lap, just hovered there, Jim could feel her moving above him, driving him mad with desire as she moved on him, barely touching his lap, then she turned, her face near his, her breasts almost brushing his face, almost worshipping him, she looked at Denning and danced over behind him, touching the tops of his shoulders, then she was away and back on the stage, she grabbed the pole, hugged it between her breasts, slid down and back up, Jim's mind was filled with fantasies he had no control over. He drained his beer in one gulp, feeling it sting the back of his throat, feeling the burn in back of his eyeballs, feeling the soothing effects take over his brain.

The music stopped and Suzie collapsed on the stage, lying flat on the floor, looking right at Jim, her arms outstretched towards him, a sleepy, sexy look in her eyes, her lips inviting him.

She rose from the floor, came to the edge of the stage and stood there, naked, waiting, looking at Denning.

"Do I get the job?" she asked.

"Way to go!" Denning exploded in applause as he grinned at her. "Baby, you never have to worry about ever working construction again! Damn right you get the job!"

***

Jim was headed for his car. He saw Suzie's car next to his, she was standing there, dressed in her jeans and tube top, her makeup washed off. She came across the lot and met him half way, throwing her arms around him, looking in his eyes then she leaned her head against his chest and he held her tightly. They parted, she looked up at him.

"I thought I was going to die in there, Jim, I thought I was going to die..."

She came into his arms again.

"I don't know if I can do this..."

"Then you should quit, right now, Suzie, you should quit."

"No...no I can do this..."

"I must say you certainly 'prepared' for the job..."

"The shave?" now she smiled, "I thought it would be a nice touch, lock me into the job..."

"Well it certainly worked, Denning hired you on the spot."

"And you?"

"Chief bouncer. We both start Thursday night."

"I know. Jim, let's go have a beer at the bar, I want to talk to you."

"See you there."

***

They were seated in the local bar at a table in the rear, both had longed necked beers. The place was still fairly packed this time in the late afternoon, everyone stopping off for a quick one on the way home from work, many had remained. Joe and Will were seated at a nearby table. Sam was busy behind the bar. Suzie raised her bottle, Jim raised his, the bottles touched, then they took long sips.

"I guess, congratulations, we're hired," Suzie said and she downed her beer in one gulp and rose to get another one, she brought three back, setting one in front of Jim. She drank one of the others quickly as well.

"Better be careful with that," Jim said.

"I needed it after this afternoon. Oh Jim, I almost died in there, the way he was leering at me and it's only the beginning, there will be a sea of men leering at me every night, Starting Thursday."

She reached across the table and Jim took her hand.

"You were looking at me, Jim, and I liked it, I danced only for you, Jim, only for you. I can get through this if I can keep you in mind. Oh Jim, I really only wanted you to see me naked. I'm not like that..."

"Suzie," Jim held her hand firmly, "I know you're not. And I am thinking of going right to Martin..."

"You'll do nothing of the sort, Jim! I'm needed on this job, we're getting close to a major bust and I have a job to do! And speaking of that, Jim Saunders!"

"I know, Chinatown."

"Chinatown! I was ready to crush your balls earlier today, I was so mad at you, Jim! I told you to stay out of there, and now there are three dead men."

"It was self defense and you know it!" Jim said, keeping his voice low, leaning towards her.

"Those men..."

"Were members of The Dragons, a ruthless gang! And I could bet those three dead men have records..."

"...yes, a mile long, assault, extortion, drugs, suspects in several ruthless murders. I'd bet on it!"

"I prevented a kidnapping! The waitress."

"We talked to her, she tried to hide behind the language barrier but we, of course, have interpreters. Still, she was too afraid to talk."

"And Jonnie Lee?"

"Still playing the part of the hysterical shop owner wronged by the gangs. I know he was there with you during the shooting, I just know that and it's your duty to report..."

"Report what?"

"Jim!"

"I saw a hostage situation and I acted to protect the victim, plus I saw the damage they had done to the store."

"Gang shootout. That's the way it's reported by the local police, so it will stand for now. But right now representatives of the Chinatown Coalition are up in arms, the mayor's office is being plagued with complaints of slow police response, claiming that the local police really don't care about what happens down in Chinatown."

"It looked to me like there was a pretty quick response. What do they want? It didn't take long for the police to arrive after the vandalism and the hostage situation began."

"And the weapon you used. What happened to it? You had not even brought yours with you. How did you obtain a firearm? And also, there were two weapons used, one a 9mm and the other, a .45."

"Look, I'll level with you, yes, I was talking to Jonnie Lee earlier. When the attack came down we were in his office above the restaurant and we were able to escape through an underground tunnel right under the street which lead to the gift shop. And Jonnie Lee supplied us with the firearms but without them that young girl would have been kidnapped and killed! We were defending ourselves. I have an in with Jonnie Lee, he wants a deal with Denning, in opposition with The Cobra. It's a good lead and I am developing it! You go in and screw this up..."

"I'm not going in, Jim, all I am saying is it is going to play hell trying to explain all this to the local authorities. We'll claim jurisdiction over the matter, right now, Martin is probably telling them it's a deep cover op and for them to lay off. Locals hate it when we become involved. They will demand to know why."

"Then it's up to Martin to come up with a good explanation."

Suzie thought about it, took a sip of her beer and set it down.

"Jim, if you really think it's worth pursuing then go ahead. But be careful, Jim..."

"We're not in the business of being careful and you know it. I'm more concerned about how you're going to handle that 'job' down at the nightclub."

"I did okay today."

"More than 'okay' I'd say. You had Denning going, really going..."

"And you? I think you were 'reacting' to my performance..."

"It was impressive. You were so scared going in..."

"I was able to just step outside myself on that stage, Jim, before I went out there, knowing I was going to be naked in front of you and Denning, I was terrified but once I got out there I seemed to come alive. I remember now what it was like when I used to dance in school, how I took to the stage, I would always be terrified but then when the music started, then I was in a different world. But of course, I was never totally naked like I was today."

Suzie reached across the table and took Jim's hand.

"I'm glad you saw me naked, Jim, I'm glad. I wish it could be..."

She took her hand away, now Jim reached over to her and took her hand in his, holding it and looking into her eyes.

"Suzie, you're a beautiful young woman, if I had not..."

"No, Jim, you have a good thing going with that young girl, I know that. It's just that I..."

She pulled away again. Jim finished his beer and they rose from their tables. Joe and Will looked across the room at them and Jim and Suzie nodded to them as they left. They walked to Jim's car and Jim was about to get in. Suzie leaned against him, pressing herself against him, her arms around his waist.

"I'm after you, Jim, I can't help it, I'm after you and I won't give up."

She stirred against him and he reacted. She smiled a knowing smile.

"Suzie..."

"See you later, Jim," she said and she brushed her lips against his face. "And be careful, Jim, you're playing a dangerous game in Chinatown."

"That's what I was hired for."

***

Later that evening Jim was seated on his bed, going over the files on Denning and the other crime organizations in Chinatown. He had had dinner earlier, steak and baked potato, at the restaurant across the street and now he sat with a cup of coffee he had bought from Starbucks. This was the second cup he had gone across the street to get. He set the material down on the bed and grabbed his cell phone. He dialed Jiang Li's number.

"Hello."

"Hello yourself."

"Oh Jim! Oh it's good to hear from you, oh Jim I have been under a mountain of books tonight! I am so tired. Oh Jim, today was wonderful!"

She laughed.

"Remember that teacher?" and she laughed again.

"I hope I didn't get you kicked out of school because of today."

"No, no problem. She was too embarrassed to report it, I am sure. And I only have a week, next week is finals week and it will be nothing but endless tests. Oh Jim, I wish I could see you but I'll be so busy. Yet I want to see you..."

"I want to see you too. Jiang Li. I got that nightclub job."

"It's a nude dance place, isn't it?"

"Yes."

"I should be angry, I suppose..."

"Jiang Li, it's the best paying job I can find, it was offered to me, it's just a job and we need money right now. I'm going to be going over to the local community college to check out the classes. We need..."

"I know, Jim, I know. I don't have to like it but I know you need a good job for now. It's just the idea of you looking at other women naked."

"I promise you will be the only one benefiting from it, Jiang Li, I can promise you that."

"Jim, do you have a camera on your phone?"

Jim checked.

"Yeah, I think so, yeah, I do."

"Oh wonderful, Jim, turn it on."

He pressed the appropriate button and he could see Jiang Li on the screen. She was in a bedroom, there were some posters on the wall behind her, a makeup table and chair. She seemed to be reclining on the bed, he could see the piles of books and papers.

"Wow! I can see you!" he said. She looked absolutely beautiful in her sweatsuit, her hair done up loosely on her head, strings of her hair falling around her shoulders.

"You're the most beautiful sight I have ever seen," he said and meant it. He wanted to jump right into the picture.

"Just wait a moment," she answered and the screen went blank. He could hear sounds in the background.

"I'm going to set the camera phone on the table," she said, "Just a moment...okay, now..."

The picture came back on. Jim was astounded. There she was, standing there in her room in front of the bed, completely naked, her hair undone and streaming around her shoulders, she was absolutely gorgeous.

She moved to the bed and posed seductively for the camera, lifting her hips suggestively as she looked right into the camera.

"Oh Jesus!" Jim exclaimed and it brought a smile to Jiang Li.

She rolled about the bed as Jim became incredibly aroused.

"You're driving me mad, Jiang Li, you are driving me completely mad!!! I want to jump through the camera right now!"

"I wish you could," she answered then she picked up the phone.

"Let me see you!" she said and Jim held the camera away from himself, looking right into it.

"You gorgeous man!" she breathed then she set the camera away from her so he could see her again as she turned her back so he could get a rear view of her. Her perfect buttocks glistened on the screen, her long, black hair trailing down her silken back, she looked over her shoulder and smiled at him.

"Take care, my love," she said with a smile. "I have to get back to my studies now."

She winked at him, did a twitch of her hips and then the screen went blank.

Jim had no more thoughts of Suzie for the rest of the night.

CHAPTER FOURTEEN

Jim awoke at eight. He shot upright, for a moment not knowing where he was. He had been having dreams, wonderful dreams of Jiang Li and every now and then Suzie would intrude as well, images of her dancing at the club, dancing over him, naked, beautiful. Then the image of Jiang Li would intrude, the image of her in the classroom, on the cell phone.

Jim reached for his cell phone and opened it up. He brought up the saved picture of Jiang Li posing for him, he had saved several poses. He wanted her right at that moment.

Jim expended his energy lifting his dumbbells, working out heavy and hard, breaking a sweat, exhausting himself. Then he headed into the shower. He headed for Stan's for breakfast. He saw Denning's Cadillac parked in the lot. He headed inside, Denning had a booth by the window and he waved Jim over. Jim slid into the seat opposite him and the waitress immediately brought coffee to him. Jim noticed Stan busy behind the counter cooking on the grill. The man had endless energy, Jim thought.

"Morning," Denning said.

Jim nodded and sipped his coffee.

"What'll it be?" Denning asked, "I'm buying."

"I don't..."

"Nonsense. You're my head bouncer. Breakfast is on me, so what'll it be."

"Steak and eggs, steak rare," Jim said.

"Good choice, gotta keep strong for the work you'll start doing Thursday night. It can get pretty rough in there. But then you look like you stay in good shape. Been hittin' the weights from the look of it. I've heard you're pretty good with your fists when you have to be. Like in Chinatown last week."

Jim had to choose. Should he reveal Jonnie Lee's desire for a meeting? This was an opening.

"Okay," Jim said. "I'm going to say this."

"What?" Denning asked, his eyes now piercing, intent on Jim.

"Jonnie Lee wants to talk a deal."

"What are you talking about, I don't know any..."

"You do. We might as well get to the point. Jonnie Lee says he can outbid The Cobra. He wants a chance to cut a deal. He feels that fight in the alley in Chinatown was me trying to make a statement. And he mentioned you, not by name, but it was you, when I went to his restaurant."

Denning's eyes were burning a hole in Jim but Jim held his gaze.

"Okay, you want to talk 'deals.' I'll say this, I know the story of the family of your pretty little Oriental gal. She is owned by The Cobra, her family owes them. You are on a thin line with her, son. I know all about The Cobra. So you're trying to get in on deals and using The Tiger Clan to ride on."

Jim was silent, looking at Denning. He had blown it. It was all over, he had opened his big mouth at the wrong time and it had cost him. He saw the bouncer job dissolving right before his eyes.

"Okay, I like it. you're smarter than I thought and I thought you were pretty smart. You understand a lot of things already. Those were Cobra who jumped you in retaliation for the mishap in the steakhouse on Market Street. Oh yeah, Jim, I also know about that. I think it went like this. Here you were, down and out, discharged from the Army, a trained warrior set out in the cold. You met the girl, the Cobra tried to jump you, you took them out, it's quite the story in Chinatown lately, foreign devil walks tall in Chinatown. So you probably went to the restaurant and Jonnie Lee sees you and figures you were there to purposely make a 'statement' to get in. He takes a chance and tries to get involved, thinking automatically that you're with me because of the upcoming negotiations with The Cobra. He wants in so he tells you to deal. Now you're a smart kid, see the chance to get in on something on the ground floor.

"I like it, you have initiative. You will do well working for me. That's the picture, right?"

"Pretty much."

"I knew it. Not many things get past this old bird."

The breakfast was set before them, Jim's steak and ham, eggs and pancakes for Denning.

"That Oriental gal you're seeing. Be careful. She belongs to Tommy Xiang, he's gunning for you. If you don't watch out you could end up gettin' your pecker cut off, they do that, you know, cut a man's pecker off, especially if he's trying to get one of their women. You won't have much of a life anymore without a pecker, you know. Is that little gal worth it? think about it. Now Suzie! Wow, that's a babe, beautiful, don't you think?"

Denning let out a hearty laugh.

"What a performance she put on. I've been after her to leave that construction job in the city to work for me, she'll turn top dollar and I'll pay her top dollar, not to mention the tips she'll make. She's one fantastic broad and she's sweet on you, you know. I saw the way she came on to you during her performance and saw her with you in the parking lot. Think about it."

"I have," Jim said.

"Okay, so you going into the city today?"

"Yeah," Jim said as he took the last bite of steak.

"So when you see Jonnie Lee tell him maybe I'll deal, we'll have to set something up. Just tell him I'll listen. It'll be good the keep The Cobra on their toes, a bidding war will be something that'll work very well in my favor. Stick around, kid, I'll teach you the ropes. My kid..."

"He's friends with my younger brother."

"Yeah, I know, my kid, he stands to inherit this one day, my whole operation but he's not really interested. Looking at college but that's good too. Meantime, I need to train someone good to run things for a few years. I like what I see in you, kid, you're smart, have good survival instincts, except when it comes to that Oriental broad. But that's your business, I can only advise."

Jim finished up his breakfast and rose from his seat, reaching for his wallet.

"I got it," Denning said as he also rose.

They shook hands and walked together out into the parking lot. Denning watched as Jim got into his car and drove away.

***

Jim bent into the stretch on the mat, he had his gi bottoms on. He had waited an hour, parking again at Union Square and walking around Market Street and then making his way to the Federal Building. He had not gone up to see Suzie in her office but had gone immediately to the training room. He had already worked out with his dumbbells that morning. He had a flash of Jiang Li's picture on his phone. He blocked it from his mind.

"All ready, I see," it was Gene's voice.

Jim looked up. Gene was also dressed in gi bottoms and held two pairs of lightweight boxing gloves in his hands. He tossed a pair down in front of Jim. Jim put them on as he stood and they bowed to each other, never taking their eyes off each other.

"You know the first rule, I see," Gene said. "Never take your eyes off you opponent, even when you bow."

Suddenly Gene stepped in and instantly landed a punch to Jim's jaw, knocking him back, staggering him, his head reeled.

"You show the respect, but you do not trust!" Gene said as he delivered a sidekick which Jim blocked as he moved to the side, Gene flashing past him but Jim whirled to deliver a punch to the side of Gene's head, wobbling him as he danced away, shaking it off.

"You're learnin'!" he said.

Gene executed a quick dive and roll tying Jim's feet up in his and leveraging him to the mat. He bore down hard and Jim could feel the pressure in his knees. Then Gene released him and rolled free. Both were instantly on their feet.

"You're playing a dangerous game over in Chinatown!" Gene said.

"That's my job, that's what I was hired for."

Gene came at Jim with a flurry of kicks but Jim moved to the side and attacked, they worked their way around the training area, trading punches and kicks, blocking, evading, attacking again then fading back.

"I'm doing my best to prepare you!" Gene said. "That little row in the alley over there last week, well..." Jim attacked and Gene defended, "...you did pretty good, they fear you and that's leverage! Use it!" another attack, then Gene came at Jim. Jim caught him with a straight jab to the chest and Gene was down, struggling for breath, "Pretty good, man, pretty good, you're coming along!"

Jim stepped over to Gene and offered his hand to help him up. Gene reached for it and then in a sudden instant Jim found himself on the floor, flat on his back, the impact knocking the wind out of him. Gene was standing over him, he was not out of breath.

"I suckered you good with that one! You have a lot to learn yet!"

Now Gene offered his hand but Jim did a back roll and came up on his feet. Both of them faced each other and bowed. Gene smiled.

"You're gettin' the idea now, you're gettin' it."

The workout was over.

***

Showered and feeling a bit sore Jim entered Suzie's office. She was seated at her desk going over a file. She looked up and smiled. She was wearing her usual gray business suit, the skirt a little bit too short, her hair done back in a severe bun, very little makeup, no resemblance to the brazen vixen on the stage at the club yesterday. A vision of her shaved charms came to mind and Jim blocked it. As if reading his mind Suzie smiled a coy smile. She rose and came to him, putting her arms around his waist and pressing herself against him.

"It's good to see you," she said.

Jim said nothing as she looked up into his eyes.

"I meant it yesterday, Jim, I am out to land you, I see what I want and I will get it!"

Jim shuffled uncomfortably.

"I'm sorry, Jim, it's just that I have trouble controlling myself around you. I wish I could have met you before you ever laid eyes on that Asian princess you are so enthralled with."

"Suzie, er, Agent Bradley..."

"Suzie will do fine," she smiled at his nervousness.

"I have to talk to you about something, about yesterday in Chinatown..."

"What about it, we already discussed it yesterday. You will work the Tiger Clan angle..."

"No, not that. Yes, I already told Denning I want to work up a connection with the Tiger Clan, so I can get in better with his organization and he went for it, admired my ambition. No, I want to talk about something that's bothering me, Suzie."

"What's that, Jim, have a seat..."

Jim was seated and Suzie took her seat behind the desk.

"You blew your cover yesterday, Suzie! You appeared on the crime scene, Tommy saw you."

"Jim, I was wearing a SWAT type assault suit, my hair was done back in this bun you see, I was wearing very dark glasses and a black cap with DEA lettered on it. There's no way Jonnie Lee will make the connection if he even ever sees me again."

"He is not stupid and he will definitely will be seeing you again. What if he comes to the club to talk a deal and you're..."

"I don't think, when he sees me on that stage, he will have any idea I'm the same woman agent on that street in Chinatown. He was too busy getting into his hysterical victim act."

"I think you underestimate him."

"Well, Jim, if you hadn't gone off on your own and caused all that trouble we wouldn't be talking about this would we?" Suzie's eyes took on the hard official look.

"And if I had not gone there then I would have missed out on a possible connection which will advance our case!"

"True, Jim, look Jim, I prepared myself, if you know what I mean, for a very good reason you know, it will highly distract anyone and they will in no way even equate me with that severe, Federal Agent with the tight bun on her head wearing sunglasses. But you're right, Jim, from now on I have to be more careful. And now, Jim, we have to take a little ride to City Hall."

Suzie rose from her chair and led the way out of her office. They went down the hallway to another room and went inside. There was a counter, a uniformed clerk was behind it, a young woman. Suzie looked at Jim then at the woman.

"We need travel clothes," she said.

"What?" Jim asked.

The woman smiled and motioned for them to follow her. Suzie went into a room on the far side and Jim into another after being given a package. He found himself in a small dressing room and he opened the brown wrapper to find a black baseball cap with the letters DEA on it. Also, a dark blue, windbreaker with DEA on the back in large yellow capital letters and a pair of dark sunglasses. He put these on and emerged from the room. He went to the counter. The young woman looked at him and smiled.

"She'll be right here," she said. "Oh, and take out your badge and place it on your belt in view."

Jim took out the badge, it had a clip and he clipped it on his belt.

"Where's your firearm?" the woman asked.

"I don't carry it."

The woman rolled her eyes.

"Oh she's gonna be pissed now," she said.

A moment later Suzie emerged, dressed in the same black swat style suit, black jacket and pants with DEA stenciled on her jacket and cap, her badge on her belt along side her firearm, a 9mm. She had her sunglasses mounted on her cap.

"Jim, where's your piece?" she asked.

"I didn't bring it, I don't carry it, you saw that this morning."

"You should travel armed, Jim, it's required."

Jim shrugged his shoulders.

"Come on, let's go," she said and she led the way out of the room and down the hall. Jim looked back at the young lady behind the counter and she just shrugged.

They went to the elevator and it began to descend.

"It's highly irregular for you not to be armed, Jim, from now on carry it!" Suzie said as she turned to him.

"It's not always a good idea. Being undercover, you don't go around with your badge and a gun showing. I don't really feel comfortable traveling armed."

"For God's sake, Jim, you traveled armed for a year in Iraq."

"That was a different story. I was in a war."

"Oh believe me, Jim, we're in a war here, believe me, we *are* in a war."

The elevator descended to the basement and Suzie led Jim to the equipment room where a .45 and holster were charged out to him. He put it on his belt after checking the mechanism and slamming in a clip.

"Now are you happy?" he asked Suzie.

"It'll be returned after we get back."

Suzie led the way through a door and they emerged into an underground parking lot. Gene was standing beside a shiny black Lincoln with blacked out windows all around. Gene was also dressed in a SWAT type suit with cap and had badge and gun on his belt. He opened the passenger door and Jim and Suzie stepped in and seated themselves. Gene got in the front passenger seat, another agent was at the wheel. Suzie donned her sunglasses, the other agent and Gene were already wearing theirs. Jim noticed a shotgun mounted on the front panel between the driver and passenger.

"Let's go," Suzie said. "City Hall."

The car moved along through the parking lot, heading up then out the entrance onto the street. Suzie turned to Jim.

"There's going to be a lot of media where we're going so keep your sunglasses on and your cap down and try to avoid any direct contact with any TV cameras. Say nothing to them, they will be trying to ask questions. If you say anything at all, just say, 'No comment.' Be polite and we'll get through them as fast as we can." She nodded to the men in the front seat. "Gene and Hank, that's Hank driving, will run interference for us until we get to the Chief's office.

There will be no media inside."

She looked straight ahead as they drove through the city. They arrived at City Hall, passing by the front steps to the large building with marble and pillared facade. There was a media circus on the front steps and several TV news vans parked in front, there was an array of microphones and cameras of all sizes. The car drove on by and circled around to the rear.

In the car, Suzie briefly took Jim's hand and leaned over to him.

"I love you," she whispered in his ear then she took her hand away.

They were at the rear of the building. Agents were waiting for them along with uniformed members of the San Francisco Police Department.

"Okay, watch what you say," Suzie warned, "We're on their turf now! Let's go!"

They quickly emerged from the car, Hank and Gene in front, they were immediately surrounded by the cops and other Federal Agents and were hurrying towards a rear entrance.

"There's someone! It's the investigators!" someone yelled and Jim looked around.

A sea of media people, cameras and mikes in hand were pouring around the side of the building and descending upon them in a thundering hoard!

"Keep moving, head down!" Suzie commanded as they pushed through the mob.

"When is the violence in Chinatown going to stop!" yelled one of the reporters, a blond woman Jim had seen many times on Channel 7 News. She looked older in person than she had appeared to be on screen.

"What are you going to do about all these firearms on the street, all the handguns!" demanded another reporter as Jim's group kept moving. A mike was right in front of his face.

"No comment," Jim said as they rushed on by.

They made the entrance and barged through. They rushed down a hallway and made it to a bank of elevators. More media were there waiting. They literally attacked them, cameras and mikes ready, a barrage of questions while Jim's group waited for the elevator to arrive.

"No comment at this time!" Suzie said.

"No comment!" Gene said.

"No comment!" Jim said, keeping his head down.

All the voices seemed to blend into one cacophony of endless noise. Suzie huddled against Jim and took his hand. Finally the doors slid open and they darted into the elevator. The media was right behind them trying to get in as the police and Federal Agents pushed them back. A mike almost got caught in the door as it closed. They were packed tight in the elevator, Suzie right against Jim, still holding his hand.

"What a zoo out there!" Suzie breathed and looked up at Jim, raising her sunglasses to look at him.

"Wow!" she said.

"What?" Jim answered.

She leaned up and whispered in his ear.

"I rather like to see you dressed like that, it's a real turn on!"

The elevator stopped. They exited quickly. They were in a hallway, more media ambushed them. More cameras, more mikes shoved in front of them as Gene and Hank led the way, pushing through the crowd.

"What about the Chinatown Phantom?" one reporter shouted as they passed. "Do they know who he is yet? Has he been apprehended?"

"Maybe the Chinatown Phantom is what's needed to bring justice!" an Asian reporter yelled as they passed.

They went through a large doorway, the police forcing it closed behind them. They were in an outer office. Several high ranking police were there in dress uniforms, captains and assistant Chiefs with symbols of their rank on their shoulder epaulets.

"Go right on in, the Chief and the Mayor are waiting," one of the assistant chiefs said and Suzie and Jim were shown on through a double door which closed behind them, Hank and Gene waiting outside with the others.

They found themselves in a plush, carpeted office with a massive picture window with a spectacular view of the city, facing north. Jim could see the tops of the towers to the Golden Gate Bridge, and the Transamerica Building. Standing behind his desk was San Francisco's Chief of Police, Dan Hayden, in full dress uniform, an imposing figure with short, steel gray hair. With him, dressed in a dark gray, three piece suit was San Francisco's Mayor, Don Grey. With them, also in a three piece suit was Martin Thomas who quickly made introductions. Jim shook hands all around as did Suzie.

"Nice to see you again, Agent Bradley," Chief Hayden said with a smile.

"Nice to see you also, Dan," Suzie said but not with a smile.

"So," Mayor Grey said, "we finally get to meet the Chinatown Phantom."

He was looking right at Jim.

"The what?" Jim asked.

"We've heard about your exploits in the past few days, Agent Saunders," Chief Hayden said. "From the fight in the back alley to the shootout in the middle of Chinatown, you're making quite a name for yourself."

"The Chinatown Phantom, I heard a reporter yelling that," Jim said.

"That's the word on the street, some mysterious stranger taking out several members of The Cobra the other day in a back alley, word's out big time, you are almost a God down there. And the shootout."

"I find it hard to believe..."

"Oh believe it, young man," the Mayor said. "The media is all over this now! We've got quite a situation on our hands."

"I still don't see how..."

"It's real, it's in our face and we have to deal with it!" Mayor Grey said and now he was dead serious, the gloves came off. "It's a media frenzy out there and we need to give them something right now!"

"Gentlemen, gentleman," Martin was now speaking in his smooth voice.

"Gentlemen hell!!!" Chief Hayden said firmly and loud. "What's the problem, Martin, can't you reign in your people? Do you just allow them to run amuck alley fighting and shooting down people on our city streets?"

"Gentlemen..." Martin was trying to say.

"That's not an answer, Martin!" Mayor Grey said, no "political" smiles now.

"My agent acted in self defense and stopped a hostage situation cold. The men who were shot had criminal records a mile long and were terrorizing a local businesses! My agent acted appropriately!"

"Standing right there in the middle of the street acting like Wyatt

Earp gunning down people is acting 'appropriately?'" Mayor Grey said.

"And just what would you have me do? Let the assholes just kidnap the young girl?" Jim's voice thundered and everyone looked at him, almost in shock.

"Listen, young man!" the chief started to say.

"Listen my ass!" Jim said.

"Agent Saunders..." Martin started to say.

"Bullshit!" Jim shouted. "And you all know this is bullshit!!! Pure and simple!!!"

"I heard there was someone else with you! Who was it? I demand to know!" Chief Hayden said, now moving right in front of Jim, eye to eye. Jim did not back down.

"I know there was someone else, there were slugs from a .45 and a 9mm found in the shooting victims!"

"Victims! You call those scumbags victims? You're an asshole!"

"Listen you young punk, just watch who you call an asshole!"

"Asshole!" Jim said again, standing firm, right in the Chief's face, their eyes burning into each other's.

"Jim..." Suzie said as she placed a hand on Jim's shoulder.

"Anytime, anywhere, asshole!" Jim offered the challenge.

"Jim..." Suzie tried again.

"Don't think you can fuck with me!" the Chief said.

"I already am!"

"Gentlemen, gentlemen..." it was the mayor now.

"Listen to the mayor..." Suzie said.

"Mayor my ass!" Jim said in a firm, even voice.

"Hey, you can't..." the mayor stammered.

"I just did, asshole, I just did! And let me tell you something..."

"You don't tell me anything!" the mayor said, his face reddening by the second.

"Jim! Stop this at once!" Suzie demanded.

Martin Thomas just stood to the side, watching, a small smile on his face.

"Stop my ass!" Jim was on a roll now. "What's all this concern all of a sudden about Chinatown? You don't give a rat's ass what goes on down in Chinatown, you know it and I know it! You are full of bullshit! All of you are full of bullshit! Bullshit! You're concerned about the shooting because it makes both of you look bad, exposing the fact that you have done nothing to stem the crime in Chinatown! It's looks bad on election day so now, all of a sudden, you give a shit! You give a shit because the media has suddenly jumped all over this like stink on shit! That's why you 'give a shit' but in reality you don't give a shit! And the second it blows over it will be back to business as usual! Well it's going to be different this time because I will be there to show them at least someone gives a shit! This is now a Federal investigation so you just keep the fuck out!"

Jim turned away, Suzie held his arm. His fists were balled up at his sides, he was ready to explode! Suzie began rubbing his back.

"Jim..." she whispered.

Jim saw his career as a Federal Agent dissolving, going down the drain of life, gone, extinct! He looked out the window, the room was silent.

"Gentlemen," Martin Thomas spoke up.

Everyone turned to look at him.

"What my agent has said is true. This is now a Federal issue and we claim jurisdiction over the Chinatown matter. This meeting is concluded, good day. Jim, Agent Bradley, let's get out of here!"

Martin led the way out the door, Jim and Suzie following. They made their way down the hall with their escort forging a pathway through the media circus. Their questions were just a din of noise in Jim's ears as he kept his head down, Suzie holding his hand as they headed into the elevator.

The elevator doors slid closed.

Martin turned to Jim.

He broke into an uproarious laugh, slapping Jim on the back!

"Good show! That's my man! Good show! I think the looks on the mayor's and the Chief's faces is the best thing I have seen in my entire life! Whadda guy we have here, right, Suzie?"

"I just have one thing to add," Suzie said as she looked up at Jim. "This!"

She leapt up, throwing her arms around his neck and before he could do anything she planted her lips on his, giving him a long, passionate, endearing kiss which completely blew his mind!

***

They were now in Martin Thomas's office. He was seated behind his desk, Jim and Suzie were present, still dressed in their combat gear. Martin was facing away from them, gazing out is window, thinking.

Suzie looked over at Jim nervously.

Martin turned and faced them at last, looking directly at Jim.

"I guess now I have to take my 'official' stance. I should be reprimanding you about your behavior in the Mayor's office. It was uncalled for, very unprofessional, Suzie!" he shot a look that could kill at her, "you are supposed to be coaching this man here on proper procedure! So why did this happen."

"It's not her fault!" Jim said. "I said what I knew was the truth and you know it's the truth, Martin!"

Martin shot him a look.

"This isn't the Mayor's office, my young, overanxious friend!" he said.

"Truth is truth and it's about time someone spoke it!" Jim answered.

"If you want to go far in this organization you're going to have to learn to be discrete, Jim."

"I guess I am not going to be going very far then," Jim answered.

A look of steel came into Martin's eyes.

"You don't want to go pissing me off at this stage in the game!"

Jim was seething. Suzie placed her hand on his thigh, her eyes imploring him to tone it down. Jim took a deep breath.

"I'm here to do a job!" Jim said, "I have made good headway in Chinatown and am working on a connection right now. And as far as my actions yesterday..."

"Jim, you did the right thing! And we can cover for you, you are a Federal officer doing his duty to defend the public and you did it exceedingly well. I have managed to claim jurisdiction over this case now, using the angle of human trafficking, a Federal offence, plus interstate transportation of human cargo and drugs, another Federal offence. The local authorities will still try to get involved. We will claim we are investigating and that we will share our findings at a future time once our investigation is concluded. I guess, Jim, we won't be needing to have any future meetings between you and the Mayor and Chief of Police. At least I hope not."

Then Martin laughed again, a booming laugh, a thundering laugh.

"Oh the look on their faces! That was too good, just too good! It was worth it!"

Suzie took Jim's hand and she was laughing now, almost hysterically, both she and Martin.

"Jim, you are too much!" she said.

Then she shook her head.

"Your boss is really going to be upset about this, you know," Martin said to Suzie. "But don't worry, I'll calm her down. Also," and he looked directly at them, "I don't want either of you reporting here again, not you, Suzie, not to your office here, nor you, Jim. You've gone deep cover now and it wouldn't do to have you recognized. It would cost the mission and it would cost you your lives. Suzie, from now on, you live in that town, you work at that club and you contact me by phone only, understand?"

Suzie nodded.

"And you, Jim, as far as your training with Gene."

"Yeah, I guess it will have to stop."

"No no, Jim, you see, Gene has just opened a private training dojo in your town, he is a sixth degree black belt, you know. That's his cover for now, karate school owner. He will even have clientele as well as being available for your private training sessions. Any questions, well you tell Denning, your employer, that you study martial arts to keep you sharp for your job. He'll buy that.

"And also, Jim, it will be important for you to be in Chinatown now to make your connections. You now have the rep as 'The Chinatown Phantom' so you have the respect when you walk among them. That's good leverage. That back alley confrontation couldn't have come at a better time. It was almost as if it was divinely created for us. The perfect setup for you. Now, Jim, you are going to have to rely on your wits and your instinct, both of you are pretty much on your own from now on.

"Suzie, Agent ."

"Yes, Martin."

"Are you sure you can deal with this, I mean, being a nude dancer is a lot to ask of an agent and..."

"No, Martin, I can handle this..."

"You're sure? Because if you in any way feel like you..."

"No. I can do this, I can."

"Jim, you keep a close eye on her. I want you to let me know if you think she can't..."

"Oh what's he going to be, my babysitter?" anger flared in Suzie's eyes now.

"Suzie! I don't like asking you to do this kind of assignment and I will have Jim watching your back and I expect you to watch his. I mean it! Take care of each other. If I think this is going to get to you, that you can't take it, I am going to pull you off right fast! Because if you break than the investigation is blown. And besides that, Agent , Suzie, I really care about what happens to my agents, and to you. Understand?"

Jim placed a reassuring hand on her shoulder and she calmed down.   She nodded.

"Don't worry, Martin, I can do this job," Suzie said.

"Okay then, you can go, Agent , and Jim, I want a word with you alone for a moment."

Suzie looked at Jim then she rose from her seat.

"I'll be right out," Jim said.

"I'll wait in the outer office," she left the room.

"Now Jim," Martin said. "About Agent Bradley ."

"I figured that's why you kept me here."

"Exactly, Jim. I want you to answer me this, what is your take on her regarding this job?"

"I'll be frank with you, Martin."

"That's what I want, you honest opinion."

"I don't think she belongs there in that club. It's killing her somehow, I can see it. I'm afraid it's going to break her, I can see it in her eyes, Martin."

"Agent Bradley is a pretty tough cookie, Jim, she's one of my best."

"Has she ever done this kind of assignment."

"Not this type, never. She wanted it, she's gung ho as they come, Jim, and she's good."

Jim noticed that Martin's eyes were misty, although his face remained stern.

"Martin, if I didn't know any better I'd say you have a fatherly concern for that girl."

Martin looked down, hiding his eyes for a moment.

"I do, Jim, I do. And I want you to let me know the minute you think she might lose it. I'll pull her from the job right then and there! I mean it."

"Then pull her now!"

"No, not yet. I'll give her this chance. If you say the word in a few days I'll pull her, of course she'll be madder than a hatter at me but

I'll pull her. Not yet though. But I can't have you worrying about her all the time either, you both have to hold up your ends. And yes, Jim, I have a fatherly concern. Actually, I consider all my agents my 'kids.' And I take it real hard when I lose one. Real hard, Jim, so you take care out there, watch your ass, watch her...what am I saying," he gave a brief laugh at what he almost said, "I mean, take care of each other out there."

Both of them rose and shook hands. Then Jim left.

Suzie was waiting outside and she rose up, taking Jim's hand.

"I know what you talked about in there," Suzie said. "He wants you to watch me, to see if I'll break..."

"I don't even want you there, Suzie, and don't get mad, I care about what happens to you!"

Suzie reached up and kissed Jim on the cheek.

"You're sweet, Jim. I appreciate it."

They left the office and headed for the elevator. Once inside Suzie turned to Jim and put her arms around his waist, bringing herself close to him. He was nervous.

"Suzie..."

"I can't help it, Jim," she said and he could feel her against him, her face close to his. He recalled her passionate kiss earlier.

"When we leave the elevator we go our separate ways, Jim. I'll be seeing you at the club Thursday night."

She pressed against him, driving him mad again. Saved by the bell, the elevator doors opened and they exited. She blew him a kiss and they went their separate ways.

***

Jim found himself once again in Chinatown. He was dressed in his regular clothes now, he had kept the firearm they had issued him with instructions to add it to his arsenal. He had put it in his car. He was walking down Kearney Street. There were hardly any tourists in Chinatown today, the shooting the day before had killed off the tourist trade for now, it seemed. In fact, for this time of day, early afternoon, it seemed almost deserted. No one looked at him as he passed people on the street, everyone was hurrying about trying to get their business taken care of and then get home as fast as they could.

Jim was now in front of the restaurant. Large sheets of plywood covered what had been the picture windows and two smaller sheets covered the door. Jim tried the handle. The door pushed open and he stepped through. The dining room was lit up and an Asian repair crew was at work fixing the place up. They did not look at him.

"Ah my young friend, you have returned," Jonnie Lee came through the kitchen entrance carrying a bowel of food. He shouted something to the cooks and went to a table. He gestured for Jim to be seated. Jonnie Lee was eating a bowl of rice and beef.

"The cook will bring you one," Jonnie Lee said.

A moment later the cook came through the door carrying the extra bowl and two beers, he set them down on the table. Jim looked around at the bullet holes in the wall.

"It's nothing," Jonnie Lee said. "The place will be back together by the end of the week, my crews work fast."

They ate quickly, saying nothing, sipping their beers, Jonnie Lee was intent on his food. Jim felt slightly claustrophobic with no picture windows with a view to the outside.

"Feels kind of confining in here," Jonnie Lee said as if reading Jim's mind. "We'll have new glass in by tomorrow. It's dusty in here, let's go up to my office."

They rose from the table and went through the kitchen, setting the bowls down on the dishwasher. Jonnie Lee grabbed two more beers.

They entered his office. The place was a mess. Judy, the waitress, and Samantha Yi were busy straightening up the room, at the moment they were putting finishing touches on the altar, the statue had not been damaged. Samantha had just lit the incense sticks. Both girls turned as Jim and Jonnie Lee entered.

"Oh Jim!" both girls said at the same time and they ran over to him, both of them putting their arms around him and hugging him, they were dressed in silk pants outfits, buttoned to their necks, both brilliant, Chinese Red. Their hair hung in long pony tails down their backs and they had very little makeup on today. Jim noticed how pretty they were without it.

"Jim, Jim," they said as they held him. He put his arms around them. He remembered the last time he had seen Samantha, she had been clinging to him and she had been totally naked.

"I can see they are very grateful to you for saving their lives yesterday," Jonnie Lee said. "They both want to please you in any way they can."

"I appreciate that," Jim said as he managed to dislodge himself from them discretely so as not to hurt their feelings. Jonnie Lee motioned for them to be seated, Jim sat down at the front of the desk, Jonnie Lee, behind it. Judy and Samantha immediately began to massage Jim's shoulders and Samantha kissed him on his neck, running her hands through his hair.

"They would both like to marry you, you know," Jonnie Lee said with a smile as he lit up a cigarette and settled back to sip his beer. The window behind him had not been broken and the office seemed to be pretty much in order other than the clutter which the girls had been cleaning up.

"Didn't take long to get things back in order, they had overturned the desk and knocked down a few shelves but nothing was missing. I think what they wanted was to install terror, to get me to give in to their territorial demands. We took care of that problem. I doubt if they will be back, they are small time players and they found out real fast what it was like to step into the big league. The shooting really killed business around here though, at least for a few days. But they'll be back."

"Back?"

"The tourists, they won't stay away forever and it will give me time to get the restaurant back together. But my gift shop across the street is doing hardly any business today. Oh well," he took another sip and a drag from his smoke, "can't be helped I guess. Just business as usual, some days you win, some days you lose."

He laughed. His eyes laughed.

"Is there anything you would like?" Judy asked Jim. Then both girls looked at Jonnie Lee. He raised his beer bottle. Judy smiled and moved away from Jim out of the room. Samantha sat in Jim's lap now, putting her arms around his neck. She spoke in Chinese to him.

"She says she would make you a wonderful wife," Jonnie Lee said. "Like I said, both of them would marry you in a split second."

Samantha was looking right into Jim's eyes. Her dark orbs penetrating, serious, Jim saw a deep longing there. And a hint of fear.

"What to do, what to do," Jonnie Lee said. "I have my share of worries. I'm glad they didn't try to question Samantha, I kept her hidden in the gift shop. Judy, the waitress, has her papers in order, so no problem there. I must admit I have grown rather fond of Samantha however, I brought her into this country a few months ago, she has treated me...well..." he smiled. "Maybe I am a little bit jealous..." he looked at Jim and Samantha and smiled again, "no, not at all. I have not yet traded her to anyone's brothel. She is a good girl, so willing to please, and good in her heart, I can tell these things. She managed to get enough money in Hong Kong to finance her way here. Perhaps I will give her as a bride to one of my sons...oh yes, I have two sons, each by a different woman, women I brought in years ago when I was just starting out. My sons are in their early twenties now, about your age. Or maybe you want to buy her, I'd offer a fair price. She would dedicate her life to you, she seems to have already committed herself to you."

"I am already soon to be married," Jim said, thinking of Jiang Li and wishing she were the one with him right now, Samantha was very distracting, an image of her naked coming again to his mind.

Jonnie Lee picked up the remote and the TV mounted high on a shelf clicked on. There was full footage of City Hall, filmed earlier in the day. Jim could see himself and Suzie, caps low with sunglasses and partially hidden behind their escort as they were hurried around the building. There was also film of them in the hallway in front of the Mayor's office. Jim stiffened, Samantha's hands settled deep into his tense neck muscles.

Jonnie Lee scanned the tube for a few moments.

"Such an uproar," he said.

Jim studied Jonnie Lee's face for any sign that he had recognized him. He saw none, the images had been fleeting, the cameras jerky and the escorts had done their jobs well.

"So they questioned you yesterday," Jonnie Lee said. "I held up my end with my 'hysterical shop owner' role, how did I sound?"

"Like a typical hysterical shop owner whose place has just been vandalized and shot up," Jim said.

"They didn't talk to you very long. I thought they were going to take you in."

"They told me not to make any plans to leave town. And now they know where I work."

"Work?"

"Which brings me to the reason for this visit," Jim said as Judy left and returned with two more beers which she handed to Jonnie Lee and Jim. They took sips. Judy moved over to Jonnie Lee and began massaging his shoulders. He took a sip of his beer and leaned his head back, closing his eyes for a moment of unrestrained bliss. He patted her hand with his then looked at Jim.

"I work at Denning's club as head bouncer," Jim said. "I talked to him. He may want to deal, he is taking a wait and see attitude right now. I think he will listen, if only to bring down Cobra's price."

Jonnie Lee nodded. "So the cops and Feds know right where to find you."

"I'm afraid so. But I'm not worried. They asked me where the firearms were and I said, 'what firearms.' They didn't buy it of course so I'll be questioned again, you can be sure of it. They mentioned firearms charges but there's no evidence."

"I took care of that, those weapons will never be found. They have 'mysteriously' ended up at the bottom of the bay I am afraid."

Jonnie Lee smiled at that one then closed his eyes a Judy hit a nerve point just right. Samantha did the same for Jim at that moment and, again, Jiang Li flashed through his mind.

"So my friend," Jonnie Lee said, "go to your boss and tell him I want to set up a meeting as soon as possible. We can't have The Cobra taking all the lion's share of the profits, now, can we? Or should I say the 'tiger's share?'"

Jim carefully extricated himself from his seat. Samantha looked up at him with disappointed eyes and a pout.

"She would prefer you to stay, you know," Jonnie Lee smiled.

"Like I said, I am going to be married soon."

***

Jim took a good look at the naked image of Jiang Li on his cell phone when he got in his car, saw her smiling face as she looked over her shoulder at him, her, beautiful, naked buttocks glistening on the screen, her long, black hair trailing down her back. Jim figured he should erase the image but found he could not bring himself to. He wasn't going to be seeing her much in the next few weeks and he had to hang on to her in any way he could.

Jim pulled out of the Union Square parking garage and headed on across the bay bridge for his home town.

***

An hour later Jim was entering the club, he had been caught up in the rush hour traffic which had begun to flow into the east bay across the bridge. Jim could see that final preparations were being made for the club's reopening. Rebecca was dancing, naked, on the stage. She looked at him as he entered, no expression in her eyes. Mike Walker was working with some of the crew on a wall while the lights flashed and the music played. Rebecca spun around the gleaming pole, her head back, her black hair trailing down about her. Jim noticed she had adopted the "shaved" look. It looked like Suzie had started a trend and Rebecca was not to be outdone. Beautiful as she was she somehow had no appeal in Jim's mind. He saw Mike looking towards her, then Mike flashed him a look and waved in greeting. He went back to work. Jack Depoli was working with him.

"Hi ya, Jimbo!" Jack yelled.

Jim nodded, then he headed for the bar. Denning was seated there sipping a beer. A TV above the bar was showing the latest news and, there again, was Jim and Suzie being hustled down the hallway to City Hall. Denning seemed not to be paying too much attention and he greeted Jim, motioning him over. The girl behind the bar placed and extra bottle of beer on the counter top.

Jim was seated.

"Have a cool one," Denning said and he glanced at the screen.

"There's a lot of talk about this 'Chinatown Phantom' right now, stalking the streets, involved in shootings, he seems the local hero to some of them," Denning was saying and he turned to Jim. "So that's what they call you over there. You've made a name for yourself thanks to that back alley brawl. But the shooting..."

"Just taking care of business," Jim said. "I may be questioned. The Feds talked to me briefly but I doubt they have anything. Self defense."

"I like it!" Denning smiled. "It may give us good leverage in our deal with The Cobra. I've heard rumblings."

"Rumblings?"

"Already. Concern that a deal will be taking place soon. Top Cobra guys want a meeting and soon."

"That's what I want to talk to you about. The Tiger Clan also wants a meeting soon. I talked to Jonnie Lee today. He wants in bad on the action."

"This is good! Nothing like a hot bidding war to drive prices down for us! Great! Tell you what, Saturday night I am throwing a party at my home, a real bash. I'll invite top Cobra reps and you talk to Jonnie Lee, invite him as well. it's time to talk business."

"There's a guy I want to try to bring in with me," Jim said.

"Who."

"A guy I served with over in Iraq, Indian guy..."

"Big guy with long, black ponytail? Yeah, he was backing you up at that fight out at the railroad tracks. So he's good?"

"One of the best, and he's looking for some good action. I'll try to get in touch with him and bring him in."

"You trust him?"

"With my life."

"You ex-Army Rangers! Great! Have him at the party if possible."

Rebecca was now dancing out on the ramp, lost in the music she rolled off the stage and came across the room to dance right up to Jim and Denning, ignoring Jim completely but smiling at Denning and flashing her shaved charms at him. She sat in his lap, putting her arm around him. He put his arms around her waist and smiled at her.

"So, sporting a new look?" Denning said as she moved on his lap, still ignoring Jim.

"Like it?" she smiled.

"My dear, you're a gorgeous babe, but you know what?"

She smiled at him, questioning.

"There's nothing like the original, you're just a copy cat, now get back up there, you're a lousy dancer and a poor imitation, now get going!" and with a slap on her buttocks he sent her back to the stage. Jim caught the intense rage that momentarily flashed across her eyes. Rebecca continued her act on the stage. Denning turned to Jim and laughed.

"That's one pissed off broad, I bet she'd bite your dick off in a split second. Suzie will have to watch herself with this one. But then, maybe a catfight on stage, a real catfight, might be great for business, as long as we can keep it controlled. Oh yeah!"

Denning's eyes flashed with inspiration.

"A cage match! Right here at this club! What a draw! And the stage is already set, that broad up there has a real hate on for Suzie, has ever since Suzie came in here and auditioned. And as I remember, out at the railroad tracks she had a little encounter with Suzie. Oh yeah, and that little Oriental gal that was with you."

"You think she'd go for it, Suzie, I mean?"

"I can only ask. Hey, a job requirement, right?"

Denning's laugh boomed throughout the room. He got up from his barstool as did Jim.

"Well, I got business to take care of, son," he said with a great big grin as he slapped Jim on the back and left the room.

The music had stopped and Rebecca was standing there, still naked, on the stage looking right at Jim. Jim noticed that Mike Walker was paying no attention. Jim headed for the door and out into the parking lot. He was about to get in his car when Mike called his name.

"Hey Jim."

Jim turned, Mike was standing there, Jim did not sense any threat.

"What's up, Mike?"

"I just gotta warn you..."

"Warn me? About what?"

"Rebecca, she's real bad news, man, I ain't even seein' her anymore. She's makin' a play for Denning."

"I guess that's her business, right?"

Mike shrugged his shoulders. "What do you think?"

"Think? About what?" Jim asked.

"The club, you think you're gonna stay on here?"

"Sure, why not?"

Mike leaned over closer to Jim.

"I gotta bad feelin' about this place, Jim, a bad feelin'."

"Like how?"

"I think there's stuff that goes on here, ya know?"

"No. It's just a job, Mike, just a job while I check out going to school."

"That's a nice broad...er excuse me...I mean that Oriental girl you got...now she's nice, not like her," Mike's eyes darted towards the club.

"Yes, she is, Mike. Real nice. Well, I gotta be going, I'm going by Dad's shop for a few minutes."

"Just watch yourself, that's all. I gotta funny feelin'."

"Well, thanks for the warning, Mike. See ya later."

Jim got into his car and drove off. As he was leaving the parking lot he saw Rebecca, now dressed, get into her car to leave.

CHAPTER FIFTEEN

Jim pulled up in front of his dad's garage and got out. He saw Denning's car parked there as well. He went inside. It was just about time to close up. His dad's head mechanic, Tony, was already pulling down the rollup as Jim walked in.

"Hi Jimbo," the Mechanic said.

"Hi Tony," Jim answered. He had known him since he was a little kid.

Jim could hear his dad's and Denning's voices. He went into the other, connecting bodyshop. His dad and Denning were talking and standing in front of a brand new, shiny Mercedes Benz. There wasn't a mark on it although Denning had been pointing to a spot. Both older men looked over at Jim.

"Jimboy!" his dad said with a smile and both men greeted him.

Jim looked over the car.

"Nice car," Jim said as he looked at Denning, "Yours?"

"Sure is, quite a honey, huh?" Denning was all smiles. "Just a little touch up work here and there."

Jim looked over the car and then at Denning. He was smiling, then he turned to his dad.

"Well, John, I gotta be going, so take care of it, okay?" Denning said as he shook John's hand and left. He patted Jim's shoulder as he passed. "Quite a boy you've got here, John, quite a boy."

"I'd say he's quite a man, myself," John answered.

Denning looked at him and then at Jim. "I'd sure say that too. Well, good day."

Denning let himself out the front door. Jim could hear Tony locking everything up.

"Busy day, Dad?" Jim asked.

"Sure was, runnin' all day, say son, why not join me for a beer?"

Jim looked over at the Mercedes.

"What's wrong with it? Looks perfectly good to me," Jim said.

"Oh, that. Denning just wanted a few extra touches here and there, he's particular. Meet you over there, okay son?"

***

Jim and his dad were seated in the dark interior of Sam's over their beers. They both took sips from the ice cold drinks. Jim noticed the big screen TV above the bar. The afternoon news report again and there Jim and Suzie were at City Hall. His dad was looking at the screen as he took another sip. Jim felt a slight tinge. His dad looked at him, studying his eyes for a moment and saying nothing.

Did he know? Had he recognized him? Or was Jim just being paranoid?

"Well, Jimbo," his dad said, "how's the club?"

"Comin' along, tomorrow night it opens again."

"I mean, how are you feeling about it, you know my opinion already, I don't think it's a good idea, you working there."

"Dad, it's just a job. It pays better than I could find anywhere else, it was handed to me, I couldn't be luckier right now. I mean..."

"I know, son, I know, you're thinking about that gal of yours and I don't blame you, but son, let me warn you..."

"Warn me?"

Jim glanced at the TV. There he was, full face but just for an instant as they cut to the reporter, the blond who had tried to pry questions from him. Had his dad just seen it? No, John was looking right at Jim, his eyes intent.

"Be careful around there, Jim, just be careful, that's all I ask."

"Don't worry dad," Jim answered with a smile and they both looked at the TV. "I've been in some pretty tough situations over there in Iraq, Dad, I can take care of myself."

"Son, there are many kinds of battlefields in this world."

There was Jim and Suzie leaving.

"Take Chinatown, Jim."

"What about Chinatown?" did Jim sound too anxious?

"It's been on the news all day long, the shooting, right there on the main street, it's a wonder more people didn't die out there. I gotta say though, son, I admire whoever it was that took down the kidnappers. Heard he was questioned by the FBI and then released. It's a case of self defense as far as I am concerned. The gangs that run that place, and the other gangs in the city and for that matter, even local thugs, son it's a full scale war out there.

"Son, Denning is a powerful man, but his wealth was ill begotten they say, although no one really knows. Working at that club, son, I don't know...I just don't like it, that place has thugs of all kinds that congregate there. And you, as head bouncer, will be at risk all the time."

"I'm used to being at risk, Dad."

"The war is over for you now, son. Look, why not work in my shop. You need money for school, I'm here to help, I know you're sweet on that gal, and she's a 'keeper' as far as I and your mom are concerned."

"Dad, the bouncer job pays a lot more than you can afford to pay me right now."

"Son, I'll pay you whatever you need..."

"No, Dad, there are guys working for you who need it more than I do, look, I appreciate what you're trying to do, Dad..."

"And son, you didn't have to move into that apartment..."

"Dad..."

"Well, son, it looks like the reason for all this is walking right through that door."

Jim looked up. Jiang Li was heading right for his table, dressed in jeans and cutoff sweatshirt, her hair trailing down her back in a loose ponytail. Jim's heart leapt into his throat at the sight of her. She came right up to him and sat herself down in his lap, planting her lips on his, her arms around his neck. Then she blushed and looked at Jim's dad.

"I'm sorry, Mr. Saunders..." she started to say and John Saunders gave out a hearty laugh. He reached over and patted her shoulder.

"My dear, you have nothing to be sorry about. And you may as well start calling me 'Dad.' I can see how things are going."

He laughed again and stood up.

"Well...Mr. S..."

"Ah ah..."

"...Dad..."

"That's better. It's 'Dad' from now on, understand?"

Jiang Li nodded, "...Dad..."

"Sounds good to me," John glanced at his watch, "And it's about time for me to get back home so I'll leave you two alone. Dinner's waiting."

Jim rose, an arm around Jiang Li and shook his dad's hand. John smiled at both of them and then left. Jim sat back down, Jiang Li in his lap, her arms around him.

"So," she said, "how's about buying a hard working girl a beer?"

Before Jim could rise to go to the bar Sam was setting two fresh long necks on the table. He smiled at them then returned to the bar to serve his customers.

Jiang Li shifted on him, arousing him greatly as they took a sip of their beers. She looked at him.

"So what..."

"...brings me here? I finished early today, took two finals. There is nothing more for me to do this evening now, I took my car to school so I decided to come here. That's okay?"

Jim kissed her. "It's always okay."

"Good. Oh yes, I also drove by that club you are working at."

"Oh?"

Momentary anger flashed across her eyes.

"Jim, really, I saw the bill board outside, I mean, really, Jim, you work at a place where totally naked women dance, you look at completely naked women all night!"

She reached under the table and grabbed his testicles and put a squeeze on them, a firm grip for such a delicate hand. "I ought to pull them off!"

"Jiang Li..." Jim could feel the gripping power on him. "I need this job, Jiang Li..."

The vice tightened on him and he didn't like the look he saw there in her burning orbs.

"You could do something else!" she whispered.

"Not for the kind of money I am making and we need it. For our future and any kids we might have unless you are going to make that impossible..."

Jiang Li looked down then released her hold. She kissed him.

"Oh Jim! I'm sorry, I hope I didn't hurt you, I'm sorry," there was almost panic in her eyes, "If I hurt them it could ruin our night..."

Jim looked at her, her eyes had softened now.

"Yes, my love, I am staying the night. I already set up the excuse with June."

They kissed hungrily right there in the chair, the sounds of the bar fading into the background.

***

Jim and Jiang Li walked up the back steps to the building where Jim lived. She had followed him here in her car and parked in the rear parking lot, next to Jim's car. They made their way down the narrow hallway to Jim's room and halted at the door. Jiang Li's arms went around Jim's neck and she pressed herself against him, shoving him against the door as her lips met his, kissing him hungrily, her tongue darting into his mouth, wrestling with his. He put his arms around her tiny waist and pulled her against him.

"I'm sorry I hurt them..." she breathed as she looked at him with misty eyes. "I'm sorry, Jim, I'm sorry, I never want to hurt you..." she kissed him again and both her arms were around him again as he fumbled for his keys. He managed to get her off him for a moment as he unlocked the door, her arms around him, pressing herself against his back, he could feel her breasts yielding against him and he was hot with desire.

They made it inside and she had her arms around him again, kissing him feverishly. Her hands went to his belt buckle, hastily undoing it, and his snaps, ripping them open and pulling down, briefs and all then pressing herself against him, he fought for control.

"I've missed you so much..." she whispered as Jim stepped back, fumbling with his shoes and stepping out of his clothes, pulling his "T" shirt over his head and standing there in front of her as she looked him over.

"Oh Jim!" she gasped as she came to him again, pressing against him, kissing his neck. "I've missed you so...missed you...missed you..."

She stepped back while pulling her sweatshirt over her head, her breasts bare. She was out of her clothes and standing right there in front of him. Jim looked towards the drawer.

"We won't need it," she read his action. "I went to the clinic today, I am protected. Jim..." she was in his arms again, he could feel her smooth skin against him, driving him wild, in total lust now, "...I want to feel the real you in me, Jim, the real you..."

Jim had her up in his arms, carrying her to the bed only two steps away, he tossed her down and she bounced, her hair falling all about her brown, smooth shoulders as her arms went wide. He sank down on her, feeling himself entering her gates as she opened herself to him.

"Be free, Jim, be free..." she gasped at his first thrust, her legs going around his waist and locking on him, hard and tight, he could feel her moving beneath him, her tiny body a writhing mass of subtle movements driving him to the brink and way, way beyond...

***

Their furious love making went on for an hour non stop then they both collapsed on the bed, lying on their backs beside each other. Jim could feel the gentle breeze wafting in through the open window on his bare skin, caressing him, cool on his damp body. Her lips were on his chest, working their way up his neck now, her arms around him. She reached down and caressed him, he was relaxed now as she fondled him, checking him.

"I'm so glad I didn't hurt them, so glad...oh Jim I am so jealous...I can't help it, those naked women..."

"Jiang Li..."

"I know, I know...but Jim, Jim, what would you do if I had a job dancing naked in front of men? What would you do?"

"Jiang Li, please, Jiang Li..."

"Maybe I'll go down there and apply? Maybe...well my breasts are too small..."

Jim reached over and kissed her naked breasts.

"Your breasts are beautiful, Jiang Li, the most beautiful breasts I have ever seen..."

"Now you lie...I saw those billboards..."

"Jiang Li, don't do this..."

"I'm sorry, Jim..."

"Jiang Li, when I find something else I promise you I will be gone from there. It's just a job, I wouldn't have accepted it if it was at the usual starting pay for bouncers, but I am the head bouncer and with more pay than I would have hoped for and we need it."

"As long as I and only I get the benefit then I suppose..." she found him beginning to respond again, he was ready and she moved over on top of him, sitting upright, her hair over her left shoulder, she sank down on him. She leaned her head back, moaning with pleasure as he arched upward, she rode him like a bucking bronco, her breath coming in gasps, on and on into the night...

***

The sun was filtering through the curtains which were partially open, the room dimly light by the early morning light. Jiang Li was on his chest, snuggled there with a smile on her face. He opened his eyes as she opened hers. She looked at him with her sleepy, sexy, bedroom eyes, her messed up hair all around her shoulders, she smiled at him, she kissed him and stirred on him. He rolled her over under him, kissing her.

She moaned with pleasure as he took her again in the morning light.

***

She was asleep. Jim dislodged her arm from him and rose up. He looked around the room. Good! All his things were well hidden, his badge, the guns were in the closet which was locked.

Getting up he went to the window, parting the curtains to look out on the street below. The bus depot was open for business now, people were seated at outside tables at the coffee house, sipping their lattes and reading their newspapers or talking on cell phones, already planning meetings when they arrived at work. A married couple in their early thirties went jogging past in their sweatsuits, their earphones and Ipods evident. The husband pulled out and checked his cell phone for the time as they ran past and off up the street. Life was beginning.

Jim felt a naked arm encircle his waist, felt Jiang Li's naked breasts against his back, felt her lips caress his shoulder. Her hand traveled down his waist, his stomach and found him ready again. She kissed his neck, moaning for him. He shut the curtains and turned, taking her in his arms as hers went around his neck, kissing his lips. Her legs went around his waist, gripping him and settling down on him, he felt himself sinking into her once again and he released right there in front of the window. She moaned as she climaxed at the same time then she eased off of him. Arm in arm they went into the shower. Jim turned it on as Jiang Li kissed him and kissed him. As the shower heated up Jim took some shaving cream and put it on his face. Jiang Li took the Bic razor in hand and stood before him. She began to shave his face then she toweled it off and felt its smoothness. She reached up, putting her arms around him and placed her baby smooth cheek against his and moaned with pleasure. Steam was rising now from the shower so they stepped in together, holding each other. He pressed her against him. They held each other tightly and let the water wash them off as she rubbed against him, driving him wild again. He bent down, putting his arms around her waist and hoisted her up, entering her again one more time.

She let out a gasp and smothered his lips with hers.

***

They sat together at a table at the latte bar across the street next to the bus depot. She sat close, her arm around him as they sipped flavored coffees and ate sweet rolls. She shared her roll with him, feeding bites to him as he fed bites to her, they were lost in the eternal dream together, existing in another world where there was no strife, no pain, no struggle. Jim's body tingled all over, a wonderful sensation and it was enhanced each time Jiang Li fed him a bite of the sweet roll or when she kissed the side of his face, or when she would place her hand on his thigh, up high and very, very close, arousing him again. Truly, they were in another world.

Jim looked at his watch. He sighed. It was time to enter the real world again. He looked at Jiang Li and gave her a kiss.

"I must be going," he said, "I have some things I have to do."

"I thought maybe we could spend the morning together," Jiang Li said.

Jim thought about it. It had been on his mind, the deception he was playing with her. A necessary deception however, lives were at stake here and he couldn't afford to jeopardize his mission. It killed him that he couldn't tell her the truth, that he had actually gotten a job with a future, a career that could take care of them for their entire life if he did well. He hated having to work at that club and he didn't blame her for being upset about it. He just needed a little more time, things had to happen just right. Their lives together depended on this. He had to bring down Denning and The Cobra, and also The Tiger Clan. As he sipped his coffee he thought about Samantha Yi, about Jonnie Lee. He was beginning to rather like Jonnie Lee for some reason but it didn't matter. Jonnie Lee was a criminal and he had to be brought down. Samantha Yi would then be deported back to China. Jim was not comfortable with this. That girl worshipped him after he had saved her life and he felt as if he was betraying her in the worst way. She was the real innocent victim in all this.

"Your thoughts, my love?" Jiang Li's voice knifed through the fog in Jim's mind and he looked over at her.

Yes, this morning he could spend with her. "Yes, we will be together this morning, Jiang Li."

A look of delight crossed her face and she threw her arms around him and kissed him. Commuters on their way into the bus depot looked at them as they passed then went on about their business.

"You can join me for a morning workout," Jim said.

"Oh, you mean back at your room? I saw the weights..."

"No, not today, somewhere else, a different kind of workout."

"I'd like that very much!" and she kissed him again.

***

Jim drove down the main street of town, looking for a certain address. Yes, there it was, the "new" martial arts school that had just been started, in fact, today was opening day. A large sign adorned the storefront, "Gene's Fight Club" it read. Amazing how it all managed to appear overnight as if by magic. Taxpayers dollars hard at work.

Jim pulled up in front and got out. He figured Gene would get the idea when he saw Jiang Li and say nothing. Jim took his gi out of the back seat and tucked it under his arm. He took Jiang Li's hand and lead her through the entrance. The place was completely equipped, wall to wall mats, hanging heavy bags, speed bags, a complete weight workout area and wall to wall mirrors. This had just been an empty hull the day before, they had moved fast, the Feds had moved heaven and earth to open this place. And the paying customers would help fund it. Just another martial arts school for the moms to bring their kids to, for out of shape business execs to try to burn off some fat, for housewives and professional women to build confidence in their ability to defend themselves, for high school kids to find positive direction, and all the while the school was a blind for it's real purpose. To train Jim and get him ready to help topple the town's ever expanding crime organization. Afterwards, the school would disappear. Or maybe not, perhaps it would remain if it turned a profit. Jim hoped so, hoped it would be there to serve the community.

"Wow!" Jiang Li said as she looked around then she looked at Jim. "You know," she whispered to him, her lips near his ear, "I didn't grow up in this town but I would swear I didn't see this school as we came up the main drive the other day. I guess I just didn't notice."

"It's new," Jim said, "but the owner is a friend of mine and he invited me down for a workout when he opened it."

"Ahem!"

Both of them looked around. Gene was standing there now, framed in the doorway to his office, wearing black gi bottoms and a black tank top, his hands on his hips. He was looking right at Jim.

"Well, don't you think you'd better get ready?" Gene said, a stern look on his face. Then he looked at Jiang Li and smiled.

"Welcome, young lady, this is an unexpected surprise for my opening day," Gene said with a wide grin. "Please, my name is Gene."

"Jill," Jiang Li said offering her hand, then looking around the dojo she did a bow, keeping her eyes on Gene.

"Ah, the lady knows the protocol," Gene said, "when bowing never take your eyes off your opponent. You've studied before."

"I had kung fu lessons when I was a younger girl," Jiang Li said.

Gene threw a look at Jim then back to Jiang Li.

"Well, Jill, welcome, and while I'm kickin' your boyfriend's butt out here on the mat you may be my guest and use the machines or whatever you wish to do."

Jiang Li looked the place over and smiled. She made her way over to one of the heavy bags and stood before it. With a sharp yell she leapt into the air and delivered a powerful wheel kick which impacted on the six foot long, two hundred pound bag. She spun and delivered a heel kick then spun and kicked with the other leg. She stepped back.

"Lady knows her stuff!" Gene said with a smile. "I can see you know how to take care of yourself. And now..." Gene threw Jim another look, "if you would just stop standing there gawking we can get down to business."

Jim hurried into the dressing room and changed into his black gi bottoms, he emerged shirtless onto the mat a few minutes later. Jiang Li was working out on the bench press machine and Jim noticed she had the pin quite low on the weight stack. There was surprising strength in her lithe body as she pumped away.

Jim faced Gene on the mat. He didn't really feel up to a workout today considering last night. He felt a bit weak in the knees. He looked over at Jiang Li. At that moment Gene caught him square on the jaw with a gloved fist sending Jim reeling to the floor.

"I can see concentration is very poor today!" Gene said as he pressed the attack.

Jim rolled and came up on his feet, not fast enough as Gene was on him in a flurry. That sweet roll Jim had had for breakfast and the coffee wasn't really making it and Jim attempted to reach deep down inside. He didn't reach down far enough or fast enough as Gene kept up his relentless attack. Jim glanced over at Jiang Li. She was watching, an amused smile on her face. Momentary anger flared through Jim and he came at Gene. His target wasn't there and a fist landed on the side of his head, Jim went down again. Gene looked over at Jiang Li.

"Whatever did you do to this man last night?" he asked and Jiang

Li smiled.

Jim was on Gene in and instant, attacking in a rapid flurry of fists and feet. Gene retreated, fending off the blows, then Jim hit him square on the jaw and Gene reeled, hit the floor and rolled, coming up on his feet.

"Now that's better!" Gene said as he came at Jim. Jim stopped him cold with a fist to the chest and Gene glanced off his glove and rolled around him. Jim stayed with him, full fighting instinct kicking in now, ready for anything. Jim leapt into the air delivering a punishing side kick to Gene's ribs then spinning into an instant reverse kick landing that one also. Now Gene was winded.

"Hey, now you're gettin' it!" Gene said and Jim kept up his attack.

Jiang Li, the room, everything seemed to disappear now, there was only the conflict, there was only his target and he attacked unmercifully, landing kicks, landing punches, Gene backing away, now struggling to defend himself, moving aside, Jim staying with him, reversing and coming at him from a new angle Gene did not anticipate. Both erupted in a flurry of punches then stopped, both completely winded, holding each other up with their gloves, forehead to forehead, struggling for breath, sweat dripping off them.

Gene gulped for air.

"Way to go, way to go, my man," he said and they parted, bowed and shook gloved hands.

"Well, he finally woke up," Gene grinned at Jiang Li who smiled back. She was working out on a leg press machine now.

"We're done for today, good job," Gene said. He turned to Jiang Li, "You are my guest here anytime." He nodded to Jim and Jiang Li. Jim went in and dressed. Jiang Li was waiting in the office, a small partitioned area with a desk and chairs arranged for the sales pitch Gene would be giving prospective students later on in the day.

"Nice place you have here," Jim said as Jiang Li rose, taking his hand. "did you have trouble 'financing' this place?"

A grin crossed Gene's face.

"No trouble at all, not at all," he said.

"I figured you wouldn't," Jim said and they shook hands. He and Jiang Li left.

***

Jim and Jiang Li drove back to the center of town. Jim walked Jiang Li to her car and they stood there, hand in hand. She looked up into his eyes.

"I wish I didn't have to go," Jiang Li said. "But I have to go home sometime or I'll arouse suspicions."

"Move in with me, Jiang Li, let me talk to your father. It's dangerous for you to be there."

"No, not yet, Jim, I can't..."

"Jiang Li, this man who is trying to claim you, he's..."

"I know what he is, Jim..."

"I know this is difficult for you. To face them, let me go with you, let me meet your father and talk to him."

"I can't do that, Jim, you don't understand...let me get through graduation first, please, Jim."

She put her arms around him and held him.

"Jiang Li, we've been seen together enough times now, they will know and I am afraid for what might happen."

"No, Jim, don't worry, please, it'll be all right, Jim."

Jim looked at her. He was worried. If Tommy Xiang suspected that Jiang Li had had sex with anyone he might kill her or worse. Jim wanted her near him. Jiang Li hugged Jim then reached up and kissed him, a long, lingering, passionate kiss.

"I love you," she said as her lips lingered near his, her hands stroking his lower back. Then they parted and she got into her car. She gave a wave as she drove away.

***

Jim was walking up Kearney Street in Chinatown, gazing at the shops as he walked along. He had stopped at Stan's for steak and eggs and coffee before driving into the city, he needed his strength after that workout with Gene, that sweet roll earlier not really making it as a meal. Jim paused a moment outside a shop. He felt as if eyes were on him, a familiar feeling down his spine, a warning. He knew he was being watched and tracked. He made no quick movement, he just walked calmly along the sidewalk. Then he saw him. The thug Jim had confronted in the steak house when he had first returned from the Army. He noticed the man was on crutches and he remembered the fight in the alley. He couldn't recall taking out the man's legs in the fight but it had been an instantaneous blur and then it had been over. The man was looking right at him, his eyes glaring. Jim approached him.

"I know you," Jim said.

"Yes, you do," the man answered.

"You trying to follow me?"

"As if I could follow anyone in this condition," the man spat.

Jim nodded to his cast. The man shrugged his shoulders.

"I made a mistake," the man said. "The girl in the restaurant I harassed belonged to Tommy Xiang. I didn't know. Now I do."

"And what about your associate?"

"He is running scared, plenty scared, he watched my punishment and thought the same would be done to him, or worse. He will not get out of line again."

"Nor will you?"

"I am not with them anymore. They cast me out. Now I am on my own, here on the street with no options. I stay with an uncle. Maybe it's for the best."

"What's your name?"

"Andy, just Andy."

Jim looked him over and nodded. A question had been answered in his mind. He had wondered why The Cobra would harass the fiancée of one of their main leaders. A mistake and now this man had paid. Well, Jim figured, he deserved it, that and the butt whipping Jim had given him in the alley.

"I want to pay them back!" Andy said.

"Pay them back?"

"For doing this to me! And casting me out, I want them to pay!" rage filled Andy's eyes. "I can help you. I've heard you've been seen with her."

"You want my help for what? What is it to me?"

"You've been seen with her and you are in danger, so is she, I just want to warn you. You are down here for a reason. To make business? You represent someone and want a deal? Maybe I can help."

"In your position, Andy, I don't see how you can help anyone. And you have no idea why I am here."

"Just the same, if you make a deal and it hurts them then I want to be part of it! I'll keep an eye out! I want payback!"

"I don't think you can help me but I'll keep you in mind," Jim said. "Are you hungry?"

"I am not too proud to beg," the man said. "Yes, I am hungry. My uncle, he doesn't have much. I was helping him make a better life when I was with Cobra and now, I am no help at all."

Jim reached into his pocket and handed Andy a twenty dollar bill.

"We'll call this an 'investment,'" Jim said. "You keep your eyes open and if you ever have anything to tell me then the investment pays off."

"Good enough, at least I will feel like I am earning something."

"I doubt you ever earned anything your whole life," Jim said as he walked away. He could feel Andy's eyes burning into his back as he made his way to the restaurant. He went inside and made his way through the kitchen, Judy greeted him with a smile as he passed through, she was on her way back to the dining room with several plates of food balanced in her hands. Jim went upstairs and right to the office door where he knocked. There was silence, then he heard someone moving. The door opened a crack and Samantha Yi peered out, he could tell she was naked, holding her dress against her. When she saw him a bright smile crossed her face and she reached out and took his hand, letting the dress fall to the floor, she pulled him inside, throwing her arms around him in an affectionate hug.

"Jim, Jim," she cooed to him, his hand went around her tiny, silken waist and he could feel her against him. She kissed him on his cheek. Jim saw Jonnie Lee sitting behind his desk, his shirt was off and he was smoking a cigarette. He was tightly muscled though slender of frame. He smiled at Jim.

"Well why don't you come in," Jonnie Lee said as Jim made his way over to the desk, holding the naked Samantha's hand. He seated himself and Samantha plopped herself down on his lap, her arms around him. Then she began working her fingers into his shoulder muscles. He looked at her and she smiled.

"In her you would have a most devoted wife, my friend," Jonnie Lee said.

Jim smiled at Samantha.

"Yes, I would," he answered.

Jonnie Lee took a long drag from his cigarette.

"Such a shame, the laws these days, a man can't smoke in his own restaurant anymore, his own place of business. But here, who would know?"

"It's a changing world," Jim said, "And that's why I am here. To discuss business."

"You could dally for a bit," Jonnie Lee indicated Samantha. "I would even leave my office for a while."

"I appreciate the offer but, as you know, I am engaged already."

"A wife is one thing, a lover like this one is quite another. She would do anything for you, you know, why I am almost jealous." Then he smiled at Samantha and spoke to her. She giggled.

"She is more than willing you know, but, oh well, to business."

He spoke to her again and she rose from Jim's lap, smiling down at him then she slid into her short dress and faded silently from the room. Finally, Jim was able to relax. Even though he had had quite a night the night before with Jiang Li he found he was still greatly aroused. Was that cheating? No, she would get the benefit of it later, he vowed to himself.

Jonnie Lee put on a red silk Mandarin jacket, buttoned it all way to the neck then sat back down.

"Ah, it's been a busy afternoon, my friend. And now, what is the word?"

"There's going to be a big party this weekend, you are invited and requested to bring your representatives with you. The Cobra will also be there. It's at eight o'clock. I'll give you directions."

"Great! Progress, I have been long awaiting this moment. I am not concerned with The Cobra. I can beat their prices. I will bring samples," he looked towards the door where Samantha had just exited. Anger momentarily flashed through Jim at the thought of Samantha being displayed as "product." And sadness, he felt sadness that in the long run, when this was over, she would be shipped back to China. He was betraying her trust in him. Such great trust and affection.

Jim took a deep breath.

"So it's set then, I will be there with my people at eight o'clock sharp," Jonnie Lee said.

***

Jim sat on the bench on the patio to his parent's house. It was early afternoon and Robbie was lifting weights, he was coming up on his eighth rep in the bench press with 235 pounds on the bar. Pretty good, the kid was getting strong fast. Jim stood over the bar, placing his fingers just under it, barely touching.

"Come on, you can do it, come on!" Jim said as Robbie struggled. The weight came up to arm's length and Jim helped guide it to the racks. Robbie sat up.

"Now your turn," he said.

Jim thought about it. A brief workout might do him some good, get him pumped up for opening night tonight at the club.

Robbie started to take off one of the plates.

"Leave it," Jim said as he sat down on the bench. He lay back and gripped the bar. He did and easy ten reps and replaced it.

"Geez, you make it look so easy!" Robbie exclaimed.

Jim spotted Robbie through a few more sets and did a few more himself, working up to five reps with 400 lbs. which absolutely astounded Robbie even though he has seen his big brother do this many times before.

"One day!" Robbie said.

"One day for sure," Jim answered as he rose and went into the kitchen where his mother was busy preparing the evening meal, a spaghetti casserole which she would cook in the oven for three hours on a low flame to blend in the flavors. Jim loved his mom's cooking.

Robbie went into living room and his mother called after him, "I want you in your room and studying, no TV! Understand? No TV!"

"Yeah, yeah, Mom," Robbie answered.

"And no lip either!"

Then she turned to Jim. She did not have a happy look on her face.

"What's wrong, Mom?" Jim asked.

"You know what's wrong!" she snapped.

"What?"

"That job! A strip club! Oh John told me all about it! A strip club, my son working at a strip club as a bouncer!"

"Head bouncer, and Mom, I am making good money for now. I need this."

"And what does your girlfriend say about this?"

"She doesn't like it much either..."

"I'd say she doesn't like it at all, she's a good, decent girl..."

"I know, Mom, and I'm going to ask her to marry me soon."

Jim's mother's face lit up in a big smile at the news.

"Now you're making sense, and you will get out of that job right away!"

"Mom, as soon as I can I will. I'm going to be going to the local college during the day starting in fall. I can save loads of money with my present job."

"You could save more if you got out of that seedy rat trap you moved into and move back here!"

"Mom..."

"Oh that's right, you have your own little 'love nest.'"

"Mom..."

"Oh Jim, I just want what's best for you, and I don't mind you having an apartment and being with Jill, she's a good girl and these are modern times. Your father and I...well...we didn't exactly wait either..."

"Mom, you're blushing!" Jim smiled.

"No I'm not! Now are you staying for dinner or not?"

"Not tonight, Mom..." and Jim could already smell the dinner beginning to warm in the oven. He wished he could stay.

"Well, I'll have plenty left over so you come by here tomorrow for lunch and I'll have a plate especially for you! Your dad's going to be late again, he's had a lot of work lately. I wish he could just retire. You could take over the shop..."

"Mom, I am just not going to work at the shop. And besides, Robbie will be able to take over in a few years, he really loves working on cars and helping Dad out. I see it, he'll end up being a great manager."

His mother frowned.

"I guess so, I just...oh well."

"What's dad so busy with that he's late coming home, I didn't notice a large amount of cars there yesterday when I went by there."

"Oh, there's always work. He won't say..."

She was thinking. Jim wondered what would keep his dad out so late. Another woman? No! Jim dismissed it from his mind, not his father, he was always so in love with his wife. Just work, that's what it had to be. Jim cursed himself for even thinking bad of his father. His father had always stressed values, the importance of the family and he had always been there for his sons, never missed a game, or not many as Jim could remember. Jim looked around the kitchen. He had a sensation of total security in here, he felt completely safe from the world. His father had provided that with his hard work. He was such a strong man and Jim had always looked up to him. It would be good if he could retire someday soon, he deserved it. Jim knew he could help out now that he had a new career with the U.S. Government. He wished he could share the news with them. But not now. Later, after this was all over with, then Jim could tell them the truth.

"Gotta go, Mom," he said as he kissed his mother on the cheek and went out to his car.

***

Jim was in the shower letting the beads of water cascade off his face, eyes closed, the steam filling the shower stall. He just stood there for a while enjoying the relaxing sensations as his sore muscles gave up their pain. He had had quite a workout with Gene this morning and then had lifted some weights with his brother. He needed this shower to put him together for tonight, his first night on the job at the club.

Finally he turned off the water and dried himself, draping the towel over his shoulders he entered the room and was astounded to see Suzie standing there right in front of him.

"My my," Suzie said with a smile as he immediately reacted. He tried to drape the towel around his waist but Suzie grabbed it away from him then stood back, admiring him. She came to him, putting her arms around his waist and pressing herself to him as he tried to back away.

"Suzie..."

"What?"

She moved against him, arousing him further, driving him mad with desire which he was trying to quell. He stepped away immediately hauling on his jeans, tucking himself in.

"Careful there," Suzie said with a smile, "Don't damage him."

"Suzie! What are you doing here, how did you get in?"

"That lock on your door is pretty simple, a hairpin works just fine."

Jim buckled his belt and stood there shirtless in front of her, his muscles glistening in the afternoon light that flooded into the room.

"I was just getting ready for work," Jim said.

"Work. I really dread this," Suzie said and she came to him, he put his arms around her and she leaned her head against his chest.

"Suzie, don't do this if..."

"No! I said I would do this...it's my job..."

"You know Martin will pull you off if he thinks..."

"Thinks I can't handle it? Is that what you're saying!"

She backed away from him, anger in her eyes now.

"Suzie! I can see it in your eyes, this is getting to you. I'm going to call Martin and tell him to pull you off now!"

"Don't you even dare!"

She was glaring at him now, rage in her eyes.

"Besides, something is going to happen tonight and I want to be there."

"What do you mean?" Jim asked.

"You'll see."

"Hey, I don't like surprises, tell me what you're talking about."

"It's just going to be a busy night, Jim, that's all. And don't you dare make that call. Understand? Don't you dare!"

Jim looked at her, she was trying to be brave but he could tell she was crumbling inside, he could see it in her eyes, she was blocking the fear well but he could see through it.

"Okay," Jim said. "I'll hold off for now. You know that Denning is throwing a party at his house this Saturday night? Representatives of both The Cobra and The Tiger Clan will be there in force. It's the big meeting we've been waiting for. Denning will probably have the dancers, including you, the main attraction it seems, there to try to entice business."

"Good, the plan is coming together. We're getting close."

"What happens to the girls, the illegals brought in by Cobra and Tiger Clan?"

"Deportation of course."

"Just like that."

"Yes, why, Jim?"

Jim was thinking of Samantha Yi and Judy, both of them had worked so hard to get out of China. He found himself wishing Jonnie Lee would go straight and marry Samantha, at least she could remain. The thought startled him.

"What's going on, Jim? Why are you so concerned about people who have no business in this country in the first place."

"I just wish...shit, Suzie, they try half their lives to get here to have a better life..."

"As prostitutes?"

"Not all of them are prostitutes, home workers, maids, etc..."

"It's not our concern, Jim. Stay focused! We're dealing with major criminal organizations here, let others handle the illegals. It's not our immediate problem. Our job is to put the assholes away who entice those girls over here in the first place. They are little more than slaves, Jim."

"And what are they in their own country, Suzie, what are they there?"

"Whatever life they were born into is their problem. Our job is to take out those who prey on them, plain and simple. If Cobra and Tiger wasn't operating, and others like them, those girls wouldn't be here in the first place."

Jim sighed and walked over to the window. He could see the commuters exiting the bus depot now, scurrying on home to their families. Many of them probably had maids, maybe maids imported through the same organizations he was trying to bring down. He turned away and pulled on his black sports shirt, collar open.

"Your sure look good in that," Suzie said with a smile. "Almost good enough to eat!"

Jim blushed and she smiled again.

"See you a bit later," Suzie said as she smiled again before turning her back and leaving the room.

Jim lay down on the bed and closed his eyes. He would need a brief nap to get him ready for tonight.

***

Jim slipped into a deep sleep. He had set his alarm clock for six. He didn't have to report to the club until eight. He found himself in a dream. Jiang Li was there with him. They were standing on a street in Chinatown together, arm in arm. They were just preparing to cross the street to go into Jonnie Lee's restaurant. She looked up at him, smiling. Jim heard a shout and he could see Suzie across the street calling to him. She was in her gray business suit and she was holding her open wallet with her badge showing. She was screaming a warning. Jim took Jiang Li's hand and was preparing to run when a sleek black limo appeared. The windows rolled down and men inside leaned out armed with MAC 10s. They opened fire and Jim heard Jiang Li scream. He saw splattering blood and saw her hair fly up as she fell.

"No, Jiang Li!" he screamed.

He was sitting upright. It had been a dream. He looked over at his clock. It was not quite six. He rose and made sure his things were secure then he went out the door and descended the stairs, going out into the parking lot to his car. He got in and drove to Stan's where he seated himself at the counter. Coffee was brought, black, and he sipped it. Stan came over to him to take his order.

"Steak and fries, steak rare," Jim said as he took another sip. He needed his strength for tonight and steak would fill the bill. Stan looked into his eyes for a moment. The waitress passed with steaming plates balanced in her hand, on her way to a table.

"I heard you start your new job tonight," Stan said.

"That's right," Jim answered.

Stan went off to grill Jim's steak and Jim relaxed with more coffee. He looked around the place. It was fairly busy tonight, early evening, Stan would close up about eleven.

The meal was brought to him by Stan personally and Jim dug in, savoring the flavor of the lean, red, meat. He had more coffee. Stan returned just as Jim was finishing his coffee. Jim reached in his pocket and Stan waved him off.

"Keep it," Stan said. "Meal's on the house. But I will give you a word of advice."

Jim looked at him.

"Watch your back over at that place, Jim. That's a bad man you're getting involved with so watch your back. Bad things go on there."

"Thanks, Stan, I'll watch myself."

"Is there something you aren't telling me?"

"No, just a job to me, for awhile."

"Okay, but watch yourself."

***

Jim arrived and got out of his car. He headed in the main entrance. The place was packed already. One of the other girls was dancing onstage in a skimpy string bikini.

"Hey Jimbo," Depoli was standing there, he had been guarding the entrance and Jim shook his hand.

"Busy night already," Jim said. "Has Suzie arrived yet?"

"Yeah, she's in the dressing room. Any directions, boss?"

"Looks like you're doing a good job so far."

Jim moved on into the club. Mike Walker was standing over by the bar, Rebecca was serving. There was a skinny young man with long hair in the DJ booth. The music was blaring and waitresses in bikinis were serving drinks, moving through the crowd which was behaving so far. Mainly business types in suits and a few working class men in "T" shirts and jeans. No one seemed too drunk yet. Jim moved on, Denning was at his own table sipping coffee and he motioned Jim over. He rose, offering his hand.

"Right on time, I see," Denning said. "So, what do you think so far? Any changes in mind yet?"

"Changes?"

"You're the boss here and they know it."

"I'll see how everything goes tonight, see how the guys handle themselves."

Jim scanned the floor. There were several more bouncers stationed around the place, keeping watch. Big men, they looked like they could handle themselves. Jim moved on towards the doorway to the hall and made his way to the dressing rooms. He knocked and the door opened a crack. A pretty young woman peered out at him and smiled. She was naked.

"Come on in, boss," she said and she opened the door. There was a row of dressing tables with lighted mirrors where several girls were getting ready, they were in various stages of undress.

"Jim," he heard Suzie call him. He saw her over at the far dressing table, clad only in a skimpy bikini bottom, topless, she turned to face him. She had her hair all teased and had been putting on the finishing touches of her makeup. At another table one of the girls was seated, naked. She was shaving herself.

"Looks like you've started a trend," Jim said.

Suzie smiled.

"The competition here is fierce. We dance for the best tips so whatever works, I guess."

She put her arms around him, hugging herself against him.

"I'm glad you're here," she whispered.

"You sure you're all right to do this?" Jim asked her.

"I'm fine, you're here, after all. And there's a surprise tonight."

"What are you talking about, you said that earlier?"

"You'll see. Now let me get ready, okay?" she kissed him lightly on the lips, then she hesitated and he could tell she wanted more. Jim turned and started to leave.

"Hey," said the girl who had been shaving herself. She stood in front of him, legs spread.

"Well, what do you think?" she asked him with a smile.

"Just lovely," Jim said and he exited the dressing room, returning to the main floor.

He went right to the bar.

"Well, what'll it be, boss?" Rebecca asked with a tinge of sarcasm in her voice.

"Coffee, black."

A cup was set before him. Rebecca leaned over.

"Where's your girlfriend?" she asked.

"What are you talking about?" Jim asked.

"That little Oriental girlfriend of yours. I saw you with her in town today. Where is she, I would think you would get her a job here."

Jim glared at her.

"That'll be enough of that, Rebecca!"

"Think so? I just figured the little slut would..."

"Okay, that's it! One more word and you're fired! Understand?"

"You can't fire me...Denning will..."

"Will back anything I do. You're a dime a dozen to him and at my word you will be gone in a split second. So enough with the trash talk."

Rebecca turned away, he cold feel the anger coming off her. He sipped his coffee and scanned the room. He heard the sound of trouble and he rose from his barstool. There was a commotion on the floor. One of the bouncers was lifting a man in a business suit from his seat, the man was struggling and swearing. The bouncer back handed the man across the face and the man collapsed in his chair.

"Hey!" Jim called and he was across the room in a split second. The young bouncer was preparing to hit the man again but Jim caught his arm.

"That's enough. What's going on!"

"This guy is gettin' outta hand, that's all!" the bouncer said.

"He hit me, he attacked me!" the man blurted, he was a balding, overweight business man, his suit now rumpled, his tie half undone.

"What did he do?" Jim asked the bouncer. Mike was making his way over but Jim waved him off.

"He was trying to climb onto the ramp! I told him to stop! But he kept on..."

Jim looked at the man.

"Sir, you've had too much to drink tonight. It's time for you to leave."

"Hey," the man said, "I've paid good money to get in here! I'm not leaving...

"Oh yes you are, right now," Jim said as he grabbed the man's arm, hoisting him from his seat. "Make it easy on yourself, sir. We'll call you a cab, you're in no condition to drive."

"Hey, my car..."

"Will be here in the morning, sir, now if you would please come calmly with me."

He eased the man across the floor, the bouncer following. He signaled Rebecca at the bar.

"Call a cab," he said and he saw her pick up the phone.

Jim escorted the man outside, passed several men who were on their way in. Another bouncer was standing beside Depoli now. They were checking the IDs of several younger men. Jim looked them over.

"Don't admit them," Jim said, "I can tell they've already had too much to drink."

"You heard the man," Depoli said and the young men turned away, disappointed, to cross the parking lot to their cars.

"Keep an eye on this one, I called him a cab," Jim told Depoli then he turned to the bouncer who had roughed the man up.

"You're fired! Get out and come back tomorrow for your final paycheck!" Jim said and Depoli and his partner both looked surprised.

"And get this," Jim said to Depoli and his partner. "There will be no excessive force used on customers. This man was just a bit drunk, that's all. Be polite and escort them out. If you have any problems get help, but be polite. Now keep an eye on him until the taxi arrives."

"Sure thing, Jim," Depoli said and Jim went back inside the club. Jim seated himself at the bar again then he saw Denning motioning to him to come over. Jim went to his table and Denning motioned for him to be seated.

"So what happened?" Denning asked him.

"I fired him," Jim answered him.

"Okay, good move, and you don't have to explain to me, you're in charge here. I saw what happened with that customer and you did right. Good job."

Jim nodded then stood and went back to his place at the bar. He indicated to Rebecca, "Always have this stool vacant for me."

"Sure thing," she answered and there was no sarcasm in her voice this time.

The dancer was through on the stage and she, now totally nude, picked up her things and hurried off stage, picking up her tips as well, there was a lot of bills on the stage, she had had a good night.

"More! More!" the audience yelled.

"It's my turn now," Rebecca said as one of the other girls, the one who had been shaving in the dressing room, came back to work the bar while Rebecca ascended the steps to the stage.

"What's your name?" Jim asked the girl.

"Debra," she said.

"Hello Debra, I'm Jim and I run things around here."

"So I've heard. Suzie your girlfriend?"

"No."

"So there's hope for me, then."

"I'll take a refill," Jim said, holding out his cup. Debra smiled and took the cup and refilled it, setting it back down in front of Jim with a seductive smile.

Jim sipped his coffee and ignored her. He watched the stage, Rebecca was beginning her dance, moving about the stage, almost unsteady.

"That broad sure can't dance," Debra said. "All she's got going right now is her looks and her big boobs, right now Denning favors her but she better not let it go to her head."

Jim knew exactly what she was talking about. He watched Rebecca, Debra was right, no talent at all. Looks, yes, talent, no. She writhed about the stage to the music, off came her top as she spun clumsily around the pole.

"Hey, bitch, you gotta do better'n that!" came a yell from the audience. One of the guys in "T" shirts and jeans was starting to get rowdy. His buddies also started getting loud, making catcalls. The other bouncers in the room looked towards Jim. He shook his head and they kept back. Jim wanted to see how far they were going to go.

"Hey, baby, let big Jack show you what a real man is!" the "T" shirt guy said again as he rose up, he was seated in front of the ramp. He went for the stage and Jim nodded to the bouncers. They were right there, blocking the man who had called himself "Jack."

Jack looked at them, a smirk on his face. His friends also rose up, in a fighting mode, their fists clenched at their sides.

"Hey big man," Jack said, "We ain't the wimps that other guy you kicked out of here was!"

"Am I going to have a problem with you gentlemen?" Jim asked as he walked over. He was already psyching himself up. On the stage Rebecca's dance went on.

"No problem at all, guy, just leave us and the little lady up there be and go on about your business."

"You are my business and you are through for the night. Now please leave or I will have to take extreme measures."

"Oh really, extreme..."

Jim had Jack spun around, a hammer lock on his right arm, jamming it up behind his back.

"Out you go!" Jim said and he hustled Jack across the room and out the door. The others went without incident, escorted by the other bouncers. Jim shoved on through the entrance, past Depoli who looked at him. Jim released Jack who immediately spun and took a swing at him. Jim caught his wrist and the man went down to his knees in pain.

"Don't make this harder on yourself, Jack!" Jim said.

Jack looked at his friends who just shrugged their shoulders.

"What a bunch of wimps!" Jack said to them. They looked sheepishly at Jim and his backup then followed their friend across the parking lot to their car.

"Gettin' a little rough in there, eh Jimbo?" Depoli said with a grin.

"Not really," Jim answered. "If this is as bad as it gets then this job is a piece of cake."

"Oh Jimbo, the night is young," Depoli smiled then turned to check more IDs. Jim headed back into the club with his backup. He returned to the bar, Debra had another fresh cup of coffee waiting for him.

"You handle yourself well," she said. "You try to show respect, at least at first."

"After that, well, I guess I have to take things to another level."

"But at least you're not a 'hothead' about it. I can tell you've been around. Military?"

"Iraq, Army Rangers."

"I figured it was something like that. You know how to lead men."

Jim looked at her for a moment.

"How long have you worked here?" Jim asked her.

"About a month, I came up from LA. Worked a few clubs there and also in Florida and Vegas."

The audience roared.

Jim looked over, Rebecca had doffed her bottoms, her freshly shaved charms evident and driving the men wild.

"Your friend, Suzie, sure started something," Debra said.

Another man was trying to climb up on the stage. Jim nodded to the bouncers who escorted him politely but firmly from the floor and out the door.

Jim went back to his coffee.

The music stopped and Rebecca left the stage.

"Your friend is next," Debra said.

Jim waited.

"You seem nervous, she your wife? Girlfriend? You jealous?"

"No, she's just a friend, but she's never done this before."

"Well, I saw her practicing earlier and she can move, that's for sure. That one's good. I am almost jealous, but there's enough for all of us."

"Enough?"

"Tips. There's plenty of tips to go around. Even that last one cleaned up pretty good."

Jim had seen Rebecca scooping the bills off the stage floor. Yes, she had done well this evening.

Suzie strode onto the stage, a see through nightie on over her black bikini, her hair teased and wild, she was quite an astonishing vixen tonight, he thought. A fast number came on and Suzie started her "thing" dancing expertly down the ramp, smiling seductively at the customers who were going wild, the place was packed now. Cheers went up.

"I'd say she's the main attraction," Debra said as she refilled Jim's cup, emptying the old coffee, never letting his cup get cold. She knew her job. "Hope she can handle it, she's a nice person."

Jim liked Debra, liked her attitude. She seemed like a good, down to earth person to him. He looked at her.

"It's just another job, you know. It isn't something one lasts too long at, not if they're smart," Debra said.

Off came the nightie, now in bikini top and bottoms Suzie spun around the pole, her wild hair falling about her shoulders as she leaned her head back.

"Such as?" Jim asked.

"What?"

"You were talking about other options."

"Yeah, like school. I've been going for four years, taking classes at the local community colleges in every town I've performed at. And saving my tips. I make good tips."

"I bet you do."

"Oh I do. Then I'll be back in LA studying for my BA in management."

"Way to go. I'll be attending the local college myself."

"You seem the type. Some of the other guys here, this is it for them. They'll burn out fast. Big dudes like that are a dime a dozen. From every high school football field in the country, the same story, big shot in high school but no direction and here they are. For you, it's different, I can tell. Now that girl up there, I hope she has some options."

"I think she does."

Off came Suzie's top now, wowing the audience to great cheers as she hugged the brass pole. Bills came fluttering onto the stage.

"She's doing pretty good," Debra said. "Look at all that cash!"

Suzie danced away from the pole, making her way down the ramp then turning and jutting out her buttocks, tucking the brief bikini bottom between her glistening cheeks and creating a sensation as more bills were tossed up onto the ramp. Then she turned her back and pranced to the main stage, moving about, catching some of the men's eyes in her seductive stare. She looked across at Jim and smiled her best bedroom smile, arousing him. She turned her back again.

"Oh here it comes," Debra said.

Off came the bottoms and Suzie danced about, her back still to the audience, letting the momentum grow.

"That girl knows what she's doing!" Debra said. "You sure this is her first time."

"She's amazing, all right."

Then Suzie turned, facing her audience, turning to each side so they could all see and the yells filled the room, vibrating off the walls and almost drowning out the music. There was a roar of excitement as Rebecca, fully nude, suddenly exploded onto the stage and crossed right to Suzie, shoving her. Suzie stumbled towards the edge of the stage, struggling to balance herself. Jim dashed across the room, plowing through several tables, knocking them, the customers and the drinks aside. He made it in time as Suzie lost her balance finally and fell into his arms. She immediately put her arms around his neck and hugged him to her, her breasts against his chest.

Customers were picking themselves up, waitresses bringing them fresh drinks on the house, the other bouncers standing by just in case. Jim waved them off as the music stopped.

"Sorry folks! Drinks on the house. Music please!"

The music started up again as bouncers set up the tables and helped the customers back into their seats with apologies.

"Hey, that was pretty good!" one customer grinned.

Rebecca stood on the stage, hands on hips, glaring down at Jim and Suzie. She pointed at Suzie.

"I challenge you to a dance off! You and me! Right now!"

"She's fired!" Jim said under his breath as Suzie was set on the floor, her arm still around him.

"No Jim, wait," Suzie said.

"I warned you, Rebecca!" Jim said.

"No! I accept the challenge!" Suzie yelled as she bounded upon the stage. Rebecca was about to bend down to pick up some of Suzie's tips.

"Leave the cash alone!" Jim yelled and he also bounded onto the stage. The music stopped.

"Okay, if it's a dance off you want then that's what it'll be! We'll work it like this, everyone for Rebecca, toss your bills over there!" Jim pointed to the left of the stage. "And all bills for Suzie, to the right!" and Jim pointed to the right.

Jim was standing between Rebecca and Suzie. Rebecca was glaring at Suzie.

"Hold on!" Denning's voice boomed across the room and he also advanced across the floor and onto the stage, waving at the audience.

"Looks like we got quite a competition going on here, eh folks?"

"Yeah!" the audience roared.

"Tell you what, folks. What do you say to an all out catfight? These two against each other in an all-out catfight! What do you say?"

The audience roared their approval, the roar filling the room.

"Yeah, that's what we want! A catfight!" several yelled at once.

Denning stood there, taking it all in, all the yells, all the catcalls. He smiled, master of ceremonies now.

"What about a steel cage match?"

"Steel cage! Right on!" came the yell.

Jim started to protest but Suzie took his hand and squeezed it. She leaned over to him.

"Don't worry, Jim, I can handle her, remember the rail road tracks? She can't fight her way out of a paper bag. I'll make it look good."

Suzie waved to the Audience, looked at Rebecca.

"Okay, you want a fight, bitch, you got one!" Suzie challenged.

"Oh you are so on!" Rebecca answered and she tried to come at Suzie but Denning held her back. Suzie, in her role, started at Rebecca and Jim, catching on, stopped her, holding her back as she struggled to reach Rebecca.

"Let me at that bitch!" Rebecca yelled, struggling to reach Suzie.

One of the bouncers ran up and placed a remote mike into Denning's hand. Denning spoke, his voice carrying over the sound system.

"A cage match it is!" his voice boomed and he waved his arms. Dramatic music began to play and everyone looked skyward. A steel cage, it looked like a large birdcage, was being lowered by pulleys from the ceiling, lowered slowly to the main stage while the audience cheered. There was a roar outside, a thundering sound, the sound of many Harley Davidsons, Jim knew the sound. A moment later a group of about ten burly bikers in cutoff jean jacket vests with insignia on them came striding into the club led by a towering giant of a man with long blond hair and a bushy, flowing, blond beard, he looked like a Viking warrior, like Thor the Thunder God himself with his piercing, ice blue eyes. He looked to be about six foot six and weighing about two seventy at least, all solid muscle. The bikers went right to the bar grabbing long necked beer bottles as fast as Debra could hand them off. Two other girls were now also helping out at the bar.

"All right, we came at the right time!" the one who looked like Thor said as he looked at his buddies and laughed. They all laughed, booming laughs as they hoisted their beers and guzzled fast, foam sliding down their chins and massive chests. They were truly barbaric looking.

"This is starting to get out of hand!" Jim said.

"Don't worry," Suzie said and she looked at the giant Viking biker. He looked at her, Jim thought he caught a twinkle in his eye. He looked at Suzie.

"You're on, bitch!" Suzie said as the cage settled onto the main stage, several of the other girls opening the cage door.

Jim scanned the floor, his guys were all in place, looking at him for direction. He nodded to them that it was all right for now.

"After you!" Rebecca said as they both headed for the cage. Rebecca paused at the entrance.

"Oh please, go on ahead," Suzie said.

"Oh no, you go first."

Suzie looked at her then started through the opening. Rebecca shoved her and she fell against the bars. Rebecca was on her in an instant as the girls shut the cage door. Jim faced the audience. He could see the Viking standing right at the stage, his buddies right beside him, occupying the front tables, the customers having thought better than to argue with them.

This was fast getting out of hand, Jim thought as he eyed the biker.

"Way to go, Zeke!" one of the bikers called to their towering leader. The giant named Zeke raised his beer to them in salute. They saluted back in kind and guzzled. The girls were bringing more beers immediately, placing them in the biker's hands and also distributing beers to the other customers who were going wild now.

Jim looked at Denning who leaned toward him.

"Don't worry, this is going to be a great show tonight. Trust me and learn," Denning said.

He picked up the mike and turned towards the stage.

"First the rules!" he said. "No hair pulling, no scratching or any kind of skin breaking whatsoever! Pure wrestling only! The first one who breaks the rule is fired! Got it?" and he looked right at Rebecca. She looked at him and nodded, smiling, then she looked at Jim. And then at Suzie.

"Let the games begin!" Denning yelled and the music started up again.

Both girls exploded at each other, entwining each other in naked, glistening limbs as they struggled for a hold. Suzie putting on a good act, not reverting to her martial arts experience as she appeared to struggle with Rebecca who was truly struggling as both women rolled about on the cage floor. They were on their feet, facing each other, their hair wild. They came at each other, Rebecca driving Suzie back against the bars as Suzie struggled to get free. Down they went, Rebecca on top of Suzie, it was making the audience go crazy now. The Bikers cheered them on, the roar growing ever louder. Jim retreated to the side of the stage, near Zeke. He looked at him. Zeke looked him over and Jim held his gaze for a moment. Zeke slowly nodded then raised his beer and cheered, looking at his buddies. The fight went on, the girls rolling about the cage, body to body, glistening with sweat. Suzie wrapped her legs around Rebecca and rocked her back so her shoulders were touching the floor. Denning in the role of referee started the count, on his knees, slapping his palm against the floor, one...two...thr.....

Rebecca tossed Suzie off her and rolled free and they went at it again. Rebecca had Suzie pinned now.

"One...two...thr..."

Off came Suzie's shoulders as she tossed Rebecca off of her, she did an expert flip, pinning Rebecca.

"One...two...three..!!! The winner!" Denning yelled. The cage door opened and Rebecca walked out, angry and defeated, leaving the stage. As Suzie left the cage Denning raised her hand in victory.

Suddenly the place erupted in chaos as several customers tried to gain the stage. Jim and his bouncers formed a wedge between the floor and the stage. The bikers got into the act. One of them picked up a chair and broke it over another customer's head, he went to the floor, out. Zeke pushed aside two of the bouncers and bounded onto the stage. Jim wheeled to see him scooping up Suzie.

"Hey!" Jim called but arms grabbed him as two bikers had him. Jim wheeled and delivered a hard right to one of the biker's jaw, sending him to the floor. Jim wheeled but more were grabbing him. Denning backed out of the way as bouncers ran into the room led by Depoli, making a pathway. The fight was on in front of the stage as fists flew. Jim downed two more of the bikers. He could see Zeke carrying Suzie out of the room and through the entrance. She had his vest on at this moment. He was carrying her bikini bottoms and top in one hand as they went out the door. Jim tried to follow. His backup was busy, the battle in full bloom as chairs flew and bodies dropped. The tamer customers were now making a bee line towards the entrance, they had had enough for the night. Jim outran them, tossing them aside as he tried desperately to get to the entrance. Zeke was already gone. Jim made the door in a mad dash and found himself in the parking lot. He saw Zeke and Suzie over by the parked bikes. She had on her bikini bottoms and top now. Jim thought it was rather strange as he charged up. Suzie stepped aside as Jim dove at Zeke who sidestepped easily. So this one knew his stuff. Jim came at him and caught a right to his jaw that jarred him. Jim shook it off, looking at Suzie who was heading inside as fast as she could run. She turned and looked at him for an instant, she blew him a kiss.

Strange!

A fist collided with his jaw again and he spun, dazed but not out!

Jim dove and caught Zeke, driving him into the lead bike which fell against the others, a domino effect as, one by one, they tumbled over. Zeke dove over the bikes but Jim stayed with him, driving him across the parking lot, away from the lights. The thought of Suzie's strange behavior briefly crossing his mind just before he expertly blocked a punch thrown by Zeke.

"Not bad but no cigar!" Jim answered as he delivered a punch which landed square. Zeke stumbled farther back, away from the lights into darkness now. There was a marsh at the end of the parking lot and trees, weeping willows. Into this Zeke stumbled, Jim right after him, right into Zeke's outstretched hand, holding an open wallet, a badge showing. Jim stopped cold.

"What the hell..." Jim said, stopping cold, reading the Federal DEA ID:

> It read: Agent Jason Bradley,
> Drug Enforcement Agency.

Jim was standing, fists still clenched, staring at the badge.

"Agent Jason Bradley? Bradley?"

"Sound familiar, bro?" Jason Bradley said.

"But..."

"Look after my little sis for me, bro, I got your back. Now let's make this fight look good!"

So this was the "surprise" Suzie was talking about.

"Name's Jim Saunders..."

"Agent Saunders, pleased to make you acquaintance. Now let's get on with this fight."

***

Jim was leading Zeke back across the parking lot into the lights. The other bouncers had rounded up all the bikers who were picking up their bikes. It appeared to be a standoff rather than a defeat. Zeke was bleeding from a well timed and aimed punch thrown by Jim just before they had stepped out of the trees and Zeke appeared to be subdued. People were crowding about now, customers, the girls, Suzie was standing there along side of Denning, who looked rather pale.

"Everything's under control, folks!" Jim yelled as he led Zeke back to his bike.

Denning looked relieved.

Jim walked into the club. Denning was now ecstatic, running around talking excitedly.

"What a show!" he said as he raised a hat full of bills, hundreds had reigned onto the stage during the cage match. The cage had returned to the ceiling where it had been hidden. Jim looked up, marveling at the construction. He hadn't noticed before. It had been hidden in rafters by a black shroud. Jim remembered how high the building looked from the outside. Now he understood as he saw the pulley system rigged on the ceiling.

Suzie was dressed in cutoff jeans and a tube top now. Denning ran up to her with the hat full of bills.

"All yours, my dear, all yours, winner take all!" he handed the hat to her and she took it, looking around at Jim, smiling. Rebecca was nowhere in sight. Suzie came up to Jim.

"My rescuer!" she said as she threw her arms around him and kissed him, pressing herself hotly against him. She looked into his eyes. The fear was gone from her eyes, Jim could see and she was almost on a high.

Jim looked around at the club. At all the broken chairs and tables. Otherwise the place was not too damaged, not as much as he figured it would have been.

"What a mess," Jim said.

"Oh, no problem!" Denning said, cheerfully, "we'll have this place up to speed again by tomorrow night for sure. These tables are cheap and I have a garage full of others. It's a tax write-off, no big loss. That's the name of the game, son, the name of the game. Well, you two run along, it's been a fantastic night! See you tomorrow, great job, son, great job!"

Denning shook Jim's hand enthusiastically.

"Go on, you two, get on out of here, the other guys will clean up this mess."

Suzie looked at Jim, smiling.

Jim could hear the roar of the Harleys as the bikers drove off.

"I'm starved, what about you?" she said. "There's a Denny's down the road."

Jim realized at that moment that, yes, he was indeed famished. It had been a long night, first night on the job.

***

Jim was enjoying his steak and fries, as was Suzie, both of them dug in enthusiastically.

"I never realized how really hungry I was!" Suzie said. She had followed Jim's car do the restaurant with hers. They had walked, laughing, into the restaurant.

"You seem to be handling things better," Jim said.

"I feel great!"

"That was quite a show."

Suzie laughed.

"So you met my little brother tonight. I told you a surprise was coming, didn't I?"

"So that was it. It was set up. Are all..."

"All of them DEA, no way. He's in deep cover. I asked him to show up and raise a bit of a scene. We even planned the 'kidnapping' so you would follow him to the parking lot and he could let you know who he is."

"So he's your 'little' brother. Funny..."

"A year younger than I. He is my guardian, the shadow who watches over me. And you too..."

Suzie leaned over the table and gave Jim a kiss. "I'm okay now, I mean with the job and all. I know I have you and my little brother to watch over me."

"What does he think..."

"About me working at the club. He knows it's part of the job but he is enraged that I have to do it. He was thinking of going straight to Martin about it.'

"He thinks like I do."

"But it's okay now, I'm not afraid anymore."

"That was quite a battle up there in that cage."

Suzie laughed again. "Oh, that. I faked it all the way, I worked Rebecca good, reeled her in and pinned her when I figured it was time to end it. I really had her thinking she almost had me pinned then I would do my escape. Then I ended it!"

"Really, but then she isn't much of a fighter, physically, that is."

"Wrestling."

"Wrestling?"

"My brother and I used to watch professional wrestling when we were kids and would constantly wrestle each other on the living room floor. We knew all the moves, when to pin, when to get out, everything, my dad would just howl with laughter watching us, he said it was better than the show on TV. We learned all the timing, everything. One time my Dad took us both to the stadium in Atlanta, Georgia, to see the show. All the great champions were there, Ric flair, Magnum TA, all of them, what a show it was. My brother and I studied every move and had a ball wrestling on the front lawn for weeks afterwards. It came in handy when I joined The Agency, it fit in with all the martial arts training. I had also had Taekwondo classes along with my brother.

"My brother. He's something else. He just kept growing and growing and then he started lifting weights out in the garage and grew even more. It was astounding! I lifted weights with him but wow, there was no way I was going to keep up with him. We would spar together but he really had to hold back to keep from obliterating me. And I was good. But him, he's in another world altogether. He joined up after serving in the Marines for four years, right after getting out of high school. We both used work construction for my dad during summers. Jason, he's a great guy. I'm glad I have you and him to watch over me."

She reached across the table to hold Jim's hand and look in his eyes.

"Really, Jim, it'll be okay now."

"That's good to hear," Jim answered but he was still not convinced. He would keep an eye on her and go right to Martin the moment he thought he should.

They had finished and they drained the last of their coffee.

"Time to get going," Suzie said, "I guess you'll go on back to your apartment."

"Yeah, got a busy day tomorrow."

"Yeah, we both do. We're going to be at that powwow out at the Cow Palace to talk to your friend, Charlie White Eagle. Think he'll bite?"

"No way to tell."

He and Suzie were walking out of the restaurant having laid their money down on the table with tip to pay for the late night dinner. Jim walked Suzie to her car and she turned to face him, putting her arms around him and hugging him close. She looked up at him.

"Thanks again, Jim, thanks for being there."

"It's my job. And Suzie, watch out for Rebecca, she'll be looking to pay you back. Don't underestimate her."

"Don't worry, Jim, I won't."

She kissed him lightly on the lips and got into her car.

***

Jim returned to his apartment and went inside, getting undressed and flopping down on his bed, covers off for it was quite a warm, late spring evening. He closed his eyes and despite the coffee, he drifted off into a deep sleep. Tomorrow would be another day.

***

Jim and Suzie pulled into the packed parking lot at the Cow Palace, a convention center just south of San Francisco where trade shows and all kinds of events went on. They had taken Jim's car, Suzie sitting rather close, leaning across the console from her bucket seat. Both were dressed casually, Jim in sport shirt and his jeans and Suzie in halter top and cutoffs. They walked together through the ticket gate and into the giant sized main floor. The place was filled with booths selling Native American jewelry and artifacts, trinkets, blankets and custom "T" shirts with pictures of wild animals, eagles, buffalos, and elk deer. Many Native Americans wore traditional dress on this day and the stadium was filled with the sound of drumming. At the center of the stadium the area was cleared for traditional dances while several groups of Indians sat around giant sized drums in covered booths, the drums thundered while the dancers performed, dressed elaborately in bright colored costumes, men in headdresses and the women in beautiful, fringed outfits, they all moved in a counter clockwise circle, stepping to the drumming while the drummers sang native songs which filled the stadium over the giant PA system.

"Wow!" Suzie exclaimed as she looked around. "This is really something."

"Sure is," Jim answered and both of them were awed at the sights and sounds, this was the first powwow they had ever been to. Jim searched the booths looking for Charlie White Eagle but there were so many.

"What'll we do?" Suzie asked him, she was holding his hand.

"We'll just have to keep circulating and looking around. He told me he would be here. You saw that bunch of Harleys parked in the lot. I recognized his so he's here somewhere."

"Hey, Bro!" came a familiar voice and Jim and Suzie looked over towards a booth. Charlie White Eagle was there, sporting jeans and a black leather vest with a Harley Davidson Eagle on the back. His black hair was trailing down his back. He truly was a hulk of a man, built much like Jim but darker complexioned.

"Hey Charlie, good to see you!" Jim said as he and Suzie went on over. Charlie came out of the booth to give Jim a firm hug and a slap on the back. He hugged Suzie.

"Good to see you too, Bro," Charlie said. "Come on, meet my relatives."

They went to the booth, there was an older woman there and two young men, tall gangly but they would fill out later, all dressed in Jeans and "T" shirts except for one young girl of about fourteen who was dressed in an elaborate, white, fringed costume.

"This is my aunt, Mary, and my two cousins, Jack and Steve."

Both boys nodded shyly and shook Jim and Suzie's hands. His aunt remained seated and shook their hands. She was very heavy and her face was lined with many years of a hard life.

"This is my little sister, Tracy. It will be her turn to dance soon."

The young girl grinned shyly at Jim and Suzie.

"Hello, Tracy," Suzie said. "My what a beautiful young girl your little sister is."

"Oh, now you've embarrassed her," Charlie said and Tracy was blushing shyly, looking away from them. "It's okay, sis, these are good people."

Charlie reached into a cooler and took out two Cokes which he offered to Suzie and Jim.

"Stick around, hey Bro? You gotta see my little sister dance and check out this place. Something else, huh?"

"Sure is, Charlie," Jim said as he looked around. Charlie looked at him square.

"Hey, Bro, you didn't come here just for the show, did you?"

"Charlie, we need to talk," Jim said.

"Sure thing, Bro."

"Alone, the three of us."

"Okay, let's take a walk, be back soon, Aunt Mary," Charlie said and they made their way across the stadium, Charlie greeting friends in booths along the way. They had their hands stamped and went on outside and over to a corner of the parking lot near the bikes.

"Knew you were here," Jim said, "I recognized your bike."

Charlie laughed, they took sips of their Cokes.

"So what's up, Bro, you got something big on your mind, shoot."

Both Suzie and Jim pulled out their IDs and showed them to Charlie.

"What the... you're both Feds? Am I in trouble or something?"

"We checked you out thoroughly," Suzie said, "and your record is clean as a whistle."

"Hey, Bro, I had no idea you were a Fed, you just got out of the Army..."

"It was kind of rushed," Jim said, "And we are too so I will need an answer. We're here to offer you a job with us."

"Hey don't I have to go through some kind of training? I mean, these jobs don't come easy."

"The military has given you all the training you'll need for this job," Jim said. "I requested you personally to work with me."

"What's up?"

"It's big, but I can't fill you in unless we have some kind of a commitment."

"Hey, Bro, you can see I'm pretty busy right now."

"Charlie," Suzie said, "this is the only time you are going to get such an offer handed to you. There are no promises yet but if it works out you could have a career with us full time, benefits, retirement, whole ball of wax."

"It's show to show," Charlie said. "And then we go back to the reservation and work on restocking, then the shows again and back. I hoped for more when I joined the service but when I got home there it still was. The same life. I had dreams of doing something else but they need me. My aunt and brothers and my sister need me."

"Charlie," Suzie said, "think about what you could do for them with a career with the U.S. Government, all the benefits. A good income."

"My aunt, she won't leave the reservation, it's her life, but my sister, my two cousins, I want more for them. You're right. I can help them. I want my little sis to go to college, and my two cousins need to go also. They need a kick in the butt and soon because they are growing up fast. We will always respect the tribal traditions but we don't have to live in complete poverty like it's been for so many generations since you belagana took over."

"Belagana?" Suzie asked.

"All of you white devils, belagana, ignorant, stupid, wasting the land, oh don't get me started."

"You're right, but what's happened is over and done with," Jim said.

"Jimbo we've had this argument many times. I know it's not directly your fault, hell, you'd put your life on the line for me and you have. I'd put my life on the line for you and now it looks like that's what I'm gonna be doing, right?"

"If you say 'yes' then, yes, you will be. We're in a war, Charlie. We can use you. This is a good career. It'll work out."

"How soon?"

"I'd like you start tonight. I have a job lined up for you, undercover with me and I need you there starting tonight, as soon as you can get away."

"Are you in, Charlie?" Suzie asked. "I have to know now, the paperwork's already been processed, Martin Thomas, our boss is just waiting, your friend, Jim, here, was very persuasive. He needs backup, we both do and I saw how you conducted yourself out on the railroad tracks a week ago. You're good and we want you. I realize it's short notice but we need to know now and you have to be ready to leave with Jim today, before the afternoon."

"What's this job you have me lined up for, Jimbo?" Charlie asked.

"Bouncer. I'll be your boss."

"Well, boss, I gotta go tell them I won't be staying. It'll be rough packing up for them but I can get some of the guys here to help out. I'll tell them I have a family 'emergency.' So, boss, be with you in a while."

"Tell you what," Jim said. "Just show up at the club on your bike around seven tonight. I'll square it with the main guy there, I already fired a guy last night and told him I was bringing in help."

"See you at seven then, I can help them pack."

***

Jim was at the club, he was about to have a meeting of his staff. Repairs had been hastily made, new tables and chairs had replaced the damaged ones. Denning was seated at his personal table drinking coffee. The DJ was busy getting everything ready in his booth. Rebecca and Debra were stocking the bar. Rebecca had a sullen look on her face. Suzie had just come in the door and had hurried through the club to the dressing room. As Jim was about to speak he heard a familiar sound. The sound of a Harley Davidson pulling up outside.

"Not again," Mike walker said.

"Don't worry, I know this guy," Jim said.

A moment later Charlie White Eagle came striding into the club, looking about in the dim light.

"Over here, Charlie," Jim said and Charlie came over.

Jim walked over to Denning's table with Charlie.

"This is the guy I was talking about," Jim said. "We served together in the war and I trust this man with my life."

Denning looked up at Charlie and then at Jim.

"Yeah, I saw him in town the night of the fight at the railroad tracks. Okay, he's hired."

Denning shook hands with Charlie.

Jim led Charlie over to the group of bouncers, Mike Walker and Depoli were among them.

"This is Charlie. He's to be considered my second in command. We go way back, served in Iraq together and were in many battles. He's good, as good as it gets."

Charlie shook hands all around, he had met Mike Walker and Depoli at the tracks already. They nodded.

"Okay, now to get down to business," Jim said. "We had an incident last night in which a customer was roughed up by one of the bouncers. That bouncer is no longer here. Now I am not talking about the biker incident. We did what we had to do, it required force and it went well. The damage was not too bad. I doubt if they'll be back. So always be polite to the customers and use as little force as possible. Remember, they are drinking and there are naked girls dancing on the stage and that's quite an explosive combination. So be respectful and keep order. The customers are here to have a good time. If they don't have a good time, they don't come back, the club loses money and we have no job. Remember that. Okay, you all know your places, the door is opening soon so be ready. Things should go smoothly tonight."

Jim motioned for Charlie to follow him. They went out the door to the parking lot and walked the perimeter.

"You have a place to stay?" Jim asked Charlie.

"Yeah, got a room on the way over, motel out on the highway a few miles down the road."

"Good. Tomorrow's a big night. Private party at Denning's place. Reps from Chinatown will be there to bid for distribution rights. I made contact with one triad, the Tiger Clan. There will be members of The Cobra there also. We're to do nothing but keep our eyes and ears open and see what we can find out. Tonight, just circulate around the club, you are second in command and no one will argue with you."

"What about Mike Walker?"

"He seems okay now. We pretty much settled things at the railroad tracks that night. Oh, yeah, that girl at the bar, Rebecca..."

"Yeah, I remember her, she's bad news. And you watch your back with her."

Jim described the catfight the night before.

"An Agent..."

"Yes, Suzie's brother, deep cover. Also, remember that we use our first names, get in the habit of it."

"Okay," Charlie said. "I guess I'll go inside."

Charlie went into the club. Jim stood there in the parking lot looking the place over. Then he turned and went back into the club.

CHAPTER SIXTEEN

Jim left the club at closing. He and Charlie had a late meal out at Denny's and then Jim had headed back to his apartment. Suzie had gone on home to her place. It had been a quiet night, a few near scuffles but nothing out of control. Rebecca had behaved herself after being told by Jim that one more incident would cost her her job. Denning had left the club early to make arrangements for his party the next night. The club would be closed, unusual for a Saturday night but Denning knew this was an important meeting coming up, to have two of Chinatown's main triads at the table to deal and Denning would profit either way. He had left the club in high spirits, slapping Jim on the back.

Jim parked his car and made his way up to his room, unlocking his door. He sensed someone there and before he could turn on the light naked arms went around him and moist lips found his, a nude body pressed against him, a bare thigh wrapping around his. Jiang Li.

He didn't even ask how she had gotten into his room and he didn't care.

***

Jim awoke from a deep sleep. It was in the dark hours before dawn. He could feel Jiang Li's thigh draped across him, her hair wild around her shoulders and on his chest. The feel of her naked, silken flesh against him brought him to life. She stirred, moving her thigh on him and she kissed his face and neck. He could see her dark eyes looking at him in the dimness of the night, street light filtering into the room outlining her there and glinting off her naked skin, covers off. She reached down for him finding him ready, she climbed up on him, riding him like a bucking bronco as he arched upwards, driving into her, she gasped with his thrusts, swinging her head, her hair flying about her shoulders as she drew in deep breaths, loving him.

"I'm yours," she gasped. "I am completely yours..." another gasp as she climaxed on him. He reached his head up and kissed her erect nipples then nibbled them lightly as she gasped.

"Oh yes..." she gasped again and fought for breath. "Oh yes, Jim, yes...yes...yes!!!"

***

The sun was not yet over the eastern horizon, light filtered into the room. Jim lay with Jiang Li. She moved on him and smiled, he was still in her, had slept in her after they had made love. He started to pull out. She instantly tightened on him.

"No..." Jiang Li moaned, "I like him in there..."

She kissed him and looked into his eyes.

"Jiang Li," Jim asked.

She kept looking at him.

"How much does your father owe The Cobra?"

"He owes then one hundred thousand dollars. And Harry Xiang wants his money soon or I will go to Tommy as payment."

The thought of Jiang Li with another man, with Tommy Xiang, the thought of her naked with him, of Tommy Xiang seeing her naked body filled Jim with a sudden rage.

"Marry me, Jiang Li, marry me now! It's your father who went into debt, you are not responsible."

"It's not that simple, Jim."

She moved on him and he stirred within her. She smiled at the result. The she was serious again.

"Jim, I have been careless! We...we have already been seen at the college by David Xiang. Jim, you are in danger being with me. Jim, you know what they could do..."

"I've heard...castrate me..."

"They would not hesitate...oh Jim, I should leave you..."

"Never!" Jim hardened in her suddenly, she gasped. "The thought of you with him...never!"

"Jim, maybe it's best..."

"No!" she was moving on him now and he rolled over on top of her, driving into her as her legs went around his waist, kissing his neck and chest...

***

It was late morning now. Jim lay there the sun caressing his body. He was looking at Jiang Li. She was dressed now, standing in front of the mirror on the dresser, brushing her hair. She looked down at him and he stirred. She smiled down at him, a sexy smile, the smile of a sexually satisfied woman. She came over to him and sat on the edge of the bed. He reached for her, drawing her too him but she resisted, pushing him back.

"I really have to go now, Jim, I have to go home, I am expected. I can't keep 'staying' at June's forever or they will definitely suspect something."

"Marry me, Jiang Li, it's your father's debt, not yours..."

"I know that, Jim, please, give me some time."

"There isn't much time, Jiang Li, you graduate next weekend, then Harry Xiang will demand payment. Stay with me, Jiang Li, I'll take care of us."

"I have to be at the graduation, Jim, I have to be there, there for my family."

"Your father wanted you in college, he wants you to think for yourself, he won't hold you to this debt. A man doesn't get his daughter educated just to give her to a drug lord."

"Perhaps he thinks I will be able to leave Tommy Xiang later and make my own way in life."

"I don't want you with him for a single second!"

Rage surged through Jim again as he thought of her naked with another man.

"You! With him! No..."

"Because I will be naked with him? And what about you, every night now you see naked women all the time!"

"Jiang Li! That's just a job!"

"You think I like you seeing other women naked? Seeing that blond one, Suzie, naked. I get so mad at times! I am so enraged at you have no idea!"

She glared at him. Jim rose up and came to her, putting his arms around her. She pushed away.

"Don't touch me!" she demanded.

"Jiang Li..."

"You with her..."

"It's not what you think..."

"Isn't it really! I think I should go!"

She pushed away and headed for the door.

"Fine, then!" Jim stormed. "Go ahead, go ahead and leave! I don't give shit! Get out of here!"

He opened the door and looked at her. She walked past him, suddenly she turned and threw her arms around him, tears were in her eyes.

"Oh Jim, I didn't mean it, Jim! Jim!" she fondled him and he hoisted her up in his arms, fully erect now and headed for the bed, tossing her down as she hurriedly pulled off her jeans, tossing them aside, her panties came next and Jim was on her in an instant, driving into her as she gasped, receiving him, kissing him, gripping his waist with her legs, gripping firmly as he rode her.

"I love you, Jim, I love you!"

***

They sat at the coffee shop sipping lattes. Or rather, Jiang Li had a latte, Jim had his usual favorite, regular coffee, black and steaming. Jiang Li was seated right next to him, leaning against him, her thigh across his. It was noon now. They had just gotten dressed a half hour earlier, they had been making furious love for hours, until the anger had left and the tenderness and love had returned.

"I have to begin final preparations for my last test. And I have to be fitted for a graduation gown this afternoon," Jiang Li said as she sipped her drink. "Will you come, Jim, will you come to my graduation?"

"If it will not get you into trouble, I'll be there."

"I want you there, Jim. I want you to see me on that field. I wish I could tell my parents. After the ceremony..."

"What then?"

"After the ceremony...oh Jim...afterwards I want them to know about us. But then my father..."

"You don't owe the rest of your life to an illegal commitment, Jiang Li, what the Cobra is doing is illegal. It's extortion and they can be prosecuted."

"It doesn't end there, Jim."

"It can."

"How would you know?"

Jim wished he could tell her. Wished with all his heart and soul he could tell her. Remaining silent was killing him. He wanted to show her his badge, tell her he could make it better but he wondered if he could in any way do that.

She leaned over and kissed him.

"I have to go," she said. "I don't know if I can see you this weekend or not. I'll call you. You have your cell phone."

The image of Jiang Li naked on his cell phone crossed his mind and he was instantly aroused. Jiang Li happened to be looking down and caught it.

"My my!" she exclaimed with a smile. "I guess he never tires."

They stood and Jiang Li was in his arms, kissing him, pressing against him as the pedestrians and cars passed. Out of the corner of his eye Jim saw Rebecca driving by, looking at them, a deadly look in her eyes. Jim kissed Jiang Li long and passionately, drinking her all in.

"I'm so sorry, Jim," she breathed as she looked up at him. "I'm so sorry, Jim, I know you're doing the best you can. I love you so."

They parted, still holding hands. Jim was about to walk her to her car but she shook her head. Slowly, their hands parted and Jiang Li was gone, bouncing off across the street, her long pony tail bobbing up and down as she went. On the other side of the street she turned and waved to him and smiled. He waved back. She was gone.

***

Jim had steak and eggs at Stan's then returned to his room where he took a long nap. He awoke without the alarm in a dead start, instantly upright. At first he didn't know where he was. It was late afternoon now. Jim dressed for the party, black slacks, a white turtle necked long sleeved "T" shirt and a tan sports coat. He thought about bringing his gun and badge. No. Too much of a chance to take. He put on dress shoes and polished them until they shown brightly, spit and polish, like the military. He went to Stan's again for a steak and baked potato dinner and more coffee. It would be a busy night. He headed out of the parking lot.

***

Jim arrived at the Denning mansion. It was a large, three story many bedroom house painted white on a great expanse of lawn with trees in the back and to the sides. The front of the house was lined with white pillars. He came to a wrought iron gate, stopping at a message box, pushing the button for admittance. There was a camera on the driveway, above the gate. The gate opened automatically and he drove on through. He drove up the winding driveway, lawn on each side, manicured, trimmed, everything in its place. Up ahead in front of the house stood a man in a white blazer. Jim rode up and stopped. The man approached him. Jim looked up at him, he was about thirty five with a pock marked face and jet black hair. Jim had not seen him before. He was built, his shoulders straining at the seams to his jacket. He was only slightly smaller than Jim. Jim noticed this as he sized him up. The pock marked man was sizing Jim up as well, noticing his shoulders bulging out of the seams, sitting in the car, his thick neck. Jim leaned out the window.

"Jim Saunders," Jim said.

"Go ahead and drive right around to the back of the house," the pock marked man said and Jim drove around the circular driveway, passing the front of the pillared mansion and around to the rear. There were other cars there, he saw Mike Walker's car and Depoli's car as well. All employees, no guests had arrived yet. He saw Rebecca's car among them and also, Suzie's.

Jim got out.

"Oh Jim, Jim..."

Jim heard her voice and turned to see Suzie bouncing towards him, dressed in very tight cutoff jeans and a tube top, her hair teased out and plenty of makeup on. She looked down right alluring in a low class kind of way, rather than the classy woman in the gray business suit she really was. She came down the back steps and through a flowered, white archway, running to him.

She reached him and threw her arms around him, pressing herself to him.

"Oh Jim I'm glad you're here, I'm so glad."

She looked almost frantic under the makeup, she had on heavy eye liner which accentuated her beautiful eyes, dazzling eyes, eyes full of life. Jim fought to control himself as she moved against him.

"We'd best get inside," Jim said.

Inside the place was ready, a bar was set up with a bartender Jim had not seen at the club. The DJ booth was set up with the same young man from the club. Party lights had been mounted. Jim stood in the main room, there was a circular staircase leading up to the floors above. Jim recognized the bouncers from the club. Mike Walker and Depoli greeted him. The girls were walking around, getting things ready, a table of food was set up, ham, roast beef, chicken, in great amounts along with other vegetables. Jim saw Rebecca there, she looked across the room at him then went on about her business. Suzie walked over to one of the tables to help.

"Hello, Jim," a woman's voice said as her hand circled his hips, lightly touching him. It was Debra. She looked up, smiling at him. She was simply dressed in tight jeans and "T" shirt and her hair was also teased to extreme.

"Evening, Debra," Jim said as she removed her hand, smiling at his reaction.

"My my," she said, "well, I must be getting back to work, the guests will be arriving soon."

She trotted off across the room. Jim motioned to his team to follow him and they went into the kitchen, the place was filled with a chef and his helpers busily preparing more food on the large stove. The kitchen was huge with a preparing island in the center. Jim motioned for his team over to the side. He sat on a counter to address them.

"Okay, this is how it is," Jim said.

At that moment Jim heard the tell tail sound of a Harley Davidson pulling up outside. Charlie was here. Jim waited. A few moments later Charlie White Eagle came walking into the kitchen to join them. He was dressed in slacks and a dress shirt. Jim's eyebrows raised.

"Bought it quickly this morning, the outfit..." Charlie said. "Kind of a pain to wear it on a bike. But oh well, Bro, here I am."

"Okay," Jim said, clapping his hands together and holding them. "Charlie and I will be outside checking cars for now. We will work outside in shifts and circulate inside during the party. Outside, all visitors will be searched. All weapons will be left in their cars. Got it?"

Everyone nodded.

"So, you know the drill, just like in the club, keep order, be polite and keep your eyes open. There are a lot things here that can be stolen and a few of the visitors may have sticky fingers, so be aware. Now let's get out there and go to work, Charlie..." Jim nodded to Charlie and headed for the main entrance. As he was crossing through the main room he noticed the pock marked man with a few more men in dark suits he hadn't seen at the club. Some of them had the tell tale bulge in their jackets, they were carrying.

"That's Tony De Angelo," Mike Walker came up to Jim. "I think he's some kind of enforcer, dangerous man."

Jim nodded then patted Mike on the shoulder.

"So you've seen him before?"

"At the club sometimes."

"Good, it's extra security. Come on, Charlie, let's get out there."

Jim and Charlie walked out to the circular driveway and stood waiting. The sun was lower in the sky now, evening was fast approaching. Jim saw the first guests driving up the driveway. Two black, stretch limos which pulled up in front of the estate. The driver got out and opened the back doors. First several extremely burly men, all Asians, exited the car and stood waiting. One extended his hand into the car. Out came a gorgeous Asian woman in a tight, very short, silk red dress. She had on exotic makeup and her hair was waist length. Another girl got out, similarly dressed. Both of them looked at Jim and Charlie, no expression on their faces. Burly men were also getting out of the other limo, and other expensively dressed, beautiful Asian women. Now the burly men waited by the second limo. Out stepped a sturdy built man of about sixty with silver hair slicked back. He was in a black suit and he held out his hand. Out stepped another beautiful Asian woman who took his arm. From another door in the stretch limo came the two sons, first David, who Jim had met in the college parking lot when he had decked his bodyguard. And then his brother, Tommy Xiang, Jiang Li's betrothed. For a brief moment Jim's eyes locked with Tommy's. Tommy was also burly, a thick neck but with refined facial features and medium length hair, styled to perfection. Jim noticed how his broad shoulders narrowed to a trim waist. Rage shot through Jim for a brief instant as he visualized Jiang Li with this man. And jealousy as well. Jim put the thoughts from his mind for the moment. He saw David Xiang looking at him but saw no expression. Jim knew David knew who he was, that he remembered the incident at the college. David looked at Tommy and Tommy looked again at Jim, this time his eyes had a calculating look to them.

Mike Walker and other bouncers stepped up beside Jim and Charlie.

"Gentleman," Jim said, "If you will please step this way, I will have to do a search for any weapons before you go inside."

Jim stepped towards one of the burly men in Harry Xiang's escort.

The man stood firm, hands at his sides. Jim stood in front of him.

"If you please, sir," Jim said, looking him in the eye. The man did not move. The man looked towards Harry. Harry looked at Jim, their eyes locked. Then Harry nodded and, came forward himself, arms wide. The others in the party followed suit and they were each patted down. All the bodyguards surrendered 9mms and .45s, placing them in the limos. After the search they all stood waiting. Jim noticed there were girls on the arms of David and Tommy Xiang. A man about to be married out with a bunch of whores, Jim thought to himself.

"Thank you for your time, gentlemen, you may now proceed inside and join the party. Have a good time this evening, gentlemen," Jim said and the Xiang party proceeded to go on inside the mansion.

The drivers pulled the two limos off to the side.

Up the driveway came a sleek black Lincoln with tinted passenger windows. Jim saw that Jonnie Lee was driving. There was a young man seated next to him and it looked like there were several people in the back seat. The car pulled up and Jonnie Lee got out. He made no show of recognition as he looked at Jim. Jim gave him the usual introduction. The young man got out of the passenger side and another young man got out of the back seat along with Samantha Yi, dressed in a black, floor length formal. She was dazzling in the dress, her hair made up, piled high on her head, expensive pearls around her neck. She came immediately over to Jonnie Lee and took his arm. She looked at Jim, no expression on her face but he saw her eyes smile at him as she held Jonnie's arm. The searches completed Jim motioned for them to go on inside.

Other limos arrived carrying members of the Latino contingent, a limo with Cubans, the Miami connection. A limo with well dressed black men with their escorts, two beautiful black women, the men had their heads shaved and wore wrap around shades even though it was getting darker outside. All were searched and ushered inside. Jim could hear the music pick up now, the party was beginning. The yard lights went on, old style streetlights from a bygone era, they came on, controlled by a timer. Jim looked around, he could see several cameras on the house scanning the area. He looked towards the trees and he could see several more through the branches where they were mounted. Jim looked over at Charlie. He was also noticing. They looked at each other, then they headed inside. Mike Walker and several others remained to greet more guests as more and more cars arrived.

Jim and Charlie entered the main room to the mansion. Jim could see the party was now in full swing. The girls from the bar were circulating through the crowd, all of them dressed in seductive short dresses now, very low cut and revealing. Jim could see Rebecca off to one side, Debra was there, so were others. He saw Suzie crossing the room. She was carrying a glass tray on one hand and Jim noticed that there were precut lines of white powder and short straws on the table. She was instantly among the guests and many were beginning to partake of the drugs offered, snorting the lines. Now the other girls were also circulating with trays. All the big wigs were partaking, their bodyguards were not, they all stood by, eyeing each other with suspicion; that was their job. More high powered guests were pouring through the main door now.

Now, through the door came Denning, a dizzy looking blond in a high fashion dress on his arm. With him was an entourage of obvious hookers in short dresses and lots of makeup. They were giggling and chatting among each other, eyeing the crowd. They immediately began circulating.

"Hello, Jim," Jim looked around. Rebecca was standing there before him, she was holding a tray of drinks and drugs, lines of cocaine, and pre-rolled joints. Her eyes already had a glazed look, she had been partaking of the party treats, he could tell.

"Hello, Rebecca," Jim said.

"I don't see your girlfriend anywhere around here," she said, "You know, your little Chinadoll..."

"That's enough, Rebecca," Jim warned.

Rebecca smiled seductively and moved on.

"Hi, Jim," and Jim turned to see Suzie standing there behind him with her tray of goodies, half used up already. She set the tray down on a table and moved over against him, her arms going around his waist, she reached up and whispered in his ear.

"I'm glad you're here, Jim, I'm glad you're here. I couldn't do this otherwise."

Then she parted from him, picked up her tray and moved right across the floor towards Harry Xiang. He noticed her, his two sons began sampling the products as she stood there, they were looking her over like a piece of meat about to be devoured. Rebecca also moved up right next to Harry, who looked at her. She smiled at him and offered him the tray. Her other arm went around his waist as she kept smiling. He smiled at her then put the straw in his nose and sampled the cocaine, one long snort. His eyes were glazed over.

Jim saw Tommy Xiang taking a drink and offering one to Suzie. She took several sips, smiling at him seductively, she brushed her thigh against his and he saw Tommy's face flush red. His escort was nowhere in sight.

Off to one side of the room Jim saw Jonnie Lee, Samantha Yi still on his arm, the two young men on each side of him. He was not partaking of the "treats," nor were his sons. He was just watching the scene unfold. He did not look at Jim, not even in his direction.

"Pretty wild, Bro," Charlie said, he was standing next to Jim.

"I'll say," Jim answered but he was concentrating on Tommy Xiang. Suzie was still talking to him. She had set her tray down and he had handed her a beer which she was now sipping. She reached up and caressed his hair, smiling all the time. He was talking to her, a big grin on his face. He looked at his brother. Harry had gone on across the room. Tommy now had Rebecca on his arm, he reached down and patted her bottom, giving it a squeeze. Debra was circulating among the crowd. She did not take any of the drinks, Jim noticed. Her tray now empty, she came towards Jim.

"How are you doing?" she asked him with a smile.

"Busy night," was all Jim said.

"See you later," Debra said and she moved off towards the kitchen, probably to get some more treats for the crowd. Jim nodded to Charlie who moved away into the crowd. Jim walked outside and stood at the entrance, at the top of the steps. The cars had stopped arriving now, all guests were here and the party was in full swing, the music blaring, the voices growing louder and louder.

Jim went back inside to check on Suzie. He didn't see her in the main room now. He also didn't see Tommy or David Xiang or several of their bodyguards, Rebecca was also absent. Jim scanned the room. Neither Suzie or these men were anywhere to be seen. Now Jim was worried. He went into the kitchen. No Suzie. Debra was on her way out the door with another tray and Jim caught her arm. She spun around to look at him.

"Have you seen Suzie?" Jim asked.

"As a matter of fact I did, she was with those Asian men just a few minutes ago. But wait, I thought I saw her leaving the room with them."

A moment's panic seized Jim.

Where had she gone? Jim hurriedly went through the main downstairs rooms then down a hallway where there were several downstairs bedrooms. The doors were open and Jim could hear sounds coming from them. He looked inside. Some of the guests and the hookers were busy on the beds already, going at it, naked and sweating. Suzie was not in these rooms. Jim hurried through the main room again, Jonnie Lee momentarily looked in his direction. Jim now headed for the foyer. He looked up the stairs. A burly bodyguard Jim did not know was standing there. Jim started up the stairs. He looked at the man.

"Did you see a blond come up these stairs?" he asked the bodyguard.

"Did I ever, none of my business of course, she was with several Asian guys."

Jim pushed on past, now bounding up the stairs in leaps. He reached the first landing. He looked down the hall. He ran down the hallway, opening doors as he went. Some rooms were occupied with busy guests and hookers. No Suzie. On he ran. At the end of the hallway was a rear stairway, not as fancy as the main one. Jim ran up to the third floor. He stood in the hallway. Sweat was pouring down his forehead. He slowly made his way along now, listening carefully as he went. He came to a door and heard a muffled sound. He cracked it open and looked in. He could see bodies, one man was partially naked and he could see legs on a bed, long, tanned, smooth legs. The man was now naked and he was starting to mount the figure on the bed.

Jim burst through the door.

Suzie was laying on the bed, naked. She looked dazed, barely conscious, her head rolled back and forth. Tommy Xiang was now on top of her, erect! Ready to enter her! His bodyguards were standing there. He heard a moan and looked over and saw David Xiang, he was on top of Rebecca, her legs spread wide, he was humping her, riding her like a bucking bronco. She looked towards Jim and smiled.

Everyone looked at Jim. Jim dashed forward and grabbed Tommy Xiang by the hair, pulling him off Suzie before he could start with her. A fist connected with the side of Jim's jaw and he reeled backwards. Another fist connected with his jaw and he was pitched to the floor. The burly bodyguards were surrounding him now.

"No, Jim, no..." he could hear Suzie moaning, there on the bed.

Jim realized he was alone and surrounded!

A foot came at his head, he caught it and twisted violently. He heard the man scream and heard the knee give way with a sickening crunching sound. Jim rolled but before he could regain his feet a fist slammed into his chest. He felt like a heavy weight was there and the room started to go dark. He fought to gain his feet. A kick landed in his ribs but he rolled to deflect the blow. He leapt to his feet, striking out he connected with one of the bodyguards. The man reeled backwards and Jim stepped in, delivering another punishing blow, another man down.

David Xiang had pulled out of Rebecca and both were on their feet. Rebecca was glaring at Jim.

"Get him!" she screamed. "Get him and hold him down!"

David was retreating back behind his bodyguards. Tommy was trying to pick himself up off the floor. Jim could see Suzie moving about in a daze on the bed, her eyes barely open, she kept moaning.

"Jim...Jim," she moaned.

"Don't worry," Jim yelled as he downed a man coming at him. He could see Rebecca glaring at him, standing next to Tommy, who was trying to pull on his clothes. Two more men barreled into Jim, he fell back across the bed, across Suzie, they were on him, he punched upward, knocking a man back. He brought his leg up and kicked out. He heard his heel connect with a man's teeth, heard the crack as the man collapsed on the floor, holding his mouth as blood spewed forth. A blow hit Jim on the side of the head and he was dazed, blacking out, he fought to regain control. More were on him, holding him down, he was lying next to Suzie. He looked over at her, she was facing him, her eyes glazed over.

"Jim...Jim..." she kept repeating to him, her voice slurred.

Strong hands gripped his arms and legs, he struggled but could not free himself. He was effectively pinned down on the bed now. Tommy Xiang stood there, partially dressed now, looking down at him. David stood next to him, both were looking at him.

"It's him, isn't it?" Tommy asked his brother, David.

David nodded.

"It's him! The one I saw with Jiang Li!"

Tommy glared down at Jim. Rebecca stumbled to his side, looking down at Jim. She smiled at him.

"So, you have been with my woman!" Tommy said.

"Make him pay!" Rebecca said, "Make him pay dearly!"

Tommy held out his hand. One of his bodyguards, the one with the broken teeth came up and handed him a switch blade knife. Tommy hit the button and the blade snapped out, sharp and gleaming in his hand. He smiled down at Jim.

"You will never defile another Asian woman again!" he said.

"Let me!" Rebecca said and he handed her the knife.

"Oh this is going to give me great pleasure!" Rebecca said as she mounted Jim, straddling him, her naked breasts quivering above him. He knew what was about to happen. He looked over at Suzie. She was looking at him with her dazed eyes, barley comprehending.

"No...Jim...not that...no...no..." she moaned.

Rebecca was reaching for his belt.

He lurched and arched upward, she wrapped her legs around him and hung on. Jim twisted hard, he freed one leg and brought it back, far back around her neck and shoved, she fell backwards, dropping the knife. Jim kicked out and landed a heel on the man's arm holding his other leg. He heard the forearm bone snap and his legs were now free. He reeled back, doing a back flip and freeing his arms. Then he saw a bodyguard go down, and then anther. Jonnie Lee was in the room with the two young men that had accompanied him. They were taking out the bodyguards. Jonnie Lee punched David and he went down, hitting the floor hard. Jim was on his feet now, he looked briefly at Rebecca, standing against the wall, hate in her eyes. He turned and landed a hard right on one of the bodyguards, he smashed against the wall, Jim on him, pummeling him. Jim spun and came at Tommy now, who was attempting to retreat, fear now in his eyes. Jim hit him hard across the jaw, he reeled and went down. The bodyguards were laid out now. David was standing over against the wall next to Rebecca, he was now shaking with fear. Jim looked down at Suzie. He went to her, he couldn't find her clothes. She moaned and moved her head from side to side.

"Oh Jim...they didn't..."

Jim lifted her up against his chest, her arms went instinctively around his neck as he scooped her up. He felt her moist lips on his face and neck as he carried her away from the bed and set her on her feet, she started to fall but he steadied her. One of the young men with Jonnie Lee brought Jim a sheet and he wrapped it around her shoulders while she leaned against him.

"It's all right now," Jim told her and she just held him.

Charlie and Mike Walker came bursting into the room, looking around. Tommy and David retreated back further into the room.

"We couldn't find you anywhere, bro!" Charlie said as he looked around. "You got everything under control?"

"With their help," Jim said, indicating Jonnie Lee and the two young men.

"My sons," Jonnie Lee said with a smile.

"You saved my life," Jim said.

"I think I saved a lot more than that," Jonnie Lee said.

"You did. My thanks," Jim extended his hand and he and Jonnie Lee shook. Then he shook hands with the two young men. He was still holding Suzie, wrapped in the bed sheet and he helped her out into the hallway, she clung to him and moaned incoherently. Samantha Yi was standing there. Charlie and Mike came out of the room behind Jonnie Lee and his sons.

"What do you want to do about them?" Charlie nodded towards the room.

"Let 'em be for now," Jim said. "I've got to get Suzie out of here now. Take over for me."

Charlie nodded and Jim headed for the back staircase with Suzie.

Jim helped Suzie down the back stairs and out a rear servant's entrance. He crossed the parking lot with her and got her into his car. Some of De Angelo's goons were watching him but he paid them no mind as he fired up the engine and roared down the driveway. When he reached the gate it automatically opened for him. He sped on through hitting the street with screeching tires.

He sped along. He realized he had no idea where Suzie lived and he didn't want to leave her alone in her present condition, it was obvious that she had been given something in one of the drinks, Rohypnol, the date rape drug perhaps.

***

They finally got back to Jim's apartment and he made sure she was covered before lifting her out of the car and carrying her up the stairs, her arm around him, head back, eyes half open.

"Oh Jim I love you Jim..." she was moaning. "I'm yours now, Jim..."

He made it into the apartment and got her down on the bed. She tried to sit up, the sheet falling away as she sat there, braced on one elbow looking up at Jim, the light went on as Jim was trying to help her to lie back. Jim looked around. Jiang Li was standing there in the open doorway looking right at them, Suzie's arm was around his neck.

"Jiang Li!" Jim blurted.

"You bastard!" Jiang Li screamed at him.

She stood there glaring at Jim, he was holding Suzie, her arm around his shoulder, her head was leaned back and she stared with half open eyes at the girl standing in the doorway.

"You lying bastard, the moment I am away you..." with a scream

Jiang Li attacked, leaping on Jim, the force of her attack driving him back against the wall as she pounded his chest with her tiny fists. She tried to knee his groin but he blocked it with his leg.

"Jiang Li, let me explain...it's not what you think!"

"All men say that, don't they!" she yelled as she hit him again and again.

He grabbed hold of her arms, held her to him as she struggled. She glared at him, total rage in her eyes.

"I hate you!" she screamed.

"No, Jiang Li, no!" Jim said as he held her.

She reached down and tried to grab him but he got her wrist in his grip.

"Jiang Li, listen to me!"

"There is no explaining to be done. You know the saying, 'one picture is worth...' you know that saying and here you are with a completely naked woman in your bed and you want to try to explain that! You bastard, I hate you, you bastard!!!"

She wriggled in his grip, squirming and struggling and glaring at him with a look that could kill.

"No, no..." Suzie was moaning, she had laid back on the bed, she was trying to rise.

"You!" Jiang Li said to her. "You little whore! So," and she reeled on Jim now, "so you have to get her dead drunk to get her into your bed! You and your little slut! I should have known, you were so buddy buddy with her, oh you bastard!"

"Now you listen to me!" Jim shook her violently now and she caught her breath, looking at him. "You just listen to me! Now!"

"Listen to him..." Suzie slurred as she, again, tried to rise. "Tell her, Jim, tell her..."

"Tell me what? That you're breaking up with me, that she is with you now? That you're throwing me away? Tell me...yes you tell me!"

"Tell her the whole story Jim, I don't have my ID..."

"Tell me what story, what's this about ID?"

"Show her, Jim, show her..."

Jim sat Jiang Li down on the bed.

"Just sit there!" he said.

"What?"

"Just sit there and watch!"

He opened the closet, out came the Heckler and Koch MP5

submachinegun, out came the .45 and holster. Out came his wallet which he opened, badge and ID showing. He shoved it in front of her eyes.

"Jiang Li, I am a Federal Agent, Suzie is a Federal Agent, we have been working at the nightclub undercover. Tonight we were at a party where there were many drug lords and major crime king pins. Someone there gave Suzie, Agent Susan , Rohypnol and they tried to rape her! I got her out of there and brought her here."

"No..."

"It's true! It's true, Jiang Li. This job at the club, it's just an undercover assignment. We're trying to nail the very people who have threatened your family. I did this for you, Jiang Li, this is a good career, with the Federal Government, I was hoping we could have a life together but now, you know what? You know what, Jiang Li, now I don't know!"

"Oh, Jim...I..."

"No, Jiang Li...I don't know now. Just leave, Jiang Li, and don't worry, we'll take care of The Cobra, you'll be free, but as far as us..."

Now the total reality was beginning to set in on Jiang Li now.

"Oh Jim, no!" she screamed and she flew into his arms. He pushed her away.

"No, Jiang Li, if you can't trust me then what's the use. I told you to be patient, to believe in me, that I was working for us, that..."

"No Jim, you can't just throw me away!" she clung to him now as the tears flowed from her eyes, she hung on with all her might. "Jim, please Jim!"

"Get out, Jiang Li, just get out!" Jim pried her away from him. Again she flew at him, locking on for all she was worth.

"Jim," Suzie was starting to get her wits about her now, she pulled the sheet over her. "Jim, it looked bad when she saw us, Jim, give her a chance, Jim, please."

Jim hesitated, Jiang Li was clinging to his neck, she buried her face in his chest, weeping bitter tears.

"Think about it, Jim," Suzie said, now fully awake. "Any woman would think the same thing, I mean look what she saw, you were holding a completely naked woman in your bed when she walked in."

Jim stood there, Jiang Li held him, crying and looking at him. "Oh Jim, I'm sorry, Jim...oh Jim please..."

"Both of you listen to me!" Suzie now demanded. "Sit down here and listen to me!"

They were seated on the bed next to Suzie. Suzie looked right at Jiang Li.

"Make no mistake about it," Suzie said to her, "I love this man here, I wish with all my heart and soul he had really been with me in this bed tonight, but it isn't so, he's so in love with you he has eyes for no one, absolutely no one else, understand?"

Then Suzie looked at Jim.

"Jim, you have to understand, when she saw us, the way it looked, any woman would feel the same. I know I would! Jim saved me from being raped tonight. Someone gave me Rohypnol and tried to rape me and Jim saved me from them. He was almost castrated as a result."

"Ca...oh God no..." Jiang Li said as she held Jim, "No, not that...the Cobra, they would do that..."

"It was Tommy Xiang, he was trying to rape her. He had whores he had brought to the party tonight," Jim said.

"And Jim's former girlfriend, that Rebecca, is with them now!" Suzie said.

"Jiang Li," Jim said, "this was told to you in the strictest of confidence. Our lives, mine and hers," he indicated Suzie, "are in great danger right now!"

"Oh God, I didn't know..."

"Now you do," Jim said.

Jiang Li leapt upon Jim, driving him back to the bed, her arms around him.

"I'm so sorry, Jim, I'm so, so sorry..." she cried and then she smothered his lips with hers. He held her to him, kissing her, running his hands through her hair.

"Oh my," Suzie said.

They both looked up.

"I have no clothes, no car, I'm stuck here," Suzie said. "My car's at the mansion."

"I'll leave," Jiang Li said.

"No," Jim answered. "We'll drive back to the party for her car. We'll take my car, just keep back out of sight and we'll have her car back."

Jim looked at Suzie.

"You just go ahead and sleep."

"I'm awake now," Suzie said, "But my head is just killing me right now. Those bastards!"

"Thank God all you got was a headache," Jim said.

***

Jim and Jiang Li took his car. They headed down the main street to return to the mansion so Jim could retrieve Suzie's car. Jiang Li sat close to Jim, her arm around him. They drove into the hills until they were about a quarter of a mile from the mansion. Jim pulled the car over.

"I'll hike the rest of the way and get Suzie's car. You drive on back to my apartment and wait there for me with Suzie. I'll be back shortly."

"But Jim," Jiang Li started to say.

"I don't want you anywhere near this place, the Cobra is there among others. Go on back."

Jim got out and Jiang Li moved over into the driver's seat. She leaned out and kissed him, letting her lips linger there with his for a long moment. Jim waited until she had turned around and driven away. Then he began his hike down the road. Before he arrived at the main gate he decided on a detour through the wooded area bordering the property. He made his way in the dark, feeling his way through the trees until the block wall that bordered the property was in sight in the distance through the trees, illuminated by the lights around the mansion and in the driveway.

Stealthily he avoided several cameras he had seen mounted in the trees in the woods, they were probably infrared. He watched his footsteps, looking for trip wires, anything was possible near this place. He found one near the approach to the wall about waist high, a thin thread like piano wire stretched taught as a violin string and barely discernable. Only someone with the combat experience of an Army Ranger like himself would think to be alert for such a trap. He traced the wire through the trees and could make out in the dim light a mounted camera several yards away. He made his way over to the tree where it was mounted keeping out of its line of sight. He carefully slipped under the wire and made his way to the wall. He was at the rear of the mansion, he could see it on the other side of the wall through the stand of trees. He could make out the multi car garage as well. He checked, he was in the clear here so he slipped over the wall and landed softly on the ground. He made his way through the trees, spotting where the cameras were. He was at the edge of the rear parking lot, there were still many cars parked there and some of the guests were milling about, some appeared to be pretty stoned from all the booze and party favors. He walked out onto the lot and made his way past the people who barely took notice of him. He walked right into the house. He made his way through the kitchen, there were guests there sampling food and drinks from trays. He made his way on through into the main room. It was still pretty full of people. The Hispanic contingent was still there. He also saw some of the burly Asian bodyguards he had taken on in the bedroom. They looked a bit ruffled and bruised. He walked right on past them. They paid no attention to him. He saw Charlie White Eagle standing by one of the doors.

"Where did you disappear to, handsome?" Debra said, she was next to him.

"I was taking care of some business."

"I heard someone say they saw you drive away."

"I had to take Suzie home. She was ill, someone put something in a drink. I came to get her car and her things, if you could show me where they are..."

"Sure, come with me, I'll show you," Debra said and she led the way across the room. Jim passed Mike Walker and Charlie and nodded to them. He did not see Jonnie Lee and his sons or Harry Xiang and his two sons anywhere. He also saw no sign of Denning.

Many of the guests were pretty drunk by now, and pretty loaded as well from the various party favors and some of them stumbled about in a dazed state, their various bodyguards keeping an eye on them and eyeing each other suspiciously. One drunken man reached out and attempted to grab Debra's butt as they passed but she skillfully and discretely brushed his hand aside. She took Jim's hand and led him up the stairs to the first landing. There were several men in the hallway making out with the hookers, right up against the walls. They passed these and continued down the hallway. Debra opened a bedroom door and peered inside. She looked at Jim and nodded. They went in. One of the Cubans was screwing one of the girls from the nightclub right there on the bed, both naked and sweating. They paid no attention to Jim and Debra as Debra led the way to another bed where clothes were laid out neatly. Jim recognized Suzie's outfit and started going through it. He found her wallet and a lump rose in his throat. He opened it and gave a sign of silent relief. It was a fake ID, no Federal

Agent identification. He found her keys and folded everything up into a roll and tucked it under his arm.

As he turned to leave he saw Debra standing in front of him, looking at him, her hands on her hips. She moved towards him and put her arm around his waist, drawing herself against him. He reacted naturally as she rubbed against him. She nodded towards the couple on the other bed.

"We could join them, you know..." she whispered to him and her hand strayed down to fondle him. "My my..." she said, "No wonder Suzie is in love with you."

Jim gently brushed her hand away as her arm went around his neck. Her lips were near his.

"We could..." she whispered in his ear.

"No, no we couldn't..." Jim whispered back as he gently removed her arm. She smiled at him.

"Okay, maybe one day..." she said and she turned and started to leave the room. She glanced over at the entwined couple who had no awareness that anyone was in the room. The man was reaching climax now, humping his partner in a frenzy. Debra sighed, smiled at Jim, then left the room. Jim followed her down the hallway. She turned to him.

"It's going to be one lonely night," she said.

Then she leaned close to Jim.

"I hate that bastard, you know," she whispered. "Denning, I hate his twisted guts. This place gives me the creeps. All the drugs, these are bad people, Jim, really bad people."

"I know," Jim answered her.

"I'd better get back down there and mingle," Debra said and she walked on ahead of Jim. Jim looked down the hallway towards the rear staircase. He headed down that way. Half way there a couple came stumbling out of a bedroom, both stoned, the girl was laughing. They had just had sex and were completely stoned. They were also both naked. They stumbled off together towards the main staircase. Jim headed on to the rear staircase and climbed up to the third floor. He looked down the main hallway and could see the large door to a room at the end. The door was slightly ajar. He made his way down the hallway and paused to the side of the door. Peering through the crack he could see that it was an office with a large, oak desk. He could make out Denning seated behind the desk, he could partially see who else was there. He saw Harry Xiang, or rather, the back of his head and also Tommy. Off to one side he saw one of Jonnie Lee's sons and the shoulder of a man, obviously Jonnie Lee. Others were there also. He heard a man speaking with a heavy Spanish accent. The Cubans. Jim flattened himself against the wall, he looked quickly to the right and left. No bodyguards evident. Perhaps some were also in the room.

"It's pretty simple," Denning was saying. "I have all the customers waiting, some are here tonight, the Cubans, the Mexicans from East Bay and Los Angeles, you guys from New York and Chicago. I have supplies here and elsewhere, ready to go."

"And we will be able to channel to you more product, pure China White, pure uncut and in great amounts," now Harry Xiang was speaking. "A carton is arriving via freighter on Thursday night at a pier in South Bay. It will be warehoused then transported to you for distribution. All we require now is payment."

"We are ready also," now Jonnie Lee was talking. "I have illegals on a boat off shore, fresh in from China ready to go out into the mainstream to work various jobs, at anything. They paid a heavy fee to get here and I need my payment. Then I will send them over to you for transport."

"There is already 'employment' waiting for them. And this one is a sample?"

Jim strained to see, he could see a woman's smooth thigh, Samantha Yi.

"This one will be remaining with me," Jonnie Lee said, "But yes, others are comparable. And also the usual regular work trade, menials, domestic workers, ready for delivery."

"I have customers lined up, all upper class and just waiting for cheap help," Denning said. "Now, gentlemen, please open your briefcases that were presented to you when you came in."

Jim could hear the snaps. He could make out some of the brief cases on men's laps.

"One million each, to cover costs and as partial payment in advance. This is satisfactory to you?"

Jim could see heads nod, one by one, as they examined the contents of the briefcases.

"I am taking delivery on Thursday night at an undisclosed location," Jonnie Lee said. "It is all arranged."

"Well," Denning said, "I am glad we could all come to an agreement rather than having conflict. I feel this will work out for everyone involved. This has been a great pleasure, gentlemen, and now, let's go join the party, shall we?"

Jim ducked back and dove into a side bedroom. It was empty. He could hear them going down the hallway. He peered out the door. He could see Jonnie Lee and his two sons and Samantha Yi on his arm.

So, it seemed Jonnie Lee favored Samantha Yi, did not want to sell her off with the rest. Jim somehow found himself relieved about it.

Jim waited for a few minutes then rejoined the party, still holding Suzie's things under his arm. The members from the meeting were now all mingling and having drinks, though Jim noticed Harry Xiang did not touch the white powder offered anymore, only beers. Jonnie Lee was having a beer, Samantha Yi on his arm. Denning was circulating among the crowd, all smiles, a beer in his hand. He also was not partaking of any of the other "treats." Jim figured he wouldn't, to Denning, it was purely product to be sold, a commodity, a tool to wealth.

"Jimmy boy!" Denning's voice boomed as he crossed the room to Jim and slapped him on the back. He turned to Harry Xiang and his sons. "This is a fine, rising star in my organization. He'll be going far soon." Denning smiled at Jim, "Sorry you couldn't be at the meeting I had upstairs. You would have learned a lot. But I heard something about you having to leave for awhile."

Jim looked into the eyes of Tommy and David Xiang then he looked at Denning.

"Suzie became ill and I drove her home. I have her things here."

A smile crossed Denning's face.

"Drove her home eh," his laugh boomed. "Okay, that's a good one. Well, hope she's doing better. Come to think of it, I didn't see her around. Well, Jimboy, next meeting we have I want you to be there for sure! Okay?"

"Sure enough," Jim answered. Yes, he thought, we certainly will be having a "meeting" and very, very soon.

Jim crossed the room after shaking Denning's hand, he could feel the eyes of the Xiang brothers on his back. He went to the bar where the bartender placed a beer in front of him. Jim watched as the bartender opened it, one could not take chances with open drinks in this place.

Jim felt a hand touch his arm and turned to see Samantha Yi standing there along with Jonnie Lee, his two sons in the background. Jonnie Lee was all smiles. Samantha Yi put her arm around Jim.

"Too bad you have a girlfriend, she'd make you the best wife a man could have," Jonnie Lee said with a broad grin. He leaned close to Jim.

"Thank you for setting this up for me," he said in a low whisper. "This is such a sweet deal."

"Thank you for showing up earlier," Jim said.

"No problem. I didn't see you so I decided to take a look around. Good thing I found you or you'd be a eunuch right now. I haven't' seen any sign of that girl who almost castrated you."

"Rebecca."

"You know her."

"We have a bit of a past."

"No good, that one."

"That's for sure, let me get you a beer," and Jim nodded to the bartender. Beers were brought for Jonnie Lee and his sons and one for Samantha Yi. She politely refused so Jim offered her a Coke which she delightedly accepted, all the time remaining on his arm.

Samantha turned to Jonnie Lee and spoke to him in her native language and he answered her. A look of concern came over her face and she held Jim's arm tighter, looking into his eyes. Jim looked at Jonnie, questioningly.

"She asked what had happened and I told her what almost happened to you," Jonnie answered as Samantha moved in closer to Jim, right up against him. She spoke to Jonnie.

"She wants to kill that woman," Jonnie said.

Jim could see the anger in Samantha's eyes.

Jim sipped his beer. He saw that people were starting to leave now, stumbling out with the help of their bodyguards. Most of the girls were now dressed in their regular clothes. Some were leaving with the guests. Jim looked at his watch. It was past two in the morning now. He yawned then finished his beer.

"Well," he said, "I gotta be going along."

He shook hands with Jonnie Lee and his two sons. Samantha Yi leaned up and kissed him fully on the lips and smiled at him. He gave her a hug and she pressed against him suggestively. He pulled away and crossed the room. Denning was talking to Harry Xiang as Jim approached. Denning grinned and motioned him over.

"Like I said, this is a rising star, this one," Denning smiled at Jim. Jim looked at Harry who extended his hand, no expression on his face, no emotion betrayed. David and Tommy came up beside him, no expression on their faces, but their eyes burned into Jim's. Jim smiled at them and extended his hand.

They shook.

"I almost feel as if we have all met before," Jim said smiling with his teeth. Tommy smiled a crooked smile, his grip firm, he was testing Jim. Jim applied pressure and he could feel Tommy's hand yield, see the hidden pain in his eyes. Jim released his hand and did the same when he shook David's.

"A pleasure," Jim said, "we should do this again sometime."

Jim turned and left the room, heading out the rear entrance. Cars were driving away, there was a small traffic jam near the gate. Jim found Suzie's car and got in. He heard a horn honk and saw Debra driving past in an old Toyota. She waved. He started the engine. He let it idle for a few minutes to let the traffic jam clear.

CHAPTER SEVENTEEN

Jim parked Suzie's car in the rear parking lot next to his own car. He made his way up the stairs and entered his apartment. Suzie and Jiang Li were both sipping coffee from Styrofoam cups. Jiang Li was immediately in Jim's arms, kissing him hotly, pressing against him.

"Oh Jim I'm so glad you made it back okay, I was beginning to worry."

"I'm fine."

"I stopped by a donut shop and bought a full plastic pot of coffee and some cups," Jiang Li said as she looked over at Suzie. "We've been talking for the past hour or so."

She smiled and Suzie smiled, looking at Jim.

"Jiang Li," Jim said and she looked up at him.

"Jiang Li, I want you to marry me," Jim said, taking her hands in his.

"But of course, we have already..."

"No, Jiang Li, I want you to marry me tonight!"

"What?"

"Tonight, Jiang Li. I don't want you to go back to your parents house now, things are really getting dangerous. Marry me, Jiang Li, I'll do what I can to protect your parents, but Jiang Li, marry me!"

"Yes, Jim, I will, but how..."

Jim looked at Suzie. He had tossed her clothes on the bed.

"We're headed for the airport right now. All three of us!" Jim said.

"What?" Suzie asked.

"We'll need a witness, and a bridesmaid, you're it. Hurry and get dressed, we're heading for the first flight to Vegas, now!"

"Jim..." Suzie started to say.

"Now!"

Suzie leapt out of the bed, Jim averted his eyes from her naked body, looking at Jiang Li. She put her arms around him, pressing herself against him and kissing him.

"That's better," she said, "From now on I will be the only naked woman you'll be looking at!"

***

Jim, Jiang Li, and Suzie were standing in the all night wedding chapel, right next door was an all night divorce court. Las Vegas, the town that never sleeps. Jim and Jiang Li were looking at rings that were on display, a girl was behind the counter helping them. Jim had brought all his money, he didn't have much but he didn't care, he had bought them return plane tickets, they had taken the first flight they could get and the flight took an hour. They had hailed a cab into town, Jiang Li had been asleep on Jim's shoulder. Suzie had dozed during the flight and in the cab. Now here they were, looking at rings. The prices ranged from three hundred dollars to over ten thousand. Some rings were downright dazzling. Jim was broken hearted that he couldn't buy one of those.

"Which one do you like?" Jim asked his bride to be.

"I like that one," Jiang Li pointed to a modest, gold ring with diamond inlay, a thousand. There was a matching ring for the man, also for a thousand.

"We'll take these," Jim said and he paid cash. Suzie was almost hypnotized by all the dazzling jewelry on display and Jim grabbed her arm, shocking her back to reality.

"Come on, now, we have a wedding to attend to," he said and with both girls on his arms they entered the wedding chapel. A middle aged, balding minister was standing at the podium in his finest robes, a Bible in his hand, he was smoking a cigarette while he studied the text. They approached and Jim cleared his throat. The minister looked up and quickly stubbed out his smoke.

"Oh, yes, so we're ready to begin," the minister stammered and he nodded to the organist. He looked at Suzie and Jiang Li and nodded again. Jiang Li was dressed still in her sweatshirt and jeans but had a white wedding veil on her head. She looked at Suzie and Suzie took her hand and led her from the room.

"That's better," the minister said sternly. "We have to do this properly you know."

Jim nodded. He was nervous, shifting from one foot to the other. In a corner was an organ, another middle aged man was seated at it, waiting.

"Relax son," the minister said. "Just take a deep breath."

Jim took that deep breath. He was exhausted, deep fatigue had invaded his entire being, he had not slept on the plane.

"Okay, now I guess we're ready," the minister said and he nodded to the organ player. The organ player nodded back and began to play the wedding song. Jim turned and saw Suzie escorting his bride down the isle towards him. Jiang Li was looking into his eyes as she approached and Jim almost started to cry, he was shaken, she was so beautiful, so trusting, so in love with him. His heart swelled with emotion, with the love he felt for her. He swallowed hard as she approached, extending her hand to him. She took his arm and the three of them stood before the minister. He began...

***

"You may now kiss the bride," the minister said to Jim and Jim turned and lifted the veil, revealing his bride's beautiful, smiling face. They put their arms around each other and their lips met for the first time as husband and wife. They held the kiss for a long time, while Suzie watched, tears in her eyes. They finally parted and Jim gave Suzie a kiss on the lips.

"Thank you," he whispered to her.

Jiang Li kissed Suzie's cheek, embracing her and thanking her. Now the final music played and from somewhere on the ceiling sparkling confetti came floating down on them, flooding the chapel as the three of them ran down the isle and through the entrance where the girl who had sold them the rings started taking pictures of them, the flashes blinding them, one after another. The girl extracted the computer chip from the camera and handed it to Jim, he thanked her and gave her a one hundred dollar bill as a tip. She was delighted and beamed up at him.

"May I give your husband a kiss?" she asked Jiang Li and Jiang Li nodded. She kissed him, thanking him again.

"Now I can get something for my kids," the girl said. "Thank you again, so much."

Jim smiled then looked again at his bride. For now, they had gone to heaven together, for now, they lived the wonderful dream.

***

They flew back on the next plane, the sun was up now, a new day. They drove up to the rear parking lot to Jim's apartment. Suzie was fast asleep in the back seat. Jim gently took her shoulder and shook her. She opened her eyes.

"We're back," Jim said.

Suzie opened her eyes and looked at him and smiled a sleepy smile then looked at Jiang Li who was smiling at her.

"Oh I am stiff and sore," Suzie said as she stretched.

They got out of the car and stood in the parking lot. It was filling up fast, it was about ten in the morning, Sunday morning and people were already arriving from church, or to go shopping, to buy their coffees and eat breakfast at the restaurants. Jim looked at his new bride, standing there in the parking lot smiling at him, a sleepy smile. They were all exhausted.

"It seems unbelievable," Suzie said as she looked around. "We were actually in Vegas just hours ago. Unbelievable! Totally unbelievable." She stretched her aching muscles, the sun was warm, summer just around the corner a week away.

Suzie looked at Jim and Jiang Li, standing together.

"Well," Suzie said, "I'm going to go get about twelve hours sleep. And Jim, Monday, don't look for me at the club. I've quit, I found out all I need to know for now. It's over at that place."

"I'm glad you don't ever have to go back there again," Jim said.

"So am I, I couldn't have hung on much longer, I'm afraid, especially after last night. Those fucking bastards! Thank God you were there, and to think..."

"What?"

"What they, what that bitch almost did to you..."

"It didn't happen. Jonnie Lee arrived just in time."

"Funny man, he is," Suzie said thoughtfully.

"Funny?"

"I realize he's a total criminal but somehow, he seems likeable enough. Too bad."

Jim thought about it for a moment. Jonnie Lee had saved both of them but his actions were going to land him in prison. It couldn't be stopped. And yes, he also found that Jonnie Lee was a likeable fellow.

"What did you find out?" Jim asked.

"Never mind for now," suddenly Suzie had a far away look in her eyes. She shook her head.

"What?" Jim asked.

"I want to look into it before I make any judgments either way. Just something I heard, that's all."

"What?"

Suzie smiled.

"I am sure you two would like to be together alone for now, so I'll be running along. It will be good to get back to my office in San Francisco. I am vacating my place here in town, it will look like I was never here, Jim. If Denning asks just tell him that after the party I was drunk and you drove me home and haven't seen me since, okay?"

Jim nodded and Suzie stepped forward and hugged Jiang Li and kissed her on the cheek. Then she came up to Jim, looking into his eyes.

"I get to kiss the groom," she said and she put her arms around Jim and kissed him fully on the lips. As they parted she looked almost longingly into his eyes. Then she smiled, Jim thought it seemed to be a sad smile. She nodded to both of them and then went to her car and drove out of the lot. Jim took Jiang Li's hand and led her to his apartment. He opened the door and picked her up, carrying her across the threshold. He set her down on the bed and lay down next to her. They were asleep almost as soon as they hit the pillows, asleep in each other's arms, they slept the long, sweet, dreamless sleep.

***

Jim woke up, opened his eyes and looked around the room. Jiang Li was sound asleep next to him. He looked at the ceiling, thinking. He was wondering what Suzie had found out. He was relieved that she would no longer be down at that club. He hated the place, hated Denning, hated Harry Xiang and his two sons. At least that was one marriage that would never happen now. He thought of Jiang Li's family. They were now at risk. But it had been plain out extortion! Jim would have to find a way to protect them. He heard a moan next to him and looked around. Jiang Li was looking at him through smiling, sleepy eyes.

"Hello, my husband," she said.

Her arm went around him and they kissed. She sat upright, looking at her ring. She smiled then stood up. She went to the table and saw Jim's cell phone. She picked it up and flipped it open.

"Oh my..." she was startled at what she saw, the picture Jim had of her when she had posed for him.

"Well, well," she said.

"I had to have some kind of inspiration to keep me going," Jim said. "I looked at it every day, many times a day."

"And also at all those other naked women," she pouted then smiled, looking at her likeness on the phone again.

"Well," she said, "let's make this a dream come true, shall we?"

With that she peeled off her sweatshirt, her bare breasts swinging free in the afternoon light filtering through the window. She peeled off her jeans and stood there in her black, brief, high riding, silk panties, her hair messed up and down around her naked shoulders. She tossed her head and smiled.

"My husband," she moaned, "I love you, my husband...I love you..."

"I love you, Jiang Li..." Jim answered as he gave himself to the experience totally and completely. Complete surrender.

***

"I'm famished," Jiang Li said.

Jim opened his eyes. It was now late afternoon. The light in the room had changed with the position of the sun. Jiang Li was lying next to him, still on her stomach, he was beside her, against her, feeling her there with him, feeling the wonderful sensations surge through him, unstoppable.

"We really should get something to eat," Jim said as he rolled over on his back. She mounted him, smiling down at him.

"Perhaps we should go have dinner soon," she said as she sank down on him and they were away again, away in a sea of blissful, union.

***

The bite of steak was mouth wateringly delicious. Jiang Li had just placed the tasty bite in Jim's mouth with her fork. He savored the flavor and looked at the exotically, intensely beautiful woman seated against him in the booth at the high classed steakhouse, filled with customers who were quite well dressed. It was early evening and Jim and his bride were seated in the booth side by side, Jiang Li in her jeans and sweatshirt, her hair done loosely back in a ponytail, Jim dressed in "T" shirt and jeans. They were having steak and lobster, the house special for this Sunday evening. Of course the night club was closed so Jim didn't have a care in the world on this wonderful evening, still their wedding day.

Jiang Li looked at her ring and then at Jim. She kissed him on the cheek and he forked out a bite of lobster and dipped it in the melted butter. He placed it in her mouth and she took it in her teeth, such a sensual movement of her mouth as she hungrily munched it down.

"My husband, my husband, my husband," she said as she groped him playfully under the table. "He's such a lively one."

Jim looked around at the customers. One couple looked over and then away immediately and Jiang Li smiled.

"So what?" she said as she kissed Jim again.

He gave her another bite of steak.

***

His arm around her, Jim escorted Jiang Li to his car. He drove back to the his apartment and parked next to her car.

"What now?" she asked him, looking up into his eyes.

"Now? Now we go into the city and I tell your father and mother that we're married."

Jiang Li looked down.

"No..."

"Why not, they are soon going to know."

"No, Jim, wait..."

"Why wait? We're married. That's now a fact. We're married and I want to walk you in there and tell them and let your father deal with it. I can't reveal my identity as a Federal Agent yet, much as I'd like to, but there is too much risk right now, too many lives at stake. This has to go down right. But I can tell them we're married, we have to do this sooner or later, you know that, Jiang Li."

He held her face in his hands, cupping her cheeks, her brown eyes looking at him.

"I want to, Jim, I really want to, but please, just wait until I graduate next Saturday. Then we can tell them, please Jim..."

Jim looked at her. It made sense, he should wait and then tell them as he revealed his true identity. He could then offer some kind of protection. Big busts were going to be going down this week, then, perhaps there would be no more Cobra to worry about. Jiang Li's father would be free. Jim railed at that. Her father should have some accounting for what he had done, which, basically, was to sell his daughter.

"Jill," Jiang Li said.

"Jill?"

"Jill Saunders, that's my American name now, Mrs. Jill Saunders, wife to former Staff Sergeant Jim Saunders, US Army Rangers, now a Federal Agent. Mrs. Jill Saunders." She smiled and moved in close to Jim, her hands going to his face, feeling the rough stubble, he hadn't had time to shave.

"Rough," she frowned. "but I kind of like it, my husband. My husband, I like the sound of that."

"My wife," Jim said, "I like the sound of that."

He kissed her.

"Jim," Jiang Li said, "I'm going to be staying at June's for the week. I'll call my parents and tell them I'll be there. Why don't you follow me over there?"

"I can't think of a better idea," Jim said. And he was relieved, he felt he could be in danger soon and it would be good if Jiang Li was not with him at his apartment, just in case anything happened.

"See you there," Jim said.

***

Jim pulled up and parked across the street from June's apartment. Jiang Li was already waiting near the front entrance. Jim walked across the street and Jiang Li flew to meet him, throwing her arms around him.

"I phoned her," she said. "I told her I had a surprise for her. She tried to pry it out of me as I drove over but I didn't budge. Come on..."

Jiang Li led the way to the steps and they knocked at the door. June opened it, smiling at them.

"Well?" June asked.

"Well what?" Jiang Li teased.

"Jill! What is going on? You said you had some kind of surprise for me, now out with it!"

"Whatever would you be talking about, would you know, Jim?" Jiang Li smiled, looking innocently at Jim. Then she raised her left hand up, displaying her ring right in front of June.

"You're engaged?" June smiled.

Jiang Li said nothing, just held the ring there and with her right hand she brought Jim's left hand up.

"You're...don't tell me...you're..."

"Married!"

"Married!" June threw her arms around Jiang Li, hugging her tightly and then she hugged Jim, kissing him on the cheek. "I am so happy for you! Married! Well, come in, come in!" she opened the door wide and Jim and Jiang Li entered.

"You must tell me all about it! where..."

"Vegas," Jiang Li said, "last night, or rather early this morning."

"Not even a full day!" June said. "And where are you going on your..."

"Honeymoon?" Jiang Li said. "Actually all day has been one long honeymoon."

She turned and put her arm around Jim, moving close to him.

"Oh my," June said, "Oh my oh my! I am so happy for both of you."

"June," Jiang Li said and she took on a serious look now.

"Oh Jill," June said, concern on her face, "Your father, how did he take it?"

"June, he doesn't know yet."

"Oh my the shit is going to hit the fan, excuse me," June said.

"June, when we talked..."

"Of course you can stay here as long as you need to, anything I can do..."

"Just a friendly place to stay," Jiang Li said.

"That is assured," and June kissed Jiang Li on the cheek. She looked at Jim. "You will stay here tonight, won't you, I will fix dinner..."

"We've just had a feast," Jiang Li said, "Steak and lobster."

"Oh. Well come on in and make yourself at home. Would you like anything to drink?"

"Coffee," Jim said and Jiang Li nodded.

June went to the kitchen. Jiang Li looked at Jim.

"Can we tell her?" she asked, "I mean about who you really are?"

"Not a good idea to tell anyone right now."

"Jim, I'm glad you told me. I am. And I'm sorry I doubted you, oh Jim, I'm so sorry...the things I said..."

"Were understandable. I had to tell you, it was really getting to me, not being able to tell you..."

They held each other and he kissed her.

June cleared her throat and they both parted.

"You'll be staying here this week also?" June asked Jim.

"I'd really like to but there are things I have to attend to this week. I'm afraid I will not be able to be around much," he looked at Jiang Li, holding her hand.

"Well, you're staying the night," June said.

They seated themselves by the picture window.

"So Jill says you work at a nightclub?"

"Sort of," Jim said, "But not for long. This week will probably be my last. Hopefully it will be."

"I told her about the 'nightclub,'" Jiang Li said and Jim felt embarrassed.

"I'm afraid so," he said. "Ideal maybe for a single guy but I am married now. I am looking into other prospects right now."

"I'll be working soon as well," Jiang Li said. "At a real job finally."

She moved closer to Jim on the couch where they were seated. She kissed him.

"My my," June said, "you two can hardly keep your hands off of each other."

***

It was starting to get dark outside. Jim and Jiang Li entered the Master bedroom, June had insisted, calling it the "Honeymoon suite." Jiang Li headed for the shower, and in an instant she was naked.

She turned on the water and, together, they entered, pressing against each other. He pressed her against the tile shower wall, enjoying her, her enjoying him. Then he pulled out, turning off the water he scooped her, soaking wet, up in his arms and carried her, both of them dripping, across the bedroom floor. He set her down in front of the bed and stepped back, looking at her. She looked at him and smiled. Then she lay down on the bed and reached for him as he descended on her.

Their lovemaking went on hour after hour, the world only existed for them, in this place, in this instant, moment to moment, this was the only reality, this was their universe, only them, together. On and on, into the night, oblivious to anything else, only each other, that was all that was, that was all there ever needed to be...

***

The first light of day filtered in from outside the window as Jim awoke. He was dazed. He looked over at Jiang Li. She was lying there next to him, sheets off, naked in his arms, her leg moved against him as she stirred at the first light. She opened her eyes and smiled, putting her arms around him, kissing him, moving against him.

He moved over on top of her. One more time, just one more time, an endless time for them.

***

The sun was up now, June had already left for work. Jim and Jiang Li sat at the kitchen table sipping coffee. Jim had on his jeans, shirtless, Jiang Li was in a short bathrobe, tied loosely around her, her hair a tangled, sexy mess around her shoulders as she smiled at him. They finished their coffee and Jim finished dressing, Jiang Li remaining in her robe. She escorted him to the door. He paused in the doorway as he held her.

"My husband," she whispered to him.

Jim undid her robe and it fell to the floor around her feet.

"My wife," he said and he stepped back to view her. "I may not see you for a few days, I want to remember you this way..."

She was in his arms, kissing him, she fondled him, exciting him all over again. He kissed her a final time. Then he headed across the street to his car, she was watching him from the partially open door, smiling at him, he could see her bare arm and shoulder and part of her naked thigh. She waved as he got in the car and drove away.

***

Jim drove to Union Square and parked. He took the walk over to Lombard Street and entered the Federal Building. He remained unarmed, he did have his ID in his wallet though. He went on up to Suzie's office and went inside. The secretary looked up at him and got on the intercom. She nodded and he went in. Suzie rose from her desk, she was dressed in her light gray business suit, her hair done up in a severe roll behind her head, a few stray strands fell about her face. She smiled and came to Jim, hugging him. Then she kissed his lips, holding him.

"This just had to be the most exhausting weekend I ever had," she said. "I can hardly believe we went all the way to Vegas and right back. It seems like a blur. So how is the married man?"

Jim started to speak but Suzie turned away, shaking her head. "I don't want to know the details, I'm happy for you, Jim. She's a jewel, it's just...oh I don't want to get started."

"It's best you don't," Jim said as she returned to her desk and seated herself. Jim was seated across from her. "I need to know what you heard," he said.

"Heard?"

"You said you found something out at that party."

A guarded look came over her and she looked away from him.

"What is it?"

"Not now," she said. "It's just something I want to check out, I'll let you know when I know more."

"Why not now, maybe I can help you..."

"No!" she sounded rather abrupt. Then her smile softened. "I am so glad I never have to go back to that club again. I'd like to cut that bastard's balls off, cut the balls of all of those pigs!"

"I don't blame you."

"So the man who almost raped me, Tommy Xiang, he was the one who was supposed to marry Jiang Li by arrangement."

"That's the one."

"Looks like that girl you used to know, Rebecca, the one who almost…you know… looks like she left with him."

"She seems to have an instinct for who can butter her bread."

"I guess you could put it that way. So Jim, you're almost done at that club also."

"Just a few more nights, then we can bust 'em good and I'll be done. As far as this…"

"Jim, you have a career here. It's yours, you've earned it. Martin has great plans for you, you'll see."

"Well," Jim started to rise from his chair. "I have to pay a visit to Chinatown."

"Jonnie Lee?"

"Yes, oh, and I have a question."

"What is it?"

"If an illegal marries an American citizen then that gives them legal status, right."

"Well, not exactly, unless it could be proved that this person had planned to marry the American citizen all along. There would be paperwork, it could be worked out, why?"

"Oh no," Jim said, "You have a little secret and so do I."

He headed for the door, Suzie joined him there and stood in front of him. She hugged him, pressing against him, looking in his eyes.

"I'm sorry, Jim, I just can't seem to help myself. You take care out there, you do have a wife to think about now, you know." She kissed his cheek and they parted.

***

Jim found himself seated in the restaurant eating a large lunch of beef and rice, a double order, he was famished. The weekend had taken a lot out of him.

As he was sipping his beer he saw Jonnie Lee's two young sons enter, dressed in suits. They were both handsome young men, both in their very early twenties. They came over and stood over his table. Jim motioned for them to be seated and they seated themselves.

"I didn't get your names," Jim said.

They introduced themselves as Charles Lee and John Lee Jr. And Charles was known as Chuck.

"Pleased to meet you, again," Jim said.

"We are not pleased to meet you," John Lee Jr. said.

Jim looked at him, his eyes were burning into his with anger.

"So what's the problem?" Jim asked. "Not that it matters, I'm not here to be liked."

"You are not liked, not by either of us!" Chuck said

"You don't have us fooled!" John Jr. said.

Jim felt the coldness rise up his spine, the tingle warning him of danger. He was found out! And he didn't have his weapon. He remained calm, hear them out, he told himself.

"Whether you like me or don't like me is no concern of mine. Business is business."

"I guess that's the way it is," Chuck said.

"You've placed our father in great danger!"

"Your father made his own deals!"

"He thinks he knows what he's doing," John Jr. said. "He always was like that, trying to be the 'bigshot.' Having his girlfriends, his underground dealings."

"He is the head of The Tiger Clan, after all."

"We're second rate, always were, me and my brother, we've been trying to legitimize it, make it more like a business brotherhood of sorts," Chuck said.

"You've both been to college."

"Yes, we both have our MBAs."

"So why deal in things that are illegal."

"We are loyal to our clan and our father!" John Jr. said as anger flared.

"Well, you have a sweet deal brewing now," Jim said.

"A deal which will destroy all of us! Our father thinks he can handle it but this is too much! He does this and we're done trying to help him," Chuck was angry, rage filled his eyes. "Things were getting better until you stepped into the picture, you and your big boss, Denning. He's a pig! And worst of all, the involvement with The Cobra. We've warned our father for years to stay out of their way."

"Your personal problems with your clan and your father is no concern of mine. We're talking about mountains of money to be made here and made fast!"

"Money! Blood money! It has to stop!" John Jr. started to rise but Chuck placed a restraining hand on his shoulder.

"No, not here," Chuck said. "He has no soul, he's just a gangster like the rest of them."

Jim liked these two young men. They had values. He wished at that moment he could have shown them his ID, tell them it would be worked out but he had to play this out.

"Your father knew what he was getting into right from the start. He's been involved in these things since way before you both were born and before I was born as well."

"Not as deep as you would think," Chuck said, "He likes to think he is a bigshot like the rest of them, but he's not. Mainly he is in legitimate businesses, and never involved in drugs! And now you show up!"

"Drugs are not the issue with The Tiger Clan, it's the importation of human bodies. He's doing them a service they have paid for."

"It's a dirty business, and he never operated on this large a scale before."

Just then Samantha Yi entered, dressed in a short red dress with a slit up the thigh almost to her hip revealing a great deal of her luscious thigh. She smiled widely when she saw Jim and came right over and hugged him, kissing him on his cheek. She smiled at John Jr. and Chuck, she went to both of them and kissed them on their cheeks then looked at Jim, smiling. She left through the kitchen. Jim watched her go.

"And Samantha," Chuck said.

"What about her?" Jim asked.

"The best thing that happened to our dad and he doesn't realize it."

"Nice girl," Jim commented.

"Yeah, we can see how you would think that, you probably want to hire her for your boss's strip club."

"There are already plenty of dancers there," Jim said. "It's not my business. I'm here to see your dad."

"He's upstairs. We're going to keep an eye on you so you'd better not get out of line."

Jim smiled and rose from his seat. These two young men were tall, almost as tall as he was, solid, obviously trained in martial arts. Jim finished the last of his beer and headed through the kitchen for the stairs.

He knocked.

The door opened a crack, Samantha Yi was standing there, when she saw Jim she smiled again and opened the door wide, hugging him close, looking up into his eyes.

"Welcome," Jonnie Lee said as he rose from his desk and came over to Jim extending his hand, they shook and Jonnie Lee slapped Jim on the back. "Good to see you!" he said. "have a seat!"

Jim was seated and Jonnie Lee motioned to Samantha who went to the liquor cabinet and took out a bottle of aged, whiskey and two glasses. She brought these to the desk along with a cup of ice cubes. She placed the ice in the glasses and poured, handing one to Jonnie Lee and one to Jim. Jim nodded to her and she smiled at him again, a seductive smile. Then she left the room.

"Beautiful girl," Jim said.

"She would make you a good wife," Jonnie Lee said.

"I already have a wife."

Jonnie Lee looked surprised. "Jiang Li..."

"Yes. We went to Vegas."

"I warned you, her family is at risk, as you know. And The Cobra will be gunning for you."

"They already tried at the party, they already know."

"Yes, and if I and my sons had not intervened you would be a eunuch right now. You'd better watch your back in these dealings. My sons..."

"Your sons?"

"They somehow don't seem to have the same knack for this business, it's not like the old days, kids these days..."

"Maybe they're just concerned for you."

"They understand nothing about risk! Not real risk. I really don't want them involved totally but they still have to have some kind of understanding of what's going on."

"Maybe they already know."

"I have tried to teach them. Each one was from a different woman, but they are my sons. I gave them education! College put all these things in their heads, not like me, I came from the streets, I had to be tough and fight my way to the top. I defeated all my rivals and became head of the Tiger Clan! They want to make more of a legitimate business out of it. Most of the old timers are gone now, others in our organization unfortunately are thinking the same as my sons. It is up to me to be a strong leader, to show them the right path!"

They took a sip of their drinks.

"You ought to marry that girl," Jim said.

"What girl?"

"Samantha. Make her a citizen, legal."

Jonnie Lee thought about it, took several sips.

"I never felt the need to be married. I have always been able to get women."

"What about your sons?"

"I adopted them as my own after they were born, they are legally mine in every way. And I always saw that the needs of their mothers were taken care of, so there was never any problem. I put them through college, now I wonder about that, they seem bent on changing everything."

"But about Samantha..."

Jonnie Lee looked thoughtful for a moment as he sipped his drink.

"Perhaps, perhaps. She is good to me, but then, she has no choice, I can send her back..."

"I know people, Jonnie, I know people, the good and the bad, I remember a young girl in Iraq. Beautiful, and a wonderful person. You can look at someone and know..."

"Like your new wife..."

"Yes, you can know and looking at Samantha I can tell. If you ever got busted by immigration she would be shipped back immediately, you know that. It doesn't take long, marry her. What would it cost? You have plenty of money. And Jonnie, you're not getting any younger, you know."

Jonnie Lee sighed and finished his drink.

"I am in great shape, I practice kung fu every morning as soon as I wake up. I am fit."

"Doesn't matter, Jonnie, but then, whatever, I..."

"I know, you are concerned, you seem to be a good man, Jim Saunders, even though we are both gangsters, there are values, we have to survive and we both know how tough this world is. You've seen combat, abroad and right here on the streets of Chinatown. You are the Chinatown Phantom, you know."

Jim shrugged his shoulders.

"Now, to get down to business," Jonnie Lee said, "I have moved the drop off time to Wednesday night, that's when the ship will be off shore at the designated spot."

"Where would that be?"

"Do you know of a place up the coast, a cove, just the other side of the Golden Gate Bridge on the Marin County side?"

"I am familiar with it, it's on what used to be an old Army base."

"It's the perfect place, don't you think? I've been there. A boat will be lowered from the ship, an old cargo steamer, and the people will be brought ashore, they have already paid a high price in China and I have received partial payment, the rest to be supplied by them as they arrive on shore. I'll have a truck at the top of the hill, waiting. Will you go there with me and oversee this? It's why I moved it to Wednesday, because of the other delivery for Cobra on Thursday night."

"Good idea, I'll be there," Jim said and he had finished his drink.

Jonnie Lee clapped his hands and Samantha Yi entered the room and brought another round of drinks to them. Then she sat in Jim's lap and spoke to him.

"She says she wants to marry you," Jonnie Lee said and then he spoke to her. She shrugged, pouted and then smiled at Jim and spoke again.

"She says she would be content to be number two wife."

"I am flattered, or rather stunned," Jim said.

Jonnie Lee laughed and spoke to her again and she kissed Jim on the cheek and then got up and started massaging his shoulders and neck. Jim leaned his head back, enjoying the sensations as his muscles relaxed, not that he hadn't been in a rather relaxed state all day from Sunday night and this morning.

"And you think I should marry her," Jonnie Lee said.

"Sure do."

They sipped their drinks and Jonnie Lee placed a cigarette in his mouth. On cue, Samantha went to him and lit it for him.

"She sure doesn't know much about American ways," Jim said. "Wait until she learns to understand English. Then she'll watch Dr. Phil and it will be all over for you."

Jonnie Lee laughed.

"People, they are stupid, most of them, they have an idea based on television on how life should be. We know better."

"Do we?"

They took another drink. Jim finished his and set the glass on the desk. He rose to his feet.

"Well, I must be getting back," he said. "I have things to take care of."

Samantha was at his side, she put her arm around him, smiling up at him. He shook hands with Jonnie Lee and Samantha gave him a kiss on his lips. He left the room.

***

Jim was out on Kearney Street, he had just left the restaurant when he saw the man on the crutches, Andy. Jim walked over to him and Andy looked up at him and smiled.

"You have anything to tell me?" Jim asked him.

He grinned wide and looked up and down the street.

"I could sure use a nice meal and maybe a beer?" Andy said.

Jim reached into his pocket and took out forty dollars. He gave it to Andy.

"I can get several meals with that, that's good."

"So..."

"It is said that The Cobra is setting up your friend, Jonnie Lee, and Tommy Xiang, the son, is out to get a certain man who has a certain interest in his bride to be. That man is on unsteady ground."

"I already know this, and what about this 'setup' as you call it?"

"A hit will come down on Jonnie Lee's private residence tonight at about ten o'clock. It's just a rumor I heard, that's all. Cobra wants the thorn removed."

"I have no idea where Jonnie Lee lives."

"I may still be hungry, in fact, there's tomorrow, will I eat then or starve?"

Jim handed out one hundred dollars and Andy told him what he wanted to know.

***

Jim arrived at his parent's house. He went inside and found his mom in the kitchen. It was now early afternoon. He knew his dad was at the garage. Robbie was out on the patio with Dave, Denning's son. Dave had stayed with Robbie while the party had been going on and now the two of them were lifting weights. Robbie glanced inside at his brother.

"So you finally decided to come home for a home cooked meal?"

his mother said.

"Afraid not, Mom, but I have news."

"So you'll be going off to that club you work at. What a cesspool that place is, it should be banned."

"It's outside city limits, Mom, on county property. The city has no jurisdiction over it at all."

"Just the same, you could find other work you know."

Jim was tempted to pull out his Federal ID but something told him not to. Especially with Denning's son there, not that the young man was a criminal like his father, but kids do talk.

"So what is it you have to tell me?" his mother asked as she continued preparing the evening meal. Jim noticed that it was spaghetti and meatballs. One of his favorites but he had no time to waste right now.

Jim held out his left hand, displaying his wedding ring. His mother looked at it absently then went back to preparing dinner. Then she stopped cold. She grabbed his hand.

"Is this what I think it is?" she asked.

"Sure is," Jim said. "We went to Vegas last weekend and got married."

A sudden look of joy burst across his mother's face and she hugged him.

"Oh Jim! You're married!" then she turned to face the patio. "Your brother just got married!" she shouted.

Robbie looked up, amazed then came into the kitchen, Dave followed. He looked at Jim, rather sheepishly, not knowing what to say, being a teenager.

Then the expression on Jim's mother's face changed.

"You didn't invite us, your family!"

"Mom, it was on the spur of the moment..."

The joy again.

"Well, soon you can have a proper ceremony," she said, "Won't you..."

"Of course we will, Mom," Jim said.

"Oh I wish your father were here right now! Why don't you go down to the garage and tell him?"

"I'll do that," Jim said. "In fact, I'm on my way right now."

He kissed his mother on the cheek, nodded to Robbie and Dave and headed out the door.

***

Jim pulled up at the garage. He didn't have a lot of time, he had to get to the club right away. Before he got out of the car he noticed a Lincoln Town car parked in front of the shop, black and shiny. He got out and crossed the street, entering through the office door. The office was empty. He heard voices out in the shop and looked through the glass window. His dad was talking to two men in black suits. They had slicked back, black hair and Jim had not ever seen them around town before. Then he saw Denning there as well.

"Hi Dad," Jim said as he walked through the door into the shop. The men looked around. Denning was all smiles.

"There he is!" Denning said and he came forward and shook Jim's hand, he patted him on the shoulder.

"Hi, son," Jim's dad said, "What's up?"

"I can see you're busy, Dad, I'll drop by the house later," Jim said, not wanting to interrupt his dad at work.

"We're just talking about fixing a fender on that fancy car outside, son, that's all. We'll be done in just a minute. Want to wait in the office?"

"Sure," Jim shrugged his shoulders and headed into the office. He waited a few minutes. Denning and the men left and his father came into the office. Jim told him the news and his father was overjoyed, shaking his hand and slapping him on the back.

"Good for you, son, good for you, that's a real decent girl you have there. It was sudden but both your mom and I kind of knew it was coming sooner or later. We could tell, just looking at you two together. Oh I'll bet your mom was a little ticked off..."

"Oh yes she was, Dad, at first but I promised we would have a 'proper' ceremony later so that made her happy."

"Good. Well, are you going to be staying for dinner?"

"No, Dad, I gotta run, got my job."

"I know."

"Dad..."

"I know, son, it's just that...that club...son, it's bad business..."

"Dad, don't worry, I'll be out of there real soon, I just needed something fast and it was an offer that came up at the time."

"Promise you won't be there long, son, it's bad business there. Son, I've known Denning all my life, we do business together sometimes, he likes the work I do on his cars, but son, that man..."

"I know, Dad, and don't worry."
"Okay, son, I just want what's best for you."
"I know, Dad, well, I gotta run."
Jim started to leave then he turned and faced his dad.
"Dad," Jim said.
"What is it, son?"
"Is everything okay, Dad?"
His dad smiled the wide smile Jim knew so well.
"Son, everything's just fine, don't worry about me. Now get outta here, I got a little more work to do."
"Mom's fixing your favorite tonight, Dad."
"Spaghetti! Well, now I am going to hurry up and get out of here."

***

Jim got in his car and drove off. He was smiling. Then he thought about something. The Lincoln Town car had not been left at the shop. And it didn't seem to have any damage, just like the other car he had seen there. But then Jim had not really checked it out. Probably just there for and estimate. Then he thought about those two dark haired men. Probably recommended by Denning, his dad was the best at what he did and people had been known to bring him cars for repair all the way from San Francisco.

***

Jim arrived in the parking lot of the nightclub. He parked and got out. The same Lincoln Town car was parked right in front of the club. Jim approached the club. He decided to check out the car. He walked around it, he saw no damage whatsoever.

Strange.

Oh well, maybe that was not the car intended for repair. Jim walked into the club. He had to talk to Denning fast. He entered the darkened interior. He saw that Rebecca was not tending bar.

"Over here, Jimboy!" he heard Denning's voice boom through the room.

He looked over, Denning was there with the same two men who had been in his father's shop. Jim walked over.

"I want to introduce you to a couple of my colleagues from back east. You'll get to know them better soon, when we starting funneling products. This is Boris Ivanovich and this one is Igor Buderin."

Both men rose and offered their hands, they had cold eyes, their ruthlessness showed through the fancy suites, the hair a little too greasy, the suits a little too overdone.

Jim shook their hands.

"Jim Saunders," Denning told them, "we were just at his dad's shop. Great guy, your dad, Jim."

"Yes he is," Jim said and he took a mental note to tell his dad to watch who he had for customers more closely.

"I won't be in to work tonight," Jim said. "I've got other work to do, setting things up."

"I was going to tell you when you came in, son," Denning said.

"What?"

"You're not head bouncer anymore. Mike has his job back. You're promoted, this work we're doing isn't doorman stuff you know. You've moved up, my boy, congratulations!"

Denning offered his hand and they shook.

"More beers all around!" Denning said. "You can stay for one, Jim boy? I know what you have to do is important but we need a little celebration!"

Debra brought the beers and they held them high, clinging the bottles together.

"To a prosperous future for all of us!" Denning said and they answered in kind. They sat back and drank the beers and Denning took out a box of Cuban cigars, lit one and passed them around. Jim, though he didn't smoke accepted one and they lit up. Jim took a few puffs and set it in the ashtray.

"I know it's against the law to smoke in bars and restaurants but who's here to ticket me?" Denning let out a big, hearty laugh. The two other men chuckled mirthlessly, their eyes remaining cold, calculating, deadly.

"Well," Jim said as he rose to his feet, "I'll be going along, I have lots to do."

He shook hands again, drained his beer, and then headed out the door. On his way to the car he made a phone call on his cell phone. Jim was forming an idea in his mind right now as he drove down the road.

***

Jim arrived at Stan's and sat at the counter.

"Hi Jim," Stan said as he came up and poured Jim a cup of steaming coffee.

Jim studied Stan carefully, the creased face, the smile but the deadly eyes that lurked there. Jim had heard stories about him. Now was the time to find out.

"Stan," Jim said.

"Yeah, Jim, what can I do for you?"

"Stan, I need to talk to you in private."

Just at that moment Jim heard the Harley thundering up outside. A moment later Charlie White Eagle came in the doorway and headed for the counter. Jim nodded to him, Charlie nodded back.

"In my office," Stan said as he did an instant study of Charlie. Stan nodded to the waitress and he led Jim and Charlie through the kitchen to a small, cluttered office, the desk overloaded with papers and several novels about Navy SEALs. Stan was seated, there were two more flimsy wooden chairs in the small office and Jim and Charlie were seated. Charlie looked at Jim questioningly.

"What do you think?" Charlie asked Jim, Jim had filled him in on what was going down tonight at Jonnie Lee's residence.

"Stan, I have to tell you something, I think, if I am right, that you are the right man to talk to. You know Martin Thomas?"

"Sure do," Stan said. "He told me to expect you sometime. It'll be good to get back to work, to my real work."

Jim and Charlie both took out their IDs and showed them to Stan.

"I already know about it, I've been waiting, Jimboy, just waiting for this moment."

"So your boat is still operational, it just isn't where you live?"

"Never has been just where I live, I always maintain it, have all these years, I take it out at night sometimes for test runs, just to make sure, Jimboy. I wasn't surprised when I heard you joined up with us. When do you need me?"

"We should get ready and back to your boat in about an hour," Jim said. He looked at Charlie, "We can leave your bike here..."

"Just run it in the back room, it'll be safe, nice bike by the way," Stan grinned, "used to run one myself. Just got tired of fixing it all the time."

"They do take work," Charlie grinned.

"Let's go, we'll take my car."

With that they headed out of the office.

***

The boat waited in the calm waters of the south bay, just off shore, it was dark, about nine thirty now. Jim had been amazed at the power in this seeming wreck of a boat, on the outside, needing paint, on the inside, cluttered but Stan had an up to date computer system. He also had weapons galore, fully automatic rifles, AK-47s, all confiscated weapons turned over to him in case of need. He had talked to Jim and Charlie as they had left the dock, on deck, Stan behind the wheel as powerful engines powered the craft across the water, the sun had just been going down. Stan had worked for the Federal Government as a kind of contractor agent, using his boat to help in smuggling investigations. Many of the weapons confiscated had been turned over to him in case he and other agents needed them. Jim and Charlie had brought their weapons along, Jim, his .45 and his Heckler and Koch MP5 submachinegun with extra ammo clips. Charlie was similarly armed. Both men were now dressed in black, black jeans, black sweatshirts and they had black hoods they were preparing to put over their heads.

"This is the place," Jim said.

They were looking at a large, three story house with steps that lead down to a dock where a large cabin cruiser was tied up.

"He probably brings 'em in with that," Stan said. "I've seen it operating before. It's fast. I tried to catch up with it once but even this boat couldn't catch it. I have upgraded the engine since then."

"How long have you been in the employ of the Federal Government, Stan, I mean, I never had any idea," Jim said. "Growing up we just knew you as Stan, the guy whose restaurant my dad took us to now and then."

Stan was strangely quite for a minute.

"Ever since Vietnam I have served in one way or another. Remember all those 'fishing trips' I used to take, leaving the diner closed for long periods?"

"We never could figure out how you could operate and be gone so long," Jim said.

"Investments, and I own the building, I could let the place sit for years and just pay the taxes which are pretty low. And with the pay I receive from the Feds, I make out real good. I keep everything low key."

"Wow, I never had any idea, but then recently, I began to really study you..."

"You'd been in combat by then and you could read people, you were always a natural, Jim, I knew that from the beginning, remember, I watched you grow up."

"So now what, Chief?" Charlie asked.

"Chief?" Jim said.

"Just a term, that's all."

"We wait."

"I'm going below for a smoke," Stan said and he went through the hatchway, he did not want to give away their position by lighting up, they had run dark, not much boat traffic in this part of the bay.

"Quite a place your friend has here," Charlie said, looking towards the house.

"I am impressed, crime has paid off well for him, I will say that. Too bad it's about to come to a quick end," Jim answered.

The house was partially lit up, there were some lights on downstairs and one room upstairs, the master bedroom perhaps, was lit up.

***

An hour had gone by and now the entire downstairs of the house was dark.

"It's time to move," Stan said and he pitched a quickly inflated rubber raft over the side. He had dropped anchor. He was armed with an AK-47 with a 30 round banana clip and also had a .45 Smith and Wesson semi auto in a holster at his hip. They pulled on the ski hoods and climbed aboard the raft. It had a battery operated motor which ran silent. They made their way to the dock, stopping at the large cruiser and tying up at its bow. They slipped aboard and made their way along the rail beside the cabin, then made their way off the boat and along the dock and up the steps. They crossed the yard, it was dark. From around the side of the house Jim could see floodlights in the front driveway. They had carefully ducked under several electronic eyes set up on fence posts and light poles that would have probably triggered an alarm and caused the entire area to light up. Stan had guided them, he used incredible stealth, he moved like a cat, silent, smooth, gliding along. They positioned themselves near a walkway at the side of the house and waited.

Jim heard a low growl and started turning. Something slammed into him then flopped to the ground. A Rottweiler guard dog. It lay still and Jim noticed a tiny feathered dart in its side.

"Tranquilizer dart," whispered Stan.

"He didn't bark when we first got here," Charlie said.

"That's when I got the first two in him," Stan whispered back.

Jim felt like a blind fool next to this seasoned ex-Navy SEAL.

"Listen!" Stan whispered.

They heard it. Then they saw several dark figures dash towards the house from several sides. The night exploded with the sound of automatic rifle fire. The place was isolated, no other houses nearby.

More gunfire!

"Let's move!" Stan said as he lurched forward, Jim and Charlie right behind him.

There was the crashing of glass, they had broken inside the house. Jim heard a woman's scream then more gunfire. They rounded the house, there were several figures outside who whirled on them. Jim, Stan and Charlie opened up on them, there was a brief exchange of gunfire, bullets flew everywhere then the figures were down. There was gunfire inside the house. Jim and his crew dashed inside the opened door. The lights were on now and Jim saw several of the dark clad figures heading down a hallway.

More screams.

More gunfire.

A dark, hooded figure stumbled back out of the hallway and fell to the floor. There was gunfire upstairs. From the hallway emerged Jonnie Lee's two sons, Chuck and Jonnie Lee Jr. They were armed with 9mms. Jim and his team covered them.

"Drop it!" Jim commanded and they dropped their weapons.

"Down on the floor!" Demanded Stan and they hit the floor.

"Hands behind your heads!" Charlie yelled and he was on them, picking up their weapons. Jim knelt over them. Jonnie Lee Jr. looked up, right into his eyes.

"Stay put!" Jim hissed. "We have this handled."

There were crashing sounds throughout the house. More gunfire.

"We can help!" Jonnie Lee Jr. was looking right into Jim's eyes.

"We're Federal Agents!" Jim said firmly.

"That's even better," Chuck said. "We want to help out! You need us!"

Jim looked at Stan.

"Go for it!" Stan said.

Charlie placed the 9mms back in their hands, letting them up.

"Keep low and let us lead!" Jim said as they all quickly moved towards the stairs. They found themselves in the upper hallway.

Several dark clad men spun and opened fire. Fire was immediately returned, they ducked into rooms, on each side of the hallway and fired from the doorways.

Chuck and Jonnie Jr. started forward and Jim grabbed both of them and pulled them back.

"Stay down!" he yelled. Then Jim charged forward, Stan and Charlie right behind him. A hand holding a weapon shot out behind the doorframe, ready to fire. A bullet hit the wrist and there was a cry of pain. Jim and Charlie dove to the floor in front of the two opposite doorways and came up firing, several dark clad men in both rooms went down.

Suddenly a giant of a man barreled into Jim, taking him back down the hallway with his momentum. From another room several more men barreled into Charlie and Stan. Stan side stepped and took his opponent down with a lethal chop to the neck at an angle to stun rather than kill. Charlie heaved and his opponent was thrown off, he went for his piece, Stan shot him and he flew back. Charlie gave Stan the thumbs up. Meanwhile Jim's opponent had a strong hold on him as they backed towards the stairway, struggling. Chuck and Jonnie Jr. were on the man as well. He broke from Jim and turned on them, one of them, before turning, pulled Jim's hood off. Jim dove at the man and both of them along with both of Jonnie Lee's sons tumbled down the stairs which were heavily carpeted, easing the fall.

"The other stairway!" Chuck Lee yelled. "They've got my dad and Samantha!"

Jim stood, so did his opponent. Jim decked him with a strong right, then a left and they barreled into the hallway. Jim attacked, feet and fists in a flurry, the opponent blocked expertly.

"Now we know you!" the man said and Jim dove at him. They crashed into the kitchen, there were several women and an older man there now, in night clothes. The women screamed as Jim and his opponent crashed through a table.

Jim could hear sirens in the distance. The local authorities were arriving. Jim slammed his fist into the other man's jaw again, the man reeled and went down.

Jonnie Lee Jr. burst into the kitchen. He looked at Jim. Jim pulled out his ID.

"Now tell me, are these people in here illegals? Answer me!"

"Yes!" Jonnie Lee said fearfully. Chuck Lee was beside him now, looking at Jim's ID.

"They've got Dad and Samantha! They went out the back stairway!" Chuck Lee said.

"Quick!" Jim yelled to Stan and Charlie.

The police were pulling up outside. Uniformed officers were coming through the doors.

Jim, Stan and Charlie ripped off their hoods and showed their Federal IDs.

The first cop looked at them and then at the scene, his jaw wide, he had his weapon drawn as did the other officers.

"Take charge here, officer!" Jim ordered. "This is a federal investigation. Take all these people into custody, all of them!"

Then he nodded to Stan and Charlie and they ran down the hallway. They were out the back door running fast through the back yard and down the steps. Jim could hear the sound of the boat engine and saw the cruiser pulling away.

"Damn!" Jim yelled as he ran towards the raft. Charlie and Stan were right beside him. So were Chuck and Jonnie Lee Jr., still armed.

"What are you doing here?" Jim said.

"You need us!" Chuck Lee said as they pulled the boat into the water. Both young men had placed the 9mms in their belts and had paddles they had probably picked up at the dock.

"Okay!" Jim yelled, "let's move fast then!"

They splashed into the water dragging the raft with them and then climbed aboard the bobbing, unsteady craft and all of them began paddling, it was faster than using the battery operated motor. The cruiser had gained momentum now and was heading out into the bay.
Paddling quickly they made Stan's boat. They were aboard in an instant, Stan abandoned the raft and fired up the engines. The craft lurched forward, Stan at the wheel. Jim and Charlie were at the bow, MP5s in hand, the boat bounced through the wake thrown up by the larger cruiser, far ahead of them and running dark. They could make out its massive dark shape ahead of them.

"I hope those upgrades on the engines were enough!" Stan said. "I've never been able to catch that one before!"

Chuck and Jonnie Lee Jr. were at his side. Jonnie Lee Jr. came forward to stand between Jim and Charlie.

"I think we're in a world of shit!" Charlie said.

"What do you mean?" Jim asked then he saw the weapon in Jonnie

Lee Jr.'s belt.

"I never really went over the book but you're probably right, well, we'll worry about that tomorrow! We need the help. You," he looked at Jonnie Lee Jr., "Why the help?"

"We, my brother and I, knew this was going to happen! We just couldn't convince Dad, he's so headstrong, knows it all but the world is changing! Now this! That's our dad out there."

"We're gonna get him back, don't worry!" Jim said.

They were at top speed now and gaining on the cruiser, now they were out into the bay where the waves were rougher, the craft bouncing over them. Jim hung on with his left, clutched his rifle with his right. Spray was hitting his face, and he was soaked but not cold, the adrenaline pumping through his veins.

"Must be what it was like on a gunboat in 'Nam!" Charlie White Eagle said.

"You'd have to ask Stan, he was there!" Jim answered.

"I figured!"

On they went, bouncing over the waves and gaining on the cruiser. Men on the rear deck of the cruiser began opening up on the smaller craft with automatic rifles, Jim could see muzzle flashes and bullets strafed the deck. Jim and Charlie White Eagle returned fire. Jim saw a man pitch overboard into the water. On they sped.

More gunfire!

Anther body over the side. Both Chuck and Jonnie Lee Jr. were also firing their weapons. Jim noticed they were good.

"Not bad!" Jim said to Jonnie Lee Jr.

"We've had lots of practice!"

More gunfire and slugs hit the deck.

"Down!" Jim yelled and they went prone, Jim took careful aim and fired a short burst. Another man fell off the rear deck. They sped on past his floating body, now they were almost on the cruiser. Jim stood up, clutching the rail. He slung the MP5 over his shoulder by the strap. They were pulling along side now, inching nearer. A man was on the side rail, bringing up his weapon. Jonnie Lee Jr. fired and the man was down. Jim glanced back at him.

"Thanks!" he yelled then he looked back at Stan. Stan nodded and he tried to inch in closer. Charlie White Eagle was now at Jim's side, both men were reaching for the rail on the cruiser.

Stan came in closer, just a foot away, the boat glanced off the side of the cruiser and Jim and Charlie were thrown back. They struggled to the rail again and leaned out, closer now, the smaller boat lurched and they almost went over the side. They hung on. Jim got a hold of the rail on the cruiser and leapt. He was on the other boat now, Charlie right behind him. A man came at him, knocking him back, he pulled a KA-BAR knife and slashed at Jim. Jim caught his arm and twisted, he brought his knee up under the man's elbow and heard a sickening crack. The man cried out and Jim pitched him over the side, relieving him of the knife as he fell. Jim placed the knife between his teeth and made his way rearward. Another man came at him as he made the rear deck, that man also armed with a KA-BAR. The man slashed. Jim took his knife from his teeth and blocked the attack, stepping in he plunged the knife into the man's gut, the man leaned towards the rail. Charlie grabbed his shirt and hauled him over the side. There were three men, one at the wheel. The other two came at Jim and Charlie, both big men, they were on them, barreling into them, they hit the side rail and almost pitched over. The man got his hand under Jim's Jaw and tried to force his head back, his other hand was on Jim's wrist so he couldn't use the knife. The man tried to bring his knee up into Jim's groin but Jim blocked it with his knee. Charlie was struggling with his man. Jim's opponent heaved and Jim felt himself being lifted over the rail. Both of them pitched over the side but Jim hung on. The man also hung onto the rail next to Jim. Stan veered his craft away from the cruiser so he wouldn't crush Jim.

Both men were hanging onto the rail with one hand while they punched at each other. The man landed a hard punch on Jim's jaw and his grip weakened, he almost lost it but willed himself to hang on. The man kicked at Jim but they were too close to land any kicks effectively. The man locked his leg onto Jim's and tried to leverage him away. Jim punched out landing one hard. The man lurched and Jim punched again. Jim had dropped his knife in the struggle, it was on its way to the bottom of the bay. Jim brought both hands up to the rail and swung away from his opponent, now he kicked for all he was worth. The man lost his grip and into the bay he went. Jim hung there for a moment, exhausted. He gathered his strength then hauled upward. A hand helped him, Charlie pulled him over the side onto the rear deck. The cruiser was spinning wildly, Charlie had taken out the wheelman who lay unconscious on the deck. Charlie grabbed the wheel and Jim burst through the cabin door, unslinging his MP5. The interior was well lit up and Jim could see two hooded men holding guns on Jonnie Lee and Samantha Yi, who was holding Jonnie Lee, they were holding each other.

"Jim!" Samantha said and there was a brief look of hope on her face.

One of the armed men wheeled on Jim and at that moment Jonnie Lee kicked out, knocking the gun from the other man's hand and leaping at him, both of them crashing across the cabin against the bulkhead. Jim fired a brief burst and the other man went down. Jim was on Jonnie Lee's opponent but Jonnie Lee had already subdued him, the man lay at his feet. Jonnie Lee looked at Jim, a look of relief on his face.

"How did you get here, Jim?" he said and then he saw the badge in Jim's hand.

"It's all over now, Jonnie Lee, you are under arrest for the illegal trafficking of human cargo!"

Jim saw a look of utter despair on Jonnie Lee's face. He looked like a defeated man, Samantha Yi came into Jim's arms.

"Oh Jim, Jim," she said as she held him, tears in her eyes.

"It'll be okay, Samantha, it'll be okay," Jim said although he doubted it. It was all over for her too.

They headed out on deck, Stan was pulling alongside. Both Jonnie Lee Jr. and Chuck climbed aboard, they had discarded their weapons. Their father looked at them, a lost man. They looked at him and then at Jim and Samantha then back at their father.

Both young men just shook their heads.

CHAPTER EIGHTEEN

Jim stood outside the interrogation room in the San Francisco Federal Building. Charlie White Eagle was with him, Gene was also there along with Martin Thomas. Suzie was not there. They had tried to contact her but were unable to do so. They stood behind the one way glass looking into the interrogation room, from inside the windows would appear to be only mirrors. Jonnie Lee sat at the simple wooden table in a stiff, basic wooden chair. There were two other chairs across the table from him. He had his head in his hands.

"I'm going in there," Jim said.

"No, Jim, I will take over from here, you have not been trained in proper..."

"Bullshit!" Jim cut Martin off mid-sentence. "I'm going in there!"

Without another word, before Martin could stop him, Jim was through the door. He closed it behind him, looking around the mirrored room. He knew Martin was watching, boiling.

Jonnie Lee looked up from the table at Jim. Then he looked down again. Jim took a seat across from him.

"You found nothing to link me with anything!" Jonnie Lee suddenly said, an attempt at strength but he was faltering.

"We've got plenty!" Jim lied, for in reality they really had only the illegals found in the house and of course, Samantha Yi. Jim knew it might not be enough but he decided to bluff his way through.

"You're facing a lot of jail time, Jonnie Lee!" Jim said.

"I was your friend! I even saved you at the party Saturday night!"

"Friendship? You're a criminal, a common criminal, Jonnie Lee. Yes, you helped me out but you have still broken a great number of laws and the Federal Prosecutor will be pushing for the maximum. I doubt if you will ever see the light of day until you are a very, very old man! You knew what you were doing, knew it was illegal, you took that chance and you lost!"

"You came and saved my life tonight. For that I owe you, I cannot have you killed..."

"Killed? A threat? Oh thank you for rescinding the death sentence, Jonnie Lee but I don't buy it! Oh, yes, murder is part of what you could be charged with, remember the Chinatown shootings?"

"I was defending my life and the life of Samantha, you were there!

You fired your weapon also!"

"I was acting in the performance of my duties as a Federal investigator! As far as I am concerned it was a gangland shootout! You are facing big time charges, the San Francisco DA's office will be looking to bringing charges of murder one! That's life, Jonnie Lee. You are in deep, deep shit!"

"What about my sons?"

"They are accomplices, the fact that they helped us out will be taken into consideration."

"And...Samantha..."

"She is in custody, along with all the other illegals in your house and will be shipped back to The People's Republic of China."

"They will kill her there!" Rage suddenly appeared in Jonnie Lee's eyes and he started to rise.

"Sit down!" Jim ordered.

He sat back down, the look of defeat coming over him as he hung his head. Jim let him sit there for a few minutes, contemplating his fate.

"Maybe some of this can 'go away,'" Jim said.

"What do you mean?"

"Perhaps, if you are willing to cooperate, we can talk a 'deal.'"

Jonnie Lee looked around at the mirrors. Then he looked at Jim.

"What do you want to know and what exchange are we talking about."

"I am not the one to make the deal, but I will tell you this, to begin with, and I am going to make sure you are released on O.R., if you decide to play with us, I will tell you this right now! Upon release you *will* take Samantha Yi to Las Vegas under guard by Agent White Eagle and you *will* marry her! And I will arrange to have papers drawn up so she can remain in this country. As to jail time, perhaps we can convince the Federal Judge to give you a reduced sentence. That is if, and only if, you give us your complete cooperation, Jonnie Lee!"

"Samantha..." then a smile crossed Jonnie Lee's face. "So, Agent Saunders, you do have a soft side."

"You'll see how un-soft that side is if you don't play ball with us!"

"She cares for you, you know. She will always be grateful for what you have just done for her."

"I haven't done anything yet, Jonnie Lee, it all depends on what you have to tell us in the next few hours!"

Suddenly the door to the interrogation room flew open and Gene looked inside, his eyes intense.

"Jim, get out here right away!"

Jim took one last look at Jonnie Lee and left the room.

Martin Thomas was standing there, a grave expression on his face, Trudy Williams, Suzie's boss was also there, tears were in her eyes.

"What's going on?" Jim demanded.

"It's Agent Bradley, Suzie..." Trudy started to say and then she broke down, going to her knees in sobs.

"What? What's going on?"

"Suzie's been shot! She in San Francisco ER right now, dying!" Gene said.

Jim felt his world caving in...

***

Jim burst through the swinging doors to the ER, Martin, Trudy, Charlie White Eagle and Gene right behind him. Already there, dressed in his outlaw biker garb was Suzie's brother, Agent Jason Bradley. He was standing there, shaking, tears running down his cheeks. Jim came up to him, Jason turned to face him.

"What happened?" Jim asked as Martin and the rest of them came walking up.

Jason could not speak. He shook as he stood there, his entire being looking as if it were about to explode. He slammed his fist into the wall, making a dent in the drywall then he went down on his knees, tears filling his eyes.

"Sis!" he sobbed.

Jim placed a hand on Jason's shoulder and he violently shook it away. Jim looked at Martin, at Gene, the rest of them. They shook their heads.

The door opened and a doctor came through in surgeon greens.

Martin came forward. Jim placed his hand on Jason's shoulder again.

"The doctor is here, Jason," he said.

Jason stood, wiped a heavy forearm across his eyes and waited.

"Is there a Jim Saunders here?" the doctor asked.

"Here," Jim said.

"She is calling for you, and her brother, is he here?"

Jim placed his hand on Jason's shoulder again, moving him

forward.

"She is calling for both of you. Although I advise against it, I will allow a short visit. We have her stabilized right now, she's lost a lot of blood."

"What happened?" Jason managed to ask.

"She took a bullet near the heart, lucky for her it missed the organ but there is other damage, internal. The prognosis is not good..."

Jim nodded to Jason and they pushed on past the doctor into the room. The gurney was dead ahead, two orderlies were standing by to move her to Intensive Care. She had an IV bottle attached to her, she looked deathly pale as she lay there, no longer the toned, athletic woman but more like a small child. Her eyes were closed.

"Sir..." a nurse said as they passed but Jim paid no attention. He was at Suzie's bedside, Jason right beside him. Jim took a deep breath. He saw she was breathing on her own, but faintly. He could see the readout of her vital signs, weak but there. He placed a hand on her forehead and smoothed back her hair.

"Jim...Jason..." she moaned, barely audible.

"We're here, sis, we're here..." Jason said as he kneeled by her side, touching her face. "Oh sis, oh sis, I..."

He started to break down again but forced himself to maintain.

"J-J-Jim..." she barely got the words out. It was barely above a whisper now. "J-J-J-Jim..."

"I'm right here, Suzie..."

"I love you, Jim...you know that..."

"I Love you too, Suzie," Jim answered and it was true, she held a place there in his heart, deep down inside. She had been the witness to his wedding, and now here she was.

"Jim, I found out something, I have to tell you..."

"Not now, Suzie, you need to sleep..."

"No, now...I have to tell you..."

Jim brought his ear near her mouth and she spoke to him. As she did Jim began to feel his world crumble, his existence began to lose meaning, what he was hearing, his life, his very upbringing in doubt now as she whispered the terrible truths to him.

Finally, she was finished.

"I'm sorry, Jim, I'm so sorry..." she said and then she closed her eyes.

"She's had enough," Jim said and Jason nodded as Jim gently

wiped her brow and smoothed back her hair. He noticed the vital signs, weak, faltering but there.

"We have to move her," the orderlies said.

Jim and Jason nodded their heads. They left the room and Jim nodded to Charlie White Eagle. Jim, Jason and Charlie headed down the hallway, Martin watching them go. Gene looked at Martin then he also followed them.

***

The four of them took Jim's car, Jason leaving his bike at the hospital parking lot. All were carrying, all had their IDs on them, on their belts in full view, even Jason in his biker garb. Their pieces were strapped to holsters at their waists, no more undercover now. They had business to get down to, hard business, especially for Jim, whose world had just caved in around him. It was like the last twenty four years of his life meant nothing now. All he had was Jiang Li waiting for him back at June's apartment.

They pulled up to the building and parked. Jim sat there for a few moments looking straight ahead. There was a familiar car there in front of the building. The Lincoln Town car. Also, another vehicle. Jim nodded to his partners and they all got out, they drew their weapons and headed for the building, a building so familiar to Jim. They paused at a side door, Jim knew the door so well, he eased it open and they stepped in. They could hear voices. The two Russians, and Asian accents as well.

"Hey!" a voice yelled and gunfire erupted, bullets flying at Jim's party.

"Federal Agents!" Jim yelled as he returned fire. Jim's partners opened fire. Burly Asian men came bursting at them, firing 9mms. One opened up with an UZI, Jim's group dove for cover as bullets ricocheted along the walls. Jim drew down on the man and got him with one shot. The man toppled to the floor.

Men were running. The Asians, it was Tommy and David Xiang. The two Russians opened fire, blocking the office they were in. The Asians were gone in an instant. The Russians had some heavy duty hardware, .44 magnums, slugs going through the outer walls, impacting on the floor. One of the Russians pulled out a MAC 10 and opened up, bullets spraying everywhere, windows shattering. Jim's group split up and took cover wherever they could find it.

"What's going on?" Jim heard a familiar voice yell, the voice he had known all his life.

As one, Jim and his group all opened fire, the two Russians were riddled and their bodies danced the dance of death for a few seconds as rounds impacted them. Down they went, hitting the floor hard.

Jim and his group burst through the office door, guns and badges held in full view. Jim's dad looked up from the desk he had been seated at in his office in the auto body shop Jim had grown up around all his life. Jim's dad with about a million and a half of cocaine on the desk in front of him. He looked right into his son's eyes, at the badge, at the gun, at the other agents there facing him.

"Oh God, oh my God no..." he said as tears of shame and guilt flooded his eyes.

Jim looked down at his dad, a coldness came over him.

"Federal Agents," Jim said, "and you are under arrest!"

***

Exhaustion and strain was evident on Jim's face, it was three in the morning now. They were back in the Federal Building looking through the see through glass into the interrogation room. Jim's dad sat there, a broken, defeated man who seemed to have suddenly aged ten years, his dynamic personality destroyed, his head hung low, hands folded in front of him.

Jim was with Martin. Charlie White Eagle was there as well as Gene and Jason. With them also were Jonnie Lee. They had just taken the cuffs off of him. He moved next to Jim and looked through the glass.

"He's your father?" Jonnie Lee asked.

Jim nodded then looked at him. A door opened and Samantha Yi was escorted into the room. She looked around, she was dressed in her red dress now and had her makeup on. She looked directly at Jim, then she crossed the room to stand in front of him. Suddenly she slapped him across the face, hard. She was stronger than she looked. Anger and rage were in her eyes as she spoke a tirade at him. Jonnie Lee pulled her away as she glared at him. Jim's heart was breaking but his face was as expressionless as stone, his jaw tightened, the muscles in his face moved, giving him away. Tears were now in Samantha's eyes and she suddenly ran to him and threw her arms around him, burying her face in his chest, her body shaking with sobs. Jim held her. She looked up at him with her tear filled eyes and Jim wiped them gently away from her cheek.

"I'm sorry, Samantha, I'm truly sorry," he said and he felt that she could understand him. He took her hand and walked her over to Jonnie Lee and placed her hand in his.

"You know what you have to do!" Jim told Jonnie Lee and then he looked at Charlie White Eagle. Charlie nodded.

"You'd better get going. Take the next plane out," Jim said and Charlie led Jonnie Lee and Samantha out of the room.

Martin came up to him.

"This is highly unusual you know, I don't think we'll be able to get away with it," Martin said.

"Sure we will," Jim said.

Martin looked through the glass.

"I'm sorry, Jim, I'm sorry it came to this."

Jim's heart was beyond broken. There sat his father, a criminal, a common criminal, the man who had taught him values as a kid, who had guided him and his brother. And he had made a deal with the devil himself.

"He made his choice," Jim said.

"You want me to handle it?" Martin asked.

"No. This is for me to do. I'll handle it."

Martin nodded and Jim walked to the entrance to the room. He entered. As he did his dad looked up then down again as Jim took a chair across from him. He looked at his dad for a good long time.

"How long have you been an agent?" his dad asked, sounding distant.

"Not long, but long enough," Jim answered.

They sat there in silence for a few moments.

"Why?" Jim asked.

His dad just shook his head.

"You don't understand..." he said.

"Don't give me that!"

"You don't..."

"I understand plenty!" now rage filled Jim's being, his eyes glared. "An agent, and a good friend, the witness to my marriage, now lies in a hospital bed dying because of the organization you are a part of. Do you know what that makes you, Dad? Do you even know what that makes you? If she dies you are an accomplice to first degree murder!"

"I-I didn't realize...I didn't know...I..."

"You knew! You had to know! You always warned me these were

bad people! I guess you would know, wouldn't you!"

"You know this is going to break your mother's heart, son!"

"Don't call me 'son' anymore! Break my mother's heart? Well, you should have seen that coming when you made your bargain with the devil! Did you think it would end well?"

"God damn it!" his father started to rise, anger in his eyes.

"Sit down!" Jim commanded, no longer a son, but a Federal Agent doing his job no matter how deeply it hurt his soul. He had to see this through.

"You don't understand, we were losing the house, you were just a little boy and your brother was just a baby! Denning offered his help, I had refused before, he had even threatened me, our family, but still I had refused. Perhaps he had arranged for my business to start to fail so he could come in and take over, I don't know...but whatever, I did what I had to do."

"No! That's not an excuse! And you taught us to be anything but what you really were!"

"I was a victim, son, just a victim..."

"I don't want to hear it! And how many other murders have you been aware of?"

"I swear, I had nothing to do with that part of it, I didn't know..."

"Oh you knew! You had to know, on some level you had to know! Just being a part makes you as guilty as the rest of them! Think about it, Dad, your facing the rest of your life in prison now! I can't save the house, look what you caused! Your ruined your own family. What will Mom do now?"

"She..."

"She what, Dad? Did she know?"

"She knew, and she always was afraid this would happen, but to be betrayed by my own son..."

"Don't you give me that shit! You're the one who went against the values you taught! My action in arresting you would be what you would have expected me to do and you know that! You thought you could save your business! Your house! And now you lose it all! We all lose here, Dad, all of us! If we had lost the house when I was a child you would have found another way, I know you would have! Or maybe not. Maybe you're not the man I looked up to after all."

There was silence. His father sat there and tears began to run down the side of his face.

"There is no way out, is there?" he looked up at his son, his eyes pleading, no trace of the man Jim had admired and looked up to.

"The Federal Prosecutor will be wanting to know everything! Perhaps she will cut a deal, perhaps not. It's up to her now. But the only way out is to come clean, completely clean and tell us everything you know."

"You know they would kill your mom, kill Robbie."

"We will protect them. I will protect them! This is over, Dad, the game is over. You have a choice. I'll leave you to think about it!"

With no further words Jim rose from the table and left the room.

***

Jim entered another room. His mother and Robbie were seated there, they had been brought in for their own protection by other agents immediately after the bust had gone down. His mother and brother both looked up at him, saw the gun and badge on his belt, they had not yet been informed of his status.

"Jim, I don't understand," his mother said. "We were picked up by these men in suits and brought here...what's going on? Why are you wearing that badge and gun?"

"Mom," Jim said as he sat between her and his younger brother, putting his arms around them. "I have something very painful to tell you."

"I already know..." the look of dread, long expected dread, was coming over her face. She broke into sobs and Jim held her. "I knew it had to happen, I knew it..."

"What, Mom, what?" Robbie asked and he looked up at Jim.

"Robbie," Jim said, "You are going to have to grow up now, real fast. I'm sorry."

Jim began his story.

"I hate your guts!" Robbie yelled at him after he was finished and he came at Jim. He landed a strong right on Jim's jaw, Jim reeled from the blow, the kid had gotten so strong. Jim went down to the floor in a daze and Robbie stood over him, fists clenched, his mother crying and begging him to stop.

"I hate you, you asshole!" Robbie yelled.

Jim looked away. Then, slowly, he rose and put his hand on Robbie's shoulder. Robbie knocked his hand away and took another swing. This time Jim blocked and grabbed his fist firmly in a vice like grip.

"That's enough, Robbie, that's enough. Maybe someday you'll understand."

Jim left the room.

***

Jim was exhausted beyond belief as he parked his car across the street from June's apartment. He got out, his heart was broken, his soul felt destroyed as he walked across the street. He needed his wife, she was all he had now, everything else was gone. It was only the two of them now, that's all he had to hold onto. He approached the apartment, he wanted to be in her arms, needing her like never before, he could see her face in his mind as he climbed the several steps and knocked at the door.

Strange.

The door opened easily! It wasn't locked. Then he knew why! The door window was broken! Glass was on the floor just inside. He went in, the lights were off, he fumbled for a switch! Panic was rising fast! He turned on the lights!

"Jiang Li! June!" and he knew the calls would not be answered.

He ran down the hallway to the guest bedroom. Things were strewn everywhere! Tables and chairs were overturned! He entered the guest bedroom. Empty, the bed in disarray! He ran on down to the master bedroom. She was there, June, lying across the bed, naked, her vacant eyes staring up at the ceiling, her throat slit, blood was everywhere, on her body, on the bed. Jim felt the world ending right before his eyes!

***

The police arrived before the Federal Agents, cars everywhere, unmarked, marked, red and blue lights flashing, an ambulance, not needed, uniformed and plain clothes officers on the scene. Even a fire truck rescue unit had arrived and the personnel were standing by in full gear.

Jim stood, his back against a wall, exhausted. He had been talked to briefly by investigators but had mostly remained silent, showing them his ID. Finally Martin arrived with Gene and Stan and Jason wearing navy blue windbreakers with DEA in bright, reflective letters on their backs, their badges and weapons on their belts in plain sight.

"You okay?" Martin asked Jim. It was now almost sunup, the light of day showing in the eastern horizon, a warm breeze was blowing.

Jim nodded.

Just then a sleek, black car showed up. Two escorting uniformed officers stepped out and opened the passenger door. Chief Dan Heyden stepped out and he stood there, surveying the scene. He walked up to Jim, Martin, Gene and Stan, he nodded to Gene, ignoring Jim and Stan.   He spoke directly to Martin.

"I want answers!" he said.

"What brings you out in the middle of the night, Chief?" Martin asked.

"It's morning! I heard about it a half hour ago! Cobra, I heard! So what have you got?"

"Nothing yet," Martin said.

"Nothing you're going to tell me, that's the story, right?"

"Like I said, nothing."

"And you, young man," Heyden said to Jim, facing him.

"Don't fuck with me!" Jim said in a low, even voice.

"You listen here..."

"I said 'don't fuck with me!'"

"You can't..."

Jim had him by the collar in a split second, driving him back towards his car and slamming him against it. The uniformed officers ran over and started to pull Jim away. Jim turned and decked the biggest one, the other one drew back and pulled out his billy club. Martin grabbed his arm. Jim grabbed Heyden again and slammed him against the car again, harder this time.

"I said 'don't fuck with me!' Get it, asshole, don't fuck with me!"

He slammed Heyden against the car again to make his point as other officers rushed up and grabbed Jim, pulling him away. Martin tried to intervene but he was restrained. Suddenly bodies were flying in all directions! Gene, Jason and Stan were wading in, tossing men aside like kingpins, Stan showing great strength in his aging, steel corded body. They grabbed Jim and hustled him aside and down the street.

"I want that man, those men, arrested!" demanded Heyden.

"Fuck you, Chief!" Martin said. "And besides, this is now a Federal investigation and you have interfered. Gene, get Jim away from here pronto and cool him off!"

"Come on," Gene said as he and Stan hustled Jim to his car.

"Cool it man! Just cool it!" Gene said.

"My wife has been kidnapped, a young girl is dead and I'm

supposed to cool it? Fuck you too!" Jim yelled.

"Jim," Stan said.

"Fuck you!"

Jim pushed them away and got in his car. He fired it up and burned rubber down the street as officers leapt aside, Gene, Jason and Stan staring after him.

***

Jim was in an exhausted frenzy, the adrenalin surging through him as he drove, almost hallucinating from lack of sleep. He knew right where he was going and he was going fast, gunning the engine, running stoplights, burning around turns, almost air born as he crested hills until he was right in the middle of Chinatown on Kearney Street. He took out a removable, flashing, revolving red light and placed it on the roof of his car, got out and scanned the street. The sun was about the break over the horizon, no one was out, a few old newspapers were blowing in the wind down the street. Jim looked over at the restaurant, there was yellow tape at the entrance, the place closed down for the investigation. Jonnie Lee and Samantha Yi should be married about now, Jim figured. Good for her, he didn't give a shit about Jonnie Lee, Lee was just a common criminal along with the rest of them.

Jiang Li!

His wife! His life and love! Gone! Where! He had to have answers and fast! He scanned the street again, the red light reflecting off the window panes of the local businesses. Then he saw him, down the street hobbling along on his crutches.

"Andy!" Jim yelled at the top of his voice and he ran down the street.

Andy was trying to get away, the flashing red light intimidating him.

"Andy!" Jim yelled again as he plunged on. He grabbed Andy and slammed him against a wall, pulling up his badge and shoving it in front of his face.

"I want some answers right fucking now and you're going to give them to me!" Jim yelled, his eyes burning into Andy's.

"I knew it! You're a cop, I knew it!" Andy said, sweat pouring off his face, fear in his eyes for he was looking into stark, cold death in Jim's glare.

"A cop who's going to kick your sorry crippled ass in about a spit second if you don't tell me what I want to know!"

"But this is police brutality..."

"It sure is, asshole, like you've never seen police brutality before so sing, pal, sing a good song and make me happy because if I am not happy you will not be happy! You think you got a bad deal having a broken leg, well I'll break everything else so talk to me! Now!"

"What do you want me to tell you?"

"First of all, where do the parents of Jiang Li live? You gotta know that!"

"I don't! Remember, I didn't even know it was her in the restaurant..."

"You didn't know her by sight but you know where she lives, she's marrying your former boss or was! Tell me!"

"I'm dead if I talk!"

Jim pulled his .45 and shoved the barrel in front of Andy's face.

"See this, asshole? What do you think this is? I'll give you five seconds...one...two..."

***

Jim was standing in front of the apartment. He had entered from the main street and gone up a flight of stairs, from what Andy had told him, and Andy had sung like a bird, a real sweet, sweet song, the family occupied the entire top floor of this building which they also owned.

Jim knocked loudly.

"Federal Agent, open up!" he commanded and he knocked again, jarring the door.

Nothing.

"Open up! Federal Agents!" he yelled again.

He rapped harder!

Nothing!

He stepped back, psyched himself up then did a heel kick on the door, it broke the locks and flew open banging against the inside wall. Jim rushed in, weapon drawn and held in both hands, he covered himself as he moved into the apartment, scanning carefully ahead.

"Hello in here!" he yelled, "Federal Agent! Is anyone here?"

There was no answer. He knew, the dread came over him. He searched the rooms, everything was thrown about, tables overturned, the beds up ended, glass shattered from cabinets, dishes lay broken in the kitchen, it looked like a tornado had come through, devastating everything in its path.

No one was there!

***

"Okay, I want answers! Talk!"

Jim was back in the interrogation room in the Federal Building sitting across from his father. His father sat there, now a broken man, he seemed to have aged in the two or three hours since Jim had last seen him.

"Okay, son, I'll tell you everything I know, all the connections, all the deals. I don't care what happens now, it's all over but take care of Mom and Robbie."

"You know I will. Maybe I can make this all go away for you but I have to have the entire truth."

"Son, you look tired," his dad said.

"I'm not! Now talk!"

His father nodded and Jim motioned towards the window. Martin entered with a woman dressed in a business suit, wearing a gun and badge and carrying a recording device and writing tablet.

"We'll take it from here, son," Martin said, "You go and get some rest. And I have to talk to you for a moment."

Martin left the room as the woman was seated, she began to talk to Jim's father.

"Breaking and entering, Jim, that's what I want to talk to you about, you just went ahead without a warrant and..."

"Broke into my in-laws apartment? Damn right I did, they've been taken right along with my wife!"

"Tell me what you know, Jim!"

"I ain't gonna tell you shit!"

"Then you know where they are being held? Come on, Jim, tell me, we have to do this right!"

"What about Denning?"

"We are getting the appropriate warrants ready right now, it's too bad the bust couldn't have come down when the shipments arrived. But we have, or will soon have, enough evidence to go get him!"

"Good! Then I can do what I have to do!"

"Jim, just tell me, you know where they are, don't you?"

Andy had indeed sung a good song. Top of the charts as far as Jim was concerned.

"And you will go in there like gangbusters and they will kill my wife and her entire family? I don't think so!"

"Jim, think about your career with us, right now you are on very thin ice here, punching the chief of police, that's assault, breaking and entering..."

"Fuck my career! I'm going to go make sure my wife is safe. I'll let you know where just before I move in."

"You'll be alone."

"Not really!"

"Jim, your eyes, you are beyond exhaustion right now, you have to rest and think things out!"

"How is Suzie doing?"

"They don't know yet."

Jim left the room.

***

Jim stood in the hospital room on the intensive care floor. He was holding Suzie's hand. She opened her eyes, looked up at him and she smiled weakly. She tried to speak.

"No, don't say anything right now," Jim said as he patted her hand lovingly. He felt like crying as he looked at her lying there. Her eyes had brightened when she saw him.

"You're going to be fine, just fine, I already talked to the doctors..."

"You know you don't make a very good liar..." she managed to whisper.

Jim shut his eyes, the tears were there and he squeezed her hand.

"Baby, hang on, just hang on for me will you?"

Tears came to Suzie's eyes and she slowly nodded her head, a hardly discernable movement but Jim knew.

"Is..." she started to ask.

"Everything is being taken care of, baby, everything."

"Your dad...what I found out...I'm so sorry...Jim...I'm so sorry..."

"Don't you worry about that. It's okay, I handled it well. We'll have to have a long talk about this sometime real soon."

"We will, real soon, I promise..."

Her voice faded and she closed her eyes and slept. Jim bent down and kissed her forehead and caressed her hair, smoothing it back. He squeezed her hand. Then he left the room.

It was now ten in the morning.

Stan was waiting in the sitting room along with Gene and Jason.

"Are we ready?" Stan asked.
"Did you tell Gene and Jason?" Jim asked.
"They know!"

Both Jason and Gene nodded. Jason was now dressed in jeans, "T" shirt and blue blazer with DEA lettered on the back in reflective yellow.

"Did you get in touch with Charlie White Eagle?" Jim asked Gene.

"Sure did. He'll meet us at the boat in an hour. Jonnie Lee and that girl are a happily married couple now. And from the information he gave us a Coast Guard Cutter is on its way to intercept his shipment of illegals."

"Good! Finally he did something right! Let's go!"

***

They arrived at the dock in the Marina where Stan's boat was tied up. Standing there waiting for them were Charlie White Eagle, with him, Jonnie Lee, Samantha Yi, now Samantha Lee, and also his two sons.

As Jim and his group approached Samantha ran to him and threw her arms around his neck, kissing his cheek and then his lips, she was all smiles, her eyes misty. He held her and smiled at her. She reached up and touched his eye lids, smoothing them, he felt so tired he just wanted to shut his eyes in her embrace. He gently moved away from her and took her hand, walking down the dock to the group.

Amazingly, Jonnie Lee was all smiles as he came to Jim, hand outstretched. Jim reached for it and Jonnie Lee suddenly landed a strong right on his jaw, staggering him. Jim shook it off, the other agents went for their weapons but Jim waved them off. He looked at Jonnie Lee.

Jonnie Lee smiled again and again extended his hand.

"Hey, I had to pay you back, now we're even, okay?"

Jim smiled and they shook hands, Samantha still on Jim's arm. Jim guided her to Jonnie Lee.

"Here's your bride, you are now a married man, how does it feel?" Jim asked.

Jonnie Lee shrugged his shoulders. His two sons came forward and shook Jim's hand.

"Thanks," John Jr. said.

"We are here to help!" Chuck said.

"We can handle it from here," Jim said.

"We want to help! We know how to fight! Something's up and we want to get in on it!" John Jr. said.

"I want in too!" Jonnie Lee said, "I owe The Cobra a few paybacks!"

"You're technically under arrest, you can't..." Gene said.

"Hang on," Jim said, "we need all the help we can get! Stan, do you have extra weapons?"

Stan nodded. "Man, I've gotta fuckin' arsenal down there!" he motioned towards the hull of his boat.

"Then let's get it on," Jim said.

***

They headed out under the Golden Gate Bridge and on up the coast, the water was fairly calm for the time of day, now just past noon.

Jim lay on deck, the sun was warm and he let himself drift away, the gentle rocking of the boat relaxing him. He was in a deep sleep.

He opened his eyes. He thought of Jiang Li, a prisoner of the Cobra. Had they taken her, sexually? Rage shot through him at thought of her being taken by them. And Rebecca. She had obviously gone with the Cobra after that party at Denning's. She would be there. Jim put the thought of Jiang Li with Tommy out of his mind. It wasn't her fault. Jim would make Tommy Xiang pay a dear price. Especially if he had in any way harmed or violated Jiang Li. Jim checked his watch. It was 2:30 in the afternoon. They were adjacent to a cliff right now, they were pretty far out to sea. There were several buildings at the top of the cliff, just as Andy said there would be. Jim could see the reflection of the sun off what appeared to be a large picture window in what was the main dwelling, it was a large estate. Jim looked over.

Jonnie Lee Jr. was at the wheel, piloting the craft.

The others were there except for Stan. Jim rose up and made his way over.

"Stan's below," Charlie White Eagle said.

Jim nodded and went down the steps and through the hatchway. Stan was seated at a computer, the screen reflecting off the walls of the dimly lit quarters.

"Check it out," Stan said.

Jim looked at the screen. There were satellite pictures of the group of dwellings on the cliff. It appeared that a winding dirt road led up through the mountains from the other side. There were no other dwellings nearby, no housing tracts or any other buildings visible. It was isolated and right against the cliff. It had an eight foot wall on three sides, the other side not needing one as it bordered the high cliff.

"What've you got?" Jim asked.

"The property shows as belonging to a corporation. I looked it up, it's a dummy corporation and is also part of another business, all registered to some import company. The Xiang family name is never mentioned. But I'll bet you anything it's theirs all right. Dummy companies formed for tax purposes to launder money."

"That Harry Xiang, he's a clever one!"

Jim turned. Jonnie Lee was standing there, Samantha at his side. She smiled at Jim and put her arms around his neck.

"She loves you, what can I say, my wife is in love with you," Jonnie Lee said.

"I..."

"I know, you already have a wife. I myself never imagined myself married. But now, well, I couldn't ask for a better wife than Samantha. I owe you a great debt, Agent Jim Saunders. I should have figured you for a cop right away."

"You did, remember, you asked me directly in the restaurant."

"That I did. I dis-obeyed my first rule, always trust my first instinct. Well, it worked out well. I still have my restaurant, Samantha is quite a business woman, she can manage it while I am in prison."

"We'll just have to wait and see what happens," Jim said.

"I got word," Stan said, "the Coast Guard intercepted the ship and took all the illegals into custody, the ship is impounded."

"There is the matter of the other ship, the one with the drugs and the meeting. It was never finalized where it would be."

"That ships out there somewhere, that's for sure. But when we're through it will have no one to deliver to," Stan said.

He worked the keys, watching the screen.

"I just tapped into NASSAU. They will be bringing up a current satelite view shortly as soon as it moves into position. There's no cloud cover today so we'll get a good picture, live, of course."

Jim studied the screen, Samantha still holding him. She felt good near him, he thought of his wife. How he wished she were here right now.

Stan lit a cigarette, took a drag and looked up at Jim.

"The no smoking policy is for new recruits. They gave up trying to reform us old timers. And this is a private vessel so I can smoke if I want to."

"No problem here," Jim said. "In fact, I could use a smoke right now."

"You're a new recruit, why we would be breaking the rules," Stan grinned as he offered Jim a Camel.

"Fuck the rules, we've broken every rule in the book in the past day or so."

Jim popped the cigarette in his mouth and Stan gave him a light. Jim inhaled deeply, he felt fuzzy headed, not being a regular smoker. He felt himself relax. Samantha began massaging his shoulders.

"It would be nice if she did that for me," Jonnie Lee said. "But I am in the doghouse with her right now. I guess I deserve it."

She looked around at him and gave him a frown then went back to working the muscles in Jim's neck.

"It would be a good idea to bring everyone down here," Stan said, "as we move a little closer they could start observing us. So far, this is just some fishing vessel and I want it to stay that way. Jim, don't go on deck without a cap and sunglasses."

Jim nodded to Tommy Lee and he headed topside to spread the word. In a few moments everyone was below decks except for Gene who was manning the helm. They wouldn't recognize him.

"I want to get in there!" Jim said, anger rising.

"No way. We will way anchor out here and appear to be fishing," Stan said.

"But my wife..."

"I'm sorry. We have no choice at this moment. It's broad daylight, we wouldn't have a chance and if we called in backup at this point they'd probably kill the hostages. We have to wait until nightfall. Okay, here it is!"

They looked at the screen. An aerial view of the coastline, a spot indicated the buildings, it looked like a private resort, walled in on three sides, the cliff at the back. Stan typed in codes. A closer view showed more detail of the grounds. Figures were moving about. Jim was alert, studying the screen. He lit up another cigarette, puffing madly, intent on the view. Closer still. Yes, armed men patrolled the grounds both inside and outside the walls. There were dogs on leashes, Rottweilers from the look of them. No sign of Jiang Li or anyone else who would be a family member or hostage. They were obviously inside somewhere, maybe in the main building.

"I don't see Harry Xiang or either of his sons." Jim said.

"Look there," Stan pointed out.

Off to the side was a helipad and a chopper was sitting on it, idle for now.

"And there," Stan indicated.

Jim saw to the side of the main building, a square structure attached to the side of the building.

"What is it?" Jim asked.

"It looks like an elevator shaft. They must have levels underground."

"I'm going up top for a look," Jim said as he grabbed a pair of powerful binoculars. Stan followed him, both of them donning caps and sunglasses. Jim was shirtless.

Once on deck Jim looked through the glasses. He had a clear view of the estate from here, the glasses brought everything up close. He traced downward and found a small beach at the bottom of the cliff. And there were people on the beach, moving about. Jim saw no pathway down as he scanned. Then he saw the doorway, cut into the face of the cliff. That's where the elevator was, all the way down to the beach. There was a flight of stone steps leading from the elevator doorway down to the beach.

"That's a man made beach there," Stan said, "the white sand is not familiar to this part of the coast. All the beaches near the Golden Gate have coarse, dark, volcanic sand. This looks to be fine. Imported. Over there, by the mounted pole."

Stan showed Jim a fishing pole mounted on the rail and beside it, a powerful telescope under camouflage netting.

"Is there anything this boat doesn't have?" Jim asked.

Stan just grinned.

Jim looked through the telescope. Now he had a detailed view of the beach. He studied the doorway to the elevator, the stone steps, then across the beach. There they were. Both sons, Tommy and David, they were naked, lying on beach towels and sipping beers. There were bodyguards, dressed in shorts and Hawaiian shirts and carrying AK-47s slung over their shoulders. There were women there as well. Jim concentrated. The woman were all naked, Jim recognized Debra. There were several Asian girls. Then Jim saw her, Rebecca, she was wading in the surf, totally naked, letting the water splash up on her glistening body.

Debra was reaching into an ice chest and bringing out bottled beers which she brought to the guards and Tommy and his brother. Tommy reached for her and tried to pinch her buttocks but she danced away, smiling with her eyes. Jim had a close-up on her face. Even from this distance he could see the hidden rage there. He studied the guards. Some were not armed. Mike Walker was there in shorts and Hawaiian shirt but carried no weapon. A prisoner? Or one of them? Jim had no idea at this point.

Jim swung the scope back to Tommy Xiang. Tommy was rising now, brushing sand off himself, finishing his beer. He approached Debra and tried to feel her breasts but she managed to move away. He looked towards the surf at Rebecca. Jim saw him get hard as he ran to her, coming up behind her and throwing his arms around her waist, pressing himself against her as the waves splashed over them. She reached up an arm around his neck and turned her head. She began kissing him then turned to face him full on, bodies locked together she reached down and fondled him, kissing him passionately. He lifted her legs around his waist, she locked them around him as the waves splashed over them again. Then he took her up in his arms and dashed back to the towel where he tossed her down and descended upon her. He began making love to her right there in front of everyone.

"I think your wife is safe for now," Stan said, he was watching through the binoculars, he had enough of a view to see what was happening.

"Rebecca doesn't even know she's doing me a favor," Jim said with disgust. Animals, fucking animals, that's all they were.

He looked again. Debra was again serving beers. So far no one had touched her. She walked over and was talking to Mike Walker, whispering in his ear. He looked around then he looked right across the water at the boat, right into the lens. Jim withdrew fast as if he could have been seen. The beach was just a spec.

"Don't worry, they can't see us from there. But up above we might be being observed so make sure you stay low," Stan warned.

Jim backed away from the telescope. He had seen all he needed to see for now.

"Stan," Jim asked as he lit up another smoke, facing away from the beach now, holding a fishing pole. Stan was next to him, also manning a pole. He was smoking as well.

"Yeah."

"Stan, did you know?"

"About what?"

"My dad, did you always know, Stan?"

"No way. I had no idea in the world. We knew the drug network operated from somewhere in town and we knew the police chief had been bought."

"No! Not the chief? I knew him since childhood."

"Sorry, but yeah, he's bought. Not the captain though, just the chief. He made many visits to Denning. But your dad, no, I had no idea, none at all. If I had, sorry Jim, but he'd have been put down a long time ago and Denning would have been in jail. It was as much a shock to me as it was to you, or, maybe not, I'm sorry, Jim."

The pain tore at Jim's soul.

They went below. Everyone was there except for Gene who still manned the helm.

"Well, Stan, he chose his path," Jim said as they settled by the computer and radio.

Stan just nodded.

A voice came across on the radio. It was Martin.

"What is going on, Stan, I know you are out there and so is Jim. What do you think you are doing. And where are you, you're blocking me, I can't get a GPS lock on you."

"It's a tough world, boss," Stan said with a grin as Martin's image came up on the computer screen. He looked flaming mad!

"Where are you, Stan? I will find you, you know that!"

"Yeah, in time, boss, in time."

"And cut that 'boss' shit! And I know Jim is there listening. Put him on!"

Stan looked at Jim, Jim shrugged his shoulders then took the mike.

"Yeah," Jim said.

"Jim, you know you're in a shitload of trouble!"

"Tell me something I don't know!"

"Jim, it's no good, what you're doing!"

"It's my wife we're talking about here, and a bunch of other innocent people."

"Yes, her family, we already investigated and we're doing all we can..."

"I bet I've done a lot more than you!"

"So you know where they are! Tell me, Jim, I can help!"

"How is Suzie coming along?"

"Quit trying to change the subject, Jim!"

"How is she?"

"She's improving. She had a bad time of it but I think she will pull through, the doctors are hopeful at this point."

"Good. Anything else?"

"We raided the club. No one there, and the mansion. No one there either but we found shit loads of cocaine in a store room. We arrested the police chief. Denning must have panicked and left just before we got there. He's a fugitive now. You've been busy, Jim. What have you got, tell me! What are you and Stan up to?"

Jim looked over at Stan, at Jonnie Lee and Samantha, at Charlie White Eagle. At Jonnie Lee's two sons. They were taking a big risk with him, they were backing him up all the way.

"No way, not now!" Jim said into the mike. Then he signed off, the screen went blank.

Jim turned to Stan.

"Nothing to do now but wait until dark I guess," he said.

"Jim, you need to get some sleep, all of us do. We have hours to go so find a comfortable place if there is one," Stan said.

"There is no way I am sleeping, I already had a nap..."

"Not enough. All of you, we sleep, Gene will take first watch, then me. But you, you will sleep all the way through!"

"And how do I sleep when I am so wide awake it isn't even funny?"

"Jim, just lie down someplace and close your eyes, then start counting in your head from one hundred down."

"Right."

"Give it a try. We used to call them 'combat naps' in the SEALS. It's how we made it through many long, intense, missions. Now go sleep, Jim!"

Stan's eyes burned into his. Jim looked around, Jonnie Lee nodded to him then put his arm around his wife. His two sons settled down right there in the cabin and closed their eyes. Jim headed topside and walked out on deck. He settled with a blanket to block the sun on the foredeck. He was used to rough surfaces, being an Army Ranger. He settled down on his side and lay still as the boat rocked gently with the waves. He closed his eyes.

Nothing. The stress wouldn't leave him.

What did he have to lose?

He started counting down, 100, 99, 98...still the stress...97, 96, 95...wait...yes, he was beginning to feel like he was sinking down...down...94, 93, 92...farther down, drifting away.

Then came oblivion, deep, dark oblivion. No thought, no dreams, just sweet nothingness as he drifted away...

***

"Jim, Jim."

He heard a woman's sweet voice, heavily accented in Chinese.

"Jim..."

He felt a hand on his bare chest, a gentle, soft hand, caressing him and he felt lips against his cheek. He opened his eyes. It was dark and he could make out her form as she kneeled over him.

Samantha had awakened him, awakened him sweetly, gently. She smiled down at him in the darkness. The boat rocked. Jim rose up and sat next to her on the deck.

"Time," she said.

Jim nodded. The others were assembled on deck, all armed, all ready. They had smeared camouflage paint on their faces. Charlie White Eagle was shirtless, his muscular torso streaked with the paint. He handed over the container to Jim.

"Here, buddy, war paint," Charlie said with a grin.

Jonnie Lee was there, also armed, along with his sons, all painted and ready. They wore ammo belts with extra clips and carried AK-47s. Charlie White Eagle and Gene had their MP5s, and holstered .45s, just as Jim wore on his belt. Jim took the container and was getting ready to paint himself. Samantha took it from his grasp.

"Me do," she said.

She began applying the paint to his torso, her hands working on him, sensuous hands. He did his face. Then Samantha stripped naked right there on deck except for her high rise, black panties.

"Me too!" she said to Jim as she stood before him on deck.

Jim gulped down hard at the sight of her in the darkness, her skin glistening, her breasts bare and quivering before him. He handed her the can. She smiled then began applying the paint.

"But she can't..."

"She's martial arts trained," Stan said. "She showed me some moves on deck a while ago and when I handed her an AK she broke it down and re-assembled it expertly. They taught her a few things in The People's Republic of China, I can see that and we need all the people we can get. Jonnie Lee protested at first but he has no vote here. Does he?" and Stan turned to look sternly at Jonnie Lee who just grinned and shrugged his shoulders.

Samantha turned her back to Jim, looking at him over her shoulder, handing him the can. Jim began applying the paint, feeling her silken skin, feeling firm muscles underneath. Yes, the lady was in shape all right.

All of them were ready now, their bodies streaked in paint, all armed. Samantha took an AK-47 from Stan and an ammo belt with clips and a KA-BAR knife. She pulled the sharp weapon and felt the blade carefully as she looked at Jim. She smiled.

"For them!" she said looking towards shore. "You know!"

Jim knew.

Stan lowered two rubber rafts, they inflated as they hit the water, they were black, netting over them to keep off any reflections. They were powered by battery, silent motors. Jim, Stan, Charlie White Eagle and Samantha took the first raft. Gene, Jason, Jonnie Lee and his sons took the second. The rafts powered across the gentle waves towards the rocky shore. They made it between the outcroppings of coral rock and beached, pulling the rafts ashore and stashing them against the cliff. Stan had set the timer on his boat, in two hours it would go off sending out a GPS signal, cluing Martin in on their location. It was plenty of time for them to do what they had to do, they hoped.

They headed for the rocks, there was a rocky path leading up the mountain side along a razorback ridge. They moved upward, keeping low, moving swiftly, silently, experts, even Samantha, Jim could see the lady knew her stuff, she was right behind him, weapon ready.

They were nearing the top now. No fence or wall on the cliff side. But there were the dogs Jim had seen earlier. He was prepared for that, he had an air pistol with tranquilizer darts. So did Stan. Now they waited, crouching low. No moon, that was good. Jim's night vision was excellent and he could tell that Stan's was also. They had chosen not to bring night vision goggles because of their bulkiness. And they prevented peripheral vision.

Jim held his hand to signal the others to keep back. Then he looked at Stan. Stan nodded. They moved on ahead, now they were at the cliff's edge, right at the back courtyard to the estate. They waited. A dark shape appeared, then another, coming around a building, sniffing the air. Then there were three coming fast, alert, ears raised. They had on spiked collars, all three Rottweilers. Jim and Stan took careful aim, they could not afford to miss. One bark and it would be all over. Jim and Stan opened fire, the silent weapons repeating rapidly as the darts flew to their targets. There was a faint yelp from one dog then they began to wobble and soon, all were down, dozing in a deep sleep.

Jim nodded to Stan and they signaled to the others.

They swiftly moved across the area, looking right and left they dashed to the wall of the main building and flattened themselves against it. There was a sound. Jim could see a guard, dressed in black, moving along the walkway near them. Before Jim or Stan could do anything Samantha was on him, slitting his throat with expert efficiency. Jim looked towards Jonnie Lee who looked to be in shock.

They moved on, stepping over the body and made the doorway. Jim knew it would be wired. Stan worked the lock, carefully. Jim heard the latch give. Carefully unlocked and the alarm, if there was one, was not triggered. Stan gave Jim the high sign and they opened the door and moved in.

They were in a lighted hallway. Stairs led upward. They took them quickly. They were at the top level now, three floors up. They halted before entering the hallway. There was another guard patrolling. Samantha pulled her KA-BAR, ready. Jim shook his head at her and pulled his. Jim darted from the shadows, silencing the guard forever. He eased the man to the floor, relieving him of his weapon, a MAC 10 which he put in his belt for future use if needed.

They made their way along the hallway, slowly opening doors, looking inside, empty rooms. They moved along. An occupied room, three men in three beds fast asleep. They moved on after taking care of them. There was a door at the end. They halted near it.

Jim and Charlie positioned themselves on each side of the door, weapons ready. Jim nodded to Charlie. He tried the doorknob. It was locked. They stepped back, Charlie low, Jim standing. Jim reared back and delivered a lightning fast kick which blasted the door right off its frame. They were in, Charlie low, Jim high. A woman screamed. The lights went on.

And older couple, Jiang Li's parents huddled against a far wall.

There was a younger girl and young man there also. The room was well furnished.

"Who are you?" the older man asked.

Jim had his badge out as he came forward.

"I am your son in law!" he said.

"Son in law? What are you saying?" the woman asked.

"I am saying I am your son in law, I married your daughter! And where is she?"

"Not here, she is being prepared to marry Tommy Xiang tomorrow!"

"I am afraid those plans are about to change!" Jim said. "Where is she?"

"In another building I think. But who are you?"

"I am a Federal Agent. We are here to bring down The Cobra for good!"

A look of relief came over the couple's face.

"At last, Mom!" the young girl said. "So, I have a brother in law."

She looked at Jim. The young man came up beside her.

"Is this for real? You're not messing with us?"

"This is for real!"

"Thank God it's over," the girl said. "I knew Jill was up to something. My name is Nancy, your sister in law." She extended her hand. "And this is your brother in law, Bobby." She nudged the young man who also extended his hand, looking warily at all the others. His eyes widened when he saw the painted, naked woman standing there, armed with an automatic rifle and a KA-BAR knife.

"Who is she?" he asked.

"A friend," Jim answered. "So tell me, where is your sister?"

"We have not seen her, Tommy Xiang said she is in another building and that there will be a marriage ceremony tomorrow. They came for us last night, broke into our home and took us by force! I knew this would happen!"

"I always knew it!" the older woman, Jiang Li's mother said as she looked at her husband. "I always told you you should have never made deals with The Cobra. And to sell our daughter!" Rage flooded her being as she suddenly started hitting her husband on the chest and shoulders. Then she collapsed into his arms, shaking with sobs. He lowered his head.

"I knew my daughter was up to something, young man!" the

woman said. "One of these days, if we survive this, we are going to have to have a long talk, you and I."

"Yes, ma'am, we sure will have that talk," Jim said as he looked at his fellow team members. "But right now we have work to do. Samantha..."

The naked, painted warrior woman stepped forward. Jim looked at John Jr. "Tell her she is to stay here and watch over this family."

John Jr. spoke to her. She pouted, obviously wanting to be in on the action outside when it hit. Then she nodded and looked at the family.

"But I know you!" the mother said looking at Samantha and then at Jonnie Lee and his sons.

"The Tiger Clan! What is this?"

"Don't worry, ma'am," Jim said, "the Tiger Clan is under our command now."

"You always were such a sly one, Jonnie Lee!" the mother said and Jonnie Lee smiled. "And I have seen this woman with you many times! I thought she was your whore!"

"She is my wife now!" Jonnie Lee said. The woman looked back at Samantha. "Poor girl! Or maybe 'poor you.' she looks like someone who will keep you in line! But she needs clothes!"

"This is not the time!" Jim said, "We have to be moving on. So you have no idea which building Jiang Li is in?"

"So you use my daughter's traditional name. No, we have no idea, we have been in here since they brought us, blindfolded."

Jim nodded and then looked at his team members. They nodded back to him.

"My son," the old man said and Jim turned to face him. "My son, you look like a fine young man, I had always hoped my daughter would be able to find someone other than Tommy Xiang, that's why I insisted on her being educated, so she would see the reality and have a choice! And she made it, I am glad. My life is over now, but for her, I am glad. I deeply regret and have always regretted becoming involved with The Cobra."

"Well, don't feel like the Lone Ranger," Jim said.

The older man looked at Jim, questioningly.

"My dad, he's involved also. I just found out last night."

"I am sorry, young man, son," the older woman said, "it seems corruption is everywhere."

"Well, maybe this time it ends," Jim said.

"Good luck to you, my son," the woman said and both she and her husband came forward and hugged Jim.

"We gotta go," Jim said nodding to his team and to Samantha who nodded back.

They left the room and headed down the hallway. Jonnie Lee was beside Jim.

"Good move, leaving Samantha there with them."

"I hope she will be safer there," Jim said.

They executed a search of the entire building but found no one else there. They headed for the front entrance, looking through the window of the door at the courtyard which was lit by flood lights. There was another building straight across, by the cliff.

"I'd bet she's in there," Jim said.

Stan nodded.

Blap! Blap! Blap!

An alarm suddenly blared across a dozen speakers set around the property.

"The alert! They must have found the dogs and sentries!" Jim said.

"Let's move!" Stan yelled as they burst through the doorway out onto the courtyard.

Dark clad figures burst from rooms on the upper levels of the other buildings, heavily armed with automatic weapons they opened fire from the walkways. Rounds impacted into the ground around Jim's outfit. They returned fire on full automatic and men dropped from the balconies, hitting the turf hard. More men poured out as Jim's team dashed across the area, firing as they went. Men streamed from the building in front of them and Jim's team opened fire, the men went down, riddled with hot lead! More appeared, more went down. Jim's outfit was gaining the building but now from the other buildings men were pouring out. Jim saw familiar faces. Jack De Poli was among them as well as other men Jim recognized as belonging to Denning. They were all here!

Jim leapt over bodies as his team dashed through the doorway to the building, taking down more men who tried to stop them. It was a blood bath!

Jim looked back and saw De Poli directing his men to circle around the building. Jim fired at them, missing De Poli but hitting others who dropped in their steps, one firing into the ground as he fell.

They entered the building and were moving down a hallway. A figure stepped from a doorway. It was Mike Walker.

"Don't shoot!" Mike screamed at the top of his voice.

He was unarmed.

Jim faced him. He shoved his badge in his face.

"You're a Fed!"

"That's right! And you have about six seconds to tell me where Jiang Li is!" Jim jammed Mike against the wall.

"Hey, buddy, I was forced to come here, so was Debra and she's upstairs!"

"Where is Jiang Li?"

The sound of gunfire was getting louder now as De Poli's men attacked the building from all sides.

"Upstairs! Denning is here too! And Rebecca! That whore!"

"I saw her on the beach! Did they harm Jiang Li?"

"No, not yet, she hasn't been touched! I heard that Chinese guy is marrying her tomorrow morning!"

"She's already married! Move!"

Jim forced Mike down the hallway ahead of him. He looked at Stan.

"We'll hold them off, you go upstairs!" Stan yelled as he and the team headed back down the hallway. Men burst through the door. Stan and the team opened up on them and they were down for good!

Shoving Mike ahead of him Jim made the stairs, taking three at a time. From the upstairs balcony men emerged, Asian and white, Jim fired on them, one fell over the balcony and did a face dive for the floor below. He hit with a splat!

Jim was on the top floor now, more men came at him and he shoved Mike down, opening fire as he did. Men went down. With a yell two black clad figures came spiraling and cart wheeling at him delivering kicks that knocked Jim to the floor. Jim managed to get off rounds taking down one of them. He clicked on empty. He was on his feet in an instant as the man came at him in a flurry of fists and feet. Jim backed up, blocking expertly and delivering return strikes, also, expertly blocked by his attacker. This guy was good!

The attacker rocked a fist across Jim's jaw, staggering him for a moment. Jim stepped in, delivering fast punches, the man did backflips in fast retreat. Two more attackers came forward and Mike met them with punches, downing one. The other one staggered him back and barraged him with a flurry of strikes. Mike took it and kept on fighting. More came at them. Jim downed his man and took on two more!

Fast moves!
Strikes!
Punches!
Kicks!

The fight was on. Jim could hear gunfire going on downstairs where the rest of the team was fighting off the outside attackers.

Jim grabbed one attacker by the head and twisted hard. He heard the neck break with a sickening crunch, the limp figure dropped to the floor.

"Jim!"

He head Jiang Li's voice scream his name. He looked down the hallway. There she was, still fully clothed in her sweatshirt and jeans.

Harry Xiang was there with his two sons. David had Jiang Li, a gun under her chin. Tommy Xiang was with Rebecca, she was clad only in bikini bottoms.

"Kill him!" Rebecca yelled.

She glared at Jim with vicious eyes. Such hatred there!

"Take him alive! I want him!" she yelled, changing her mind.

Mike had just finished with his opponent and stood next to Jim. Jim did a quick reload and had his .45 trained on David Xiang.

"Drop it!" Jim yelled. "You have no chance, drop it!"

"You drop it!" Harry Xiang yelled at him. "Or she dies!"

"I blow her head off, you see!" David yelled.

"Your bitch is as good as dead!" Rebecca said. She drew a knife, a long, curved blade and looked wickedly at Jim. "but first she will watch as I 'take care' of you!"

"You bitch! I'll kill you!" Jiang Li yelled.

"Shut the fuck up, bitch!" Rebecca yelled. "Drop the gun, Jim, or she dies right now!"

"We aren't fuckin' around here!" Tommy Xiang yelled.

"No we aren't you traitorous bastard!"

Denning stepped into the hallway, armed with a 9mm. He had Debra by the arm. She was naked. Tears were in her eyes.

"He forced you didn't he!" Jim yelled.

Debra nodded her head, almost falling but Denning jerked her upright.

"The lady has been downright entertaining! I just love college girls! Especially when they submit! Now drop it, you bastard!"

Jiang Li yelled in pain as David jammed the barrel of his weapon further into her chin.

"Okay, okay..." Jim said and he dropped his weapon.

"Take them!" Denning now ordered and men stepped forward taking Jim and Mike and hustling them forward, jamming their hands behind them.

"Oh this is going to be fun!" Rebecca said as she approached Jim, pressing herself against him. She brought the knife to his groin, pressing the blade hard against him.

"No, no!" Jiang Li screamed.

"Your lover soon will no longer be a man!" Rebecca said. Her breasts were mashed against him, he felt himself responding, he raged against the feeling as she pressed harder against him.

"Let's go!" Denning commanded.

"Wait a minute!" Rebecca said.

The gunfire went on outside, the battle still raging.

"Kiss me!" Rebecca said, her face near Jim's. "Kiss me and mean it!"

"No way!" Jim said.

She pressed the knife harder against him.

"She dies if you don't!" Rebecca hissed.

Jim bent down, pressing his lips against hers, she kissed him, forcing her tongue into his mouth, moving against him.

Jiang Li lowered her head, tears in her eyes.

Jim finished. He looked over at Jiang Li.

"I'm sorry, Jiang Li," he said.

"Oh Jim! I love you! Let them kill me! Get away, Jim, get away!"

"He won't!" Rebecca said, as she parted from him, glaring at him. She looked at her knife then at his groin and she smiled.

"Let's get moving!" Denning commanded again.

Tommy Xiang grabbed Rebecca's wrist and pulled her along as they fled down the hallway, Jim and Mike in tow.

They ran down a rear flight of stairs and out a back door, across the rear of the compound heading towards the chopper which was warming up on the helipad, a passenger craft, doors wide open.

From around the corner of the buildings Jim's team burst into view. The gunfire had stopped now, they had all survived. There was one more building to pass. The team aimed their weapons in their direction but Stan waved them off, still, they approached. David Xiang kept the barrel of his weapon under Jiang Li's chin. As they passed the edge of the final building Samantha burst forward, her body striking David Xiang, he lowered his weapon away from Jiang Li. She leapt away from him, Jim instantly whirled and dropped the man behind him, Mike broke free also and took down his guard. A man came at Jim, diving at him. The man was big, he grabbed a hold of Jim. Stan and the team burst forward. Denning's escort opened fire as did Stan's men. Stan took a hit in the shoulder and spun to the ground, Gene took a hit in the side and went down, firing as he went, more of the Cobra men dropped.

Jim drove back with his elbow and caught his man in the stomach, the man let go of him, Jim spun and downed him with a right cross to the jaw, as the man went down Jim caught him full in the face with his knee then spun away from him.

Charlie White Eagle, Jason and Jonnie Lee and his sons dove in among the Cobra now, hand to hand combat ensued. Jiang Li did a flying wheel kick downing a man, Samantha moved in, jamming her KA-BAR into a man's gut then extracting it and moving on, now right beside Jiang Li.

Rebecca broke away from Denning at dove at Jiang Li. Jiang Li leapt at her, so did Samantha. Jiang Li delivered a punch, spinning Rebecca around to fall towards Samantha. Samantha caught her and wheeled her around, Rebecca struggled. Jiang Li spoke to Samantha in her native tongue. Instantly, rage filled Samantha's eyes for she had been told of Rebecca's intention towards Jim. She screamed and punched Rebecca, then drove her back, delivering kicks to her, spinning her along.

Tommy Xiang rushed forward and grabbed Jiang Li, pulling her along with him.

"What about me?" Rebecca screamed as Samantha hit her again.

"Screw you, bitch!" Tommy Xiang yelled. He and David were retreating towards the helicopter. His father and Denning had already made it and were standing in the entrance. The team was in the fight all the way, hand to hand they battled, kicking, punching, smashing. Jim started towards the chopper, it was about to lift off, he could see Jiang Li in the entrance struggling with Tommy Xiang, Denning was right beside them, gun in hand. He started firing. Jonnie Lee caught a slug in the torso and spun. Samantha screamed when she saw him go down, she delivered one more finishing punch to Rebecca and ran to him. Rebecca lay still on the ground. The rest of The Cobra were down now. Jim looked over at Jonnie Lee, he was struggling to rise.

"Go after her!" Jonnie Lee yelled as Samantha and his sons ran to his side. He was fading fast. Samantha threw her arms around him, easing him to the ground. Stan was on his feet running towards Gene who was looking pale as he lay on the ground. Stan looked at Jim.

"Go!" he yelled and Jim ran on.

Denning started firing at Jim but the chopper was starting to lift off, his aim was spoiled. Jiang Li struggled with Tommy. Jim leapt up and grabbed the landing strut as the chopper lifted into the air. He hung on, he was below the bird, out of sight for now. Charlie White Eagle ran forward, took aim and fired. Harry Xiang pitched forward and fell through the entrance, hitting the ground hard.

The bird gained altitude fast, heading out over the ocean now!

Jim gripped with his arms and legs. He looked down, he could see the team mopping up the area, Samantha was holding Jonnie Lee, Stan was helping Gene, Charlie White Eagle stood there, watching Jim, looking helpless, Rebecca was out cold on the ground. Samantha rose up and looked skyward. Now they were fading from view as the chopper headed farther out to sea.

Jim looked down. He could see Stan's boat anchored off shore, just a dot in the water now. Farther out he could see several ships. He heard a cry and saw David Xiang cart wheeling past him on his way down. Jiang Li was scrapping, he could tell. He had to get up there. David continued his journey down, down, down until there was a splash. That was it for him.

Jim started to climb. The bird shifted and his legs dropped, now he was holding on with just his hands, swinging freely in the air. The bird started to rock from side to side, Jim fought to maintain his grip as he moved hand over hand, trying to pull himself up. They must have known he was still hanging on. He made it up the side. The doorway was still wide open and he could see inside. Jiang Li was now involved in a struggle with Tommy Xiang while Denning watched, trying to get a hold on her as well. Jim climbed upward, almost to the entrance.

Denning saw him.

"You bastard!!! Now you'll pay!" Denning yelled as he tried to stomp Jim's hands. Jim moved fast, pulling himself up. He got a hold of Denning's leg. Denning kicked out and Jim lost his grip. He hung on, now with only one hand as the bird swung wildly about. Jim felt his grip weakening. Denning's foot stomped down on his fingers, Jim felt the pain shoot through his hand and forearm but he hung on.

"You haven't got a chance, you bastard!" Denning yelled.

Jim got his other hand up, pulled hard. Just at that moment the bird shifted, it actually aided him as he used the momentum to swing his legs up. He was at the doorway now. Denning fell back and Jim was in the door. Denning leapt at him, he hit Jim with a right. He was strong, that was for sure. Jim was pitched backwards but hung on swinging himself back inside and landing a foot in Denning's chest. Denning fell back and Jim was on him. He saw Jiang Li struggling with Tommy Xiang, giving him a good fight.

Denning lunged back at Jim, getting a strangle hold on him, driving him back to the entrance. Jim hit the floor, his head hanging out as Denning got his palm under Jim's chin, trying to force his head up to break his neck. Jim got his palm under Denning's chin.

"Give it up, asshole!" Jim said through clenched teeth. "Your game is up!"

"Not yet it isn't! And you'll be dead!" Denning glared down at him, pure hatred in his eyes.

Suddenly Jiang Li fell across Denning's back, Denning lost his hold on Jim and Jim twisted out of his grip, kicking out with a thrust kick which sent Denning back against the far bulkhead. Jim was on him, landing a right, then a left!

"Here's one for corrupting my dad!"

Jim planted another strong right which pitched Denning on his side. Jim stayed on him, smacking right into Tommy Xiang and Jiang Li. The bird pitched again and both Denning and Jim were pitched towards the opening again. This time Denning was through the entrance. He reached for the side of the door. Jim planted a foot in his chest and hesitated, looking into Denning's fear filled eyes.

"So long, asshole!" Jim said and he shoved. Denning flew out into empty space, he screamed all the way down.

Now it was between Jim and Tommy Xiang.

Tommy backed up, fear in his eyes. He looked towards the cockpit and called out. The pilot appeared, a big man, almost as tall as Jim.

Jiang Li was at Jim's side now, Jim pushed her back. The bird kept level, on autopilot for now. both men dove at Jim. He spun, taking out the pilot, downing him, the man pitched through the doorway and out into the air, plunging down.

Panic seized Tommy Xiang now!

No one was left to fly the bird!

Tommy dove at Jim and they tumbled backward. At that moment the bird pitched. Jiang Li screamed. Jim and Tommy hit the bulkhead opposite the entrance and rolled. The bird was now spinning out of control, around and around it went, the scenery a blur out the entrance. Jim shoved and Tommy flew back, Jim was on him, they collided with Jiang Li. All three of them flew out the open doorway, Tommy got a hold on Jim's leg, both Jim and Jiang Li got a hold on the frame as the bird continued to spin wildly. Jim tried to shake Tommy off but Tommy began to climb up, grabbing Jim's waist. Jiang Li started to lose her grip, she screamed.

"Hang on, baby!" Jim yelled.

Tommy was on Jim's torso now and he locked his hands around Jim's neck, his eyes burning into his with rage. Jim pulled up, managing to get into the cabin again. He kicked Tommy off of him and was back at the entrance. He extended his hand to Jiang Li. She grabbed for it and found a strong grip. Tommy came at Jim, trying to kick him out the door, the spin continued, the bird arching downward heading right towards the water, spinning and descending. The surface was coming up fast. Jim pulled and Jiang Li climbed over him into the cabin. Tommy headed for the cockpit and grabbed the controls, they were heading downward now, skimming the water almost. The bird lurched and rose again then circled wildly, Jiang Li was pitched towards the doorway again. Jim kept his hold on her, the bird leaned over to the left, the door side, near the surface and both Jim and Jiang Li were pitched out the door. They flew through space and splashed down in the water, the impact hard, they bounced on the surface once, the impact knocking them cold. The bird flew crazily on, hitting the surface then rising again. Soon it was out of sight.

Jim was dazed. He was on his back. He opened his eyes, he felt himself drifting. He had no awareness of who or where he was at that moment. Then it came ratcheting back to him suddenly in brutal detail. He looked over. Jiang Li was face down in the water, drifting.

"Jill!" he called and swam to her, rolling her over. She gasped and spit out a spout of water, coughed then grabbed on to him.

"Baby!" Jim called, relieved.

But now they were adrift in the ocean, far from Stan's boat, it wasn't even in sight. Jim kicked his legs, they had to stay afloat. He could see the cliff line in the distance, a far swim.

"Are you okay, baby?" Jim asked her as she held him, both of them kicking. She nodded.

"It's cold!" she said. It was getting cold, even though it was almost summer the water off the Northern California coast was always cold. Both of them were starting to shiver.

"We've got to try for shore!" Jim said, "It's our only chance!"

"It's so far!"

"Just take easy strokes, try to relax, I'm right here, just stay beside me."

Both of them began the swim, easy strokes but the cold was beginning to take its toll.

"Come on, baby, we can make it," Jim said.

Jiang Li continued to swim, Jim could feel the cold eating into his bones now, his arms began to weaken. He saw Jiang Li began to falter. He knew they couldn't make it but he kept on.

"Come on, baby, come on..." he grabbed her arm and tried to help her along.

"Oh my love, I can't go any farther..." she started to relax, to drift.

He grabbed her.

"Come on, baby, no going to sleep now!"

He felt despair, to come so close and now to die by drowning because they were too cold to keep going.

He heard it then, the sound of a chopper swooping low overhead. A Navy Air Sea Rescue chopper turning and heading back to hover over them. A line was dropped.

"It'll be okay, baby, it'll be okay now," Jim said as he grabbed the life preserver on the line and got it around Jiang Li.

Men in floatation vests splashed down into the water next to them, securing them together on a line. One of the men gave the thumbs up and Jim and Jiang Le were yanked out of the water, she clung to him, arms around his neck. As they drifted above the surface, being slowly reeled up to the rescue craft Jiang Li looked into Jim's eyes.

"I love you, Jim Saunders!" said.

"I love you too, Jill Saunders," Jim answered and their lips met.

All was right with the world now. They were pulled aboard by strong arms.

"Good to see you!" it was Martin who spoke. The strong arm that had grabbed him belonged to Jason , the fortress had been secured. He and the Navel personnel hauled them aboard and blankets were thrown over them as they huddled together in the cabin, the craft heading back to base.

All was well.

CHAPTER NINETEEN

It was a bright sunny day, Saturday, on the football field of San Francisco State University. It was graduation day and a large crowd was assembled, all the families of the graduates, all dressed up in suits to fit the occasion. Jim was seated with Jiang Li's family, his family was not in attendance, his father was still in custody pending his case. He had cooperated and perhaps there would be a deal but the decision had not come down yet. Had they been there Jim still wouldn't have been seated with them. He had a bitter taste in his mouth still. The betrayal had cut him to the bone. Denning's son was living with Jim's family until further notice. Orphaned at seventeen through no fault of his own. Jim was dressed in his Sunday best, a brand new suit, dark gray in the accepted Federal Agent fashion. He had his weapon and ID on him. The weapon strapped to a shoulder holster. He was an accepted full time Federal Agent now. Stan had recovered from his injuries, Gene would be released next week from the hospital. Stan was there with Jim along with Charlie White Eagle, they also were dressed in dark gray suits befitting their status as Federal Agents. Nothing had been mentioned about the tactics they had used. It had all gone away. The remainder of The Cobra, those who had not been killed in the shootout, had all been rounded up. De Poli had been killed in the conflict. Mike Walker and Debra had been rescued, they had had no part in any criminal activities. They were also present. Rebecca had been taken into custody and was facing a barrage of charges which would put her away for years to come. The wreckage of the helicopter belonging to The Cobra had been found down the coast, a total, smoking loss, it had gone down and burst into flames. There was no sign of the only surviving member of The Cobra, Tommy Xiang. The shipment of drugs had been waylaid by the Coast Guard and the vessel had been impounded, the drugs seized. It all pointed to The Cobra and Denning. Suzie was out of intensive care and was recovering nicely. Jim and Jiang Li had visited her, she was beginning to get back to herself and was angry that she could not attend today's ceremony. In the center of the field the stage had been set up and all the dignitaries were present in black robes and caps. Former graduates who were now professors.

"I am so proud," Jiang Li's mother said, she was seated next to

Jim, on his right. And to his left were Jiang Li's brother and sister, her father next to his wife. He was beaming with pride. And he was greatly relieved, such a great burden had been removed. Also with the family was Jonnie Lee and his wife, Samantha and also his two sons. He had recovered from his wound as well.

People were starting to get restless now, so far it seemed the ceremony had been delayed.

The music began to play over the PA system and the candidates marched onto the field, single file, all dressed in their black robes and hats. Some were wearing gold sashes, they were honor role students. Jiang Li was among them in her robe and gold sash, marching along with the others in the middle of the line. As they marched across the field she searched the audience, an anxious look on her face until her eyes rested on Jim and her family. All waved to her and she beamed with Joy. All was right with the world now.

The line halted near the podium and the Dean of the school gave a brief speech on the accomplishments of the graduating class. Then the line began to move as names were called. Each graduate stepped up and shook the hands of the dignitaries and received their diploma from the President of the College along with a congratulatory handshake as photos were taken. The line was moving along, Jiang Li now near her time, ten people back, then nine, then eight.

Charlie White Eagle nudged Jim's shoulder and nodded to the far end of the field.

Jim looked.

A figure was sprinting across the field, far in the distance dressed in black and carrying something in his right hand. No one seemed to be paying attention. Jim was on full alert as he honed in on the running figure.

It was Tommy Xiang!

And he was carrying a gun!

Jim bolted from the stand, pushing through the crowd, Charlie White Eagle and Stan right behind him. As they burst onto the field they all drew their weapons as the crowd suddenly became aware of the situation and screamed in panic. The graduates looked around, confused as to all the commotion. Jiang Li saw Jim and his group running towards her and she had a questioning look in her eyes.

"Down, Jill!" Jim roared as he ran full out, motioning with his hands. "Everybody down, now!"

The dignitaries looked confused but Stan was on them, pushing them to the ground, showing gun and ID as was Charlie, long pony tail bouncing off his shoulders as he ran.

"Down! Everybody down!" Charlie yelled as he waved his badge in his left hand and everyone started to drop to the ground.

Jiang Li still stood there, confused as Jim bolted forward. Tommy Xiang was closing the gap, not caring, only with his target in mind as he ran on, gun raised now.

"You betrayed me! Now you die!" he yelled at the top of his voice.

He started firing the weapon as people screamed in panic. Jim dove on Jiang Li bowling her over. He rolled free, Stan, Charlie and Jim had their weapons trained on Tommy Xiang and all at the once, all of them opened fire, Tommy Xiang danced the dance of death as rounds impacted into his body. He flew back, the gun flying, he seemed to dance in the air as more bullets hit him then he was down. The three agents were on him in an instant, pinning him to the ground although it was not needed for Tommy Xiang would never cause trouble again, ever!

Security was running onto the field now and into the stands to try to calm the crowd, some of them had started to stampede and more security joined in to quell the panic.

Jim rose up, gun still in hand and he searched the crowd, the graduates. They were starting to rise up now. Jiang Li was still lying on the ground, still.

"No!" Jim yelled and he heard a woman scream behind him. He turned. Jiang Li's mother, father and brothers were bolting across the field towards the still form of their daughter.

"My baby! My baby!" her mother kept yelling as they ran.

"Jill!" sweat poured from Jim's brow as he ran to her still form. She must have caught a round, they had been too late!

Jim dove next to her, grabbing her up in his arms. She moved now, putting her arms around him and looking into his eyes, her eyes misty.

"You sure hit awfully hard you know, I'm not a running back!"

She smiled and Jim held her to him tightly, tears in his eyes as she held him.

"Oh kiss me you big fool!" she said as her lips met his.

***

Two months had gone by. It was mid-summer now, July and it was sweltering in the little church in Jim's home town. Jim was standing at the altar in front of the minister. Next to him was Charlie White Eagle, his best man for this time he was doing things right all the way. Also in his party were Mike Walker, Jason and Gene, now fully recovered. Jonnie Lee was also in the party. He had been put on probation and would have to tow a tight line from now on. All wore white tuxes, befitting a summer wedding. Then there were the bridesmaids. Among them were several college friends of Jiang Li. Also there were Suzie and Debra, dressed in their formals along with Samantha Yi, now Samantha Lee. Jiang Li's younger sister carried the flowers. Seated in the audience were Jim's family, his dad and mom and brother as well as Denning's son, now a member of the family. Jim's dad had been given immunity after a full confession which had busted wide open the crime wave in the town which had led to the arrest of the town police chief. Jim had started to get close to his family again and his brother was starting to come around. His dad had told his younger brother that it was he, his dad, who had been in the wrong and that Jim had done everything right. He had told both young boys, Robbie and Denning's son, that he had taught his sons to do the right thing even if he, himself, hadn't and that he was proud of his older son.

Healing was taking place.

Also in the audience were Stan and Martin. Seated with Jim's family was Jiang Li's mother and her younger brother. Both Jim's mother and Jiang Li's had tears in their eyes.

Now the music began.

Jim looked down the isle to see his father in law escorting his bride, dressed in white with a veil covering her face. They slowly marched down the isle and Jim felt tears welling up. Charlie put a firm hand on his shoulders.

"Easy now," Charlie said quietly.

The bride was escorted to the altar and surrendered by her beaming father who smiled at Jim.

Jim and his bride turned to face the minister. The words were said.

"And you may kiss the bride," the minister said after the vows and Jim gently removed the veil. Jiang Li looked up at him, misty eyed as he bent to kiss her, their arms going around each other.

***

The bride and groom entered the reception hall together as people cheered and rice was thrown, they were arm in arm as they made their way to main table where the best man and the rest of the wedding party sat. It was an afternoon of celebration as they feasted and cut the cake. The music played and Jim danced with his new bride in his arms, as she beamed up at her husband and kissed him occasionally. For them, no one else existed.

"May I cut in?"

Jim turned to see a smiling Jonnie Lee standing there. Jim surrendered his bride to him and then he accepted a dance from Samantha Yi.

"May I cut in?"

Suzie stood there and Jim nodded to Samantha and took Suzie in his arms. They danced around the hall. Jim could see the sadness there in Suzie's eyes.

"I'll be going to Los Angeles," Suzie said. "It's my new assignment. I hope you have a wonderful life, Jim."

"You made it all possible," Jim said and Suzie kissed him lightly on his lips, looking in his eyes. Then she parted, the tears were starting to flow.

"Goodbye, Jim," she said and she hurried from the room. Jim watched her go.

"Hello, handsome," Jim turned. His wife was there and he took her in his arms and they danced. Then he whispered. In her ear.

"Why don't we sneak out of here?" he said.

"I think that's a wonderful idea, Mr. Saunders."

"Quite right, Mrs. Saunders."

And they quietly fled the room.

The music played on as they darted to their car. It was no use. The quests poured from the hall cheering the couple. Jiang Li took the flowers and closed her eyes. She made the toss and every girl scrambled for the bouquet. Debra caught it, she was standing next to Mike Walker. She turned to look at him, smiling as they took each other's hands.

The bride and groom got in the car and drove away. the party went on and on...

AFTERWARD

I hope you enjoyed this saga. Writing it was quite a journey for me. A few notes of mention.

First to note, the town where Jim grew up does not exist in the east bay, it was a composite of many towns throughout America.

Second, the Federal Building in San Francisco is no longer on Lombard Street. It is down on Sixth street, south of Market Street. When I began writing the first draft I found out about the new location. I decided for the sake of the story to use the old location. Call it creative license.

This is a self published work, I am both writer, and also the editor so please excuse any typos or misspellings you may find. I have done my utmost to keep this copy as clean of errors as possible.

A book is never written by only one person really. I may have been the one putting the words down but I had a lot of help. I want to thank David Kong for his valuable assistance as well as John Chase for his knowledge of weaponry. I owe a debt of gratitude to my sensei, the late Gus Johnson, grand master and seventh degree black belt, combat veteran, special forces, Vietnam War. I want to thank Gene Orro. Recognize the name, Gene? Oh yeah, any resemblance between anyone in this work of fiction is absolutely coincidental. I also owe a debt of gratitude to Lambert Cheung, author of the RED PHOENIX LEDEND series for his invaluable help on this project.

Well, dear reader, thank you for joining me on this journey.

Don't get in her way!

PATRICK L. DEU PREE

Deputy Ronda Miller / The Protector

THE BLACK JADE TRILOGY
BY
PATRICK L. DEU PREE

Other novels by Patrick L. Deu Pree

And enjoy this epic si/fi saga

Don't miss these two fantastic si/fi fantasy thrillers from author Lambert Cheung

Made in the USA
Las Vegas, NV
29 September 2025